BEN CHEETHAM

ANGEL OF DEATH

HEAD
ZEUS

First published in the UK in 2014 by Head of Zeus Ltd.

9 7 5 3 1 2 4 6 8

A CIP catalogue record for this book is available
from the British Library.

Paperback ISBN: 9781781853986
Ebook ISBN: 9781781853955

Typeset by Ben Cracknell Studios, Norwich.
Printed and bound by CPI Group (UK) Ltd, Croydon, CR0 4YY.

Head of Zeus Ltd
Clerkenwell House
45–47 Clerkenwell Green
London EC1R 0HT

www.headofzeus.com

For Clare

Chapter One

Angel examined her face in the cracked mirror, combing her fingers through raven-black hair that framed intensely blue eyes and uncommonly pale cheeks. 'You're beautiful. You're beautiful,' she murmured, as though repetition would make the words true. But she wasn't beautiful. Not any more. Her once crystal-clear eyes were yellowish and laced with spidery veins. Fine lines and dark shadows marred the surrounding skin. The cute dimples that used to appear when she smiled – not that she ever smiled these days – were gone. In their place were two sharply etched hollows, like knife cuts.

She ran her tongue over lips that appeared unusually full and sensual in her otherwise gaunt face. The best blowjob lips in the business, that's what Deano called them. On the day they'd met he'd told her, 'Those juicy babies are gonna be your ticket out of this life.' She'd believed him at the time, just like she'd believed him later when he said he loved her. She didn't believe him any more. She'd heard him say those words, or words like them, to too many other girls. She knew him now for what he was – pure poison. He'd given her nothing but had taken everything, and she'd let him. Wilfully, pathetically, she'd sold her last chance, her last grain of hope, for an earful

of his sweet bullshit and a veinful of smack. The knowledge made her burn with hatred.

Angel's fingers curled into a fist. She hit the mirror hard enough to send a jolt of pain rocketing up her wrist. When she drew her knuckles away from the glass, she left behind a bloody smear. She closed her eyes, letting the pain wash through her, using it to block out the hate like she had so many times before. But this time it wasn't enough. The hate kept on growing, expanding like waves from a limitless ocean. Violent visions flashed across the screen of her mind. Visions of herself lashing out at a faceless figure, punching, clawing and tearing. And as she did so, tears streamed from her eyes. Not tears of sorrow but tears of pleasure. It felt good, better than any sex she'd ever had. She began to rock back and forth. A low moan escaped her lips.

The daydream dissolved like a wisp of smoke as the bedsit's door creaked open. Eyelids snapping up, Angel jerked around to see Deano poking his head into the room. 'Grace, baby, it's—' he started to say.

'I asked you not to use that name,' Angel broke in sharply.

Deano dismissed her words with a crooked smile that showed a mouthful of stained and chipped teeth. The years hadn't been kind to him either. He was a big man, although not as big as he used to be. Slowly, the smack was wearing him away, eroding a few millimetres here, a centimetre there. He was still handsome in a rough sort of way, but his complexion was pimple-blotched and his hair was fast thinning. 'What does it matter? There's no one else around.'

'Please will you just call me Angel. Will you do that for me?'

'Alright, alright. Anything to stop your whining.' Deano

squinted through the dingy gloom of the room. 'Look at the state of you. You've been crying again, haven't you? What's up? Actually, don't bother telling me. Just sort your face out. It's time to get back out there. Five minutes. I want you on the street in five minutes, or I'm really gonna give you something to cry about.'

Deano headed back outside, his footsteps thumping the bare floorboards as heavily as his fists would thump Angel if she didn't get her arse and all the other parts of her body that helped pay the rent into gear. Four or five years ago he would have kissed her tears away and sweet-talked her into doing what he wanted. There was no need for any of that bullshit now. He had her exactly where he wanted her, and both of them knew it. It wasn't just the smack. She knew plenty of other people she could score from. It was the things she'd told him. Thinking back on it, she wanted to slap herself for having opened up to him, for being so weak and stupid. But at the time she'd needed to talk, to confide in someone, otherwise she might have done something even more stupid. She hadn't told him everything. There were things she couldn't bear to think about, never mind talk about. But she'd told him enough.

After rinsing the blood off her knuckles at a sink in the corner, Angel put on lippy and mascara. She shrugged off her dressing-gown and slipped into a miniskirt, boob-tube and over-the-knee high-heeled boots. Picking up a can of pepper-spray and slinging a handbag over her shoulder, she hurried after Deano. As usual, he was lurking in the ginnel alongside a boarded-up terraced house a couple of streets away. A boy of maybe eighteen approached him at the same time as Angel, shoulders hunkered against the raw wind coming off the River Tees. He handed Deano a couple of crumpled tenners, and Deano's hand emerged from the shadows holding a small foil wrap. The exchange happened fast, then the boy was hurrying away.

'Looking fuckable,' said Deano, approvingly surveying Angel's freshly applied slap before dropping his gaze to her outfit that left little to the imagination. Leaning forward with a sneering smile in his eyes, he added meaningfully, 'Angel.'

Hate surged up in Angel again. She had a sudden wild urge to empty the can of pepper-spray into Deano's eyes. Oh, how she would have loved to see the fucker scream and squirm. She saw herself doing it, then saw herself grinding a heel into his throat, crushing his windpipe. The far-off wail of a police siren brought her back to the moment with a slight start. 'Where do you want me?'

'Over by the bridge.' Deano scanned the street uneasily as he spoke, ear cocked towards the sound of the siren. The wailing faded away and his gaze returned to Angel. 'Do me proud, baby, and later we'll do a bit of you know what.' He rustled the foil wraps in his pocket. The sound, so repulsively yet irresistibly familiar to Angel, sent a shudder through her. It had only been a couple of hours since her last fix, but already the craving was growing. Her veins itched with it.

Angel tottered towards the Transporter Bridge, whose blue frame dominated the Middlesbrough skyline, straddling the Tees like a steel-limbed horse. She passed a scattering of other girls all dressed, like her, in high heels and revealing clothes. Most of their heavily made-up faces were familiar. Some of them smiled and nodded hello. She spotted a new girl scarcely old enough to be out of school, her eyes glazed with a tell-tale sheen. The girl shifted nervously as Angel neared her. There was a bruise on her cheek, probably put there by one of the other girls protecting her patch. The girls looked out for each other, but that didn't stop fights from frequently breaking out over who worked the most lucrative spots. Angel gave her a smile, not of sympathy – her heart was too hardened by bitterness and anger for that – but of understanding. She knew what the girl was feeling. She'd been there herself not so many years ago. She didn't offer any words of reassurance. Some whores liked to take new girls under their wing, impart their wisdom. Not Angel. The idea repulsed her. Nothing this life had taught her was worth repeating.

A black BMW with tinted windows crawled along the kerb. One of the other girls lifted the hem of her skirt, exposing her bare crotch. But the car didn't stop. She shoved her middle finger up at it, mouthing, 'Fuck you.' The Beamer pulled over by Angel and the young girl. The driver-side window came down just enough for a massive hand adorned with chunky gold rings to beckon the girl. Flicking Angel a tense glance, the girl hurried to the passenger door and ducked into the car, which accelerated sharply away in the direction of the Transporter Bridge.

'Hope that little bitch isn't thick enough to let him take her over the river,' said the girl who'd been snubbed.

The other side of the Tees was a lonely mixture of heavy industrial land and the Seal Sands nature reserve. If you got into trouble, there was no one to hear you scream except the wildlife. Some girls came back robbed and raped. They were the lucky ones. In Angel's time, there had been two girls she knew of who never came back at all. Angel went there

5

occasionally, but only with her most trusted regulars who were willing to pay extra to indulge their vice in the safety of isolation. She stared after the fast-receding car, trying to make out the number plate. She caught the first three letters before the car turned from view. 'B... A... D,' she read aloud, a frown gathering on her brow.

'Bad.' The other girl shook her head. 'That can't be good.'

Another kerb-crawler pulled into view. The girl yanked her skirt up again. This time the car stopped. Angel continued to her patch – a corner between two warehouses a couple of hundred metres from the river. She sparked up and took a drag, watching the bridge's gondola ferrying cars towards the north bank. She couldn't be certain, but she thought she glimpsed the Beamer amongst them. A car pulled into the kerb. She flicked away her cig and ducked down to greet her first punter of the night.

The next hour went by in its usual way – a couple of blow-jobs, a handjob, straight sex that was over in less than two minutes. Even as Angel serviced her punters, her eyes kept shifting towards the bridge, watching for the Beamer or the girl. But there was no sign of them. Minute by minute, her uneasiness grew. She kept thinking of the number plate, and the more she thought of it, the more the letters seemed like some sort of omen. She returned along the street. 'Has she been back?' she asked the skirt-lifting girl, who shook her head in reply. 'What do you reckon we should do?'

'Sod all. What else can we do?'

Angel briefly considered going to Deano, but she knew what his response would be. *What the fuck do I care?* Her heart heavy with foreboding, she headed back to her corner. Her mind flashed back to when she'd first worked the streets. The things that had happened to her. So many bad, ugly, twisted things she'd lost count. Sometimes she wondered how she was still alive, or even if she deserved to be.

A familiar car was waiting for Angel: a red Volvo estate. Its middle-aged driver had the unmistakable look of a family man – balding and grey, a little overweight, glasses, shirt and tie. His name was Kevin – or at least that's what he said it was – and he was one of Angel's regulars, an easy customer who liked a bit of domination, but nothing too kinky. As soon as she saw him, she knew what she had to do. 'Hi there, lover. What's it to be tonight?'

'The usual.'

Angel ducked into the passenger seat. 'You're not in a rush, are you?'

'Why do you ask?'

'Fancy taking a trip to the other side of the river? I'm in the mood for a drive.'

Kevin glanced uncertainly at the bridge. 'It's already late. The wife will start to wonder where I am.'

Angel's long red fingernails crawled up Kevin's thigh. 'I'll make it worth your while,' she purred. 'No extra charge.'

Still Kevin hesitated. Angel grabbed his crotch and gave it a hard squeeze. 'OK,' he groaned, his face wrinkling into a pleasurably pained grimace. She let go and, shifting the car into gear, he accelerated towards the bridge. He paid the toll and drove onto the gondola.

'Come on, get a fucking move on,' muttered Angel, twisting to look at the bridge operator.

'You alright, Angel?' asked Kevin. 'You seem a bit tense, like.'

7

Angel forced a smile of pouting promise. 'I'm fine, lover. I'm always fine, you know that.'

The thick steel cables that the gondola was suspended from vibrated as well-greased wheels cranked into motion nearly fifty metres overhead. As the gondola advanced across the broad, dark waters towards the north bank, Angel got out of the car and leaned against the railings, staring at the vast sprawl of petro-chemical refineries. Flames spouted from their chimneys, illuminating colossal tangles of steel pipes. The thought came to her, *What the hell are you doing? What's this girl to you?* The answer was obvious – *Nothing.* And yet she had to do something. She didn't understand why, but she felt it in her heart. Maybe it was because something about the girl had reminded her of herself. Or maybe that wasn't it at all. Maybe it had more to do with the anger that was simmering inside her, ready to go off like a grenade at the slightest provocation.

There was a dull, heavy thunk as the gondola connected with the north bank. Angel returned to the car. 'Where are we going?' asked Kevin, accelerating away from the bridge.

'Head towards Seaton. I'll tell you when to stop.'

As they drove, Angel scanned the roadside. 'Slow down,' she said, whenever they came to a layby or anywhere else a car might pull over.

'Are you looking for someone?'

Angel didn't reply to Kevin's question. They were nearing the muddy tidal estuary of Seal Sands – pretty much the final place the Beamer could have pulled over before hitting the coastal town of Seaton Carew. They passed a small car park on their left. No Beamer. To their right a narrow lane angled away from the main road. It led, Angel knew, to a car park popular with bird- and seal watchers during the day, and lovers, doggers and stoned kids during the night. She gestured towards the lane, and Kevin turned onto it, his tongue running excitedly over his lips. He expelled a huff of breath upon reaching the car park. 'Bloody hell, someone's already using it.'

The Beamer was parked at the edge of the estuary. Its tinted rear windscreen gleamed in the Volvo's headlights. 'BAD,' Kevin said, reading its number plate. 'What kind of dickhead has a reg like that?'

'Stop the car,' said Angel.

Kevin shoved the gearstick into reverse. 'We can use the other car park.'

'I said stop!'

Kevin took his foot off the accelerator, but kept the engine running. 'What's going on, Angel?' A little quiver in his voice suggested it had dawned on him that maybe he'd stumbled into something he wanted no part of.

'Wait here.'

'Listen, I don't want to get into some kind of trouble.'

Angel's nostrils flared. It was on her tongue to snap back, *Don't be such a pussy!* But she resisted, reflecting that she should know better than to expect anything more from Kevin – or for that matter, any man. 'Nothing's going on, baby,' she reassured him. 'I know the owner of that car. I'm just going to say hi, that's all.'

Looking unconvinced, Kevin cut the engine. 'OK. Make it quick, though.'

Nothing much scared Angel, but her heart began to pound as she approached the Beamer. Her highly developed whore's instinct for sniffing out danger screamed that something dodgy was going on. It was impossible to tell if there was anyone in the car, but a faint light seeped from the edges of the doors. She raised one hand to knock on the driver-side window. Her other slipped into her handbag and curled around the pepper-spray. Before she could knock, the window came down a few centimetres. A puff of sickly sweet ganja smoke wafted out as a deep voice barked, 'Fuck off.'

Stooping, Angel found herself looking into a pair of eyes glassy with dope and hard with threat. 'I'm looking for a girl you picked up—'

A mouthful of gold teeth flashed from the Beamer's interior as its driver broke in. 'I said fuck off, bitch.'

As the window slid back up, Angel caught a glimpse of two parallel scratches still glistening with blood on the man's cheek. Her already pounding heart surged at the sight. She took several hesitant steps away from the car. The scratches didn't necessarily mean her instincts were right. She'd been with plenty of men who got turned on by being hit during sex. Men like Kevin who desired to be dominated and humiliated. The Beamer's driver wasn't one of those men. It was plain from his voice and eyes that he was the type who liked to dish it out rather than take it. Angel had been with plenty of that kind too. She still had the scars – both visible and invisible – to remind her.

Angel came to a stop as a savage burst of anger burnt away her fear. She felt suddenly as if her head was on fire. Her barely concealed breasts rose and fell as she sucked the night into her lungs. This fucker, this bad boy, thought that because the girl was a nobody, a nothing, he could do what he wanted and there'd be no consequences. Well he was wrong. There would be consequences, painful consequences.

She scanned the ground and stooped to snatch up a chunk of concrete. Without pausing, she ran at the car and hurled the chunk at its driver-side window. The glass shattered with a loud pop. The driver reeled sideways, one hand flung up to protect his face, the other groping at something on the passenger seat. He let out a shrill yell as Angel emptied the can of pepper-spray into his eyes. She yanked open the door and dragged him out of his seat, her wiry muscles straining against his bulk. She saw what he'd been reaching for – there was a handgun on the passenger seat. Ducking into the car to grab it, she found the girl stretched out unconscious on the back seat, her skirt half torn away, blood crusting her inner thighs, her face a battered mask. She didn't appear to be breathing.

Her eyes a crucible of rage, Angel twisted towards the man writhing in agony at her feet. He blindly tried to defend himself as once, twice, three times she stamped her long, sharp heel into his face, ripping deep gouges. 'You fuck!' she shouted, spittle flying from her mouth. 'You sick fuck!'

She would have continued to stamp and stamp until the man's face was as unrecognisable as the girl's, if Kevin hadn't come sprinting over, crying out, 'Stop! For Christ's sake, stop!'

Angel jerked her eyes up to Kevin's, and he lurched to a halt as if he'd come up against a wall of flames. He spread his hands, palms out. 'Please, Angel. You'll kill him.'

'And why shouldn't I?' she snarled. 'The bastard deserves it.'

'Why? What's he done?'

'He's killed her, that's what.'

His face as pale as the moon, Kevin asked, 'Killed who?'

'The girl.' Angel gestured at the car. 'She's in there.'

Kevin edged around Angel. He reached for the back door handle, but hesitated. He pulled his sleeve down over his hand, then opened the door. 'Oh Jesus,' he gasped on seeing the girl. He felt for a pulse in her neck. His eyes widened. 'She's alive!'

'Are you sure?'

'Her pulse is weak, but it's definitely there.' Kevin pulled out his mobile phone.

'What are you doing?'

'What do you think I'm doing? I'm phoning for an ambulance.'

Angel snatched the phone away. 'No you're not.'

Kevin looked at her in stunned silence for a second. 'But she'll die if I don't.'

'No she won't, because you're going to take her to hospital.'

Kevin's forehead contracted. 'I can't do that, Angel. If I'm seen with this girl, it... well, it would—' His voice snagged in his throat at the thought of what it would do to him if word of this got back to his wife.

'I don't give a shit what it'd do to you. You're taking her.'

'No I'm not.'

Kevin recoiled back against the car, his chest heaving as Angel aimed the gun at him. Her voice as hard as the steel the nearby factories produced, she said, 'Yes you are.'

'OK, OK, I'll do it. Just stop pointing that thing at me.'

Angel lowered the gun. A groan from the prostrate man drew her attention. He was struggling to sit up, his muscular, tattooed arms trembling from the effort. She drove her heel into his face again, sending him crashing onto his back. 'Bitch,' he choked out, blood dribbling between his lips.

'Keep your fucking mouth shut unless you want more of the same,' snapped Angel. She looked at Kevin. 'Get her into your car.'

As Kevin hooked his hands under the girl's armpits and pulled her from the car, she exhaled a whisper of a moan. Her eyelids fluttered and cracked open a fraction. Angel leaned over her like a mother over a child. 'That's it, come on, open your eyes.'

The slitted eyes closed again.

'Hold on, baby girl, we're going to get you to hospital.'

The girl's limbs dangled like broken twigs as Kevin carried her to his car and laid her on its back seat. Breathing heavily, he turned to Angel. 'You coming?'

'No.'

The creases on Kevin's forehead deepened. His eyes flicked between Angel and the man at her feet. 'What are you going to do?'

'You don't need to worry about that, all you need to worry about is getting her to hospital. Oh, and if I find out you've dumped her somewhere and rung for an ambulance, I'm not going to be best pleased.' Angel patted the gun. 'You get me?'

Kevin nodded, his tongue darting dryly across his lips. 'You're not going to do anything crazy—'

'Get the fuck out of here,' cut in Angel, her eyes flashing.

Flinching from her fury, Kevin ducked into his car. He accelerated away, wheels spitting gravel. Angel waited until he hit the main road before returning her attention to the Beamer's driver. His eyes glared at her from between swollen pouches of flesh, glistening with hate but also fear. It sent a thrill through Angel almost as heady as a hit of junk to see

13

his fear, to know that, for once in her life, she was the one with the power. 'On your belly.' Her voice was calmer. The anger was still there, but she was controlling it now, not it her.

Groaning, the man slowly rolled onto his belly.

'Now crawl to the river. Crawl like the worm you are.'

The man dug his fingers into the cracked concrete and dragged himself forward. The light from the Beamer's interior only stretched a few metres. At the edge of its reach, estuary mud glistened palely in the moonlight. When her heels sank into the mud, Angel said, 'Stop.'

The man lay panting, agonised tremors vibrating through his body.

'Roll over,' said Angel. 'I want to see your face.'

The man heaved himself onto his back again. He stared up at Angel, his mud-smeared face invisible except for the red-laced whites of his eyes and the gleam of his gold teeth. 'You don't know who the fuck I am,' he gasped, his voice cramped with pain.

'Yeah I do. I've known you all my life.'

Angel took aim. The man flung up a hand as if he might ward off a bullet with it. 'Wait! Fucking wait! I've got money.' He fumbled out his wallet and tossed it to Angel. 'There's more than a thousand quid in there. It's yours.'

Angel took out the money and shoved it into her handbag. She didn't look to see if there was any identification – she already knew all she needed to know about the man – she just threw the wallet into the estuary. Again, she took aim. Again, the man raised a hand. 'Why are you doing this?' he asked, panic sucking at his voice.

Angel studied the man with a cold fire behind her eyes, greedily drinking in his fear, savouring its bittersweet taste. 'The same reason you did what you did. Because I can.'

The fear in the man's eyes was joined by a hopeless rage. He spat a glob of phlegm at Angel, which left a bloody snail-trail down her thigh. 'Fuck you, bitch! Fuck all you slags. I'd kill the lot of you if I got the chance.'

'Well you're not going to get the chance.'

Angel pulled the trigger. Nothing happened. She pulled it again. Still nothing. 'Shit.' The word whistled through her teeth as she thought, *The fucking thing's broken*. Another thought came to her. *The safety must be on*. A quick examination of the gun revealed a catch marked 'Safety' above the trigger. She flicked it.

'Please, I don't want to die!' pleaded the man as Angel took aim again. An ear-splitting shot rang out. The gun's recoil jerked her hand upward. The muzzle flash set pinpoints of light dancing in front of her eyes. The man screamed and flailed in the estuary slime, clutching his right shoulder. As her vision cleared, Angel took careful aim at his chest. The man just had time to cry out some incomprehensible final words before a second bullet punched the breath from his lungs. He lay gurgling like the estuary for a moment, then fell silent.

Angel closed her eyes and drew in a slow, deep breath. The night tasted good. It felt good against her skin. She felt good. Strong and alive! Every sensation in her body seemed to be heightened almost to the point of ecstasy. She hugged herself, moaning, swaying. She wasn't sure how long she stood there immersed in the throbbing whirlpool of her mind, but when she opened her eyes the tide was lapping at the man. Soon it would cover him, and as it receded it would draw him out to sea, hopefully never to be seen again.

Slipping the gun into her handbag, Angel approached the BMW. She considered burning it out, but dismissed the idea, realising she almost certainly wouldn't have time to get back to town before a passer-by alerted the police. With her jacket sleeve, she rubbed the door handle she'd touched. She didn't know whether doing so would erase her fingerprints, but she figured it was worth a try. Keeping her hand covered, she reached into the car and switched off the interior light. Then she started walking.

It was at least six miles back to town. Angel hadn't gone far before her ankles started to throb. She took off her boots and continued barefoot, keeping her eyes and ears peeled for vehicles. A fragmentary hedgerow ran alongside the road. Whenever she saw approaching headlights or heard the rumble of an engine, she ducked out of sight until the vehicle had passed. Her mobile phone rang. She flipped it open and 'Deano' flashed up on its screen. She wasn't surprised. He rang several times a night. He said he did it because he cared about her, which of course was bullshit. The only thing he gave a toss about was making sure his property was in working order. The temptation not to answer was strong, but the consequences wouldn't be worth it. She put the phone to her ear and said in a hushed tone, 'I can't talk right now, Deano. I'm with a punter.'

'Where?'

'The Thistle Hotel. He's a businessman. I reckon I'm onto a good little earner. I'll call you as soon as I'm done.'

'Make sure you work him for all he's got.'

'I always do, baby.'

Angel hung up, reflecting that it was a lucky thing for her the dead man had attempted to buy his way out of trouble. Three or four hundred quid of the thousand would be enough to keep Deano sweet. As for the rest, she would find some way of getting it to the girl, assuming she survived her injuries.

Dawn was beginning to crack by the time Angel reached the Transporter Bridge. She paid the toll and leaned wearily against the gondola's railings. She could feel the beginnings of withdrawal symptoms setting in – her teeth chattered as if she had a fever, and bitter mucus ran down the back of her throat. It wasn't just withdrawal, though. For hours she'd been on a high unlike any she'd ever known, but now she was coming down, and she was coming down hard. She scratched the track marks on her arms, itching for the oblivion of heroin. Glancing around furtively, she slipped a hand into her handbag and touched the gun. The feel of the plastic grip sent a little shuddering thrill through her. Wrinkles of indecision spread over her face. She'd intended to toss the gun into the Tees, but now that it came to it she was reluctant to do so. She closed her handbag. She knew it was crazy to keep the gun, but she couldn't bring herself to get rid of it. Not with the memory of the feeling that had coursed through her body as she pulled the trigger so fresh in her mind.

An orange glow crept across the water, followed by the emerging sun. Angel blinked, tears rising in her eyes. She'd seen the sunrise hundreds of times before during her nocturnal existence. But she'd never seen it like this, so brilliant and blazing. Her trembling subsided as its faint, cleansing warmth washed over her. Then the gondola passed into the shadows of the industrial units on the south bank, and the moment was gone. Not that it had really been anything other than a fleeting illusion. The sun was for other people, not her. She'd learnt, or rather been taught, that hard lesson a long time ago.

Angel felt as though she was wading through deep water, but even so she walked fast, dragged along by the heroin itch. She found Deano crashed out on the bed, his tracksuit bottoms around his ankles, a fresh track mark where he'd injected the big artery in his groin. The veins in his arms had collapsed years ago. Angel had bad veins too. Recently there had been times when she'd missed by so much that blood had streamed down her wrists. So she too had taken to injecting her groin, or as Deano called it, 'opening the window'.

Deano's eyelids fluttered but didn't open as Angel slipped a hand into his pocket and pulled out a small lump of black tar heroin wrapped in cellophane. She took a shoebox full of drug-taking paraphernalia from under the bed, tore open an alcohol swab and cleaned her hands and a bent spoon. She dissolved the lump on the spoon over a lighter, then placed a little ball of cotton-wool in the solution. When the ball had puffed up, she inserted a syringe into it and drew up all the dirty-brown liquid. Spreading her legs as if for a punter, she felt for the pulsing femoral artery. She slid the needle in and pulled the plunger a millimetre. Blood swirled into the syringe barrel. Slowly, she depressed the plunger. The rush was instant, enveloping her like a lover's soft, warm embrace, soothing away all the pain and memories. Eyeballs rolling, she lay back next to Deano. As sweet oblivion stole over her, she replayed in her mind the moment the man had died. That was one memory she wanted to hold on to. Always.

Chapter Two

Stephen Baxley wandered around the grounds of his ungainly mock Tudor mansion saying goodbye to everything. He said goodbye to his Aston Martin. He said goodbye to his horses. He said goodbye to the swimming pool, the tennis court, the sprawling landscaped gardens. Then he headed inside the house.

The entrance hall's ornate beamed ceilings, chandeliers and faux-antique furnishings reeked of tasteless extravagance. Stephen entered the study, its wood-panelled walls stuffed with unread leather-spined books. He locked the door, poured himself a large whisky from a crystal decanter and sank it in one. He poured another and took it to his desk, which was strewn with papers. His gaze skimmed over a letter, lingering on the words 'foreclosure' and 'court action'. A spasm twisting his face, he yanked open a drawer and took out a sheet of writing-paper whose black letterhead read 'SB ENGINEERING'. Pen in hand, he stared at the letterhead for a long moment. Finally, lips pale and compressed as if every word was a knife slashing at his mind, he wrote, 'Dear Jenny. Please forgive me for telling you this in a letter, but the words are simply too painful to say to your face. I've been forced to declare the business bankrupt. I tried everything I could to save it, but failed. I've failed you, I've failed the children…'

Stephen broke off from writing to empty his glass. Whisky dribbled down his chin. He didn't bother to wipe it off. He pressed pen to paper again, but no words appeared. His hand trembled as if struggling against some invisible resistance. Suddenly, he jerked it up and stabbed down, tearing the paper, scratching a deep gouge in the desk. Eyes shining wildly, he stabbed the letter again, snapping the pen, the jagged end of which pierced his palm. Blood spattered the papers as he thrust them off the desk, along with a reading lamp whose glass shade shattered across the parquet floor. He ground his forehead against the desktop, digging his fingers into his scalp, emitting a low, anguished groan.

'Everything OK in there? I heard a noise like something breaking.'

Stephen's head snapped up as Jenny's voice came through the door. He took a deep breath to steady himself before he spoke. 'Everything's fine, darling. I dropped a glass, that's all.'

'Do you need a hand cleaning it up?'

'No thanks.'

'Are you almost done for the day?'

'I've just got one or two more things to sort out.'

'Well try not to be too long. Charlotte's getting hungry.'

'Don't wait for me.'

A note of displeasure that suggested this was an all too familiar topic of conversation entered Jenny's voice. 'You know how I like us to sit down and eat together as a family, Stephen. We talked about this last week and you said—'

Irritation sparked in Stephen's voice. 'For Christ's sake, Jenny, I know what I said—' he started to snap, but caught himself. He drew in another long breath and continued in a softer, if slightly forced tone, 'Look, just give me ten minutes. Then I'll be all yours for the evening. I promise.'

'OK, Stephen.' The way Jenny said his name was full of significance. It meant there was going to be an argument if he broke his promise.

As his wife's footsteps moved away from the door, Stephen picked up a framed photo of her, himself and their two children, Charlotte and Mark. It was one of a set that had been taken by a professional photographer four years ago. Charlotte would have been eleven and Mark nineteen or twenty. Stephen was squatting in front of Jenny with his arms around the kids' waists. All four of them were casually dressed – the photographer had wanted to avoid the stuffy formality of many family portraits. All four of them were smiling, but Mark's smile didn't look quite real, at least not to Stephen. There was something strained and awkward about it. There was a certain stiffness about the way he held himself too, as if he'd rather be anywhere else but there. Stephen had angrily pointed this out to Jenny on first seeing the photos. As usual, she'd defended Mark, saying his smile looked perfectly genuine to her. She'd been lying, of course. But there was no point arguing with her. There never was when it came to Mark, reflected Stephen. The little shit couldn't do any wrong in her eyes.

Stephen would have kept the photo somewhere out of sight if it hadn't been for Charlotte. The photo captured her perfectly. He often found himself staring at her face with its laughing, liquid-blue eyes and frame of auburn hair,

wondering how he'd ever managed to create something so beautiful. Tenderly, he ran his fingers along the contours of her features. His breath came in a shudder. She'd had everything, every luxury money could purchase, and now she would have nothing. Nothing! The thought tore at him like a howling madman. His fingers curled into a fist, nails pushing deep into the wound on his palm. He knew what it was like to have nothing. His childhood had been a pitiless, degrading struggle against poverty. He'd sworn his children would never know that sort of life. But the last few years had been one long string of cancelled orders, failed deals and bad investments. The economy was going down the drain, and it was taking him and his family with it, all the way back to the sewer he'd spent half his life climbing out of.

Stephen shook his head, tears spilling down his cheeks. 'No. I won't let it happen. I won't, I won't, I won't.' The words hissed through his teeth like escaping steam. For several minutes he chanted them to himself. Then, as if a solution had suddenly occurred to him, the tension drained from his features. He raised his eyes, and for a moment seemed to be looking through the ceiling to some other place. His gaze returned to the photo. 'Don't worry, my sweet little girl. You won't have to find out. None of you will.'

Placing the picture face down on the desk, Stephen reached for the phone and punched in a number. A male voice answered. 'Hi, Mum.'

'It's not Mum, Mark. It's me.' Stephen's voice was flat and emotionless.

'Dad.' Mark sounded surprised, as if his father was the last person he'd expected to be calling. 'What do you want?'

'Can you come over?'

'What? Right now?'

'Yes, right now.'

'I've only just got in from uni.'

'This is important.'

A note of concern came into Mark's voice. 'Has something happened?'

'Look, Mark, I don't want to go into this on the phone, except to say that this is something that concerns us all. So just get yourself over here and I'll explain everything.'

'OK,' sighed Mark. 'I'll be there as soon as I can.'

Stephen hung up without saying goodbye. He reached for the whisky again, but hesitated. As much as he thirsted for the warmth of its liquid embrace, it was going to take a clear head and a steady hand to do what must be done. His eyes unblinking, his movements curiously stiff, like a wind-up toy set in motion, he turned to a TV screen split into four quadrants. CCTV cameras showed the front gate, the front door, the back garden and the garage. He switched off the CCTV. Then he made his way to the large living room. It was decorated in muted tones of misty blue, chosen by him to match Charlotte's eyes.

Charlotte was stretched out on the leather sofa, watching the oversized plasma television. It showed a helicopter's bird's eye shot of several figures in white plastic suits milling around a car at the muddy edge of a river. A warm breeze smelling of cigarette smoke wafted through the open French doors. Stephen looked past Jenny, who was smoking on the patio. He looked past the manicured lawns and flowerbeds. He looked past the patchwork quilt of brown moorland and green fields to the sprawling cityscape of Sheffield. A ripple disturbed his features. He knew the city as well as he knew anything. In his teens, he'd explored its every cranny and dark corner, and the things he'd found had destroyed and remade him in their own image. Those things had touched every part of his life, except Charlotte. She was the one pure passion of his existence, and he would never allow anything to change that.

'What are you watching?' Stephen asked, more for something to say than because he was interested.

Charlotte flinched, twisting towards him. 'Dad! You shouldn't sneak up on people like that.'

'Sorry. I didn't mean to.'

A slight frown marred Charlotte's china-smooth skin. 'Are you OK? You look really pale.'

Stephen tried to force a smile, but one wouldn't come. 'I'm fine, sweetie.' He stared at Charlotte intensely, as if etching every detail of her features onto his mind.

She squirmed a little. 'Why are you looking at me like that?'

'Because I love you. I love you more than anything.'

Charlotte turned on her best daddy's girl smile. 'More even than you love Mark?'

'A thousand million times more. More even than I love my own life.'

'So does that mean I can have a new iPhone?'

A tick so faint as to be scarcely visible pulled at Stephen's mouth. 'You can have whatever you want, sweetie. You know that.'

Charlotte jumped up to wrap her arms around Stephen. 'Thanks, Dad. You're the best!'

He hugged her back, briefly closing his eyes as he inhaled

the scent of her hair. 'Now go tell your mum to put the food out. There's something I need to take care of in the garage. I should only be a couple of minutes.'

A smug smile playing at the corners of her lips, Charlotte headed for the patio. Stephen's attention was drawn to the television by a voice saying, '...divers recovered the man's body earlier today. Police have yet to formally identify the dead man, but they believe him to be Ryan Castle, a thirty-three-year-old local man whose car was found at a nearby nature reserve. They further believe that Castle, a known drug dealer with a history of violent crime, may have been the victim of a deal gone wrong. Castle was killed by gunshot wounds to the chest—'

Stephen picked up the remote-control and turned the television off. As he headed out the front door, the newsreader's words echoed in his head. *Killed by gunshot wounds to the chest. Killed by gunshot wounds to the chest.*

'Stephen.'

Flinching at the sound of his name, Stephen looked towards the wrought-iron gate that separated the long driveway from the quiet lane beyond. A man in a dark grey suit was standing beside a black Jag on the other side of it. The man was bald with a natural tonsure of salt-and-pepper hair and a slightly jowly, almost babyishly smooth face. A deep frown cut Stephen's forehead. Edward Forester. That phoney bastard was the last person he felt like talking to. But he knew from experience how persistent Edward could be when he wanted something. Sucking in a tight breath, he approached him. Edward smiled, showing unnaturally white and even teeth. There was something about his smile – some quality of rigidity

– that made it seem more a habitual reflex than a genuine expression of emotion.

'Save your smile for the voters, Edward,' said Stephen, his voice cold and hard. 'What are you doing here?'

The smile disappeared like water from a tap being turned off. 'I've been trying to contact you all week. Why haven't you returned my calls?'

'Because I've got nothing to say to you.'

'I thought we were friends.'

'Friends?' A slight, humourless curl came to Stephen's lips. 'You don't know the meaning of the word.'

A ripple crossed the smoothness of Edward's face. 'Christ, they're true, aren't they? The rumours I've been hearing.'

'Goodbye, Edward,' said Stephen, turning away from the gate.

'Don't turn your back on me,' snapped Edward. 'I've a right to know what's going on.'

Ignoring him, Stephen headed towards the garage. Edward's angry voice pursued him. 'I'm warning you, Stephen. Don't make a fool of me.'

Stephen lifted the garage door, revealing his Range Rover and his Aston Martin. He ran his hand lightly over the sports car's sleek bodywork. Other than Charlotte, making money and one or two vices, there was nothing he loved more than opening up its throttle on the leafy lanes surrounding his property. The thought of someone else driving it and getting the same pleasure from it that he did was enough to make him feel nauseous. Shaking his head as if to say, *No way*, he took a couple of petrol canisters from a shelf. He unscrewed one and sluiced its contents over the vehicles. The sound of an engine starting up then receding into the distance, told him Edward had left. *Lucky for him*, he thought. He approached a tall, rectangular metal box, opened it with a key, and removed a double-barrelled shotgun and a cartridge belt. He strapped on the belt, broke open the shotgun, chambered two cartridges, and snapped the barrel shut. Holding the shotgun in one hand and the full canister in the other, he returned to the house.

As quietly as possible, Stephen set down the canister in the hallway and closed the front door. Shouldering the shotgun, he padded along the hallway. The sound of cutlery being laid came from beyond the half-open kitchen door. He peered through the gap.

Charlotte was sitting at the table with her back to him. *That's good*, he thought. *That way she won't see what's coming or have time to be afraid.* His eyes lingered on her hair a moment, before shifting to Jenny, who was spooning pasta into bowls at the cooker. She was still a good-looking woman, even though she was carrying a little extra weight these days. Not that she'd ever really been his type. Did he love her? Probably not, but he needed her. She'd looked after him better than his own mother had. Without her steadying influence, he'd never have been able to build up the business to what it was – or rather, to what it had been a few years ago. And she'd given him Charlotte. In return, he'd given her a life beyond most people's wildest expectations – holiday homes in Tuscany and Florida, a yacht, endless hours in beauty salons, a face-lift, a tit-lift, an arse-lift, a two-million-quid house. And now all of it was gone, or soon would be. Their whole world was about to come crashing down around them and there was nothing he could do about it. Well, not quite nothing.

Stephen took aim at Charlotte's head, and without hesitation, pulled the trigger. The boom of the shotgun, amplified by the confined space, set his ears screaming. Charlotte was flung across the table as if she'd been hit by a charging bull. A millisecond later, she vanished in a cloud of smoke from the gun's muzzle. Jenny's almost unearthly screaming rose above that of Stephen's eardrums. Mechanically, he advanced into the kitchen. Jenny staggered backwards, flinging her hands up in front of her terror-contorted face. Aiming for her chest, Stephen pulled the trigger at point-blank range. As if she was an empty sack, Jenny was punched into the air and thrown against the cupboards. She landed face down in a heap of quivering, twisted limbs. Blood instantly began to pool on the tiled floor. For a few seconds, she made a guttural rattling sound in her throat. Then there was silence, deep and terrible.

Stephen stooped over Jenny to check for a pulse in her wrist. He couldn't find one. He started to turn towards Charlotte, but hesitated. He didn't want to see her as she looked now. He wanted to remember her forever – even if forever wasn't that long – as she'd looked in the lounge, her blue eyes and auburn hair shining in the evening sun. Besides, he told himself, no one could survive a wound such as she'd suffered.

Taking care not to look at Charlotte, Stephen sluiced petrol over his wife and daughter's bloody bodies. He backed from the kitchen, dribbling a trail of petrol into the living room. After dousing the three-piece suite, he headed upstairs, emptying the last of the petrol over the landing.

Stephen entered the master bedroom, which was dominated by an ornate four-poster bed draped with crimson silk sheets. He shoved aside a rack of suits in the walk-in wardrobe, revealing a safe. He punched a combination into the electronic lock. Inside the safe there was a bundle of papers and a thick wad of fifty-quid notes. He retrieved an unmarked manila envelope. Carefully, almost fearfully, he opened the envelope and withdrew a similarly unmarked DVD. He inserted it into a slot on the side of the television at the end of the bed. A gloomily lit scene that had obviously been filmed on a handheld camera appeared on the screen. He stared at it with glimmering, heavy-lidded eyes. His tongue flicked out like a lizard tasting the air, as the camera swung around to focus on a group of shadowy figures.

Chapter Three

As Mark drove through the city's well-heeled south-western suburbs, one question kept repeating itself in his mind: *What was going on?* It had to be something bad. Why else would his dad phone him out of the blue? It wasn't as though they had anything to say to each other. Not that they were on bad terms. There was just no connection between them – no love, no hate, merely a kind of emotional void. It had been like that as long as he could remember, which was OK with him – or at least he told himself it was – because, try as he had many times before, he just couldn't bring himself to like his dad. There was something about him, though nothing he could point his finger at, that made his skin crawl. The rare occasions they touched, be it an awkward handshake or an accidental brush of arm or thigh, everything inside him would coil into a tight ball.

Charlotte and their dad's relationship was the exact opposite. She always seemed to be hugging him, snuggling up on the sofa with him, or laughing at some joke only the two of them shared. For years it had eaten Mark up inside to see the two of them together. He'd agonised endlessly during therapy sessions over why things were so different between him and his dad. He used to think it was because there was something wrong with himself, that he was abnormal in some way. On the advice of his therapist, he'd tried to talk about his feelings with his parents. But the words had stuck in his throat like fishhooks when faced with his dad. And the most he'd ever got out of his mum was a dismissive, 'There's nothing wrong with either you or your father. You're just very different, that's all.'

Mark agreed with the second part of what she'd said. He and his dad were very different. Thank Christ. But as for the first part, well, that was another matter. The older he got, the less he saw himself as the 'abnormal' one. A view that had taken deeper root after he moved out of the house. Every time he returned home he noticed more and more how his dad struggled to meet his eye, and a suspicion started to grow in him that he was hiding something. Some secret. Recently, he'd even begun to wonder whether his dad really was his dad. He'd sat in front of a mirror with a photo of his dad, inspecting every angle and line of both their faces. And the more he scrutinised, the more differences he discovered. His dad had hazel-brown eyes, a hooked nose, thin lips and a sharp jaw. His mum had deep blue eyes, a blunt nose, small but full lips and a round fleshy jaw. Charlotte was a mixture of these features, whereas with his blue-grey eyes, button nose and dimpled chin, Mark's only easily discernible resemblance was to his mum.

Mark suddenly found himself wondering whether this was the reason his dad had called him. Maybe he'd decided it was time to reveal that he wasn't his real father. Mark hoped so. He hoped that somewhere out there, there was a man he could love in the way that sons are supposed to love their fathers. The thought brought a stab of guilt. Stephen might not have provided him with love, but he'd provided him with a beautiful house to grow up in, an expensive education and every other material thing he could want, including the flat he lived in and the car he was driving. What had this fantasy father figure provided him with? Nothing, that's what. Unless he was ignorant of his child's existence – which Mark couldn't believe his mum would have allowed to happen – he'd chosen not to be a part of his life. Stephen might be distant and cold, and there might be something about him that wasn't quite right, but whatever he was, he was there. That had to count for something. Didn't it? Of course it did, and yet at some deep, almost subconscious level he couldn't help but hope that there was a grain of truth in his suspicions.

Mark slammed a door on his thoughts, telling himself they were as absurd as they were destructive. In truth, he knew the most likely reason for his dad's phone call was the business. Sure, he might be a bit of a daydreamer. And, sure, he might have been insulated from the everyday worries that affected other people. But he wasn't completely detached from reality. He read the newspapers. He knew there was a recession on and that it had hit the manufacturing sector hard. Added to which, Charlotte had phoned him a few days ago to moan about their dad working late every night. At the time he'd been more irritated by her whining than concerned about the reasons behind it.

Mark passed the city limits and wound his way through a valley of fields enclosed by dry-stone walls, and scattered houses. He turned onto a lane that led to a tall gate set into an equally tall wall. He punched a code into the keypad. An electronic motor whirred to life and the gate slid aside.

It was twilight, but the downstairs windows were dark. That struck him as odd. His mum always liked to have the house brightly lit up. Unlike her children, she'd been raised in the inner city. And she remained a city girl at heart, easily spooked by the rural night.

Mark's eyes were drawn to a flickering, bluish light in his parents' bedroom window. A new thought came to him. Maybe there was something wrong with his mum. Maybe she was ill in bed. A familiar sense of choking anxiety rose inside him. His mum was the most important person in his life. Where his dad had given him material possessions, she'd given him love and the confidence to be who he was rather than who his dad expected him to be. When he'd told his parents he wanted to study art, his dad had scoffed at the idea, calling it a Mickey-Mouse degree. His mum had stuck up for him, defending his right to make his own decisions. Despite his dad's contempt for his choice, he hadn't protested it much. In fact, it seemed to Mark that he was relieved his son harboured no desire to work alongside him. Of course, it was different with Charlotte. Dad had been grooming her for years to follow in his footsteps, teaching her all the ins and outs of his business.

You're doing it again, Mark reprimanded himself, concentrating on breathing slowly and deeply as his therapist had taught him. *You have to stop torturing yourself like this. There's nothing you can do about the way things are between you and Dad. And there's nothing wrong with Mum – at least, nothing serious. If there was, you'd be at the hospital now, not here agonising over the same old shit.*

The anxiety faded and Mark approached the front door. It wasn't locked, but then it rarely was. There was no need out here, especially not with the high garden walls and CCTV cameras. The first thing he noticed on entering the hallway was the smell of petrol. Another smell lurked underneath it. His nostrils flared as he inhaled its acrid stink, which was vaguely reminiscent of burnt meat. The second thing he noticed was the noise from upstairs. It was a small, tremulous noise, like a child sobbing. Something about it made him shiver as if someone had stepped on his grave. His frowning gaze ascended to the lighted rectangle of his parents' bedroom doorway.

'Mum! Dad!' he called. No reply. 'Charlotte!' Still no reply.

What the fuck's going on here? Mark wondered. He reached for a light-switch, but hesitated as it occurred to him that maybe the lights were off for a reason. He didn't have a clue as to what that reason might be. It didn't sound like Charlotte crying up there. When she turned on the waterworks it was loud enough to shatter glass. Maybe it was one of his parents' friends' kids. The thought reinforced his suspicion that this had something to do with the business – pretty much all of his parents' friends were connected to the business in some way.

Prickles of unease creeping over his scalp, Mark climbed the stairs. *Something's very wrong here*, his brain hissed at him. *Why didn't anyone answer you?* A lurid picture flashed through his head of his parents and sister bound and gagged. *You're letting your imagination run away with you again*, some other part of his brain retorted. *Whatever's going on, there'll be some perfectly simple explanation for it.* But still his body was tensed and ready for flight as he approached his parents' bedroom. He peered around the doorframe, and what he saw threw his heart into wild palpitations. His dad was standing at the end of the bed, shotgun pressed to his shoulder, its barrel aimed at the doorway.

Instinctively, Mark jerked back. As he did so the muzzle flashed white, then orange. The boom of the shotgun rolled over him like thunder. A large section of the doorframe disintegrated, spraying him with a storm of splinters. A sledgehammer seemed to hit his right shoulder, punching the breath out of his lungs, spinning him like a top. He clutched at the bannister, barely managing to stop himself from pitching over it. Through hazy layers of fear and tears, he saw his dad emerge from the doorway. His face was bloodless and blank, his eyes as empty as black holes. With a strangely robotic movement, he swung the shotgun's barrel towards his son.

For an instant, paralysis seized Mark. *I'm going to fucking die*, screamed his brain. Struggling for breath, he managed to gasp out, 'No!' His left hand darted out to grab the barrel and shove it away. Father and son strained against each other, limbs trembling, eyes bulging. Even if his right arm hadn't dangled uselessly at his side, Mark's strength would have been no match for his father's. Slowly but surely, the barrel inched towards his face. With one last desperate effort, Mark threw his body against the gun, forcing it floorward. There was another eardrum-lacerating boom, and it felt to Mark as if someone was dragging a white-hot razor along his left shin. As he collapsed down the stairs, a whoosh of flames leapt up, enveloping his dad's trousers. Tumbling head over heels, he glimpsed his dad slapping futilely at the flames on his legs.

Mark landed in a winded heap at the bottom of the stairs. Seeing that the flames were giving chase, he grabbed the bannister and hauled himself upright. He limped towards the kitchen as the petrol pooled by the front door ignited. A piercing scream sliced the air as, in a final crazed attempt to kill his son, Stephen threw himself over the bannister. Flaring like a comet, he hurtled towards Mark. His scream cut off abruptly as he hit the floor headfirst behind him.

A burst of flames searing his back, Mark half staggered, half collapsed into the kitchen. He kicked the door shut, blocking the fire's advance. Then he sagged against the work-surface, his temples throbbing as his brain struggled to assimilate what had happened. He felt as though he'd like to close his eyes and sink into oblivion – not just to escape the pain of his wounds, but to escape the pain of knowing that his dad had tried to murder him. His dad had tried to murder him! His own dad! It was beyond insane. It was so incomprehensible as to scarcely seem real. It was real, though. The blood streaming from his arm was real; the pain radiating through his body and mind was real.

Mark knew he had to keep moving. He had to find medical attention. Of even more immediate concern, the door wouldn't hold the fire for long. Already its paint was blistering and flames were licking at its edges. He found himself wondering whether he cared. Did he really want to continue living in a world where this could happen? *Yes*, exclaimed something inside him, perhaps the same deep-rooted survival instinct that had given him the strength to fight his father. Another thought struck him like a fist, jerking him fully upright, eyes wide and searching. Where were his mum and Charlotte? Had his dad tried to kill them too? In one horrifying instant, he got his answer.

'Oh God no!' cried Mark, the words tearing out of his throat as if formed from broken glass. 'Please no. Please, please.' He threw himself towards his mum, landing on his knees in a slick of still-warm blood. 'Mum! Mum!' He felt her wrist for a pulse. He put his ear close to her mouth, listening for breath. There were no signs of life. How could there be? There was a hole in her chest big enough to push his fist into. His gaze transferred to Charlotte. Not that he recognised her blood-masked face, but he knew from her clothes and hair that it was her.

Mark began to shake violently. Vomit pushed up his throat, spewing from his mouth and nose. He collapsed beside his mum, moaning and clutching at her. There was nothing left inside him. There was nothing left outside him. Everything was gone. His whole family had been blasted into a bloody ruin of flesh and bone. Better to die with them than to live on with the pain of the loss. He squeezed his tear-filled eyes shut, the rushing crackle of flames filling his ears. In his mind's eye, he saw his father's monstrously blank face peering over the gun sight. 'Come on!' he shouted hoarsely. 'Kill me! Kill me and get this over with!'

As if in response, a barely audible groan came to his ears. He snapped his eyes open, half expecting to see his dad risen from the dead like some horror movie bogeyman to finish him off. His dad wasn't there, but what he did see astonished him almost as much. Charlotte was twitching as if an electric current was being passed through her. She was alive! It seemed impossible. The top left quarter of her skull was gone. But there was no denying what he saw. Suddenly his survival instinct kicked in again, ordering him to get up and help his sister. Slowly, painfully, he obeyed.

Mark hooked his good arm around Charlotte. She was a slim little thing, but her limp body seemed as heavy as a sandbag. His breath coming in agonised gasps, he somehow managed to lift her and carry her towards the back door. Halfway there, his injured leg buckled. As he fell, he twisted his body between the floor and Charlotte. He cradled her head against his chest, taking care not to touch her wound. He lay for a moment trying to catch his breath, but his lungs seemed reluctant to inflate. He tried to get up, but was too weak. He saw that the fire had broken through the door. Tongues of flame were leaping into the room. Smoke swept like storm clouds across the ceiling. There was maybe a minute, maybe only seconds left before it would light up Charlotte's petrol-soaked body like a struck match.

'No.' The word hissed through Mark's gritted teeth. He clawed at the floor, dragging himself and his sister centimetre by centimetre towards the back door. He didn't know what had driven his dad to murderous insanity. And at that moment, he didn't care. All he cared about was making sure his dad didn't achieve what he'd planned. Even in the midst of all that agony and anguish, it lent him a perverse kind of strength to think that he would be depriving the bastard of his final gesture of power over his family.

Grunting and spitting with the effort, Mark grasped the door handle and hauled himself upright. As he opened the door, the heat of the fire sucked the cool night air into the house. The influx of oxygen made the flames momentarily shrink. Then they roared up fiercer than ever.

Mark knew there was no time to be gentle with Charlotte. He grabbed her arm and dragged her outside. They were about five metres from the house when the petrol ignited. The windows blew out, showering them with glass, knocking Mark off his feet. This time, as he lay fighting to hold on to consciousness, he knew he wouldn't be getting up again. He barely had sufficient strength to take out his mobile phone, dial 999 and murmur the address to the operator. He let his head roll towards Charlotte. His lips formed faltering words. 'Hold on, sis... Don't... die.'

Chapter Four

The mobile phone's ringtone wormed its way into Jim Monahan's sleeping mind. With a phlegmy grunt, he switched on the bedside lamp and reached for the phone. Seeing Amy Sheridan's name, he put the receiver to his ear and asked in a rasping, smoker's voice, 'What's the crack, Amy?' Even before she replied, he knew it had to be something big for her to disturb him when he was off duty.

'We've got a multiple shooting.'

'Where?'

'A house just off the Ringinglow Road. Out towards Hathersage.'

A veteran of over three decades' service, Jim wasn't easily surprised, but his eyes widened a little. He'd been expecting Amy to say the Manor or the Wicker or one of the other inner-city areas where gun crime, although relatively uncommon compared to many major cities, was certainly not extraordinary. Back when he was in uniform, he'd dealt with thefts from vehicles belonging to hikers and climbers who frequented the moors and gritstone crags to the south-west of the city. But in all his years on the force he'd never been called to a shooting anywhere near the Ringinglow Road.

His first thought was that they might be dealing with the fallout of a home-invasion gone tits up. There were some big pads out there. It wasn't unknown for gangs of burglars to cross the Snake Pass from Manchester and turn over four, maybe even five houses in a night. 'How many shot and how many dead?'

'Can't say for sure right now. There are two in hospital, both with severe and one with possibly fatal wounds. There may be two dead in the house. The house is on fire. I think the worst of it's been extinguished, but firemen are still working in the building. I'm texting you the address.'

Jim's phone beeped as the address came through. 'Got it. See you soon.' He reached for a pack of cigarettes and lit one, reflecting as he often did that his ex-wife, Margaret, would have flipped her lid if she'd caught him smoking in bed. There weren't many upsides to divorce – especially not when your wife of twenty-odd years had done a runner with another bloke – but that was one of them. He retrieved his trousers and shirt from where they'd been slung over a chair. He spat on his fingers and rubbed at a stain on the shirt. He'd been on his own five years now and he still hadn't got his head around the washing-machine. Today was the anniversary of his and Margaret's breakup. The date was carved into his brain. But if someone had asked him when their wedding anniversary was, he would have struggled to remember.

As Jim pulled on his trousers, he caught a glimpse of himself in the full-length wardrobe mirror – hangdog brown eyes and craggy features, grey-flecked moustache, fast-food belly. It occurred to him that there was a time when he would have been disgusted by what he saw, but not any more. The woman he loved was gone. A lonely retirement was looming. What reason did he have to take care of himself? For that matter, what reason did he have to care about anything?

He headed down to the kitchen and flicked the kettle on. As he waited for it to boil, he lit another cigarette with the end of his old one. A twinge of guilt passed through him at the thought of keeping the job waiting. It quickly faded. *Let it wait*, he thought bitterly. *Let them all wait. I've been kept waiting my whole life, and for what? So I can be alone?* His gaze travelled the kitchen. There were still signs of Margaret's homely touch – a calendar on the wall, a vase on the window-ledge. But the calendar was five years out of date and the vase contained only dust. He closed his eyes, sucking hard on his cigarette.

Not for the first time, Jim wondered why he didn't just jack the job in. What with all the government budget cuts, an application for early retirement would almost certainly be accepted. He recalled the contempt he used to have for those old cops who were simply waiting on retirement. In other lines of work that might have been OK, but in this job it could cost lives. This job demanded everything of you. If you weren't in it heart, soul and brain, you shouldn't be in it at all. He waved his cigarette-holding hand as if to brush away the line of thought. If he wasn't a cop, what the hell would he do? He'd asked himself that a lot recently, and he hadn't been able to come up with any answers he liked. His passion for the job may have deserted him, but the idea of not doing it any more left him with a cold, shrivelling feeling in his balls, as if he was straddling a deep chasm.

After warming himself up with a few swigs of tea, Jim headed for his car. He drove at a steady speed through the quiet city streets. He didn't need to punch the address into the satnav. He knew the streets as well as any taxi driver. A couple of miles out of the city, he spotted the flashing lights of emergency service vehicles illuminating the sky above his destination.

A constable stopped him at the end of a lane. Jim flashed his ID and the constable drew aside a cordon of blue-and-white-striped tape to let him through. He pulled over at a driveway marked by twin stone posts, noting the CCTV camera mounted on one of them. A heavy-looking gate had been cut off its hinges and balanced against the garden wall. The driveway was clogged with police vehicles, fire engines, an ambulance and several unmarked cars. The fire-blackened house was lit with silver-white halogen floodlights. A haze of smoke hung in the air, creating an eerie effect. Firemen were buzzing around, hunting down any remaining pockets of flames. A procession of flashlight-wielding constables, some of them armed with MP5 submachine guns, was scouring the garden. A forensics tent had been erected on the lawn. Overhead, a helicopter circled, no doubt scanning the surrounding fields and woodland with an infra-red body-heat detector.

'Where's DI Sheridan?' Jim asked a constable.

'In the kitchen, sir. You'll have to go round to the back of the house. The firemen are finishing up in the hallway.'

'What about the DCI?'

'He's on his way, but he won't get here for a while yet. He was visiting relatives for the weekend in Harrogate.'

The news inspired mixed feelings in Jim. On the one hand, he drew a small measure of satisfaction from the fact that he wouldn't have to see Garrett's studiedly grave, self-important face anytime soon. On the other, in Garrett's absence he was the senior detective. In his current frame of mind, he doubted if he was up to taking control of such a complex crime scene.

Jim headed down the side of the house. A forensics officer in a plastic suit and shower-cap was kneeling on the lawn not far from the back door, taking samples of what appeared to be patches of oil. Jim knew it wasn't oil, though. Halogen lights made blood appear black. His eyes followed a blood trail towards the back door, where they came to rest on a pair of legs in heeled boots caked with soot. He lifted his gaze to meet Amy Sheridan's keen, inquisitive eyes. Her face rarely gave much away, but there was a hint of paleness around the grim line of her lips that suggested she'd seen something that had pierced even her rhino hide. His gaze moved past her into the burnt-out shell of the kitchen, where more forensics officers were busy taking photos, measuring distances, bagging evidence and marking where it had been found with little numbered flags. 'It's that bad, is it, Amy?'

In reply, Amy stepped outside, her nostrils pinching as she sucked in a lungful of smoky air.

Jim gave her a moment to recover herself, then said, 'Tell me what we know.'

'This place belongs to a Stephen and Jenny Baxley.'

A faint frown of recognition crossed Jim's forehead. 'Baxley. Why does that name seem familiar?'

'Stephen Baxley owns one of the largest engineering firms in Sheffield.'

Jim nodded as his memory was jogged. 'SB Engineering. He's got a factory over at Attercliffe. So what else do we know

44

about this guy? Has he got a record?'

'We're still running the background checks.'

Jim pointed at the bloodstains. 'What's that about?'

'That's where the firemen who were first on the scene found the Baxleys' fifteen-year-old daughter, Charlotte, and twenty-three-year-old son, Mark. Charlotte had been shot in the back of the head. She was unconscious, but alive. Mark had been shot in the right shoulder and left leg. He was conscious, but barely able to speak. Before being taken to hospital, he managed to say a few words that indicated his parents were dead in the house.'

'And are they?'

'So it seems. There are two bodies in there, one male, one female, but they're too badly burnt to visually ID.'

'Assuming it is them, do you have any hunches as to what we're dealing with here?'

'Well let's just say I don't think we've got burglars to thank for this mess.'

'Why?'

'For starters there's an Aston Martin sitting in the garage. It's got to be worth well over a hundred grand. Why would burglars leave it behind? Then there's the murder weapon. Right now it looks like Jenny Baxley and her children were shot with Stephen Baxley's shotgun.'

'What about Stephen Baxley? Was he shot too?'

Amy shook her head. 'The exact cause of death hasn't yet been established.' As Jim rubbed thoughtfully at his chin, she continued, 'I know what you're thinking. You're thinking the same as me, that Mr Baxley lost the plot and tried to off his family.'

'That's one possibility. Or maybe it was the son.'

'He called this in.'

'That doesn't mean he didn't do it.'

'What about his injuries?'

'Maybe he shot himself to make it look like he's innocent.'

Amy's brow creased. 'You seriously think he could've shot himself not just once but twice?'

'It's unlikely,' conceded Jim, 'but I've seen crazier things. I'm just tossing theories around. We can't discount anything right now, including the possibility that this is the work of some very clever, very dangerous thieves. And let's not forget that Stephen Baxley was a wealthy man. Men like him don't get where they are without making enemies along the way. Have you checked the CCTV?'

'We tried hooking its hard drive up to our computers, but it seems to have been damaged by the fire. It's been sent off to the techies to see if they can retrieve the recordings.'

'Good. Right, enough gabbing. Let's get inside and see what we can see.'

Jim pulled on a pair of latex gloves and headed into the house. With a slight reluctance in her step, Amy followed. The kitchen looked like the inside of a blasted-out bunker. A section of the ceiling had collapsed, exposing charred floor joists that radiated a faint heat. Cupboard doors hung off their hinges. Pots, pans and other cooking utensils bobbed around in several centimetres of scummy water on the tiled floor. Nose wrinkling as the water seeped into his shoes, Jim picked his way through the wreckage. A forensics officer was squatting next to the corpse of a woman, her face burnt beyond recognition, a gaping wound in her chest. The stench of roasted flesh was enough to make even Jim's jaded eyes water. 'What's her story?' he asked. As the forensics bod turned to him, he recognised the pale, squinting eyes of Ruth Magill, the senior pathologist.

Ruth removed a half-face dust mask. 'Hell of a mess we've got on our hands here, Jim. I could hardly believe it when I got the call. This kind of thing, well, it just doesn't happen around here. In answer to your question, she was shot by someone standing just inside the kitchen door, and thrown against those cupboards.' She directed the almost invisible purple beam of an ultraviolet torch at some scorched cupboards, revealing a faint spray of blood spatters. 'A cluster of shotgun pellets penetrated her heart. Death would have been instantaneous.'

'Do you think it's Mrs Baxley?'

'Can't say for sure, but she fits the description.' Ruth held up a baggie containing the dead woman's few surviving strands of hair. 'Red-haired, about five-five or six, hundred and sixty pounds or so.' She pointed at several rings on the corpse's fingers. 'And she's married – or rather, she was married.'

With a meaningful glance at Amy, Jim said, 'Those look like expensive rings.'

Ruth aimed the torch at the blackened remains of the dining table and a chair lying on its side. 'Someone else was shot there. There's more blood, and there are shotgun pellets embedded in the chair.'

'That's where the daughter must have been sitting when she got it in the head,' said Amy.

Jim grunted cautious agreement. 'Where's the other body?'

Ruth headed into the hall, brushing aside a furl of soggy,

smoke-grimed wallpaper. The second body was even more badly burnt than the first. The eyeballs had melted, and the flesh had blistered and cracked away, providing glimpses of the bones beneath. The head rested at an unnatural angle, like a broken corn stalk. 'Jesus,' murmured Jim, putting the back of his hand to his mouth.

'Not even he could bring this guy back from the dead,' said Ruth. 'His neck's broken at the base of the skull.'

'Was that the cause of death?'

'It would have been more than enough to kill him, but we won't know for sure until the post-mortem.'

Jim glanced up at what was left of the landing bannister. 'Do you think he fell from up there?'

'Again, I can't say for sure. But his injuries are consistent with the injuries he would've sustained if his head was stretched upwards and backwards as a result of hitting the floor chin first from that kind of height.' Ruth beckoned for the detectives to follow her upstairs, warning, 'Tread lightly. We're not supposed to be up here. The fire's damaged the joists. We're waiting for the firemen to set up floor supports.' On reaching the landing, she pointed at the floor. 'That's where the shotgun was found.'

'What sort of condition is it in?' asked Jim.

'The wooden stock was badly burnt. The rest is undamaged.'

'Any chance of recovering prints?'

'There's every chance. Fingerprints can survive a pretty severe exposure to fire and water.' Ruth pointed at a door-frame. 'Take a look at this, Jim. I almost missed this because of the fire damage, but if you look closely you can see that the wood's been splintered by the impact of shotgun pellets.'

'And the damage is at roughly shoulder height,' Amy added.

The floor creaked ominously as Jim entered the bedroom, which was palely illuminated by the exterior floodlights. 'Careful, Jim,' cautioned Ruth. 'No one's been in there yet.'

Jim's gaze travelled the fire-gutted room, taking in the collapsed four-poster bed and the rows of singed clothes visible through the door of the walk-in wardrobe. Testing the floor with each step to make sure it would bear his weight, he edged into the wardrobe. He peered inside the safe, whose interior had been shielded from the worst ravages of the fire by its thick metal door. His eyebrows drew together.

'What is it?' asked Amy.

'A safe.'

'Anything in it?'

'A few thousand quid.'

'Well I'd say that seals it. This isn't a robbery gone wrong.'

'Looks that way.' Jim briefly closed his eyes, rubbing his forehead. When he was younger, being around death used to make him feel alive in some perverse way. Now it just gave him a kind of weary, empty headache. Resisting a strong urge to head outside for a cigarette, he said, 'OK, so what's the scenario? Mark comes to the bedroom, where his father's lying in wait for him. The mother and daughter have presumably already been shot. Which begs the question, why shoot Mark up here?'

'Maybe Stephen didn't want him to panic at the sight of the bodies?' suggested Amy.

'Maybe,' Jim agreed tentatively. He made as if aiming a shotgun. 'Bang. Mark gets it in the shoulder. His father approaches him to finish the job. Mark manages to grab the gun. The two of them struggle. Mark's shot in the leg.' Returning to the landing, Jim dropped onto his haunches and ran his fingers over the floor until he found what he was looking for. Taking out a Swiss Army penknife, he dug at the parquet tiles, dislodging a shotgun pellet. He stood up and handed it to Ruth. 'Father and son struggle some more. Father falls over the bannister. Mark goes downstairs and drags his sister outside.'

'Sounds about right.'

'But that doesn't mean it is right. What we need to do now is map out the timeline of events. For instance, how and when did the fire start?'

Ruth held up the pellet Jim had given her. 'This might be the answer to that particular question. We found an empty petrol can up here. If the floor was doused with petrol, a gun blast in a downward direction could have ignited it.'

'That makes sense, assuming the house wasn't already on fire when Stephen Baxley shot his son. Of course, all this is dependent on whether that human pot-roast down there is actually who we think it is.'

A fireman appeared at the front door and shouted upstairs, 'You shouldn't be up there. It's not safe.'

'OK, mate, we'll be down in a second.' Jim turned to Amy. 'Make sure no one goes near that safe. I don't want any of those firemen being tempted into pocketing that cash.'

'What are you going to do?'

'I'm heading over to the Northern General to find out what the situation is with the Baxley kids.'

'Scott Greenwood's already there. Last I heard, Mark and Charlotte were both in surgery. I'm sure Scott would've been in contact if the situation had changed. Besides, the DCI's expecting you to coordinate things here until he arrives.'

Jim rubbed his head again. The throbbing in his temples was strengthening, as was the urge to get outside, get away from this house of death, and above all get away from the weight of responsibility. He cleared his throat, which was raw from breathing soot. 'I've seen all I need to see here for now. And I'm sure you and the other detectives on site can handle things.'

'OK, but I'm telling you, the DCI won't be happy.'

It was on the tip of Jim's tongue to say, *Fuck Garrett*, but he held the words back. He motioned for Ruth and Amy to go ahead of him. As they made their way cautiously downstairs, the fireman asked, 'How much longer before my men can get to work on securing the joists?'

'Not much longer,' answered Ruth. 'We're about ready to move the bodies.'

'I'll talk to you later, Ruth,' said Jim, heading out the front door. With a glance at Amy, he added, 'Call me as soon as that background check comes in, or if there are any other developments.'

Amy raised her eyebrows in reply, as if to say, *Surely that goes without saying.*

As he returned to his car, Jim found himself supressing an urge to break into a run. He ducked into the driver's seat and reached for his cigarettes. He sucked in a lungful of smoke, coughed that out and sucked in another little ration of nerve-calming nicotine. *Christ, look at you*, he thought, catching a glimpse of his bleary-eyes as he reversed the car. *You're so far over the fucking hill that you're rolling down the other side.*

Chapter Five

Angel lay in bed studying the handgun. 'GLOCK 17 AUSTRIA' was engraved on its barrel. She took aim at her reflection in the dressing-table mirror, wondering if the number on the barrel corresponded to how many bullets the gun took. If it did, that meant there were fifteen bullets left in the magazine – assuming, of course, that Ryan Castle hadn't fired any rounds. 'Ryan Castle.' She said the name slowly, savouring the feel of it on her tongue. The bastard's face had been all over the evening news, which she and Deano had watched whilst crunching dry toast – coming down the other side of a heroin high always left them unable to stomach anything more substantial.

Deano hadn't been best pleased. Castle's BMW had been caught on CCTV cruising past an industrial unit south of the Transporter Bridge. That meant coppers would be sniffing around the area, talking to the girls and generally fucking up business. He'd soon brightened up when Angel gave him three hundred quid of what she'd stolen from Castle, plus the rest of the previous night's take. He'd gone off to see his supplier and stock up on Mexican brown, telling her he didn't want her to work the streets tonight. 'The Old Bill will have scared off the punters anyway,' he'd said, 'so there's no point risking getting hauled in for questioning.'

Angel's thoughts turned to the girl Castle had beaten within a millimetre of her life. There had been no mention of her on the news. If the police had connected her to the shooting, they were keeping quiet about it. Angel wondered what had become of her. Maybe she was lying in a hospital bed. Or maybe Kevin had lost his nerve and dumped her somewhere. She dismissed the thought with a shake of her head. Over the years she'd got good at reading people. Kevin was a coward, but he wasn't a heartless bastard. He wasn't an idiot either. He'd known Angel's threat to him wasn't empty, just as he'd known what she intended to do to Castle. He would have taken the girl to hospital, but he'd have made damn sure no one saw him leave her there. And now, no doubt, he was holed up somewhere, pissing his pants, hoping and praying his car hadn't been caught on CCTV too.

Angel got out of bed. Whatever had become of the girl, she had to know. She felt a strange kind of responsibility towards her. As if by saving her life – if that was what she'd managed to do – she'd somehow become responsible for it. She frowned at the gun. The weight of it in her hand was strangely reassuring. She felt a powerful reluctance to part with it, yet she realised it would be crazy to carry it with her. She was known to the local police, albeit under a false identity. If they picked her up for questioning, it would be game over.

Angel retrieved her heroin spoon from the shoebox. Dropping to her haunches in a corner of the room, she prised up a loose floorboard with the spoon's handle. There was a plastic bag stuffed into the floor cavity. She opened it, revealing a roll of banknotes with an elastic band around them. Her emergency money. She'd scraped it together over the past few months in case she needed to get away from this place, Deano, or some other trouble, fast. There was nine hundred and eighty quid. She knew the amount off by heart. She was certain Deano didn't know about it, but she counted it every day anyway to be sure. She winced at the thought of what would happen if he ever found it. As far as he was concerned, he owned her and everything she considered hers. So hiding money from him was the same as stealing from him. On more than one occasion, she'd seen the way Deano dealt with girls he believed were holding money back from him. It wasn't pretty, and nor were their faces once he'd finished with them.

Angel put the gun in the bag, slid the bundle into the cavity and replaced the floorboard. She pulled on jeans, trainers and a hooded sweatshirt. A pile of unopened bills and junk mail lay by the door. She opened an envelope, tossed its contents aside and replaced them with the remaining six hundred or so quid of Castle's money. Putting the envelope into her handbag, she made her way out of the bedsit.

As Angel stepped outside, her eyes were drawn to a police car at the end of the street. Two coppers were talking to Roxy, one of the oldest pros in the game around Middlesbrough. There was every chance Roxy had seen the girl get into the car with Castle, but no chance she'd tell the coppers. Nor would most, if any, of the other girls. If whores were good at one thing besides servicing the desires of punters, it was keeping quiet when the police came around.

Angel headed in the opposite direction. She caught a bus to the nearby James Cook University Hospital. Standing outside

A & E, from where she could see the reception desk through the glass doors, she phoned directory enquiries on her mobile. 'Can I have the number for Accident and Emergency at James Cook Hospital, Middlesbrough?' The automated operator service gave the number, telling her to 'press 1' if she wanted to be put through. She pressed 1, and when the receptionist picked up, she said, 'I'm calling to find out if a girl was brought in last night.'

'What's her name?' asked the receptionist.

'I don't know. She's about sixteen or seventeen years old, skinny, blonde. She was wearing a short white skirt and a black vest.'

'Can I ask who you are?'

'I'm a friend. I just want to find out if she's OK.'

'Hold the line please.'

The receptionist hurried from behind the desk. A minute or so later she returned accompanied by a policeman. She came on the line again. 'A girl fitting that description was admitted last night. She's on ward sixteen.'

The girl was alive! To Angel's surprise, hot tears of joy pushed up behind her eyes. She hadn't cried those kinds of tears in more years than she could remember. 'How is she?'

The receptionist glanced enquiringly at the policeman, placing her hand over the receiver. They exchanged a few words, then she said to Angel, 'I'm sorry, I can't give that information out over the phone. You're welcome to visit her. Normal visiting hours finished at 8 p.m., but in special circumstances such as this we try to be as flexible as possible.'

Angel thanked the receptionist and hung up. The policeman jotted something down on his notepad – Angel's mobile phone number, no doubt. That didn't matter. No calls made on it could be traced back to her. It was one of Deano's cloned phones, which he changed every few weeks. She knew she should turn around and head back to the bedsit. The receptionist's invitation was obviously a trap. But still she hesitated to leave. She felt a strong desire – almost a compulsion – to see the girl. It wasn't enough simply to know she was alive – people with brain damage that left them unable to talk, walk, or even move, were technically alive. No, she had to know exactly how she was doing. And then there was Castle's money. She'd promised herself that she would get it to the girl, and it was a promise she intended to keep.

Angel skirted along the building until she came to another door. She headed through it, pulling up her sweatshirt's hood. A sign listed the locations of the various clinics and wards. Ward sixteen was on the ground floor. An arrow pointed her in its direction. More arrows led her along a series of quiet, antiseptic-smelling corridors to a pair of double doors with windows at head height. She peered through the windows. Just inside the doors a nurse was sitting at the nurses' station doing paperwork. Doorless rooms, each of them containing eight beds, branched off from one side of a corridor. A whiteboard on the wall outside each room listed bed numbers and the names of their occupants. There was no sign of any police.

Angel lingered by the doors, pretending to fiddle with her phone in case anyone came along. After a few minutes, a red light lit up on the wall opposite the desk. The nurse extinguished it, then made her way to a room near the far end of the corridor.

Her pulse beating hard in her throat, Angel entered the ward. The beds in the first room were occupied by women reading or sleeping. The girl wasn't among them. She moved on to the next room. The girl was in the bed by the outer wall, staring blankly at the ceiling, her face a patchwork of bruises and bandages. A low moan escaped Angel's lips as the thought came to her. *The bastard's turned her into a vegetable.* The girl's head turned towards the sound, and recognition flickered in her features.

Relief lifting the corners of her mouth, Angel started forward. Her step faltered as the girl darted her eyes warningly at a curtain surrounding the opposite bed. Dropping silently to her haunches, Angel saw a pair of regulation police boots behind the curtain. She straightened, her gaze returning to the girl. A flicker of some kind of understanding passed between them. It seemed to Angel that the girl was trying to thank her with her eyes. She could feel the warmth of the girl's gaze creeping under her skin, touching parts of her that she'd long since thought dead, and blotting out, if only for a brief instant, the coldness in her heart.

Angel glanced at the whiteboard. The girl's name was Nicola Clarke. With one final lingering glance at Nicola, she turned towards the exit. She paused to grab a pen off the nurse's desk and wrote 'Nicola Clarke' on the envelope of money. She left the envelope on the desk and hurried from the hospital.

Sitting on the bus back to the bedsit, watching the dreary streets pass by, Angel thought to herself that even if she was caught and spent the rest of her life in prison, it would be worth it just for that one moment of warmth.

Deano was waiting for Angel. As she stepped through the door, his fist caught her full in the face, knocking her to the floor. 'You stupid little bitch!' he bellowed, a vein throbbing between his eyes. 'What the fuck have you done, eh?'

The salty metallic taste of blood filled Angel's mouth as she flung up a hand to ward off the next blow. 'What you talking about?'

'You know what the fuck I'm talking about.' Deano pulled up his t-shirt to reveal the gun stuffed into the waistband of his tracksuit bottoms. 'Where did this come from?'

Angel realised there was no point lying. Whatever else Deano was, he wasn't stupid. He knew as well as she did where the gun came from. He just wanted the satisfaction of hearing it from her mouth. Well, she wasn't going to give it to him. Let the bastard do his worst. She gave Deano a look that said she could take whatever he could dish out. In reply, he flashed a scowling grin at her. Her defiance was like a bone to a hungry dog. Some men acted out their frustrations through sex, some through violence. Deano fell into the latter category. He liked nothing better than an excuse to beat up on someone physically weaker than him. Angel knew this, just as she knew he would go easier on her if she told him what he wanted to hear. Twenty-four hours earlier she probably would have caved in and confessed what had happened. But things had changed since then. She'd changed. She knew now what she was capable of. Deano was a thug, but he wasn't a killer. It wasn't her who should be scared, it was him.

'Tell me I'm wrong, Grace,' said Deano, swatting aside her hands. 'Tell me you know fuck all about that dead guy.'

Fire flared in Angel's eyes. 'I told you not to fucking call me that.'

Deano replied with a punch that snapped Angel's head backwards. 'Don't you realise what you've done? If the coppers find this thing here, we'll both go down for murder. Accessories after the fact, that's what they call it.' He wrapped the fingers of one hand around Angel's throat. His other hand hovered threateningly over her. 'I want to know which of those bitches gave you the gun.'

A murmur of satisfaction passed through Angel as she realised that Deano thought she was hiding the gun for some other girl. It probably hadn't even crossed his mind that she'd killed Castle. In his eyes, she was just another scared little lost girl who he could bend to his will. Well maybe she was lost in more ways than he even knew, but she wasn't afraid. Not now. Not any more. A thin line of blood trickled from her mouth as her lips curled into a grin. 'I'm leaving you, Deano.'

His heroin-ravaged features twitched as though the words had hit him physically. He'd thought he had her so far under his thumb that she would never dare try to get away from him. 'You don't leave me. You're my girl.' He spoke quietly, with a tremor in his voice.

Angel knew what that tremor meant. It meant she was going to pay in bruises and blood for wounding Deano's pride. But she didn't care. Her head was dizzy from being hit, but also from the elation of knowing Deano no longer had any power over her. 'Where's my money?' Her voice was hoarse with pain, but steady.

'Your money?' Deano let out a small, choking laugh, looking at Angel as though he couldn't believe his ears. 'Your fucking money?'

Deano's fist twitched, and Angel knew what was coming. 'Don't.' There was a razor-sharp edge to her voice. Her eyes burnt a warning fire.

Deano hesitated, uncertainty flickering on his face. He blinked hard, as if it had suddenly occurred to him that maybe Angel wasn't hiding the gun for someone else. Then he shook himself free of whatever he was thinking. 'Or what?' he shouted as his fist thundered into her face. 'Or fucking what?'

Over and over again, Deano hit Angel, concentrating most of his punches on her body – after all, her face was worth a lot of money to him. At first, each blow was like an explosion, blinding Angel with searing pain. But after a while a merciful numbness stole over her. She felt as if she was falling, dropping further and further away to some dark place where Deano couldn't reach her. She didn't even realise he'd stopped beating her, until she heard his voice in her ear. 'You're my girl. My bitch,' he rasped breathlessly. 'Say it. Say you're my bitch.'

'No.' A bloody bubble inflated from Angel's lips as she spoke. Her body might be weak and battered, but inside she felt strong.

Deano's voice came again, with a cockiness that stirred a spark of anxiety in Angel's chest. 'You're forgetting that I know your name. All it would take is a phone call, and Grace Kirby would be in all sorts of trouble.'

The words were more painful to Angel than all of Deano's blows combined. They reached inside her and tore a convulsive groan from her throat. They filled her with such hatred for Deano that in that instant, if she'd had the strength, she would have snatched the gun from him and put a bullet in his head.

'Now say you're my bitch.' Deano's voice was almost gleeful.

As if dredging the words from the bottom of a well, Angel said, 'I'm your bitch.'

Deano patted her cheek. 'Good girl. Now you just lie there and think about how you've made me feel. I know I act the tough guy, but I've got feelings too. And it hurts me right in here,' he thumped his chest, 'when you say you want to leave me.'

Angel closed her eyes. She didn't want to think, but her inner voice sneered, *Leave him, hah! What made you think you could leave him? And even if you did, what difference would it make? You'd still be you. You'd still be a cheap fucking whore. That's all you're good for.*

The numbness was fading, leaving in its wake a trail of hot, throbbing pain. Her eyes snapped open at a soft sizzling sound. A familiar vinegary smell filled her nostrils, unleashing a sudden overwhelming craving. She glanced at the heroin bubbling on Deano's spoon, then looked into his face with pathetic, pleading eyes. 'Have you got one for me?' she asked as he drew the solution into a hypodermic. He darted a frowning glance at her as she continued, 'Come on, Deano, please. I...' Her voice faltered as one final fragment of her shattered self-respect reared its head. But the heroin itch was too intense, too all-consuming to be denied. 'I'll do anything you want. Anything!'

Deano's mouth spread into a smug smirk. 'I know you will, baby, but you've got to learn. You've been a bad girl, and bad girls must be punished.'

Setting the gun aside, Deano slid his tracksuit bottoms down and felt for the artery in his groin. He hit himself up, then lay back on the bed, mouth hanging open, eyelids drooping half shut. Like a lover being teased to the point of madness, Angel was racked by shudders of desperate yearning. She tried to sit up, but her body seemed glued to the floor. She closed her eyes. The flowers of swollen flesh and the itch of craving vied with each other as to which hurt most, wringing low moans from her dust-dry throat. Slowly, ever so slowly, she took out her mobile phone and keyed in a number. The phone rang in her ear. One, two, three rings. *Oh God, please pick up*, she thought. Four, five, six rings.

She bit back a sob as a weary-sounding woman's voice came down the line. 'Hello?'

Angel made no reply, but she pressed the phone closer to her ear.

'Hello, who is this?' continued the woman. 'Hello?'

A moment of silence passed. Then the woman's voice came again, full of a trembling, tentative excitement that might have been fear or hope. 'Grace, is that you?'

Tears pushed at Angel's eyes. Her lips trembled with the effort of holding them at bay.

'It is you isn't it, Grace? Please don't hang up. You don't have to say anything, I know it's you. I know you're alive and that one day you'll come back to me. A mother knows these things.'

Angel couldn't hold back her tears any longer. As they burst forth, she hung up and curled into a foetal ball. An image of her mum as she'd looked the last time they'd seen each other filled her mind: worn, angular features, dark, permed hair, eyes like a sad old cat, prematurely lined smoker's mouth. The image was fainter than it had once been, like a time-faded photo, but it still evoked a confusion of emotions in her. Uppermost amongst these was a heart-squeezing love, but there was also a toxic undercurrent of anger, resentment and even hate. *A mother knows these things.* The words rang in her mind, and her inner voice retorted bitterly, *A mother knows what she wants to know, and is ignorant of what she wants to be ignorant of.*

Chapter Six

When Jim arrived at the Northern General's main entrance, Scott Greenwood was waiting for him. DI Greenwood's rugged, steely eyed face marked him out as exactly what he was: a hard-working, no-bullshit cop. The sight of him always reminded Jim of himself – or rather, it reminded him of the way he'd been a few years ago, before his life turned to shit. The force was full of people like Scott Greenwood. Lately, Jim had found himself avoiding them. There was nothing he used to love more than a pub busy with cops drinking away the stresses of the day. Nowadays he preferred to drink alone, with only a picture of his ex-wife for company. He kept imagining Margaret turning up at the house, begging him to take her back. He wouldn't give her an answer straight away, not after everything she'd put him through. He'd make her sweat a little before saying yes. Then he'd kiss her, and she'd promise never to leave him again, and everything would go back to the way it was before. Jim shook his head. Pathetic.

'What's the prognosis?' he asked.

'It's not good,' said Scott, turning to go into the building. 'The girl's still in surgery. She's got several shotgun pellets embedded in her brain. The surgeon reckons she has about a two per cent chance of surviving the operation to remove them, and even if she does she may well be brain-damaged.'

Jim shook his head again. 'Fifteen years old. What a fucking waste,' he sighed. 'How about her brother?'

'He's stable. He came out of surgery half an hour ago, but he hasn't come round from the anaesthetic yet.'

They caught a lift up to the Critical Care Department, where a constable was standing guard outside one of the rooms. Jim peered through an observation window. Mark Baxley was lying in bed, hooked up to oxygen, a heart-scanner and an IV bag. His right shoulder was heavily bandaged. His waxy grey face was stitched and swollen where it had been lacerated by splinters of wood and glass.

'How long before he wakes up?' Jim asked the duty nurse.

'Normally you'd expect a young, healthy patient to start showing signs of responsiveness an hour or so after general surgery,' she replied. 'But that doesn't mean he'll be fit to talk to you.'

Jim turned to his colleagues. 'You head over to the crime scene, Scott. I'll stay here.' As Scott turned to leave, Jim said to the constable standing guard, 'Go get yourself a cuppa.'

When he was alone, Jim sat down and expelled a breath that seemed to come from his shoes. Somewhere nearby, someone let out an agonised wail. The sound gave him a sinking feeling in his stomach. *How many times*, he mused, *have you sat in this place, surrounded by pain and death?* But of course the answer was obvious – too many. He just didn't have the stomach for it any more.

Jim found himself wondering whether it would have been better for Mark Baxley if he hadn't survived. After all, what sort of life did he have to look forward to? A life without trust, that's what. A nightmare of loneliness and paranoia. Jim had seen it many times before in people who'd survived an attempt on their life by friends, spouses and the like. He'd watched as they withdrew from the world and locked themselves in the worst kind of prison – a prison of their own minds. Over the years, he'd built barriers of a different kind around himself – barriers to keep his emotions at bay so that he could view cases dispassionately and from every angle. In the past some people – people who didn't understand him – had called him cold and cynical. Margaret understood him better than anyone, but that hadn't lessened her need for a love that at some point he'd lost the capacity to give. He knew that was why she'd left him, even if he couldn't admit it to himself. The job had ripped out his heart. Losing Margaret had taken everything else.

Suddenly, Jim knew he had to leave, not just the hospital, but the city, the job, everything. He had to get away before it was too late, before the last vital spark in him was extinguished. His head spinning with a confused mixture of excitement and anxiety, he stood and took a few hesitant steps towards the exit. He paused at the sound of a moan from Mark Baxley's room.

The nurse moved from behind her desk and entered Mark's room. Pinching the fingers of Mark's left hand, she called his name. He moaned again, feebly trying to pull his hand away. His eyelids flickered open. First the whites, then the pupils rolled into view. A hoarse voice slurred, 'Cha... Charl... Charlotte.'

'Your sister's in a coma, Mark, but she's alive.'

Mark gave out a whimper and a light that seemed to hold both relief and triumph came into his heavy-lidded eyes.

'Have you got any pain anywhere?' asked the nurse.

Mark slowly shook his head. 'I'm thir... thirsty.'

The nurse poured water from a jug into a cup and held it to Mark's lips. He took a sip, dribbling most of it down his chin. The nurse dabbed him dry with a paper towel. 'That's all for now. I don't want you to choke.'

The nurse checked Mark's vital signs, compared them to readings on the heart monitor, then made a notation on his chart. 'I know it's hard, Mark, but try to relax. A doctor will be by to see you soon.'

As the nurse left the room, Jim asked, 'Is that true about his sister?'

The nurse nodded. 'The doctors say it's a miracle. There was about a one in a hundred chance she'd survive the operation.' Her voice dropped. 'Mind you, there's still a long way to go before she's out of the woods.'

The word *miracle* sparked a little fire of contempt inside Jim. As far as he was concerned, there were no such things as miracles. There were only things that happened. Some of those things were beyond human control, but that didn't mean God had anything to do with them. 'Can I speak to Mark?' The question came automatically, even though it was the last thing he wanted to do.

'Yes, but only for a few minutes. And don't press him too hard. He's very weak.'

Jim drew a chair up to Mark's bedside. As Mark's head lolled towards him, Jim resisted the urge to turn away from the mute pain shining out of his eyes. 'Hello, Mark, I'm Detective Inspector Jim Monahan of the South Yorkshire Police Homicide and Major Incident Team,' he began, his tone businesslike. 'I realise this is a difficult time, but I need to ask you some questions. Someone will take a full statement later when you're feeling stronger. For now, I just want to hear what happened.'

'Da—' Mark winced on the word as though it tasted bitter. He licked his scorched lips, before continuing in a strengthening voice, 'Dad shot Mum and Charlotte. Then he tried to kill me.'

'Did you see him shoot your mum and sister?'

'No. He—' A choke came into Mark's voice. Whether from pain or emotion, Jim couldn't tell.

Jim picked up the glass of water. 'Here,' he said, putting it to Mark's lips.

Mark swallowed a mouthful. 'Thanks.'

'Now take you time and tell me exactly what happened.'

Starting with the phone call, Mark gave Jim the full story. Jim jotted down the main points, pausing occasionally to give Mark another sip of water. He glanced up, frowning, when Mark got to the part about the strange sobbing he'd heard on entering the house. 'Do you think it was your dad?'

'No. I never saw Dad cry in all my life. It sounded more like a child.'

Jim's eyebrows drew closer together as he wondered whether there was another body waiting to be discovered. 'Could there have been someone else in the house other than your parents and sister?'

'There could have been, but I don't think there was. The telly was on in my parents' bedroom. That's probably what I heard.'

'Probably,' agreed Jim, thinking, *Christ, I hope that's all it was.*

His voice cracking, Mark recounted the fight with his father, and the discovery of his mother and sister. By the time the tragic, horrific tale was finished, tears were streaming down his cheeks. Again, the rawness of the emotion in his eyes almost made Jim flinch from his gaze. He reached to give Mark's wrist a squeeze, but stopped himself. He'd spent his entire working life learning how to separate truth from lies. The fact that Mark's story tallied so closely with his own reconstruction of events, coupled with Mark's obvious relief at hearing his sister was alive, was enough to convince him that what he'd heard was the truth. But technically Mark was still a suspect, and sympathy for a suspect would only serve to cloud his judgement.

'Can you think of any reason your father might have had to do what he did?'

'No.'

'Are you sure? Think carefully. Did he ever mention troubles with money or his relationship with your mother?'

'He never mentioned anything about anything to me. We barely spoke.'

'Why? Had you fallen out?'

Mark shook his head. 'That's just the way it was, the way it's always been between—' His tears suddenly overwhelmed his speech.

'OK, Mark, we're done for now.' Jim's tone was still businesslike, but despite himself, a gentle note had crept into it. *You're going soft in your old age*, he thought, making to stand.

Mark lifted a hand to touch Jim's arm. 'Stay with me. Please. I… I don't want to be alone.' His voice was awkward, almost as if there was something shameful in his words.

Jim stared uncertainly at Mark. He knew he should get back to the crime scene. Garrett would be there by now, and no doubt severely pissed at his absence. More importantly, Mark's story had opened up several lines of enquiry that urgently needed to be followed. But he couldn't bring himself to deny the request of this man who was only just a man, this man who'd gone through, and was still going through, a hell that made Jim's problems seem as nothing.

'OK, but I've got to make a phone call.'

Jim left the room and dialled Amy Sheridan. 'I was just about to call you,' she said. 'The DCI's going to brief the team and he wants you here for it.'

Jim glanced through the observation window at Mark. The sense of duty instilled into him by decades of loyal service urged him to say he'd be there as soon as possible, but the desperation in Mark's eyes caused him to bite the words back. 'Tell him I won't be able to make it.'

'He's not going to be best pleased.'

'Yeah, well he'll just have to lump it.' It felt good, liberating even, to go against his superior's orders, especially when that superior was a smarmy careerist like Garrett. 'Listen, Amy, I've spoken to Mark Baxley, and he had some interesting things to say.'

Jim relayed the details of his conversation with Mark. When he got to the part about Mark hearing what sounded like a child crying in the house, Amy hauled in a breath and said, 'Bloody hell.'

'My thoughts exactly. Any developments at your end?'

'The background check brought up some info on Stephen Baxley that's almost as interesting as what his son had to say.'

'Such as?'

'I'll fill you in when I see you. Right now, I'd better look into what you've told me. Mind you, the firemen still aren't letting us upstairs. Apparently the damage is worse than was first thought.'

Jim told Amy he'd see her soon, then returned to Mark's bedside. Mark gave him a glance that was part gratitude, part relief. Neither of them spoke. For the moment, there was nothing else to say. As he sat watching Mark's eyelids grow heavier, Jim asked himself whether he'd been serious about walking out on the job. Or had it just been a crazy moment? He wasn't sure. All he knew was that he had a duty to at least follow up on the leads he'd been given. After that... well, he would just have to see. Maybe it really was time to call it a day, time to try and salvage something from life, some small fragment of happiness. But even if it was, he was still left facing the same old question: if he was no longer a policeman, what the hell would he do with himself? It made his head pound to think about it. *So stop thinking about it,* he told himself. *Just concentrate on getting through the night.*

When Mark's eyes finally drooped into sleep, Jim padded from the room. The constable had returned from wherever he'd been on his break. Giving him a nod, Jim headed for the lift.

Chapter Seven

During the drive back to the crime scene, Jim sifted through the details of what Mark had told him, searching for chinks in his story. There were none, so far as he could tell. And if there were, they would soon be rooted out by forensic examination of the shotgun, and a simple check of Mark's phone records. When he reached the lane, he found it clogged by media vans with satellite dishes on top, ready to transmit details of the grisly events to the nation. He squeezed past them, sounding his horn at a clutch of journalists.

He parked up and walked towards a lorry marked 'Major Incident Command Unit', but his step faltered as he caught the sound of Garrett's voice from inside it. His nose wrinkled with annoyance. He'd never particularly liked any of his previous DCIs, but he'd respected them. He couldn't bring himself to like or respect Garrett. Every time the guy fixed him with his phony earnest eyes it raised his hackles. The feeling was mutual. He knew Garrett considered him a dinosaur, a relic whose time had passed. That much was obvious from the way he often gave the plum assignments to younger team members. And maybe he was right to do so. Maybe his most senior detective had become out of touch with new policing methods. But he was still in touch with the streets – something Garrett had never been. And he could read criminals' minds like Garrett could read Detective Chief Superintendent Knight's moods.

'Ah, to hell with him,' muttered Jim, continuing past the lorry towards the house. He'd get the details of the briefing off Amy.

A fireman barred his way at the front door. 'Sorry, I can't let you in. It's not safe.'

'Do I look like I give a shit?' Jim stepped around him into the hallway. Noting that Stephen Baxley's body had been removed, he headed upstairs.

'Hey guys, you'd better get out of there,' the fireman called to his colleagues. 'Some idiot's gone upstairs.'

The master bedroom's floor sagged noticeably where the weight of the charred four-poster bed rested on it. Hugging the walls, Jim edged towards the television. He pulled on a pair of forensic gloves, then took out his penknife and prised open the DVD drive, revealing the edge of a disc. He snapped the blade shut and opened out the screwdriver attachment. The television's fire-warped casing cracked as he twisted out the screws that held it together. He levered the casing apart and disconnected the DVD drive. Then he took apart the drive and removed the DVD. He returned downstairs and sought out Ruth Magill. Finding her stooped over the corpses in the forensics tent, he showed her the DVD. 'Got anything I can watch this on?'

'You can use my laptop. What's on it?'

'If I knew that I wouldn't need to watch it. I took it from the master bedroom's television.'

Arching an eyebrow, Ruth gently admonished him. 'Naughty boy. How did you know it was there?'

Jim recounted his conversation with Mark Baxley as he followed the pathologist to her car. She booted up her laptop and inserted the DVD. Grainy colour footage of what appeared to be some sort of basement popped up on the screen. A date and time flickered in the corner of the footage: '22:43, 1/9/97'. A windowless, whitewashed brick wall, foam-insulated pipes and quarry-tiled floor swept before the camera's lens as it swung round to focus on a group of figures. There were four adults – three men and a woman – standing in a row. Although the camera cut off their heads, their genders were easily determined because all of them were naked. The woman was slim with small breasts, narrow hips and a triangle of dark pubic hair. To her right was a stocky, pot-bellied man whose barrel chest was covered with curly black hair. And to his right was a slim man with a wisp of white-blond hair between his nipples. A purple blotch like a mole was visible on his left hip. To the woman's left was a man with broad shoulders and muscular arms. His body was as hairless as an egg. His hand groped at his erect, circumcised penis.

Two more figures were lying on cushions on a rug. One was a strikingly beautiful, full-lipped girl of fifteen or so, wearing white cotton underwear. A dull needle of memory prodded Jim's brain at the sight of her straight black shoulder-length hair and almost luminescent blue eyes. He knew those eyes, but where from? The question was thrust from his mind as the girl bent over the second figure – a cherubic-faced boy of about eight or nine with curly blond hair falling over his forehead, partly covering glassy, drugged-looking eyes. The boy was dressed in navy-blue pyjamas. He exhaled a barely audible moan, his head lolling sideways as the girl began to unbutton his pyjama top. Then the boy was coming out of his pyjamas and tears were coming out of Jim's eyes. 'Oh God,' he murmured, in a voice thick with horror.

He closed his eyes tightly, unable to bear what he was seeing. They snapped back open seconds later as the laptop's speakers emitted a soul-wrenchingly small sobbing noise. The boy was weakly pulling away from the girl, curling up into a bundle of tears.

'Give him some more medicine, Angel.' The voice too came from the laptop, crackling with slight distortion. It unmistakably belonged to a man, well spoken, with the barest hint of a local accent.

The girl's mouth was drawn into a tight line. There was a kind of despairing defiance in her eyes as she shook her head.

'Do it.' The voice was soft, but the accompanying images lent it a chilling menace.

Still the girl hesitated to obey. The hairless man whipped the back of his hand across her cheek. She stared up at her assaulter, silent tears running from her eyes. What she saw drained all the defiance from her face, leaving only fear. With trembling reluctance, she picked up a brown medicine bottle. The boy's sobbing choked off as she pushed it into his mouth.

The DVD seized up suddenly. Ruth ejected it from the laptop and examined its underside. 'Looks like it's been warped by the heat.'

A despairing rage swelled Jim's eyes. 'It never ends. No matter what we do, it never fucking ends.' His shoulders quaked as sobs welled up within him. He bit his lip, fighting to gain control of his emotions. 'Sorry, Ruth, I don't know what's wrong with me.'

Ruth gave him a look that said, *There's no need to apologise.*

'Christ, I haven't cried like that in years,' continued Jim, sweeping his hand across his eyes. 'Not even when—' *Not even when Margaret left me*, he'd been about to say, but he swallowed the words. He couldn't allow himself to think about her. Not now. He had to get his head straight, concentrate all his energies on what needed to be done. The case had suddenly got bigger than the Baxley family. A thought occurred to him. 'Has the Baxley house got a basement?'

'Not that I know of.' Ruth gestured at the screen. 'Maybe this is behind what happened here.'

Jim's brow wrinkled doubtfully. 'That footage is fifteen years old. If Stephen Baxley was going to kill his family and himself over it, I think he'd have done so before now.'

'Maybe he was being blackmailed.'

'That doesn't seem likely either. Even if one of those men is Stephen Baxley, it's impossible to ID him.'

'Difficult, but not necessarily impossible. There are identifying features.'

Motioning for Jim to follow, Ruth got out of the car. She led him back to the forensics tent and picked up a clipboard. 'Stephen Baxley, five foot eleven, approximately one hundred and forty-five pounds,' she said, reading from the uppermost sheet of paper. 'I'd say that rules out the big-bellied man, unless Stephen Baxley had dropped a lot of weight since '97.' She resumed reading. 'Brown hair, hazel-brown eyes.'

'And that rules out the blond-haired man,' said Jim. 'So we're just left with the circumcised man.'

Ruth unzipped a bodybag, revealing the man's corpse. With scissors and tongs, she carefully cut and peeled away the melted remnants of his trousers and boxer-shorts. 'Well whoever this guy is, he's not circumcised.'

'Assuming he's Stephen Baxley, that would seem to rule out blackmail.'

'Maybe there's an undamaged copy of the film somewhere out there in which Stephen Baxley is identifiable.'

'That's a possibility,' conceded Jim. 'What about the woman? Could she be Jenny Baxley?'

'I'd say that's extremely unlikely. The body shape and hair colour are too different.'

Jim heaved a sigh. 'I'd better go give the DCI the good news. Mind if I borrow your laptop?'

'Go ahead.'

A note of awkwardness came into Jim's voice. 'Oh, and Ruth, I'd really appreciate it if you didn't mention the way I reacted to the DVD to anyone.'

'Of course I won't, Jim,' Ruth replied in a tone that said, *Surely that goes without saying.*

'Thanks.'

Jim went over to the operations lorry. He rearranged his face into its usual inscrutable veteran's mask, then knocked on the door. Amy poked her head out. 'Hello, Jim,' she said, her eyes flicking warningly over her shoulder at Garrett. The DCI was studying a whiteboard with four close-up photos of faces stuck to it. Jim recognised Mark Baxley. The others were of a sharp-featured middle-aged man, a good-looking woman of roughly the same age, and an auburn-haired teenage girl with pretty blue eyes and a petulant mouth. Jim guessed that they portrayed Stephen, Jenny and Charlotte Baxley.

Garrett glanced towards Jim. 'Ah, Detective Monahan, good of you to finally grace us with your presence.'

'Sorry, sir. I felt it was best if I stayed with Mark Baxley and heard everything he had to say.'

A ripple of disapproval disturbed the surface of Garrett's clean-shaven, bespectacled face. 'I don't care what you thought best. You shouldn't even have been at the hospital. I wanted you here to coordinate things in my absence.'

Garrett began to lecture Jim on his duties as the senior DI. As Jim listened, the DVD footage spooled through his brain like a waking nightmare. It made his blood burn to think that the perpetrators might be out there somewhere right now doing the same to other children. *Shut your patronising gob*, he felt like snapping. But he limited himself to, 'There's something you need to see.' He set the laptop down on a table and flipped it open.

Garrett's look of irritation at being interrupted quickly turned into one of shocked disgust as the DVD began to play. When it was over, his voice uncharacteristically shaken, he asked, 'Where did you get this?'

Jim told him, adding, 'I think Stephen Baxley was watching it when his son entered the house.'

'Mark isn't his real son,' said Garrett. 'Stephen Baxley adopted him when he was only a few months old.'

'So who's the real father?'

'We don't know. There's no father's name on his birth certificate.'

'Does Mark know?'

'I've no idea. Seeing as you've already established a relationship with him, I was going to ask you to find out.' Garrett gestured at the laptop's screen. 'But this complicates matters.'

'Maybe this is a blackmail case,' suggested Jim. 'Maybe someone was using that film to put the screw on Stephen Baxley, and it tipped him over the edge.'

'Maybe so, but I prefer not to deal in speculation, especially when there are other factors at play that could explain what happened here.'

'What other factors?'

'DI Sheridan will fill you in on the details on the way to the Northern General. I have a press conference to prepare for in...' Garrett glanced at his watch, 'less than twenty minutes.'

'So you still want me to talk to Mark Baxley?'

Garrett nodded. 'And when you're done with him, I want you both to get to work on reviewing missing-children cases from the time that footage was filmed. But before you do anything else, get that DVD to forensics. I want to know who's handled that thing.' His mobile phone rang. His lips compressed as he looked at it. He headed out of the trailer, putting the phone to his ear. His slightly fawning voice drifted back. 'Hello, sir... Yes, sir... Of course, sir...'

'Must be the DCS,' Jim commented wryly to Amy. 'Can you print out the faces of the kids in that film?'

'Shouldn't be too difficult.' Taking care to touch only the edges of the DVD, Amy removed it from the laptop and inserted it into a PC. Jim resisted the urge to avert his gaze as the film began to play again. As much as he despised the sight of it, he needed to fix every detail in his mind – the position of the pipes, the size and shape of the quarry-tiles. But most of all, he needed to memorise every possible identifying feature of the perpetrators.

Amy paused the film on a close-up of the boy's face and clicked 'Print Screen'. She repeated the process for the girl.

'Play it again from the beginning,' Jim said, fishing a hand-held tape recorder from his jacket pocket.

Guessing his intention, Amy said, 'I can extract the audio and download it to my iPhone. That way there'll be no background interference.'

As Amy plugged her phone's USB cable into the PC, Jim asked, 'So what are these other factors Garrett mentioned?'

'Stephen Baxley was about to be made bankrupt. The bank started foreclosure proceedings on his home and business this week.'

'Well that certainly gives us motive.' Jim huffed air sharply through his nostrils. 'What is it with these bastards? Why can't they just put a gun to their own heads? Why do they have to try and take their families down with them?'

'Arrogance, pride, narcissism. They can't imagine their families would want to live on in a world without them.'

Jim studied the printouts, wondering if their subjects were alive and, if they were, what sort of lives they led. Meanwhile, Amy continued, 'Or maybe he was so bitter about losing his business that he just wanted to take his anger out on someone. We know from his record that he's capable of violence when things don't go his way.'

'He's got previous?'

'Back in '88, Stephen Baxley and a business associate were arrested for assaulting a man over an unpaid debt.'

'Who's the business associate?'

'Bryan Reynolds.'

'As in *the* Bryan Reynolds?'

'The very same.'

Jim blew out his cheeks in astonishment. Bryan Reynolds was a name familiar to every copper in South Yorkshire. He was a major player in Sheffield organised crime. He ran – or rather, was suspected of running – a sophisticated drug-dealing network. Recently several mid-level dealers had been arrested in simultaneous raids across the city. The 'drug supermarkets', as the newspapers called the fortified flats and houses the dealers sold crack and heroin out of, had Reynolds's name stamped all over them. But such was the respect and fear he inspired that, no matter what threats were made or deals offered, none of the dealers had given him up. 'How did a man like Stephen Baxley come to be knocking around with Reynolds?'

'Baxley doesn't come from money. He grew up on Park Hill in the same block of flats as Reynolds. They went to the same school. Only difference is Reynolds dropped out at fifteen whereas Baxley went to college. Things went wrong for Baxley when he didn't get the grades he needed for university. In '88, Reynolds got him a job collecting for a loan-shark. He'd only been at it a few weeks when he and Reynolds put some bloke in a coma for missing payments. They were remanded on charges of GBH and malicious wounding. Both pleaded innocent, but shortly before it came to trial Reynolds changed his plea to guilty and copped for the whole charge. He was sentenced to three years, of which he served eighteen months.'

Jim arched an eyebrow. The surprises just kept on coming. 'Very charitable of him. He must've had a soft spot for his old schoolmate. So what happened next?'

'Reynolds went on to become the scumbag extraordinaire we all know and love. Baxley married Jenny Shaw. She must have had a positive influence on him, because he returned to college, got his grades and went to university. After graduating in '92, he worked at Phoenix Engineering, before starting up SB Engineering in '96. As far as we know, he had no further contact with Bryan Reynolds.'

'Maybe not, but he was certainly no stranger to criminality.'

'That's assuming Baxley is in that film, off or on camera.'

'Why the hell else would he have it in his possession and be watching it just before he tried to murder his...' Jim trailed off, his brow wrinkling as though something had occurred to him.

'What is it?'

Jim shook his head as if to say, *Nothing.* 'What about Jenny Baxley? Did the background checks turn up anything on her?'

'No arrest records. Not even a traffic ticket. She's clean as a whistle. So are Mark and Charlotte.' Amy pointed at the printouts. 'You don't think she could have been involved in that, do you?'

Jim considered this in frowning silence. The idea was almost too vile to contemplate. He heaved a sigh. 'Are you done?'

'Almost.'

Amy unplugged the USB and checked the audio file transfer had worked. They left the operations lorry and walked over to a van marked 'Scientific Support'. Jim gave the DVD to a forensics officer, explaining where it had come from and what the DCI wanted done with it. Then Amy and he headed to his car.

They rode in silence. Jim glanced at Amy. Her inexpressive face gave away nothing of what she was thinking, but he wondered if, like him, the images from the DVD were swirling through her mind. He wondered too at the strength of his feelings. It was as though what he'd seen that night had punched a hole through some internal dam and he could no longer control the flow of his emotions. And the primary emotion that overtook him when he thought about the DVD was rage – an almost painful fury at the knowledge that the perpetrators had got away for so long with what they'd done.

They were a couple of miles from the Northern General when Amy's phone rang. She spoke briefly to the caller. 'Right... OK... Thanks for letting me know.' She turned to Jim. 'That was Scott Greenwood. Mark Baxley was telling the truth about the phone call. Just after 8 p.m. a call was placed from the Baxley house to Mark Baxley's mobile phone. Also the techies have managed to get the CCTV hard drive working. It seems the cameras were off at the time the killings took place. Of course, neither of those things puts Mark in the clear.'

'No, but they sure as hell go a long way towards backing up his story.'

They parked up and made their way to the Critical Care Department. Jim asked a nurse how Charlotte Baxley was doing, and was informed that her condition was still life-threatening. Mark looked to be asleep, but his eyes flicked open when they entered his room. 'This is DI Amy Sheridan,' said Jim, indicating his colleague.

'Hello, Mark,' said Amy. 'I know you probably just want to sleep right now, but I'm afraid we need to ask you some more questions.'

'I'm more tired than I've ever been in my life, but I don't want to sleep,' said Mark. The look in his eyes suggested that the world behind them was haunted by horrifying images. His gaze moved to Jim. 'Thanks for before. For staying with me.'

'No problem.'

'So what do you want to know?'

'Well, firstly, do you know that your father's business is in financial difficulties?'

'No. Dad never spoke about money with any of us, not even Mum. But I kind of suspected something was up. He'd been working late a lot recently. In the past he always made sure he knocked off at a reasonable hour, so he could spend time with Charlotte and... well, just with Charlotte really. How serious is it?'

'The business is bankrupt,' put in Amy.

'Bankrupt,' Mark repeated in a hollow voice. His forehead twitched as he tried to assimilate the realisation that not only had he lost his parents, but he was also going to lose everything their money had paid for. 'So that's why the fucker did this. He lived in terror of being poor. Mum told me he used to have nightmares about losing his money and being forced to go and live in the flat where he grew up. He said he'd rather die than end up back there. Well, fine, if he would rather have died, but what made him think he had the right to... to do what he—' Mark choked up. Tears flooded his eyes. 'Sorry.'

'No need for apologies, Mark,' said Amy, a gentleness in

her tone that contrasted with her usual staunchly professional demeanour. Glancing at her, Jim caught a glimpse of someone he didn't know, someone tender and warm. He recalled that she had two young children, a boy and a girl. He couldn't remember their names, but he remembered the way her features softened whenever she talked about them. Like many officers, she had two faces – one for work and one for home. He too used to have two faces, but over the years his 'home' face had been eroded away until all that was left was the stern, unreadable mask he wore to work. Now, though, it seemed that mask was slipping and something new – he didn't understand exactly what – was being revealed. He waited for Mark to regain his composure, dreading what he had to ask next. The thought of piling more misery on the poor kid weighed upon him like a heavy hand.

'There's another thing, another question I need to ask you, Mark,' Jim began in an uncharacteristically hesitant voice. 'It's about your… It's about Stephen Baxley. Did you know he wasn't your…' He cleared his throat as though something was stuck in it.

Mark was watching Jim intensely, and suddenly his eyes grew big. 'You're going to ask me if I knew he wasn't my real dad, aren't you?'

'So you knew.'

'Not until now, but I suspected it more and more in the last few years. It wasn't just that he loved Charlotte so much more than he did me, or even that I don't look anything like him. It was something about the way he looked at me. Like…' Mark searched for the right words. 'Like he'd rather I didn't exist. I mean, what sort of father looks at their child like that?'

His eyes veered away from Jim's, a blank look in them, as though he was unsure how to feel about what he'd just learnt. He wasn't surprised to know his dad had lied to him. But his mum… she was the only person he'd ever really trusted. How could she have kept the truth from him for so long? And why had she felt it was necessary? Had she been trying to protect him? If so, her failure couldn't have been more complete.

'I need a couple more things from you, Mark.' Jim handed him the printout of the girl's face. 'Do you recognise her?'

Heaving a sigh, Mark focused on the photo. His forehead puckered as if the sight of it pricked his brain like a thorn. Voice vibrating with uncertainty, he said, 'I don't think so, but…'

'But what?'

'For a second she seemed familiar, but I don't know her.'

'Are you sure? Take your time.'

Mark studied the photo a moment longer, then shook his head. 'No. I've never seen her before. Who is she?'

'That's what we're trying to find out.' Jim handed Mark the other printout. 'What about him? Do you recognise him?'

The furrows on Mark's face deepened. He looked bemusedly at Jim, as if to say, *Is this some kind of joke?* 'Of course I recognise him. He's me.'

A steely glint came into Jim's eyes, as though a suspicion had been confirmed.

'I've never seen that photo before,' continued Mark. 'Where did you get it? And what's it got to do with that girl?'

'I found it at the house. I'm not yet exactly sure what it's got to do with the girl.' Looking at Mark's ashen pallor, Jim felt the lie was necessary. The time would come soon enough when he had to find out the truth, but not tonight. Tonight he'd been through enough – well, almost. 'One more thing, Mark, then we're done for now.'

At a glance from Jim, Amy started the audio file from the DVD. 'That's it!' Mark exclaimed at the sound of sobbing. 'That's what I heard when I went into the house. Who is that?'

'You don't know?'

'No. Should I?'

Give him some more medicine, Angel. Do it. Isolating the voice from the DVD's images stripped it of its gut-wrenching impact, but none of its insidious cruelty. Mark's face twisted in a look of uneasy disgust. 'What is this?'

'I'm afraid I can't tell you that right now. Do you recognise the voice?'

'Yes, it's my—' Mark bit down sharply on the word 'dad'. 'It's Stephen.'

'Are you absolutely certain? Do you want DI Sheridan to play it again?'

Mark shook his head. He pressed his hand to his mouth, swallowing hard as if to force back down rising vomit.

'Are you OK?' asked Amy. 'Do you want me to fetch a nurse?'

'No. I just need some water.'

Amy poured Mark a glass. He took a few sips, then rested his head against the pillows and took a slow breath. 'Sorry, I suddenly came over feeling sick. I think I need to close my eyes and rest.'

'You do that.' Jim stood to leave, but hesitated. 'Who had access to the safe in the master bedroom?'

'Only Stephen. That's where he kept the cash he used to dole out for Mum's and our weekly allowances. I told you, he was extremely controlling about money. If you ask me, the fucker got a kick out of knowing we were totally dependent on him.'

As Jim and Amy strode towards the lift, Amy asked, 'Why does it matter who had access to the safe?'

'Maybe the safe was open because that's where Stephen Baxley kept the DVD. I'm trying to figure out whether or not his wife knew about its existence.'

Amy thumbed over her shoulder towards Mark's room. 'Let's hope for that poor bastard's sake that she didn't. I wonder why Stephen Baxley put the DVD on for Mark to see? Do you reckon he got some kind of power kick out of knowing that was the last thing Mark would ever see?'

'I'm not sure I want to know what the bastard got out of it.'

'You guessed the boy in that film was Mark, didn't you?'

Jim nodded. 'When I thought about when it was made and how old Mark is, it seemed like the logical conclusion. I just couldn't bring myself to say it. The thought that some-one could do that to a child they're supposed to love, it's just too...' He shook his head, signifying his disgust was beyond words.

'Mark obviously has no memory of what happened.'

'They had him drugged up to the eyeballs. The poor little sod wouldn't have had a clue what was going on.' Jim ground his knuckles against the lift wall. He felt like hitting something – hard. He closed his eyes and the shadowy figures from the DVD emerged like phantoms from his raging brain. And he knew the only way he would ever drive them out was by hunting them down and bringing them to justice.

'You look done in, Jim. Why don't you go home and get some sleep? I'll cover for you with Garrett.'

Jim shook his head. He was tired, but not in the way Amy meant. He was tired of the job, of manning a seemingly endless conveyor belt of misery. He wanted off. He wanted out. But the look he'd seen in Mark's eyes – both as an adult and a child – pinned him in place like a butterfly to a board. 'Thanks for the offer, though.'

The cindery glow of dawn touched the chimney pots of Pitsmoor's terraced houses as they drove to South Yorkshire Police Headquarters, a squat, rectangular concrete-and-brick building on the edge of the city centre. Jim pulled over outside it. 'I'll see you later.'

Faint lines of confusion spread across Amy's forehead. 'I thought you wanted to keep working.'

'I do.'

'So what about those old case-files the DCI wants us to review?'

'You'll have to start without me. There's someone I need to see.'

'Who?'

'Bryan Reynolds.'

The wrinkles on Amy's brow grew more pronounced. 'I don't think that's advisable, Jim.'

'Maybe not, but I'm going to do it anyway. Don't worry, I'm not going to do anything stupid. I just want to look into his eyes and gauge his reaction to the news of his old pal's death.'

'Perhaps I should come with you.'

Jim shook his head. 'There's no point both of us getting in shit with the brass. Besides, Reynolds and I go back a long way. I know how the bastard operates. He won't speak to me if you're there. If I'm alone, it'll get him wondering if maybe

I've come to deal for information.'

'OK, but call me as soon as you're done with him.'

'Ditto you if you find anything in the files. Pull Reynolds's file as well.'

'What do you want me to tell the DCI?'

'The truth,' said Jim with a crooked little smile, knowing it would get up Garrett's nose big time.

Amy got out of the car. Flicking her a wave, Jim accelerated away. He lit a cigarette, thinking about Bryan Reynolds. The guy was a sociopath of the worst kind. Friendship, love and affection were alien to him – or at least, Jim had thought so before tonight. The knowledge that Reynolds had done time for Stephen Baxley had changed his thinking. The two men obviously shared some sort of deep connection. The question was, did that connection have anything to do with the DVD? Reynolds kept a string of women. He made a great show of lavishing gifts on them. But maybe, like the legitimate businesses he owned, they were a front designed to hide his real nature. Maybe he and Stephen Baxley had shared a mutual fantasy, a mutual perversion that had forged a lifelong bond. That was why Jim wanted to be the one to tell Reynolds about Baxley's death. He knew it might be the only chance he would ever have to see behind the macho, arrogant mask Reynolds presented to the world.

Chapter Eight

Angel didn't realise she'd passed out until she came round. The blue fingers of dawn were pushing through the curtains, crawling across the floor towards her. Cold sweat filmed her forehead. Mucus streamed from her nostrils, mingling with the blood crusted around her mouth. She wiped it away with a hand that trembled as though a fever was raging inside her. A raw pain gnawed at her guts. She glared at Deano's sleeping form. She wanted him to feel something of that pain, but she was barely strong enough to push herself upright, let alone hurt him. Besides, she knew that if she attacked him, physically or verbally, she would only get it back ten times over. She staggered to the bathroom and examined her face in the mirror. Her upper lip was split and swollen to twice its normal size. Lavender-dark bruises were flowering on her cheekbones and jaw, but Deano had been careful to avoid hitting her nose or eyes. Her upper arms and back had taken the worst of the punishment. With arthritic slowness, she removed her t-shirt, revealing a blanket of bruises.

She bent to swallow cold water from the tap. After rinsing the sour taste of blood out of her mouth, she tried the other tap. As usual, there was no hot water. She turned on the electric shower and stood beneath the warm trickle of its limescale-clogged head, arms hugged around herself. As her blood drained down the plughole, she felt life seeping back into her bones. The water didn't stop her from wanting to claw at her itching flesh, though. Only one thing could do that.

After drying herself with a grubby towel and squeezing the water out of her hair, Angel re-dressed and returned to the bedroom. Deano didn't stir as she sat down on the bed. Nothing short of a grenade exploding outside the window would wake him before midday. She forced herself to eat a slice of bread, even though her cramping stomach wanted to reject it. Her gaze came to rest on the corner of an envelope poking out from underneath the pillows. She knew what it contained without opening it – a fresh supply of smack. She also knew that Deano would know exactly how many wraps there were, and that she'd be in deep shit if she took one without permission. The tendons of her neck stood out like whipcords with the force of will it took to resist cooking up a hit. In a futile attempt to take her mind off the envelope, she switched on the television.

The morning news was showing an aerial shot of a large house set in equally expansive landscaped gardens. Something big must have gone down, judging by the number of emergency service vehicles in the driveway. As the camera homed in on burnt-out windows, Angel reached for the remote-control. She didn't like the news, partly because it bored her, but mostly because it depressed her. She already had enough violence and death in her life without wallowing in other people's misery. She hesitated to switch over, knowing she should keep watching to see if there had been any developments in the

Ryan Castle murder case. Turning to Deano again, she felt in his tracksuit pockets and pulled out a cigarette packet and lighter. She sparked up, inhaling deeply. The nicotine wouldn't ease her cravings, but the act of smoking was one more thing to distract her mind from them.

'... on the outskirts of Sheffield is believed to be the home of a prominent local businessman and his family.'

Hearing the newsreader mention her home city, Angel peered closely at the television, trying to see if she recognised the area. But all that was visible were fields and grazing sheep. Wherever the house was, it was a far cry from the congested streets of Hillsborough where she'd grown up. The newsreader said something about a police press conference, and the live footage cut to a video clip of a grim-faced detective. 'I can confirm that shortly after 8 pm yesterday a call was made to the police control room from an address close to the Ringinglow Road,' he told a wall of journalists. 'Officers were dispatched to the scene and it was discovered that a man and a woman were dead in the house. It is our belief at this stage that the woman died of shotgun wounds. The exact cause of the man's death has yet to be established. A teenage girl and a young adult male were found outside the house, both suffering from serious shotgun wounds. They were taken to the Northern General Hospital, where they remain in a critical condition.'

'Can you also confirm whether you're looking for anyone else in relation to this shooting?' asked a journalist.

'The investigation is at a very early stage,' answered the detective. 'All I can say right now is that a full forensics team is at the house seeking to establish exactly what happened and identify all the individuals involved. I would, however, like to reassure people that, at this time, we have no reason to believe this is anything other than an isolated event.'

So in other words you aren't looking for anyone else, thought Angel. The implication of this was obvious – someone at the house, almost certainly one of the men, had gone on a murderous rampage. It was the same old story. She'd seen it a thousand times in a thousand forms, but it always amounted to the same thing: there was nothing more dangerous than a man angry and disappointed at life. *Other than perhaps a woman sick and tired of being beaten down by men*, a voice in her head added.

The news cut to a live shot of a reporter standing in front of a cordon of police tape. 'The names of the victims still haven't been released,' said the reporter. 'But since that press conference we've learnt that the house behind me is the home of local businessman Stephen Baxley, his wife Jenny and their two children, who can't be named for legal reasons. A representative of South Yorkshire Police has also informed us that a resident of the address was a lawful holder of a shotgun licence.'

The reporter began to speculate on the obvious possibilities these revelations might hold, but Angel wasn't listening any more. At the mention of Stephen Baxley's name, her body had stiffened as if she'd been poked with an electric cattle prod. She stared at the screen without seeing it, her face deathly pale. *Stephen Baxley!* The name was like a hand reaching out from the past – a past she'd been running from her whole adult life – to grip her throat. She rocked like someone in a trance. Twisted, perverse images were rushing at her, overwhelming her consciousness. She saw a young boy with curly blond hair and drugged blue eyes. She saw a group of figures hovering over him like vultures over their prey. Finally, she saw Stephen Baxley, his lips repulsively moist, an infinitely more repulsive light in his eyes. She heard his voice as though he was right there in the room. 'Take your underwear off, Angel.' And as she obeyed, hate ate at her like acid – hate for Stephen Baxley, hate for the other figures, hate for herself.

The cigarette burnt down to Angel's fingers, searing the images away. She twisted round, her eyes desperately searching. Spotting the gun, she snatched it up and pressed the barrel to her temple. She closed her eyes, her breath coming sharp and tight. Her knuckles whitened on the grip. Ten seconds passed. Twenty. Thirty. *Pull the trigger*, she muttered inwardly. *Just fucking do it. No more pain, no more sorrow. A bullet in the head. Quick, simple, easy!* The final word tolled like a warning in her brain. Yes, suicide was easy – too easy, both for her and for those who'd driven her to the brink of it. It was time to stop running. It was time to start fighting back.

She lowered the gun and looked at it. Fifteen bullets. More than enough to go round, even if Stephen Baxley was still alive. She swore a silent oath to herself. They would pay. Every one of them. For what they'd done to her, and for what they'd made her do to the boy. Oh, how they would pay! But first she had to deal with Deano.

Angel looked at him with eyes like cold stones. She knew he'd never let her go. His pride wouldn't allow it. But neither could she allow him to give her name to the police. That would end her plans before she'd even had a chance to properly formulate them. Her gaze returned to the envelope. She pulled it from under the pillow and emptied its contents on to the mattress.

There were fifty cellophane wraps of Mexican brown. She picked up three of them. A triple dose would easily be enough to kill him, especially with the amount of junk he already had in his system. She melted the sticky coal-black lumps and drew the solution into Deano's syringe. Very gently, she spread his legs and felt for the pulsing artery.

Angel started to move the needle towards Deano, but hesitated. Sweat that had nothing to do with withdrawal symptoms stood out on her upper lip. She'd been swept along by a tsunami of rage when she killed Castle. This was different. Sure, Deano was grade-A scum. And sure, she hated him. But her hate was tempered by other feelings. If only for a brief instant, things had been good between her and Deano. He'd adored her and taken care of her. She shook her head vehemently. No, he'd groomed her for his own pleasure, just like those other bastards who'd plucked her off the street as a fifteen-year-old runaway. And as soon as she was out of the picture, he'd do the same to other girls. She couldn't allow that to happen. A glance at her battered face in the mirror gave her the final push she needed. She slid the needle into Deano, drew the plunger slightly to make sure she'd hit his vein, then depressed it.

Deano gave out a soft moan. His eyelids fluttered but didn't open. Angel watched until the rise and fall of his chest became indiscernible. She didn't feel the way she had done after killing Castle. She didn't feel anything much at all. Neither she nor anyone else would grieve for Deano. No one would even come looking for him. As far as she knew, he had no family, and he certainly had no friends. His customers would wonder where he was, but they were hardly likely to report his disappearance.

It might be weeks or even months before someone found his body. And even then, few questions would be asked. After all, junkies died in this neighbourhood practically every day of the week.

Angel cooked up a hit that was weak enough not to knock her off her feet but strong enough to ease her craving. After shooting up, she rifled through Deano's belongings until she found her money. She put it in her handbag, along with the gun, the Mexican brown and some needles. Then she concealed the worst of her bruises with a thick layer of makeup. After peering out of the window to make sure there were no police about, she headed outside.

As she made her way to Middlesbrough Railway Station, there was a purpose in her step and a steel in her eyes that made early-morning commuters shift out of her path. 'When's the next train to Sheffield?' she asked the ticket-seller.

'8.20, platform one,' came the reply. 'Arrival time in Sheffield is 10.20 a.m.'

'How much for a ticket?'

'One way or return?'

'One way,' Angel replied without hesitation. She paid for her ticket and walked onto the platform. A shudder passed over her, but not because of the breeze blowing along the tracks. In a few hours, for the first time in nearly fifteen years, she would be home.

Chapter Nine

Bryan Reynolds's house was different from Stephen Baxley's in every respect except one – it too was worth a cool couple of million. The four-storey, flat-roofed ultra-modern house with its glazed walls, galvanised-steel balconies and panoramic roof terrace was set well back from the road, behind tall gates. A tank-like Hummer with mirrored windows was parked in its driveway. Two heavily muscled pit bulls eyeballed Jim through the gates. Reflecting that the leafy Ranmoor street was about as far as you could get, in lifestyle if not distance, from the sinkhole estates where Reynolds had grown up and where he still plied his trade, Jim hit the intercom button and held it down. An angry, broad Sheffield voice cut through the buzzing. 'You'd better stop pushing that button or I'll come down there and shove it up your fucking arse.'

'Sorry, Mr Reynolds, did I wake you?' asked Jim, unable to keep a note of satisfaction out of his voice.

'Yeah you fucking did. Who is this?'

'Detective Jim Monahan.'

'Monahan,' repeated Reynolds, obviously searching his memory to put a face to the name. 'Look up at the camera.' Jim lifted his gaze towards the CCTV camera on the gate, and Reynolds continued, 'Oh yeah, I remember you. You tried to pin some bullshit drug charge on me a while back. What do you want?'

'Just a friendly chat. I've got some information about an old friend of yours that might interest you.'

'I haven't got any old friends.'

'Are you sure about that, Mr Reynolds? Think carefully. I'm talking about someone from way back.'

The intercom was silent a moment. Jim could almost hear Reynolds's brain whirring into motion. Reynolds wasn't an educated man. If any of the students at the nearby university were ever unfortunate enough to meet him, they might have thought him stupid. But they'd have been very, very wrong. His intelligence was simply of a different nature to theirs. He was a master of bluff and bullshit. But he was also as cold and calculating as a snake, with a mind that could weigh up all the angles as fast as any copper. Faster. That was how he stayed ahead of the game when most of his contemporaries were in prison or dead.

'Are you alone?' asked Reynolds.

'Yes.'

The intercom buzzed and the gate clicked open. Reynolds's voice crackled down the line, 'Come on up to the house.' He chuckled as Jim glanced warily at the bulldogs. 'Don't worry about my girls. They won't bother you. Just don't make any sudden movements.'

The dogs sniffed at Jim's ankles as he approached the house. Reynolds met him at the door, wearing a loose kimono. He was in his late forties but had a better body than most men half his age. A hairless, tanned, heavily muscled chest showed through the kimono. He had close-set blue eyes and the broken-nosed, angular face of an old wolf. His scalp glistened pink through thinning blonde hair scraped back into a limp ponytail. The dogs jumped up at him, wagging their stubby tails. Stroking their broad, flat heads, he looked Jim up and down. A smirk flickered at one corner of his mouth. 'You've put on some weight since I last saw you.'

Resisting an urge to yank open the kimono and check for identifying features, Jim forced a return smile. 'That happens when you get old.'

'Speak for yourself, mate. I'm as fit as I was when I was twenty-one.' Reynolds patted his washboard stomach. 'Fitter.' Motioning for Jim to follow him, he crossed the minimalist white entrance hall and started up the steel-and-glass spiral staircase. 'Do you know what my secret is?'

'You work out and eat right.'

'Yeah, I do all that stuff, but that's not it.' Reynolds stopped halfway up the staircase and turned round. His eyes were still amused, but something else was lurking in them too, something that made Jim tense up as if in anticipation of having to defend himself. 'Sleep. That's the secret to a healthy life. If I didn't get a solid eight hours a night, I'd soon end up looking like... well, like you. No offence, but I'd rather be dead than look like you.'

'None taken. Sometimes I'd rather be dead than look like me too.'

Reynolds chuckled. 'You're alright, copper.' He continued up the stairs to a large, unlived-in-looking lounge furnished with beige leather sofas, Persian rugs and oriental art. In one corner there was a well-stocked glass bar. The room had the opulent but tacky feel of an expensive Las Vegas hotel suite. 'How do you like my little pad? Not bad for a Park Hill boy, eh? What kind of place have you got?'

'I'm not here to talk about me.'

'I'll bet you live in some pokey semi, don't you? And I'll bet you've got some dumpy little wifey who spends half her life keeping it clean.' Reynolds clicked his tongue thoughtfully, his gaze running over Jim's creased, stained shirt. 'Or maybe not. Maybe wifey realised she was pissing her life down the drain looking after you and decided to move on to greener pastures.' He gave Jim that same crooked smile, baring two rows of white and gold teeth. 'I'm right, aren't I? I can see things in people's eyes. It's a gift I've got.'

Usually, Reynolds's words would have been like empty air to Jim, but after the events of the night they grated on his nerves. There was an unpleasant kind of relish in his voice as he asked, 'What else can you see in my eyes?'

A slight frown came over Reynolds's chiselled face. 'OK, copper, enough of the shit-talking. Let's get down to business. What's this information you've got for me, and what do you want in return?'

'I don't want anything in return – well, not money anyway.' Jim paused to let his words sink in, knowing Reynolds's mind would be working overtime, asking itself, *If this bastard doesn't want money, what the fuck does he want?*

Reynolds's frown intensified. 'So come on then. Let's hear what's so important that it's disturbed my beauty sleep.'

'Is the name Stephen Baxley familiar to you?'

'You know it is, copper,' Reynolds replied, with an impatient sigh. 'Otherwise you wouldn't be here asking me about him

'When was the last time you talked to Mr Baxley?'

'I'm not obliged to answer your questions, but being as I'm a nice bloke who's always happy to help the police, I will do.' There was a sarcastic edge to Reynolds's voice.

With an equally sarcastic tone, Jim countered, 'I appreciate your cooperation, Mr Reynolds.'

'Now let me think.' Reynolds puffed his cheeks. 'It's got to be twenty-odd years since I last spoke to Stephen. Why? What's the silly boy done? He's not gone and got himself into some sort of trouble, has he?'

'No, he's not in any trouble. He's dead.'

Jim searched Reynolds's face for the effect his words might have. Reynolds blinked. Just a blink, nothing more, but it was enough to tell Jim his revelation had pierced Reynolds's armour of unfeeling arrogance. As if they too sensed their master's hurt, the dogs nuzzled his shins, whining. He shushed them sharply. 'How did he die?'

'Well it wasn't of natural causes.'

'Yeah, I'd worked that out. What I can't work out is what this has got to do with me.'

'We're talking to anyone who's got history with Stephen Baxley. When we ran a CRC, your name came up. That was a nice thing you did, taking the full hit on those assault charges in '88. I didn't think you had it in you. Baxley must've been a real close friend.'

Reynolds turned away from Jim. 'What about his wife?'

'Jenny Baxley also died in the same incident.'

'And their kids?'

'Mark and Charlotte are being treated in hospital.'

'Will they live?'

'I really couldn't say. You seem to know a fair bit about Stephen Baxley's family, considering you haven't seen him in so long.'

'Yeah, well he was a Park Hill boy done good. I've always kept an eye out for him in the news.' There was a trace of heaviness to Reynolds's step as he approached the bar. He poured himself a glass of fresh orange juice and gulped it down as if his throat was burning with thirst. 'You'd best leave now, copper.' He looked at Jim in the mirrored wall behind the bar. 'I'm done talking.'

The same light Jim had seen on the stairs was back in Reynolds's eyes, but it was no longer laced with amusement. Scenting that things could turn nasty, Jim was half tempted to prod Reynolds a little more, see if he could provoke him into totally losing his cool. There was nothing he would have liked better than an excuse to haul Reynolds down the station. Not that he thought it would serve any real purpose. Reynolds's thousand-quid-an-hour lawyer would have a field day with the fact that his client had been questioned without probable cause or even reasonable suspicion. Still, it would put a smile on his and a lot of other cops' faces to see the bastard locked up, if only for a few hours.

As if he'd read Jim's mind, a knowing, humourless smile tugged at Reynolds's mouth. 'You can show yourself out, I'm going back to bed. You should too, Monahan. Remember what I said, if you want to look half as good as me, you've got to get eight or nine hours solid a night.'

Jim returned a crooked smile of his own. 'I'll bear that in mind.'

As Jim turned towards the stairs, he caught a movement out

of the corner of his eye. Beyond glass doors a man in jeans and a black bomber jacket was leaning against the balcony railings with his back to the room, smoking a cigarette. He was built like a brick wall. A lattice of pearly scars crisscrossed the crown of his shaved head, clearly the result of an axe or machete attack. Taking a mental note of his physical description, Jim descended to the front door. The bulldogs followed him all the way to the street. He shut the gate, resisting the impulse to snatch up a couple of stones and fling them at their snub-nosed faces.

He hadn't got any new information out of Reynolds, but then he hadn't expected to. What he had got was confirmation that Reynolds and Baxley's relationship went well beyond that of estranged childhood pals. Reynolds's muted yet intense reaction to the news of Baxley's death had made him even more curious as to the true nature of that relationship. Reynolds had been lying when he claimed not to have spoken to Baxley in twenty-odd years, of that Jim felt sure. What he had to do now was find some way of breaking open that lie. His instincts told him that could be the key to cracking the case, and he always listened to his instincts. His phone rang. He put it to his ear. 'What's up, Amy?'

'I think I've found the girl.'

'That was quick work.'

'She was top of the pile. Her name's Grace Kirby.'

'Grace Kirby!' Jim exclaimed in recognition. 'I remember her. She went missing back when DCS Knight was doing Garrett's job. I didn't work the case, but everyone in CID was given a photo of her.' He closed his eyes, sifting through the thousands of faces he'd dealt with over the years. 'Long, dark hair, blue eyes, slim, pretty.' *No, not pretty*, corrected his mind, *beautiful. She was seamlessly beautiful in the way that only children can be, her face untouched by the corruption of the world.*

'That's her.'

'I knew I knew that girl from somewhere.' Jim pressed a hand to his stomach as it emitted a grumble of hunger. 'Fancy a bit of breakfast at Joe's Cafe? It's on me.'

'Sounds good.'

'I'll see you there in ten. Bring a copy of the Kirby girl's case-file and Reynolds's file with you.'

Jim drove back into the city centre through streets rapidly filling with rush-hour traffic. He parked outside a backstreet greasy-spoon not far from Police Headquarters. 'Usual, is it?' asked the woman behind the counter as he entered the cafe. He nodded, dropping wearily onto a chair at a Formica table. Margaret had always watched his diet for him. Saturday was fried breakfast day. The rest of the week it was cereal and toast. But after she walked out, he'd quickly got into the habit of eating a full English every day. Not that he had a particular love of fried food, but as with smoking in bed, he drew a small measure of satisfaction from knowing it would incur his ex-wife's disapproval. He heaved a sigh. Christ, could he get any more pathetic?

'Heavy night?' asked the woman, setting down a steaming mug of tea in front of Jim.

'Heavy like you wouldn't believe.'

Amy entered the cafe. She ordered coffee and scrambled eggs on toast, then sat down opposite Jim. She placed a wad of photocopied papers on the table. He leafed through Reynolds's file. A tattoo of a red devil on the back of Reynolds's right shoulder and a six-centimetre-long scar on his left buttock where he'd been stabbed in prison were listed under 'Identifying Marks'. He skimmed over the remainder of the file. That eighteen-month stretch had obviously made a big impact on Reynolds – although not in the way intended. Prior to it, he'd been in and out of court, getting slapped on the wrist for burglary, car theft and other petty charges. In prison he'd made contacts with older professional criminals who'd recruited him into organised crime. In the years since his release, his name had been linked to loan sharking, gambling, prostitution, protection and drug-dealing rackets. He'd also been picked up on suspicion of GBH in 2002 following an incident at his strip-club, The Minx. But investigators had never been able to make anything stick.

The file made for depressing reading. Jim turned his attention to Grace Kirby's file. She stared up at him from a photograph paper-clipped to the first page: high-cheekboned, full-lipped, hair as black and glossy as coal. She was smiling, but there was a sadness about her eyes, as though she was sorry about something – maybe something she'd done, or maybe something that had been done to her. He looked over the case-notes.

Grace was fifteen years old when she'd gone missing on the sixth of February 1997. Her mother, Linda Kirby, had reported her disappearance after she failed to return home from school. Most of Grace's clothes were gone from her bedroom, along with several hundred quid her mother had kept in the house, leading officers to conclude that she was a runaway – a belief reinforced by the fact that she'd gone missing on two previous occasions. The first time, she'd returned home of her own accord after twenty-four hours; the second time, she'd been spotted after a couple of days in a fast-food restaurant by a family friend.

Because of her history, Grace wasn't classified as a critical missing person. Constables spoke to Jay Longford, the boy she was last seen with – he claimed not to know where she was – but a full-fledged search wasn't initiated until three days had passed. Police and volunteers trawled the city streets, fliers were posted, dozens of people were questioned. All these efforts had generated only one paper-thin lead. Grace's favourite hangout at the time was a playground at the corner of Wellington Street that was a popular haunt for skateboarders and drug dealers. A week before her final disappearance, she'd been seen there by a school friend named Tara Riley talking to someone wearing a grey mac. Unfortunately, Tara hadn't seen that same someone's face. An appeal had been made for whoever it was to come forward, but it went unanswered.

A runaway fifteen-year-old with limited resources can only stay off the police radar for so long. So when Grace still hadn't been found after several months, the obvious conclusion was that an adult or adults were keeping her hidden. The question was whether she was being kept willingly or against her will. If the latter, chances were she would never be seen again – at least, not alive.

Over the next few months there were several reported sightings of Grace in Sheffield, but none of these leads came to anything. The case remained open, but by the end of the following year, with no new leads, active investigation was closed. Apart from the man in the mac, only one other 'person of interest' was mentioned in the case-file – Ron Kirby, Grace's father. At the time, Ron was a groundsman at Hillsborough Stadium. He was also an alcoholic with a criminal record that included convictions for drink-related crimes such as common assault, disturbing the peace, criminal damage and indecent exposure. On several occasions Grace had turned up at school with suspicious bruises and burn marks. Her teacher had reported the matter to social services after her parents refused to come to the school to discuss it. Social workers had also met with a wall of silence. In the end, although they were well aware Ron Kirby was a hard drinker with a violent temper, they'd decided not to pursue the case.

Jim studied a photograph of Grace's parents. Ron looked like an aging football hooligan – burly tattooed forearms, close-shaved grey hair. Like her daughter, Linda had obviously once been beautiful – far too beautiful for a Neanderthal like her husband – but her beauty had been worn away by life, leaving a timid shadow of its former self. Her face was thin, almost gaunt, and there were dark shadows and deep lines under her eyes. With her hunched shoulders and large, damp pupils, she looked like a frightened mouse. Not exactly the type of woman to speak out about abuse she and Grace might have suffered at the hands of Ron.

Jim's gaze returned to Grace. Was it possible she was still alive? It came back to the same basic questions as in '97. Had she been abducted against her will? Or had she been picked up and groomed for sex? If the former, statistics indicated that she was long dead. If the latter, there was a small chance she was still alive. He'd seen many times how easy it was for children from loveless and abusive families to fall under the sway of someone who offered them affection. Like a junkie, they sometimes came to crave that affection so much they were willing to do anything for it.

Jim's line of thought was broken by breakfast being set down. With a smile of thanks, he reached for his knife and fork.

'So what happened with Reynolds?' asked Amy. Between mouthfuls of bacon and egg, Jim recounted the details of their meeting. When he'd finished, Amy said, 'Do you think he was telling the truth about Baxley?'

'Was he bollocks. There was something between those two, some sort of bond that went beyond friendship. I'm certain of it. The question is, what is it that connected two blokes who moved in such different circles?'

Amy indicated Grace's photo with her knife. 'Maybe if we can find her, we'll find the answer.'

'Maybe. But even if by some chance Grace Kirby is alive, how the hell are we going to find someone who's managed to stay unfound for the past fifteen years?'

'I don't know, but I'd say the best place to start looking is here.' The tip of Amy's knife moved to Grace's parents.

Looking at Linda Kirby's grief-stricken face, Jim sighed at the thought of stirring up all the old hurt and anguish. But even worse than that was the thought that they would also be stirring up hope – hope that was almost certainly false. Suddenly he was no longer hungry. He pushed his plate aside. 'Come on then, let's go do some work.'

'Shouldn't we report to the DCI first?'

'What for? So he can put someone else on this?'

'We've only glanced through the case-file. There might be other angles to this we don't know about. We should really speak to someone who worked the case.'

Amy was right, Jim knew. But something within him urged him to act without delay. He had the sense that time was running out. *Grace Kirby's been missing fifteen years*, an inner voice said. *What difference will a few hours' delay make?* The answer was obvious – none. But this wasn't only about the case clock, it was about his own internal clock. He could almost hear it ticking in the centre of his brain, pushing him, compelling him. He tapped the photo of Grace's parents. 'You said it yourself, Amy, this is the best and only place to start looking. If you want to talk to Garrett, fine. But I'm moving on this now.'

Picking up the files, Jim approached the counter to pay. Amy frowned after him. With a slight shake of her head, she stood and followed him to his car.

Driving against the flow of rush-hour traffic, they headed out of the city centre along the Penistone Road. The Kirbys' house was a two-up two-down mid-terrace in the shadow of Hillsborough Stadium, its stone front black with industrial-era soot. 'You think they still live here?' asked Amy as they parked up.

'People like them don't move house.'

Jim knocked on the door. A moment later, Linda Kirby opened it in a dressing-gown and slippers. She looked the same as in her photograph, except the wrinkles around her eyes and the sadness in them had deepened with age. She opened her mouth to speak, but before she could do so a man's voice boomed down the stairs. 'Who the bloody hell is it knocking me up at this time of the morning?'

'Sorry to disturb you, Mrs Kirby,' said Jim. 'I'm Detective Inspector Jim Monahan. This is Detective Inspector Amy Sheridan.'

'This is about my Grace, isn't it?' Linda's voice vibrated with anxiety, but Jim noted that she didn't seem particularly surprised by their presence.

'Yes.'

'You've found her, haven't you?'

'No, but some new information concerning her case has come to light. Do you mind if we come inside?'

Looking as though she wasn't sure whether to be relieved or disappointed, Linda motioned them into the house. 'Are you deaf, woman?' came another roar from upstairs. 'I asked you a bloody question.'

'It's the police, Ron,' replied Linda. 'They're here about our Grace.'

The detectives followed Linda into a neat little living room furnished with a three-piece suite that was as old and worn as its owner. The fireplace had been turned into a shrine to Grace. Dozens of framed photos of her cluttered its hearth and mantelpiece. More hung on the wall above. In some of the pictures Grace was a chubby-cheeked toddler, in others she was a smiling young child, and finally she was a sulky-eyed teenager. Linda took a pack of cigarettes out of the pocket of her dressing-gown. She lit a cigarette and spoke through it. 'So what's this new information?'

'We believe your daughter's case may have some bearing on another case we're investigating,' said Jim. 'I'm afraid as it's an on-going investigation that's all I can really tell you right now.'

'Back at the door you seemed to think we'd found your daughter,' said Amy. 'May I ask what led you to that conclusion?'

'I know Grace is alive. She phoned me last night.'

Jim and Amy exchanged an astonished glance. 'What did she say?' asked Jim.

'She didn't say anything.'

'So how do you know it was her?'

'I know because I know. It's a mother thing.' She turned her watery blue eyes on Amy. 'Have you got children?'

'Two. A boy and a girl.'

'Then you know what I'm talking about. I didn't have to hear her voice. I just knew.'

'What time was the call made?' asked Jim.

'About eleven o'clock.'

'Did you get the caller's number?'

'Yes. I think it's a mobile phone number.' Linda took a scrap of paper with a number written on it from the mantelpiece and handed it to Jim. He jotted it down, then passed it to Amy, who did likewise before returning it to Linda.

'Have you tried ringing it?'

Linda shook her head. 'I know my Grace, she won't answer if I do. She's a very independent little girl, and she's stubborn too...' she glanced towards the hallway, her voice dropping low, 'like her dad. When she's ready, she'll call again.'

At the words 'little girl', a glimmer of sympathy passed through Jim. Linda was obviously unable to picture her daughter as anything other than the child she'd been when she disappeared. Her mind was stuck in limbo, frozen in a moment that existed only in history. He wondered whether, if Grace suddenly turned up alive, Linda would even be able to accept her as her daughter. 'Is this the first silent phone call you've received?'

'Yes.'

'If it was your daughter, why do you think she would suddenly decide to get in touch now after all these years?'

'I don't know. Maybe she's thinking about coming home. Maybe she just needed to hear her mother's voice.'

'Is she giving you her guff about Grace phoning?' The voice came from the doorway. Jim turned towards its owner. Ron Kirby had put on a fair bit of weight since his case-file photo. He wore a string-vest that bulged like a sack of grain over tracksuit bottoms. His broken-veined cheeks, craggy nose and rheumy eyes told of a diet of alcohol, cigarettes and greasy food. His brawny arms were tattooed with, amongst other things, Sheffield Wednesday's blue owl insignia and a list of the club's honours. Lines of meanness spread from the corners of his eyes as he looked from his wife to the detectives.

'I take it you don't think it was your daughter, Mr Kirby,' said Amy.

Ron grunted out a phlegmy laugh. 'Course it bloody wasn't. It was just some dirty little perv.' He prodded a thick, tobacco-yellowed finger at his wife's head, causing her to wince. 'That's the only place Grace is still alive.'

Linda lowered her eyes, fidgeting nervously with her cigarette. Jim felt a prickle of anger, both at Ron's callousness and at Linda's apparent inability to stand up for herself. Keeping his voice carefully businesslike, he asked, 'What leads you to believe your daughter's dead, Mr Kirby?'

Ron gave Jim a frowning smile, wagging his finger as if the question was a trap he didn't intend to fall into. 'Oh no, you're not leading me down that rabbit hole. I had a gutful of your lot's snide little questions when Grace first ran off.' He jerked his chin at Linda. 'It took me and her years to get back to some kind of normal life. So unless you're here to tell us something new, you can bloody well bugger off and leave us alone. Do you hear me?'

'I hear you and I understand.' Jim vainly tried to catch Linda's downturned eyes. 'Thank you for talking to us, Mrs Kirby.' He proffered a card with his name and number on it. 'If you get any more strange phone calls, or if anything else out of the ordinary happens, or even if you just want to talk, please don't hesitate to contact me.'

Ron snatched the card out of Jim's hand. 'Why would she want to talk to you? You lot are about as much use as tits on a nun. You proved that back in '97. If we get any more of them calls, I'll deal with them my way.'

Jim shot Ron a brief, hard look. His eyes softened as they returned to Linda. 'Sorry to have bothered you. If and when we do have something new to tell you, we'll be in touch.'

The detectives made their way to the front door, which Ron slammed emphatically behind them. 'He's a real piece of work,' said Amy. 'I think I'd have run away too if I had a dad like him.' She sighed. 'Christ, it depresses me to see a woman like that waste her life on a tosser like him. Why do you think she stays with him?'

'Who knows? Maybe her parents were the same way. I sometimes think these things are passed down through families like diseases.' Jim sparked up a cigarette, lifting his face to the pale morning sun.

'What do you reckon to this phone call business?'

'I reckon we should look into it. It's probably just a coincidence, but it's all we've got to go on right now.'

'Pretty big coincidence, don't you think? News goes out about what went down at the Baxley house. A few hours later, Linda Kirby gets a silent phone call. I'm thinking, what if the news spurred Grace into getting in touch?'

Jim squinted at Amy. 'Do you buy into what Mrs Kirby said about being able to sense it was her daughter?'

'As a cop, no. As a mother, I'm not sure. I can tell you this, often when one of my two needs something from me, they don't even have to say it, I just know.'

Jim took a thoughtful drag, then flicked his cigarette away. As they drove to the station, tiredness settled over him like a thick blanket. Catching a glimpse of his red-rimmed eyes in the rear-view mirror, Reynolds's words came back to him. *Sleep. That's the secret to a healthy life.* A wry smile crossed his lips. Reynolds was the last person in the world he'd ever expected to be taking advice from, but he was right. If he didn't get some sleep soon, he'd be no use to anyone. 'Does your offer still stand?' he asked.

'You mean about covering for you?'

'Uh-huh.'

'Sure, go home, get a few hours' shut-eye.'

'Thanks, Amy.'

Jim dropped Amy at Police Headquarters, then turned in the direction of home. By the time he got there, he was almost asleep at the wheel. He dragged himself upstairs, undressed and crawled between the sheets. But when he closed his eyes, his mind began to empty itself of the night's events. He saw the burnt and bloody bodies. He saw Mark Baxley's desperate, agonised eyes and Linda Kirby's tired, sad eyes. But most of all he saw the basement, the naked figures and their victims. Over and over, the sickening footage looped through his brain.

With a sigh, Jim got out of bed and retrieved his cigarettes. As he smoked, he booted up his computer and googled 'SB Engineering'. He clicked a link to the company's website. According to the PR bumf, SB Engineering was one of the UK's leading contract manufacturing companies. The 'About' section boasted that the company had expanded rapidly since it was founded in 1996, and currently employed 230 people in 160,000 square feet of hi-tech workshop space.

Jim navigated back to Google and scanned further down the list of links. One entitled 'SB Engineering: Does Their Success Prove The Government Was Right?' caught his eye. It led to an article on a financial blog published on 18/03/2010. The article began, 'Thirteen years ago I wrote about how Stephen Baxley was granted a multi-million-pound interest-free government loan to help get his then fledgling company, SB Engineering, up and sprinting. The loan, whose exact amount and repayment timeframe has never been made public, matched capital raised from private investors. With the general election looming, I thought it would be a good time to revisit the issues raised in that article.' The author went on to question whether it was right for governments to use tax money to kickstart businesses, congratulating SB Engineering on its success, but stressing that it had not changed his opinion that politicians driven by short-term electoral pressures were poorly qualified to pick long-term investment prospects.

The author was someone called Peter Nichols. Jim signed up to receive email alerts when the blog was updated, reflecting that Nichols would probably soon be publishing another article about SB Engineering, along the lines of 'I told you so'.

Jim made his way downstairs to the sofa. He lay studying the printouts of Grace and Mark's faces. His thoughts returned to Margaret. They'd intended to start a family but had always found reasons for putting it off. At first it was money – or rather, the lack of it; then it was their careers. And then, suddenly, it was too late. He wondered, as he often had, whether Margaret would have left him if they'd had children. He sharply dismissed the thought. It was pointless. She was gone and that was all there was to it. It was up to him to find something to fill the hole she'd left in his life. But what? When Margaret had first walked out, things had got so bad he'd sought help from a counsellor. The counsellor had told him that over time his pain would ease, but it hadn't. Even now after five years, the hole was as cavernous as it had ever been.

Jim flipped through his notepad until he came to the phone number Linda Kirby had given him. He stared at it, brow furrowed. It would be a crazy move to ring the number without even knowing if it was registered to a name, and especially without the back-up of recording and tracing technology. At best it would put the phone's owner on their guard, at worst it would prompt them to get rid of the phone. But in his mind the clock was ticking like a bomb, pushing him to make something happen. He picked up the photo of Grace. If she was alive, what had become of her? Had she got away from her abusers? Or was she still caught up in their sick fantasies? If the former, maybe news of Stephen Baxley's possible death had given her the confidence to consider coming out of hiding. If the latter, maybe she was looking for a way out, a way back to the life her abusers had stolen from her. Either way, Jim wanted her to know the path was open, and that if she took it, she would get all the help he could give. Slowly, he picked up the phone and dialled.

Chapter Ten

When a voice announced over the loudspeakers that the train would soon be arriving at Sheffield, Angel's eyelids jerked up. She stared out of the window at the sprawl of housing estates and industrial plants that made up north-east Sheffield. Her memories of the landscape were hazy, seeming almost to belong to another lifetime. But she recognised the blue-green roof of Meadowhall Shopping Centre, under which she'd whiled away many Saturdays with friends. And she noted the absence of the Tinsley Cooling Towers, which had stood like sentinels watching over the endless streams of traffic flowing along the M1.

Angel compressed her lips, struggling to keep her breathing steady as the concrete rampart of Park Hill loomed into view. Swinging smoothly around a final curve in the track, the train drew into the station. Angel's gaze swept over the people waiting on the platform. She knew it was absurd, but she half expected to recognise some of their faces. She pulled up the hood of her sweatshirt before getting off the train.

Looking around herself in a daze, she headed out of the station. It was like revisiting a dream. Everything seemed different yet the same, not quite real, but real enough to evoke echoes of the warnings that had rung in her ears the last time she was in Sheffield. Warnings not to contact her family or friends. Warnings never to return. Warnings that to do so would have dire consequences for her and her family. She knew the names of some of the people behind those warnings. Others had maintained a shadowy anonymity. But all of them had one thing in common – they were people with power and influence, people who thought they could do whatever they wanted and get away with it. Well, she was going to teach them otherwise.

Angel's phone started to ring. Brow pinching, she snatched it out of her handbag. A mobile phone number she didn't recognise showed on its screen. Who the hell could be calling? Only Deano knew the number belonged to her, and it obviously wasn't him. She'd made two other calls on the phone – to James Cook Hospital and to her mum. The hospital had certainly passed her number on to Cleveland Police, and her mum would almost certainly have dialled 1471. So it had to be the police or her mum. She didn't want to speak to either of them, but she did want to hear her mum's voice again.

She put the phone to her ear and waited for the caller to speak. Silence. Several seconds passed. More silence. She resisted the urge to ask, *Who is this?* It occurred to her that perhaps that was exactly what whoever it was wanted her to do. She felt certain the caller wasn't her mum. Her mum was a simple woman. It would never cross her mind to use such a tactic to try and goad her into speaking. So it had to be the police. Didn't it? Another possibility occurred to her, one that made her heart thump in her chest. Maybe it was her dad.

This was exactly the sort of thing *he* would do. Then a man's voice came over the line.

The voice had a smoke-roughened edge, like her dad's. But there was also a gentleness to it that her dad had never possessed. 'Who am I speaking to please?'

Angel made no reply. The caller repeated his question. Again, she said nothing. Then came a question that sent her heart and mind into overdrive. 'Is this Grace Kirby?'

She stifled a sharp intake of breath, telling herself it had to be the police. But how could Cleveland Police have found out her real name? There was just no way. The only person up there who knew it was dead.

'This is Detective Jim Monahan of South Yorkshire Police,' continued the man.

South Yorkshire Police! Reflexively, Angel's free hand dove into her bag and curled around the Glock's grip. She jerked her head from side to side as if expecting to see a clutch of police officers bearing down on her. How the hell could South Yorkshire Police have got her number? The answer was as obvious as it was painful. Her mum must have contacted them. She could have slapped herself for phoning her. That moment of weakness had put everything at risk. Her plans. Her family. Everything! What if the people she was out to exact revenge on had contacts in the police? Word might already have got back to them. This Detective Monahan could be in their employ. She drew a steadying breath, telling herself that all the police had to go on was a mother's gut instinct. That didn't exactly constitute hard evidence. They were probably just making enquiries to placate her mum. More importantly, there was no way they could know she was back in Sheffield.

'If this is Grace I'm talking to, I want you to know that I'm here to help you,' said the detective. 'It's not too late. You can still go home.'

A lump Angel couldn't swallow formed in her throat. *Home*. The word filled her head with a storm of mixed emotions and memories, an almost schizophrenic clash of wants. She wanted to vent years of pent-up anger on her mum for not protecting her from her dad's drunken rages. She wanted to look in her dad's eyes and tell him she would kill him if he ever again laid a hand on her or her mum. But most of all she wanted to fall asleep in her mum's embrace and wake up to find the last fifteen years had been just a bad dream.

The detective spoke in a reassuring tone. Part of Angel wanted to trust him, to believe he was telling the truth. But it was only a tiny, almost imperceptible part. Other men had spoken to her in equally reassuring, if more insidiously seductive tones in the past. They'd promised to help her and take care of her, but done the exact opposite.

'All you need do is talk to me,' the detective was saying. 'You don't have to do it now. You can call me anytime, day or—'

Angel cut him off, deciding that there was no point beating herself up about phoning her mum. In fact, it might have done her a favour. The phone call from this detective was a warning that she hadn't been nearly cautious enough. From now on, things would be different.

As Angel made her way to the high street, her eyes continually shifted from building to building. Old ones had been torn down, new ones had been or were in the process of being built, but many familiar sights remained, haunting her with memories. Her gaze lingered on a cafe her mum had always taken her to when they went shopping; a pub she vaguely recalled being dragged to by her dad after a Sheffield derby match; a chippy she used to eat in with her mates. As though she'd walked smack into an invisible wall, she came to a stop at the corner of a backstreet. She couldn't see if it was still there from where she was, but at the far end of the street there used to be a bar called The Minx. A seedy-looking place with blacked-out windows. Not the kind of place you'd expect a respectable businessman like Stephen Baxley to be familiar with. But that was where he'd first taken her on the night her life had changed forever.

As abruptly as she'd stopped, Angel started walking again. She went into a chemist's and bought hair-dye, scissors and a set of non-prescription brown contact lenses. From a clothes shop she bought a black hooded top and matching jeans. She wandered around until her whore's eye saw what it was looking for – a hotel that was big enough for its customers to remain anonymous, and rundown enough to hire out rooms by the day or hour. She paid for a couple of nights and signed a false name.

Angel's room overlooked a busy roundabout encircled by office buildings, shops, bars and nightclubs. There was a double bed with some white towels folded on it, a dressing-table with a kettle and a small supply of coffee sachets, teabags and biscuits, and a windowless bathroom. In other words, it was identical to a thousand other hotel rooms she'd spent a thousand other nights in. The only difference was that this time there was no punter to service. She was hungry and bone-weary. But before she attended to those needs, there was another need that was more powerful. She took out a wrap of

Mexican brown. After shooting up, she lay for several hours in the soft clutch of her high, cut off from pain and fear.

It was mid-afternoon when Angel rose and went to the bathroom. She cut her hair boyishly short, then dyed it red – an intense blood-red to match her mood. She drank a cup of tea and ate a couple of biscuits as she waited for the colour to take. She'd never dyed her hair before. Its jet-black colour was the one thing about herself that she'd always loved. With the contact lenses in, she barely recognised herself. She didn't much like her new look. It made her appear younger yet somehow less attractive. But it was a small price to pay if it helped her achieve her purpose.

After changing into her new clothes, Angel put her heroin and her needles into a plastic bag. She knotted the bag and stashed it in the toilet cistern, then exited the hotel. She hailed a cab and told the driver to take her to Brightside Lane. The taxi left the city centre behind and entered an industrial area of towering steel mills and cavernous warehouses interspersed with pockets of sooty terraced housing. Angel stared out of the window, her eyes glittering with a strange intensity, as if she was watching for some sort of sign.

'Stop here,' Angel said, her gaze fixing on some tall, dirty-white letters on a factory building. The letters read 'SB Engineering'. Stephen Baxley hadn't told her he owned the factory. He'd never really told her anything about himself besides his first name. She'd gone through his wallet while he was sleeping and found a business card with 'Stephen Baxley CEO' and his company's name printed on it. At the time, she didn't know what CEO stood for, but she guessed it meant he was someone important. She'd also found a photo of Jenny

Baxley. She still recalled the acid bite of jealousy she'd felt at the sight of her. It was the only time she'd felt jealous over a man.

Noticing a couple of police cars parked outside the factory, Angel paid the cabbie, got out and hurried on her way. The flat was a mile or so from the factory – close enough that Stephen Baxley could visit easily, but far enough away that there was little chance of anyone he knew seeing him there. As far as secrecy was concerned, it also had the advantage of being situated on a dead-end street of otherwise derelict terraced houses overlooking an equally derelict foundry. The flat where Angel had lived for almost eight months after running away was above an empty corner-shop. It was only a few miles from her parents' house, but back then it might as well have been on the other side of the world.

The shop was still empty but had obviously been occupied at some point of late. The steel plates welded over its windows and the CCTV camera overlooking its steel-reinforced door suggested it had peddled something entirely different from newspapers and cigarettes. Two metal tubes protruded from the door. Angel had seen similar setups at drug dens in Middlesbrough. Punters put their money into one of the tubes, and the other spat out heroin, crack or whatever else their poison was. From the look of it, the property had recently been raided by police. The CCTV camera's wire had been cut. The door bore the marks of a battering-ram. Most tellingly, a scrap of blue-and-white tape dangled like a banner of shame from the tubes.

Angel looked up at the flat's barred window. Her mind flashed back to the seemingly endless days and weeks she'd spent lounging around the flat's cramped confines, watching

TV, reading whatever books and magazines Stephen Baxley brought her, eating whatever food he prepared. She'd lived like a hermit in the one-bedroomed flat, every part of her life controlled by Stephen, only going outside when he took her to his friends' parties – not that they were parties in the sense that she'd understood the word. No presents had been given, unless you called ecstasy pills and wraps of coke presents.

She closed her eyes, racking her memory to recall the journey from the flat to the house where the parties had been held. She saw herself in the passenger seat of Stephen Baxley's Mercedes, watching the passing city through its tinted windows. Holding the picture in her mind, she started walking. The car turned left. After a short distance, it turned left again. It followed the same road for half a mile or so, before making a right, passing the Northern General on its left. Angel walked fast, pausing occasionally to study some feature of the landscape – a thin line of woods, a green expanse of park, housing estates, more trees, more houses, a light industrial estate with a supermarket. Her calves ached. Beads of sweat wormed their way down her cheeks. One mile, two, three miles passed. Suddenly there were ploughed fields to either side of the road. Maybe a mile to the north more houses were visible. A dark line of trees marched across the western horizon.

Angel headed towards the trees, walking more slowly – not because she was tired, but because there were fewer landmarks to guide her memory. After passing some farm buildings, she paused at a fork in the road, her forehead wrinkled. 'Which way? Which way?' she muttered, closing her eyes, looking into a place in her mind that she'd done everything she could to avoid for the past decade and a half. She saw trees sweeping by on her left. *Nearly there, Angel*, she heard Stephen Baxley say. She felt the touch of his warm, damp hand against her cheek. Her eyes snapped open. Little shudders of revulsion running through her, she took the right-hand fork.

After another ten minutes or so, she stopped at the end of a gravel lane on her left that ran between two islands of trees separated from the main body of woodland by a couple of fields. The lane's entrance was marked by a white post that stood out in her mind like an exclamation point. A sign with 'Treetops Farm' painted on it in black lettering hung from the post.

'Treetops Farm,' murmured Angel, her chest suddenly tight with the knowledge that she'd found what she was looking for.

The house was hidden from the main road by the trees, but an image of it emerged from her memory like a ship from a bank of fog. It was a large red-brick house with tall chimneys, a pillared porch, windows like eyes and a door like a big black mouth. She recalled vividly how, the first time she'd stepped through the door, for a crazy moment she'd had the feeling that the house was swallowing her up.

Angel started along the lane but after a short distance stepped off it into the trees. Moving with the wary alertness of a stalking cat, she picked her way through brambly under-growth. She took out the gun. Just the weight of it in her hand eased some of the tightness inside her. She crouched behind a tree at the edge of a broad lawn. The house was a perfect image of rural tranquillity. It looked the same as she remembered, right down to the flower pots on the patio. There were no cars in the drive. The windows were dark and hung with net curtains, making it impossible to tell from a distance whether anyone was in. She resisted the temptation to dart across the lawn for a closer look. The daylight was softening into evening. Soon enough the house's lights would tell her whether it was occupied or not. Then she could creep to the windows under cover of darkness to find out if the same couple still lived there.

'Marisa and Herbert.' Angel's lips curled around the names as if they tasted sour. Their faces came to her, like looking at a grainy photograph. Her finger itched at the Glock's trigger as she recalled the warm smiles and friendly eyes that hid their real selves. 'Soon,' she told herself. 'Soon it will be time.' *Unless they don't live here any more*, said her mind's voice. She thrust the thought away. She couldn't allow herself to consider that possibility. They had to still live here. They wouldn't move. Not after everything that had happened at this place.

Angel settled down on the damp ground, shivering as the sweat lathering her body cooled. Half an hour passed, an hour, another hour. The daylight dropped to dark, but still no lights came on inside the house. *Have patience*, she kept telling herself, *they might be out for the evening. Even if they're on holiday, you'll just have to keep coming back day after day for as long as it takes*. 'As long as it takes,' she repeated softly, over and over, like a mantra.

She fell silent at the sound of an approaching vehicle, hunkering down even lower as a pair of headlights swept into view. A Range Rover drew up to the house and two figures got out, a man and a woman. The man was several inches shorter than the woman, stocky, and wearing a flat cap. The woman was slim and tall. A scarf was tied over her hair. Angel squinted, but it was too dark to properly make out their faces. They climbed the steps to the front door and entered the house. A light came on in the hallway, but now the man was out of sight and the woman had her back to the doorway. The sound of a dog barking came from inside the house. The woman stooped and Angel caught a glimpse of long, floppy ears and brown-and-white fur. The woman ruffled the dog's coat, then turned to close the door. Angel only saw her face for a second, but it was all she needed. Her heart suddenly hammering, she rose to her feet. 'Now's the time.' The words hissed through her teeth, sharp and low. 'Now's the fucking time.'

Chapter Eleven

Mark couldn't breathe. Something was being pushed into his mouth, something cold and hard. Bitter liquid dribbled down his throat, making him gag. He tried to raise his hands to his mouth, but a heavy weight seemed to be pinning them down. He jerked his head from side to side to no avail. Waves of pounding dizziness crashed over him. A dense grey fog swirled in front of his eyes. He felt his eyeballs rolling back into his head, and the horrifying thought came to him, *I'm passing out. I'm dying.*

He heard a voice that was slow and garbled, but which he recognised as belonging to Stephen. 'Take your underwear off, Angel.'

The words pierced Mark's brain like an injection of adrenaline, wrenching his vision into focus. He caught a glimpse of several indistinct figures who seemed to be floating amongst shadows. Then a face blotted them out, so close that all he could see of it were moist purple lips and a fat pink tongue slithering around a mouthful of overlapping, yellowed teeth. The mouth formed words that echoed as if they were coming at him from across a yawning chasm. 'Are you certain he won't remember anything?' The voice was accentless and thick with longing.

Mark's eyes snapped open. He hauled in a breath, wondering where he was. The pain in his shoulder reminded him. He couldn't seem to get enough air into his lungs. He groped for the emergency cord. 'I can't breathe,' he gasped as a nurse hurried into the room.

After a quick check of Mark's vital signs, the nurse said, 'You're hyperventilating.' She took his hands. 'I want you to look into my eyes, Mark, and breathe with me. In, out, in, out.'

Gradually, Mark's breathing returned to normal. 'I had a dream.'

'About what happened to you?'

Mark started to shake his head, but changed his mind. Maybe the dream was about something that happened to him, not recently, but a long time ago. Perhaps it was some kind of memory trying to surface. *Are you certain he won't remember anything?* The words hit the back of his skull like an axe. He pinched the bridge of his nose. *Remember what? What can't I remember?* Panic nibbled at the edges of his overstretched nerves again. He forced himself to take a slow breath. 'I need to talk to the police.'

'I'll fetch the constable.' The nurse turned to approach the policeman stationed outside the door.

'I don't want to talk to him,' said Mark. 'Tell him to call Detective Monahan.'

As the nurse left the room, Mark reached for the beside telephone and dialled a number. A woman answered. 'Hello.'

'This is Mark Baxley. Can I speak to Doctor Reeve, please?'

'Hold on one moment. I'll get him for you.'

A man came on the line, his voice quick with concern.

'Mark, I saw on the news what happened. They said you'd been shot.'

'I'm OK, well, not OK but...' Mark tried to find the words to describe how he was doing. 'I'm alive. I need to see you. I think I'm beginning to remember.'

'Beginning to remember what?'

'I'm not sure. Maybe the reason why I am like I am.'

****

At the sound of knocking, Jim rose from the sofa and headed to the front door. After phoning the mobile number, he'd lain awake mulling over Linda Kirby's claim that she could *feel* it was her daughter on the other end of the line. He'd felt something too. There had been a peculiar intensity to the silence of whoever it was he'd spoken to that had made his neck prickle. It was only a feeling, an intuition that barely amounted to a hunch, but still he was unable to dismiss the idea that maybe, just maybe, Linda Kirby was right. One thing he was almost certain of was that the silent phone call she'd received hadn't been a random thing. Why else would the number's owner have refused to identify themselves to him? And why else would they have stayed on the line after he identified himself as police? The questions opened up another possibility – if it wasn't Grace Kirby, maybe it was someone who had something to do with her disappearance. And perhaps, for some related reason, that same someone had been spurred into making the call to Linda Kirby by news of Stephen Baxley's death.

Jim recognised Amy's outline through the door's frosted glass. 'Sorry, did I wake you?' she said, when he opened it.

'No such luck.'

Jim motioned for Amy to come inside. She shook her head. 'You're needed at the hospital. Mark Baxley's got something to say, and he wants to say it to you. I was about to head home when the call came in. But I thought I might as well come pick you up, seeing as I'd planned to drop by here anyway.'

'Why? What did you want to see me for?'

'Just to find out how you're doing. You didn't seem like your usual happy self earlier.' There was a half-jokey tone to Amy's voice – Jim was never the happiest of people – but the concern in her eyes was serious.

'I'm fine,' came the reflexive response.

'Are you sure, Jim, because—'

'Because what?' Jim cut in, frowning. 'Why don't you just say it? You don't think I'm up to the job any more, do you?'

'That's not it at all. I'm just trying to look out for someone I consider a friend.'

Jim felt a twinge of guilt at the hurt he heard in Amy's voice. 'I'm sorry.' He heaved a sigh. 'Truth is, I'm the one who's starting to wonder whether I'm up to it.'

'Of course you're up to it. You're one of the best detectives we've got.'

'I very much doubt that, but thanks for the compliment. In any case, fit for duty or not, I'm not sure I want to do the job any more. I'm just so tired of all the shit that goes with it.'

'The job's a bastard. Always has been, always will be. But you still love it. I saw the way you were out there today. You were as eager as a dog with a new bone.'

Jim made a dubious sound in his throat. It seemed to him that his eagerness was more like that of a dying man clinging to life for fear of what waited on the other side. 'I've been thinking about applying for early release.' *Early release.* Coming from someone who'd spent his whole working life locking others up, the irony of the phrase brought a faint smile to his lips.

'Seriously?'

'Yes, seriously.'

'But what would you do with yourself?'

That was the big question. The question to which Jim had no answer. He shrugged.

'You're not ready to retire, Jim. This case has just got you thinking you are. What this Baxley guy did to his family – it's almost impossible to wrap your mind around it.'

'You're right, this case has got to me. But I've been thinking about retiring for weeks, months even.'

'Look, just do me a favour. After this case is done, take a holiday and think things over before you mention this to Garrett.'

'Which case are you talking about? The Baxley house killings will probably be wrapped up when the forensics come back. The Grace Kirby case could drag on for another fifteen years.'

'I think you're right about the killings. A little birdy told me they've lifted two sets of prints off the shotgun. Nothing's been officially confirmed, but the word is they belong to Stephen and Mark Baxley.'

'That was quick work, even considering that Stephen Baxley's prints are already on the database,' Jim said with a wry edge. 'It's amazing what can happen when someone with a bit of money gets topped. So whose prints are where?'

'Apparently Stephen Baxley's are on the trigger and barrel, but Mark's are only on the barrel. Stephen's were also the only prints on the gun box and the petrol canisters.'

Jim showed no surprise at the news. 'I'd say that just about wraps things up as far as who tried to kill who.'

'We still don't have confirmation on the identity of the bodies. Forensics is struggling to get DNA samples from the Baxley house to match against the bodies.'

'Even so, I don't think we're in for any surprises. Do you?'

'No.'

'Any news on the DVD?'

'It only had one set of prints on it – Stephen Baxley's. And it's too heat-damaged to recover any more of its content.'

Disappointment curling the corners of his mouth, Jim pushed his feet into his shoes and reached for his jacket. As they headed to the unmarked car, Amy said, 'I really can't imagine what Mark's got to say that he hasn't already told us.'

'I've been wondering that same thing. All I can think is he must have remembered something new.'

'Oh that reminds me, I managed to track down the owner of that mobile phone number.' Jim turned sharply interested eyes on Amy, as she continued, 'It's registered to a Lillian Smyth of Cargo Fleet Lane, Middlesbrough.'

'Have you spoken to her?'

'Yes. She says she didn't make the call.'

'Well of course she bloody does, but that doesn't—'

'Hold on, Jim. Before you go getting your hopes up, there are a couple of things you should know about Lillian Smyth. Firstly, she's sixty years old. Secondly, she recently received a phone bill full of calls she claims not to have made. Her mobile phone provider has detected discrepancies between the radio fingerprint of the phone that was used to call Linda Kirby and the mobile identification number of Lillian Smyth's phone.'

'What does that mean in English?'

'The call was made with a cloned phone.'

A thoughtful frown spread over Jim's forehead. He associated cloned mobiles with criminals who wanted a phone that couldn't be traced to them. And there was only one person he knew with easy access to such technology who also had a link, however tenuous, to Grace Kirby. 'Bryan Reynolds,' he muttered.

'You think Reynolds made that call?'

'I don't know. Maybe. The question is, why would he do such a thing?'

'If the Kirbys' daughter is alive, maybe he thought news of Stephen Baxley's death would bring her out of hiding. Perhaps he was trying to feel them out, or even put the frighteners on them.'

'I might be tempted to think you're right, except for one thing. Unless my judgement has completely gone to pot, the first Reynolds heard about Baxley's death was when I spoke to him. And that call was made hours before then.'

'Which brings us back to Grace Kirby.'

Jim heaved a sigh. 'Come on, we'd better get a shift on.'

When Jim and Amy arrived at the Northern General, they were met by a tired-looking Garrett, a middle-aged male doctor in a white coat, and a man somewhere in his fifties wearing a dark blue suit and matching tie. Jim took one look at the suited man's keen, direct eyes, neatly trimmed silver-grey beard and wire spectacles, and decided he was most likely some kind of senior medical bod. His suspicion was confirmed when Garrett introduced the men. He motioned first to the white-coated doctor. 'This is Doctor Vincent Goodwin, the consultant looking after Mark Baxley.' Then to the other man. 'And this is Doctor Henry Reeve, a clinical psychiatrist who's been treating Mark since his early teens. They've been fully briefed. Chief Superintendent's orders.'

Jim eyed the psychiatrist curiously. 'Treating him for what?'

'Jenny Baxley first brought Mark to me when he was four-teen,' said Doctor Reeve. 'She was worried because he was having problems sleeping. And when he did sleep, he suffered with night terrors.'

'What was he having nightmares about?'

'Night terrors aren't dreams. They're more like an intense fear reaction – screaming, shouting, thrashing around. Suffer-ers aren't fully awake during attacks, so they have no memory of what happened the next day.'

'Well what brings them on?'

'Stress, exhaustion, certain drugs.'

Jim's thoughts turned to Grace Kirby pushing the medicine bottle into Mark's mouth, as Doctor Reeve continued, 'Mark had become very withdrawn. He was having difficulty forming relationships, particularly with other children and his father. From what we now know, the reasons for this seem fairly clear.'

Jim cocked an eyebrow as if to say, *No shit, Sherlock*. 'Did you never suspect Mark might be being abused?'

'I considered it of course. But nothing Mark said suggested that was the case. He simply seemed to be an emotionally insecure, fragile young boy. It's not uncommon for adolescents to experience these kinds of issues – especially boys from wealthy families, where the pressure to succeed is that much greater. And Mark responded well to treatment in every regard except his relationship with his father.'

'Stephen Baxley wasn't Mark's father,' Jim pointed out bluntly. He turned to Doctor Goodwin. 'So how's Mark doing?'

'Considering what he's been through, he's in remarkably good physical shape,' said the doctor. 'The injury to his leg is superficial. It shouldn't keep him off his feet for more than a day or two. The injury to his shoulder is more serious, but again shouldn't cause any complications. It seems to me that it's not the injuries we can see, but those we can't see that have the potential to cause him serious problems.' The doctor glanced meaningfully at Doctor Reeve.

Taking his cue, the psychiatrist said, 'I'd agree entirely with that assessment, especially considering Mark's psychological history. Even with the right treatment, lifelong emotional and social problems are common following a trauma of the magnitude Mark's experienced. But it's far too early to predict how he'll react in the long-term. In the short-term, the mind tends to respond in a limited number of ways. Most commonly, in order to protect itself, it will simply shut down. The shutdown can range from emotional numbness to a complete catatonic state. Alternatively, the mind can be thrown into overdrive.'

'What do you mean, 'overdrive'?' asked Amy.

'Well, rather like a rat in a maze, the mind scurries around seeking a way out of its pain, becoming increasingly hysterical and irrational. A mind in overdrive is a dangerous thing. Stripped of logic and consumed by fear, it can easily be tipped towards psychosis and suicidality.'

'All of which means we have to tread extremely carefully,' Garrett said to Jim. 'Listen to what Mark has to say, but don't divulge anything to him without first getting Doctor Reeve's opinion. Is that clear, Detective?'

Pushing down a jab of irritation at Garrett's patronising tone, Jim nodded. 'Is there anything else I should know?' he asked the psychiatrist. 'I don't want to go saying or doing anything that might push Mark over the edge.'

'I'm sure you'll do fine, Detective Monahan. And I'm look forward to getting your insights into Mark's mental state.'

'I wouldn't get your hopes up on that score. Psychological insights aren't really my thing.' Jim flashed Garrett a sidelong glance. 'I'm just a plain old-fashioned copper.'

Catching the ironic glimmer in Jim's eyes, Doctor Reeve smiled. 'I don't believe that for a second. I've never met a police officer yet who isn't also a brilliant instinctual psychologist.'

Jim headed towards Mark's room. Amy made to follow him, but Doctor Reeve said, 'We think it's best if Detective Monahan talks to Mark alone. We don't want to overwhelm Mark with too many faces.'

Mark was sitting up in bed, pale and drawn. There was an almost feverishly intense sheen to his eyes.

'You wanted to talk to me, Mark?' said Jim.

'I wanted to thank you. Out of all the police I've spoken to since... since *it* happened, you're the only one who hasn't made me feel like I'm under suspicion.'

Jim had no doubt Mark's gratitude was genuine, but from the look on his face, that obviously wasn't the main reason he wanted to talk. 'Your story added up. The details all rang true. I've merely treated you accordingly.'

'And I really appreciate that. I also appreciate that you're the only officer who's been anything like honest with me. That's why I wanted to ask you if you know about something else that happened to me. I don't mean the other night, I mean something way back in my past.'

'What makes you ask that?'

'I had a dream.' Mark's voice grew hesitant. Something painful flickered through his eyes. 'Actually I'm not sure it was a dream, I think it might have been a memory that was pushed so far back I didn't even know it was there. I don't know why, but I think it's got something to do with the picture of that girl you showed me.'

'Was she in your... for now let's call it dream.'

'No... I don't know... Maybe...' Mark trailed off, haunted uncertainty hazing his eyes.

'Why don't you just tell me what you saw?'

Jim was careful to keep his face poker-straight as Mark recounted his dream. 'So what do you reckon?' Mark asked. 'Am I remembering something that happened or is it just a dream?'

'I'm really not qualified to say. Did you recognise the voices?'

'The first belonged to Stephen Baxley. I've never... or at least, I don't think I've ever heard the second voice before.'

'What did it sound like?'

'It was a man's voice. Well spoken, no accent.'

Jim chewed over what he'd been told. He badly wanted to push Mark to see if he could recall any further details about the face he'd seen, but he reluctantly heeded Doctor Reeve's warning. 'I have to talk to my DCI, Mark. It should only take a few minutes, then we can talk some more.' He left the room and said to the doctors, 'I need a moment alone with my colleagues.'

'Doctor Goodwin and Doctor Reeve can hear whatever you've got to say,' said Garrett.

'Then perhaps Doctor Reeve can answer this for me. Is it possible for someone to lose a memory, then recover it again years later?'

'That depends on why the memory was lost in the first place,' said the psychiatrist. 'There's a school of thought that some experiences are so horrific the brain seals them away in its darkest recesses, where they remain unless some powerful trigger unlocks the memory. I assume Mark thinks he's remembered something about the abuse he suffered as a child.'

Jim nodded. 'And I'm inclined to think he has too.'

Doctor Reeve took on a cautioning tone. 'As I said before, a mind in overdrive is not to be trusted. When thinking becomes distorted, the mind is prone to attacking itself with false memories. What exactly did Mark tell you?'

'That he had a dream in which he saw several figures but was unable to make out their faces.' Jim tapped his temple. 'I think there's a lot more locked away in there. Possibly enough to break this case wide open.'

'Let's assume, just for the moment, that you're right, Detective. In that case, we have to proceed with extreme care. Memory is like a ball of string. Pull on it in the right place and the whole thing unravels easily. Do it wrong and it becomes an impossible knot.' Doctor Reeve's face creased in thought. 'As I understand it, Mark was drugged at the time he was abused.'

'We believe so,' said Garrett. 'In the film, he was seen being forced to drink something from a medicine bottle.'

'Rohypnol is usually swallowed by dissolving it into a liquid,' said Doctor Goodwin.

'The date-rape drug – you think that's what Mark was given?' asked Amy.

'There are lots of drugs that impair memory, but Rohypnol is probably the easiest to get hold of on the street.'

'If Rohypnol was used, it's no surprise Mark remembered nothing of what happened to him, especially considering his age at the time,' said Doctor Reeve. 'That's not to say no conscious memories of the event were formed, but they would have seemed so unreal and disconnected as to be instantly relegated to his subconscious mind. Where, of course, they remained buried until recent events exposed them – or one small part of them at least. Hopefully, with the right therapy, the rest can be brought to the surface. But I'm afraid there are no guarantees. It may well be that what Mark remembers now is all he'll ever remember.'

Jim glanced towards Mark's room. 'I'd better get back in there. I told him I'd only be gone a few minutes. What should I say to him?'

'As little as possible. I'd suggest you make up some excuse about being called away on an emergency and leave.'

'You know, Doctor, I really don't think Mark's as fragile as you suspect. In fact, I reckon he's as tough as they come. He fought tooth and nail for both his own life and his sister's, when most people would have lain down and died. I think he can handle the truth.'

'You may be right, Detective, but I'm not willing to take that risk without having had the chance to properly assess him.'

'I understand, but as a policeman, my instinct is to move fast while the memory is still fresh in Mark's mind.'

'This memory and any other fragments of memory associated with it were never fresh in his mind to begin with. They've festered in his subconscious for most of his life. And until I decide on the appropriate therapy procedure to follow, there they will stay.'

Jim gave the psychiatrist an unconvinced look. 'Have you considered that it might actually do more damage than good keeping what we know from him?'

A note of impatience came into Doctor Reeve's voice. 'And have you considered that, quite apart from the risk to Mark's health, if we tell him too much too soon, instead of triggering lost memories, it might lead to the creation of false ones?'

'You do realise that in a case like this every second is invaluable. Even as we stand here arguing, Mark's abusers could be out there doing the same thing to other kids.'

'I'm fully aware of that, Detective, but even so, my primary duty of care is to my patient. I have to consider his needs before anything else.'

Jim opened his mouth to shoot off another reply, but before he could do so, Garrett put in, 'Just do as Doctor Reeve says, Detective Monahan.'

Jim's breath whistled through his teeth with frustration. Turning sharply on his heel, he headed back into the room. No matter how Doctor Reeve dressed it up, it didn't sit right with him keeping Mark in the dark. It wasn't just about wanting to dig up more memories. As far as Jim was concerned, Mark had a right to know, especially now that they were all but certain of his innocence. And whether he found out now or later, he would probably still never recover emotionally. Who the hell would from such a devastating revelation?

'I'm sorry, Mark, an emergency has...' Jim started to reel off the suggested excuse, but trailed off with a shake of his head. Mark had been lied to enough in his life. Jim had already contributed one small lie to the list. He wasn't about to add another, not after Mark had found it within himself to trust him. He sat down at the bedside, an almost apologetic look in his eyes. 'You were right, Mark, something else did happen to you many years ago, something...' He vainly sought a word to describe just how despicable that something was. Swallowing his revulsion, he continued, 'The girl whose picture I showed you is called Grace Kirby.'

'Grace Kirby,' Mark repeated, small crinkles forming at the corners of his eyes.

'Is the name familiar?'

'No.'

'Are you sure?'

'No, but then I'm not sure of anything. I keep getting the feeling that this is some awful nightmare I can't wake up from. I keep thinking maybe I'll wake up and it won't be true.'

'This is a nightmare, Mark, but you're not dreaming.'

The lines etched into Mark's face spread. 'I know, but it's just so hard to believe that anyone – even a bastard like the man I thought was my dad – could do this to their own family.'

Thirty-odd years on the force had given Jim a pretty good understanding of what humans were capable of doing to each other. 'It's not as uncommon as you might think. Every day hundreds of people die at the hands of those who are supposed to love them. And thousands more suffer neglect, exploitation and abuse.'

'Is that what happened to me? Did I suffer some kind of abuse?'

'You remember the sound you heard when you first went into your parents' house? Well you were right, it was a child crying.'

'Grace Kirby?'

'No. It was you.' As Mark screwed up his face in confusion, Jim continued. 'What you heard was the soundtrack from a DVD we found in the master bedroom's television. On that DVD was a few seconds of a film made in 1997 of you and Grace Kirby being sexually molested.'

At first, Mark merely sat and blinked as the news sank in. Then, in a half-choked whisper, he breathed, 'It was them. My so-called father and the man from my dream or memory or whatever it was. It was them, wasn't it?'

'Neither Stephen Baxley nor the other man you described are visible on camera in the film. Although Stephen Baxley can be heard talking off-screen.'

Mark squeezed his eyes shut, clasping his hands to his head as if to keep it from splitting apart. 'I should have known. The way he was with me, the way he couldn't bear to touch me, it wasn't because of who I was, it was because of what he'd done to me. Every time he looked at me, it must have reminded him of what a warped bastard he was.' His eyes snapped open as though something had occurred to him. 'So who is visible on camera?'

Jim hesitated to reply as Doctor Reeve's warning about creating false memories came back to him.

'Is my—' Mark started to say, but he sucked the words back into his mouth, as though he dared not ask the question in his mind. Shivering with apprehension, he managed to free his voice. 'Is my mum?'

Jim summoned up an image of the woman in the film – small breasts, narrow hips, dark pubic hair. Jenny Baxley was – or rather, had been – a redhead with a busty, hourglass figure. 'No.'

'But she could have been there off-screen.'

'It's possible,' conceded Jim. 'But I don't think she knew about the DVD. I think Stephen Baxley kept it in his safe, to which you say she had no access.'

Mark's expression said he desperately wanted to believe Jim was right but was still tortured by uncertainty. His eyes widened as another thought struck him. 'Exactly what date was the film made on?'

'The first of September.'

Relief flooded into Mark's eyes. 'Then my mum couldn't have been there. Charlotte was born on the twentieth of October that year. Mum spent the last couple of months of her pregnancy in hospital with pre-eclampsia.'

'Are you sure about that?'

Mark nodded. 'She was really ill. She could have died.' His pale lips twitched with a spasm of self-reproach. 'What the fuck's wrong with me? How could I have even thought she might have been there?'

'Betrayal is the most destructive force in the world, Mark. It makes you doubt everything that's gone before.'

Mark's features twitched as he struggled with the turmoil in his mind. He steadied himself with a shuddering breath.

'So apart from Stephen Baxley, who do you know for certain was involved?'

'We don't. Their faces are hidden.'

'Well how many of them are there?'

'I'm not going to tell you that, Mark. That's something you need to try and remember on your own.'

Mark closed his eyes again, trying to summon up the shadow-wreathed figures from his dream. But all he could see was Stephen Baxley's face staring at him with cold, accusing eyes, as if he was the one who'd done something wrong. He flinched away from the image, quivering with impotent fear and rage. 'I can't remember,' he cried. 'Why can't I remember?'

'It'll come back to you, Mark. And even if it doesn't, I'll catch the perpetrators. No matter what it takes.' Jim's voice was full of steely promise.

Mark clenched his hands as if he wanted to hit something. 'What about Grace Kirby? What happened to her?'

'We don't know that either. She's been missing since February '97. Seven months before the film was made.'

'How old was she?'

'Fifteen.'

'So she's got to be dead, right? A girl that age can't have survived on her own.'

'You're right. Chances are she's long dead, but...' Jim's voice faded into uncertainty.

'But what? You think she's still alive?'

Jim sighed. Grace's fate was as wrapped in shadows as the figures in Mark's mind. 'Honestly, I don't know what to think.'

Mark hugged his good arm across himself, shuddering. 'How many lives has that... I don't even know what to call him any more. How many lives has he destroyed?' Self-disgust twisted his features. 'To think there was a time when I would've done almost anything for his affection. I used to follow him around like a puppy, helping him with whatever jobs needed doing. But nothing was ever enough for him. That's why he wanted me to see that DVD. Just killing me wasn't enough. He wanted me to know that even though I wasn't his, he owned me.' He shook his head violently, as if to clear away unwanted images. 'Oh God, I feel as if I'm falling apart.'

Jim put his hand on Mark's arm and squeezed as though trying to will some of his strength into him. He wanted to do more. He wanted to tell him he would get through this. But he knew that would have been a lie. He'd seen things that had left him in awe of the endurance of the human spirit. But he'd also seen people who'd suffered far lesser traumas than Mark disintegrate almost in front of his eyes. 'You've got to keep it together, Mark. Because when your sister wakes up she's going to need you. Do you hear?'

Mark nodded, getting hold of himself with visible effort.

'Good lad. I'm afraid I've got to go now.'

'Couldn't you stay just a bit longer? You could tell me more about Grace Kirby. Maybe that would help me remember.'

'Sorry, Mark, but I've already stayed longer than I should have. I'll try to get to see you again tomorrow. In the meantime, don't try to force the memories to return. Let them come on their own. Often the harder you try to recall something, the more elusive it becomes. At least, that's my experience from doing this job for thirty-odd years.' He wrote a number on the back of a business card, then gave it to Mark. 'Anytime you want to talk, don't hesitate to call. My home number's on there as well, in case you can't reach me on my mobile.'

Jim felt Mark's eyes follow him from the room, full of the anxious hope that he might change his mind. He would have liked to sit with Mark, talking about Grace Kirby and about Mark's life in general. Often the clues that solved cases were hidden in the mundane details of people's daily lives. But those details would have to wait for a time when the two doctors and Garrett weren't hovering at his back.

'You were in there a long time,' said Doctor Reeve, with more than a hint of suspicion in his voice. 'I thought we agreed you were simply going to tell him an emergency had come up, and leave.'

'No, Doctor, that's what you agreed on.'

'From that, I take it you've gone against both my wishes and those of your commanding officer.'

'You take it right.'

A tut of disapproval came from Garrett, but Doctor Reeve raised a quietening hand. 'So what did you tell Mark?'

'Only what he deserved to know. That we have evidence he was sexually abused as a child. I didn't reveal anything about the people involved, except that one of them was Grace Kirby. I'd already shown him her picture, so all I was doing was putting a name to a face.'

A faint angry flush crept up Doctor Reeve's neck, but his voice remained controlled. 'It makes little difference that you didn't reveal specifics, Detective Monahan. What you've told Mark is more than enough to potentially create a conflict between his memory and reality. I only hope that in the process you haven't also managed to damage the connection between his mind and reality.'

'Well he seemed to have a firm grip on his situation, but then what would I know. Like I said, I'm just a simple copper.'

Doctor Reeve stared at Jim a moment longer, his mouth set in a thin, unamused smile. Then he turned to Doctor Goodwin. 'I think it would be in Mark's best interest if Detective Monahan had no further contact with him.'

'I have to say I agree,' said Doctor Goodwin. 'I realise the detective was only doing his job, but I simply can't allow anything that might compromise the recovery of a patient. I'm afraid I must ask that Detective Monahan has no further contact with Mark while he's under the care of this hospital.'

'I understand and apologise, Doctors.' Garrett flashed Jim a look that said, *You're in deep shit.* 'Thank you both for all your help.'

'Anytime,' said Doctor Goodwin. 'Now if there's nothing else, I think we'd better check on the patient.'

As the doctors entered Mark's room, Garrett gave Jim a narrow-eyed look. 'I think we need to have a chat, Detective. I'm late for a meeting with the Chief Superintendent and Edward Forester at his constituency office. But I'll see you back at headquarters in an hour or two.'

Jim's mouth spread in a thin-lipped smile as Garrett hastened away. It amused him in a sour sort of way to picture Garrett sweating under Edward Forester's questions. Forester was the Labour MP for Sheffield South-East, and a renowned political operator who traded on his reputation as a straight-talking Yorkshireman. It was in his interest to keep a close eye on the investigation. A lot of his constituents would be out of a job if SB Engineering went under, and even in a rock-solid Labour seat like Sheffield South-East, that kind of thing could affect votes.

'I don't know why you're smiling,' said Amy. 'You'll be lucky if he doesn't bring you up on disciplinary charges for pulling that little trick.'

'No he won't. He needs every copper he's got in the field right now.'

'Maybe, but keep on like you are and when this is over he'll be out for your head.'

'I hope you're right, Amy. I hope this is over one day. And as for Garrett wanting my head...' Jim made a noise in his throat that suggested the possibility held little fear for him.

As they headed back to the car, Amy asked, 'So what are you going to do with yourself while you wait for the DCI?'

'I thought I'd take a closer look at Grace Kirby's file. It could be worth talking to some of her childhood friends and finding out if any of them remember seeing her with a man fitting the description of the one from Mark's dream.'

Amy cocked a dubious eyebrow. 'Not much of a description to go on, a posh voice and a gobful of crooked teeth.'

'I know it's a long shot, but it might turn something up.'

Amy's mobile phone rang as they ducked into the car. She put it to her ear. 'Hello?'

'Is that Detective Inspector Amy Sheridan?' The voice had a distinctive north-eastern accent.

'It is.'

'This is Detective Sergeant Debra Kennedy of Cleveland Police. I understand you've been making enquiries about Lillian Smyth's mobile phone. I thought you might be interested to know that a clone of her phone was used by someone we suspect may have been involved in a murder.'

'Hang on, Debra. I have a colleague with me who needs to hear this. I'm putting you on loudspeaker.' Quickly filling Jim in on what had been said, Amy slotted the phone into a holder on the dashboard.

'Hello, Debra, this is DI Jim Monahan. So, what's this about a murder?'

'Ryan Castle, a mid-level drug dealer, was found two nights ago shot to death at Seal Sands, a nature reserve near Middlesbrough.'

'I read about that,' said Amy. 'Sounds like a drug deal gone bad.'

'That's what we thought, but there have been some developments that suggest otherwise. The night following Castle's murder, a woman placed a call on a clone of Lillian Smyth's phone to James Cook Hospital in Middlesbrough. She wanted to know if a sixteen- or seventeen-year-old, slim, blonde-haired female had been brought in. A girl fitting that description had been admitted the previous night. A prostitute named Nicola Clarke. She was found unconscious outside Accident and Emergency. Her blood has since been matched to blood found on the back seat of Castle's car. According to her, Castle picked her up alone and beat her unconscious during intercourse. The next thing she claims to remember is coming round in hospital.'

'Do you believe her?' asked Jim.

'I believe she was unconscious when Castle was killed. She took a hell of a beating. That's not to say I don't think she knows who killed him.'

'Have you got a recording of the phone call?'

'We've got more than that. Shortly after the call was made, we believe the same woman was caught on CCTV entering the ward Nicola Clarke is on. She left an envelope for Nicola containing six hundred quid. We've since pulled Castle's finger-prints off several of the banknotes.'

'What does the woman look like?'

'She's white, around five-four or five-five, slim, late twenties or early thirties.'

Jim and Amy exchanged a glance, both thinking the same thought – the description could easily match Grace Kirby, if she was still alive. 'What about her hair?' asked Jim.

'She had a hooded top on. Give me your email and I'll send you a file of the phone call and the CCTV.'

Amy told Debra her email address, then fetched a laptop from the boot. 'Have you got any idea as to the woman's identity, Debra?' asked Jim, as they waited for the laptop to boot up.

'We're working on the assumption that she's a prostitute. We think she may have followed Castle and Clarke out to Seal Sands in another car, which was subsequently used to take Clarke to hospital. We're canvassing prostitutes who work the same streets as Nicola, but they're as tight-lipped as priests when it comes to protecting their own. What's unclear is why the woman didn't know Nicola was at the hospital.'

'The obvious answer is that she wasn't in the car when Nicola was dumped outside A & E.'

'That's our thinking too.'

'What do you know about the gun that was used to shoot Castle?'

'We recovered two nine-millimetre rounds from the scene,

but no gun. We have it from a reliable source that Castle carried a Glock. So it looks like he may well have been shot with his own gun.'

'I've got your email, Debra,' said Amy. 'I'm going to open the voice file.'

Amy clicked on the email attachment and a recording of Debra's suspect talking to a hospital receptionist began to play. The woman had a broad north-eastern accent, but a couple of times during the conversation Jim caught a vague undercurrent of something more like a Yorkshire accent. 'We've had the recording analysed by a phonetics expert,' said Debra. 'He thinks the voice belongs to someone who's lived in the north-east for a lot of years but originally comes from somewhere further south, possibly Huddersfield, Leeds, Barnsley, Doncaster or—'

'Sheffield,' put in Jim.

'Exactly. Which is why I'm so eager to find out what your enquiries are about.'

'Before we get into that, I'd like to have a look at the CCTV footage.'

Amy opened the second file. Jim squinted at a pixelated colour image of a slim, hunch-shouldered figure with a distinctly female body shape. Hood up and head down, the woman quickly passed along a corridor out of the camera's field of view. The footage cut to another camera pointed at a set of double doors with circular windows. The woman appeared at the doors. She peered furtively through the windows. The camera caught her face as she glanced over her shoulder. Amy paused the footage and zoomed in on the woman's face until the pixels started to blur her features.

Jim held the photo from Grace's case-file next to the laptop's screen. The woman's eyes were sunk so deep that they looked black. Her cheeks were gaunt and colourless, and her nose had a bump over the bridge as if it had been broken at some point. In contrast, the fifteen-year-old Grace's cheeks were round and flushed like ripe fruit, and her nose was straight as a knife. Both the woman and Grace had full, pouting lips, and there was something similar in the line of their jaws. 'What do you think?' he asked Amy.

'It could be her, but then again…' Amy spoke into the phone. 'We're not sure about the woman's identity, Debra. We're going to have to lift an image from the CCTV file and run it through facial recognition software.'

'Who were you hoping to see?' asked Debra.

Amy gave her a brief rundown of the case they were working.

'That's a hell of a situation you've got there,' said Debra. 'I don't envy you your task. Could you email me a copy of Grace Kirby's case-file?'

'Will do.'

'Thanks. Obviously I'll contact you at once if there are any new developments up here.'

Amy promised to do the same, thanked DS Kennedy and hung up. Jim's gaze was still bouncing between the photo and the CCTV image. 'The more I look at them, the less similar they seem.'

'The facial recognition program will pick up any similarities.'

'I can think of someone who might be able to give us a faster, more accurate answer.'

'Linda Kirby?' When Jim nodded, Amy continued, 'I'll come with you.'

'Go home. You've just pulled a double shift.'

'I don't think you should go see Linda on your own. I don't like the look of her husband. I get the feeling it wouldn't take much for him to go off big time.'

Before setting off for Hillsborough, Amy forwarded DS Kennedy's email along with a message explaining the situation to everyone on the Homicide and Major Incident team. 'So what's your take on the Castle murder?'

Jim stared at Grace's photo as though trying to read the mind of its subject. 'I think he fucked with the wrong girl.'

Chapter Twelve

Angel studied the house, debating whether she should wait for its occupants to go to bed before making her move, or simply knock on the door and shove her gun in the face of whoever opened it. She couldn't see an alarm box, but the dog would almost certainly alert its owners if she tried to break in. On the other hand, if she knocked on the door, the occupants might look out of a window to see who was calling. In which case, there was a chance – albeit a tiny one – that she would be recognised. And then the door would remain closed, while the police or someone else with the power to hurt her far worse than they could was called. As much as she was tempted by the idea, she decided the direct approach was too risky. She would wait and hope she could gain entry via a window without disturbing the dog. After all the years of feeding her habit, she had enough experience of breaking and entering to know how to smash a window quietly.

Angel scrunched her thin shoulders against the cold. It was a clear evening and the temperature was dropping faster than the light. She warmed herself with the thought of what she would do to Herbert and Marisa. *Herbert and Marisa* – those names had been burnt into her brain like acid on glass since the night Stephen had introduced her to them. She'd giggled upon first hearing the name Herbert. *He's a right Herbert* was one of her dad's favourite terms of abuse for royalty, politicians, the rich and anyone else he considered too big for their boots. But she hadn't laughed later when Herbert raped her for the first though not the last time.

A light came on at the back of the house. The dog ran out into the garden. It was some kind of spaniel. It cocked its leg against one of the trees that fringed the lawn, then wandered in Angel's direction, sniffing at the ground. It jerked its head up suddenly. Angel held herself as still as possible. The sodding thing was staring right at her. With a low growl, it warily approached her. She picked up a dead branch, gripping it like a baseball bat. A metre or so from where she was hidden, the dog stopped and began yapping furiously. She offered a silent apology to the animal. She didn't want to hurt it, but it was only a matter of time before its owners came to investigate the racket. She sprang out, bringing the branch down with all the force she could muster. There was a loud crack as it broke across the dog's skull. The animal collapsed, letting out a high-pitched whine. She silenced it with another blow. Then she concealed its body and herself amongst the trees.

Five minutes passed. Ten. Marisa appeared from behind the house. 'Oscar!' she called out. 'Here, boy!'

A tremor passed through Angel. Marisa's voice was the same as she remembered – loud and mannishly deep, with a cut-glass accent. The mere sound of it had once been enough to make her wince.

Marisa made her way along the edge of the garden, peering

into the undergrowth. 'Oscar! Oscar! You come here or you're going to be in trouble when I find you.'

Angel's mouth was suddenly dry. Cold sweat prickled her back as memories came at her like bullets. She was fifteen years old again. Herbert was writhing on top of her, grinding his lips against hers. She couldn't move, and not just because Marisa was pinning her arms. She was groggy and loose-limbed. There was a salty aftertaste in her mouth from the wine she'd been given when she'd arrived at the house. She'd blacked out not long after drinking it, and when she came round the first thing she saw was Herbert's pudgy face swimming above her, his thick lips contorted into a grin of lust.

Angel took a slow breath, seeking that same brutal calm she'd found in killing Castle, chasing the images away with the flame of her desire for vengeance. Marisa was close enough now that her bobbed brown hair and narrow, horsey features were clearly visible. She flinched to a halt as Angel stepped into view with the gun levelled at her face. The two women stared at each other, Marisa's eyes swollen with shock, Angel trembling with nervous rage.

Marisa broke the silence. 'What do you want?' Her voice was frightened but controlled. There was no hint of recognition in it.

'Turn—' Angel's voice caught in her throat. She freed it with a sharp rasp. 'Turn around and go back into the house.'

'If it's money you want, we don't keep much in the house.'

'Turn the fuck around and do as I say.'

Marisa reluctantly obeyed. Angel followed a couple of paces behind her. When they reached the back door, Angel warned her, 'You say one word other than what I tell you to say and I'll put a bullet in you.'

They entered a large kitchen with a stone-flagged floor, a beamed ceiling, an oak dining table and an Aga. Warmth flowed from a log-burner in a tall fireplace. It was a cosy scene at odds with the images that gnawed at Angel like hungry rats. 'Go into the hallway,' she whispered.

Angel recalled how the first time she'd stepped into the hallway, she'd gazed wide-eyed at the landscape paintings and portraits hanging on the walls, the glittering crystal chandelier suspended from the high ceiling, and the grand staircase with its ornate rails. She'd been apprehensive, not because she felt in danger, but because she felt way out of her league. The hallway was bigger than the house she'd grown up in. What could she possibly have to say that would be of interest to people who lived in a house like that? She needn't have worried on that score. Herbert and Marisa hadn't invited her there for her conversation.

Angel's gaze lingered on an oak panel under the staircase. You wouldn't have known it from looking, but the panel was a door. If you pushed on it in the right way, it slid back to reveal a stairway leading down. The low babble of a television drew her attention to a half-open door. With the gun's barrel, she prodded Marisa towards it.

Nothing much had changed in the lounge since Angel had last been there. The room was full of the same valuable-looking antique furniture. Dark red leather sofas were positioned on either side of the fireplace. A thick rug covered the floorboards between them. As far as she could tell, the only new addition was a cabinet with a television in it. But there was one thing missing. Whenever she'd been there before, a silver box had stood open on the coffee-table, displaying a colourful array of pills, capsules and powders. Herbert had never been able to get it up without the help of Viagra and cocaine. Ketamine had quickly become Angel's drug of choice. Not because it aroused her, but because it numbed her to what was happening.

Herbert wasn't in the room. Angel gestured with the gun for Marisa to return to the hallway. 'Call Herbert.'

Marisa gave Angel a searching look. The questioning fear in her eyes suggested it had occurred to her that maybe this wasn't just a simple robbery. Angel could see her trying to work out who she was, but no suggestion of recognition came into her features. Angel had screwed so many men that their faces had all blended into one more or less homogenous mass over the years. Doubtless it was the same for Marisa when it came to all the girls and boys she'd raped.

'Herbert.'

It gave Angel a thrill of satisfaction to hear the tremor in Marisa's voice. In the past, Marisa had been the one in control. Now the tables were turned.

'What is it, darling?' Herbert's voice – a thin, reedy voice at odds with its owner's stocky physique – came down the stairs.

'Tell him to come here,' hissed Angel.

'Can you come here please?'

Heavy footsteps sounded on the stairs. Breathing out an annoyed sigh, Herbert said, 'I was about to get in the bath. If this is about that bloody dog, I'll—' He broke off with a sharp intake of breath on seeing Angel. He'd changed into a dressing-gown, tied loosely at the waist. He clutched its hems together as if shy of showing his darkly hairy chest. Angel almost let out a caustic laugh. On every previous occasion she'd been to the house, Herbert had always been the first to get naked. She motioned for him to stand beside his wife. 'W...W... What is this?' he stuttered, the blood leaching from his cheeks. 'What do you w... want?'

'I'll get to that in a bit.' Angel was invigorated by Herbert's fear, her voice strong and commanding. 'Right now, I want you to open the basement door.'

'This house hasn't got a basement,' said Marisa.

A smile like a blade thinned Angel's lips. 'Lie to me one more time, bitch, and it'll be the last thing you ever say.' She pointed at the oak panel. 'Now open that fucking door.'

Marisa and Herbert exchanged a glance. At that moment, both of them knew they were in serious trouble and it showed.

'Do as she says,' said Marisa.

Herbert pressed the panel at mid-height. There was a click, and as the panel slid aside, the basement exhaled a faint, stale breath. He switched on a light, illuminating cobwebby bare-brick walls and a flight of steep, narrow stone steps with an iron handrail.

'You go down first,' Angel told Herbert. 'Try anything funny and I start shooting.'

Angel's heart pounded against her ribs as she followed Herbert and Marisa. She'd only been down those stairs once before. Her body had walked out of the basement later that night, but her mind had remained trapped there. She'd spent the years between then and now trying to blot out the memories of what happened, of what she'd done. But there was no blotting it out. It was as though she was stuck in a nightmare from which there was no waking up. As she stepped into the basement, she half expected to be confronted by a naked, ketamine-addled ghost of her fifteen-year-old self. But, of course, no such thing happened. If it had, she would have screamed at herself, *Don't do what they want. Don't fucking do it!*

Angel's gaze swept over the whitewashed walls, the racks of dusty wine bottles, and the bits of old furniture. The rug and cushions were no longer there. Neither was the video camera. But then that hadn't belonged to Marisa and Herbert. It had belonged to a man whose name she didn't know. A man who, unlike Angel, had wanted to make sure he never forgot that night. Herbert and Marisa, Stephen Baxley, they were perverts of the worst kind. But that man was something more than a simple pervert. The first moment she'd looked into his eyes, some instinct of self-preservation had told her he would have given no more thought to killing her than crushing an insect under his heel. There would have been no pity, no remorse, just a slight distaste at having dirtied his shoe. More than all the others, he was the one she wanted to track down.

'Look here,' said Herbert, mustering enough courage to meet Angel's eyes for a fraction of a second. 'I don't know what you want, but whatever it is, you're not going to get away with it.'

Now Angel did laugh, an empty, harsh sound. 'Who said I gave a shit about getting away with it?'

'Who are you?' asked Marisa.

'Don't you recognise me?' Angel pulled back her hood. 'Take a good look. Imagine me with long black hair and blue eyes. Then try to imagine what I might look like if I hadn't spent the last fifteen years shooting myself full of junk to try and forget you sick fucks.'

Marisa scrutinised Angel for a long moment. Finally, a light of recognition flickered in her eyes. 'Angel!'

'Who?' said Herbert.

'The girl Stephen was infatuated with.'

Herbert's eyes bulged as he remembered. 'It was you! You murdered Stephen. And now you're here to do the same to us.'

'That wasn't me,' said Angel.

'Liar!' Herbert clapped a hand over his mouth as though he couldn't believe what he'd said.

'Believe me, I wish it was me who'd killed that bastard, but it wasn't.'

'So what's this about?' said Marisa. 'Is it blackmail? Because if it is—'

'I don't want your fucking money,' broke in Angel, her lip curling at the idea. 'I want names.'

'What names?'

'Don't fuck with me. You know what I'm talking about. I want the name of every scumbag who's ever come to one of your little parties. But most of all, I want the names of the two men other than Stephen Baxley and your husband who were in this cellar *that* night.'

Marisa compressed her lips into a silent line. The fear in her eyes had been replaced by fatalistic defiance. The air between her and Angel seemed to vibrate with tension. Herbert opened his mouth to speak, but snapped it shut again as Marisa shot him an acid glance.

'I'm going to count to five,' said Angel. 'And if I don't start hearing names by the time I'm finished, I'm going to put a bullet in one of you.' She began to count with slow relish. 'One... Two...'

Marisa held Angel's gaze with grim intensity. Herbert's panicky eyes darted back and forth as if looking for a way out.

'Three... Four—'

'Wait!' gasped Herbert, holding up his hands, palms facing Angel. 'There's a book in my desk, in a hidden compartment—'

'Don't you say another word, Herbert!' growled Marisa, shaking her finger at him as if she was scolding a naughty child.

'But it's just a list of clients. Even if she went to the police with it, what could they do?'

Marisa shook her head and heaved a breath. 'You always were a bloody fool. You just don't get it, do you? She's not here to find evidence to put us in prison. She's here to kill us.'

Herbert's bottom lip trembled. Fat tears welled into his eyes. 'Oh God, oh God.'

'For Christ's sake, Herbert, are you really going to let a common slut reduce you to a blubbering wreck? Stand up straight and look her in the eye.' Marisa glared at Angel. 'You don't have a clue what you're getting into. The people in that book will destroy everything and everyone you care about before they let you hurt them.'

'They can't hurt me any more than I've already been hurt.'

A smile of disdainful superiority curled Marisa's lips. 'Oh what a pathetic, ignorant little cunt you are.'

A quiver passed down Angel's arm into the gun. Marisa's smile was as oppressive as the basement, leaching away her confidence, making her doubt whether she had the strength or the will to carry her plan through. Then the images of what had happened there came crashing back in on her. And she knew that regardless of strength or will, regardless of anything, she had to do what she'd come to do. 'I may be a junkie and a whore, but at least I'm not a child-rapist.'

'Mark Baxley might feel differently. That is, if he could remember what you did to him.'

A pained rage sucked Angel's face white. 'I only did what you and your friends forced me to do. What I had to do to survive.' Her forehead twitched with uncertainty as the full import of Marisa's words swept over her. 'Mark Baxley.'

'Oh, yes, didn't you know? Didn't Stephen tell you? That little boy was his son.'

A kind of dazed horror clouded Angel's eyes. 'You people aren't human. You're…' She strained to find the words to express the depths of her disgust. 'You're the slime of the earth.'

'You should be grateful to us. You're only alive because we let you live.'

'You should have killed me and put me out of my misery.'

'Believe me, if it had been up to me, I'd have shot you full of drain cleaner and dumped you in the sewer where you belonged. But Stephen wouldn't hear of it.' A patronising sneer came into Marisa's voice. 'He was quite intelligent for a working-class type. But when it came to you, he was a love-blind fool.'

'Love?' Angel's voice was shrill with incredulity. 'He let you rape me. He forced me to take part in the rape of his son! Is that what you call love?'

'No, that's what I call business.'

'Is that what that night was about, business?'

'Business, money, pleasure. It all comes down to the same thing – getting what you want. Nothing else matters.' Marisa looked at Angel with a pitying contempt. 'That's what you people with your poor pathetic lives pretend not to understand.

166

Until you have a taste of it yourselves. Then, all of a sudden, you're like rabid dogs, ready to bite anyone who gets in your way.'

Angel had heard enough. She panned the gun back and forth between Marisa and Herbert. 'Take your clothes off.'

Marisa crossed her arms. 'No.'

Angel's finger twitched on the trigger. 'Take your fucking clothes off!'

'OK, OK!' cried Herbert, pulling off his dressing-gown. He shivered in awkward nakedness, his penis shrivelled with fear to almost nothing.

Marisa gave him a look of utter contempt. 'You're almost as pathetic as her.'

'I'm trying to save our lives!'

'I've already told you, Herbert, nothing you say or do...' Marisa trailed off with a sigh. 'Oh, what's the bloody point?' Her gaze returned to Angel. 'Either shoot me or fuck off. Because you're not going to get another word—'

Marisa was cut off by the concussive boom of the gun. The bullet slammed into her chest, punching right through and shattering a wine bottle behind her. A whoosh of air flew out of her lungs as she hit the floor. She tried to take a breath, but choked on the blood flooding her throat. More blood pooled from under her blouse. With a piercing scream, Herbert threw himself down beside her, pressing his hands against the wound, vainly trying to staunch the bleeding.

'Where's your desk, and how do I open its hidden compartment?' Angel demanded to know.

Herbert showed no sign of having heard. Wail after wail burst from him. His naked body shook and streams of foaming saliva flowed from his mouth, as though he was suffering a seizure. Angel repeated her question, but there was no getting through to him. She took aim at the back of his head and pulled the trigger, splattering Marisa with blood and skull fragments. He collapsed across her body in a deathly embrace. A silence almost as deafening as the gunshots descended over the basement. For a long moment, Angel stared at the corpses. Then, like someone surfacing from a dive that had taken her far deeper than she'd expected, she sucked in a great, gasping breath. Her gaze travelled the basement again. She hated the place almost as much as she hated its now dead owners. She would have liked to tear it apart brick by brick, so that no one would ever be able to go there again. But even if she'd been able to do so, she knew it would accomplish nothing. Whether or not the basement physically existed, it would always be a part of her and she a part of it.

Angel climbed back up to the hallway. She turned off the basement light and slid the oak panel shut. A grumble rose from her stomach, suddenly making her realise that she was hungry. Hungrier than she had been in years. She went to the kitchen. There were the remains of a cooked chicken in the fridge. She tore at the meat, gulping it down like a ravenous dog, only stopping when her stomach began to cramp. She drank some milk to settle it, then started searching for Herbert's desk.

There was a study on the ground floor, its walls lined with books. A desk with a computer on it occupied the centre of the room. There were three drawers on either side of the desk. She emptied their contents on the floor, feeling around for any catches or levers that might open a hidden compartment. There were none. She shoved the monitor and keyboard off the desk and rapped her knuckles all over its surface, listening for hollow sounds. Again, there were none. With a grunt of effort, she tipped the desk over and checked its underside. Nothing. She returned her attention to the drawers, stamping on them as hard as she could. But they were too strong to break apart that way.

Angel frowned thoughtfully at the desk, then ran from the study to a rack of keys she'd noticed in the hallway. Plucking a key from a hook labelled 'Garage', she headed for the back door. To one side of the house was a detached garage. After lifting its door, she groped around in the gloom for a light-switch. The garage contained a silver Mercedes and a mud-flecked scrambler motorcycle with a helmet on its seat. An array of tools hung on the walls. She took down an axe and returned to the desk.

She hacked the drawers apart first. When that turned up nothing, she started on the main body of the desk. With manic urgency, she struck blow after blow, until the desk was reduced to little more than firewood. Lathered in sweat, she flung aside the axe, shouting, 'Fuck! The bastard lied to me.' She shook her head. No, Herbert had been telling the truth. The way Marisa had reacted told her that much. In which case... In which case, fucking what? Her temples were throbbing so much she could barely think. She massaged them. 'In which case...' she murmured. 'In which case, he must have meant another desk!'

Retrieving the axe, Angel dashed upstairs and darted from room to room. One of the bedrooms clearly belonged to a teen-age boy. The bed was unmade. The floor was strewn with clothes and motorbike magazines. Band and movie posters papered the walls. She wondered whether Marisa and Herbert had a son. And, if so, whether he knew what went on at his parents' parties. The possibility was as chilling as it was repulsive.

Whoever the bedroom's occupant was, they might return home at any moment. Angel quickened her search. There were dressing-tables and chests of drawers, but no desk. That could only mean one thing – the desk was in some other place entirely, maybe another house, or an office. She nodded to herself. An office, that had to be it. Herbert must have meant his work desk.

Angel went into the master bedroom. Water was flooding into the room from an en-suite bathroom where the bath was running. Herbert's clothes were slung over the end of a king-size bed. She rifled through his trouser pockets, but they were empty. Next she checked the top drawer of his bedside table. It contained a fat leather wallet, inside which was several hundred quid and a business card with 'Winstanley Accountants and Business Advisors' printed on it, along with a telephone number and an address on the Fulwood Road. She'd heard of Fulwood but never been there. Her dad had despised it and all the other well-to-do south-western suburbs. As far as he was concerned, they weren't the real Sheffield. But then what the fuck did he know? His ambition had never stretched further than getting pissed with his mates and caring for the pitch of his beloved Sheffield Wednesday.

Taking the business card and flinging aside the money, Angel headed back to the study. She flipped the computer monitor upright, booted up the hard drive and logged onto the internet. As she'd done many times before when Deano had sent her out to meet punters at various locations around

Middlesbrough, she googled the address and brought up a map. The Fulwood Road started in Broomhill, not far from Sheffield University and the Children's Hospital. The hospital was familiar to her. She'd been taken there for various childhood ailments, but never because of any injuries inflicted by her dad – her mum had always kept a store of antiseptic creams, plasters and bandages to treat those.

Angel returned to the key rack and unhooked a bunch of keys marked 'Office'. She turned to leave, but hesitated. Fulwood was on the opposite side of the city. It would take hours to get there on foot, and she couldn't risk travelling by bus or taxi. Two of the remaining sets of keys on the rack were marked 'Car' and 'Motorbike'. She'd never learnt how to drive, so the Mercedes wasn't an option. She knew how to ride a motorbike, though. A boyfriend from her school days had owned a small Honda. He'd taught her on factory wasteland in Burngreave. One time when a passing patrol car had spotted them, he'd also shown her how easy it was to outrun the police on a motorbike.

On her way to the garage, Angel grabbed a torch from a hook next to the back door. She stowed it in the compartment under the scrambler's seat, along with a flat-bladed screwdriver and a hammer. She pulled on the helmet, hit the kickstart, and twisted the throttle. The motorbike jumped forward, almost throwing her off the back of the seat. She braked and took a moment to familiarise herself with the controls, before opening up the throttle again.

At the fork in the road, Angel turned right. She misjudged the speed at which she could take the bend. The bike skidded into a grass verge and flipped sideways into a weed-choked

171

drainage ditch. She lay dazed, hidden from passing vehicles. After a while, she picked herself up and checked for injuries. Her clothes were torn in several places and blood seeped from scratches beneath them. But nothing seemed to be broken. She stood the bike up and set off again at a slower speed.

After a couple of miles, Angel came to the busy Penistone Road. As she rode towards the city centre, the streets became increasingly familiar. Her gaze was drawn to a house where a school friend had lived; a park she used to play at; a shop she'd once stolen sweets from. Her eyebrows tightened as Hillsborough Stadium loomed into view. As a young child, she'd loved the stadium simply because her dad did. Later, when things got really bad at home, she'd hated it for the same reason. She eased off the throttle as she neared her parents' street. Their house looked the same as she remembered. Same front door. Same blue-painted windowsills. It gave her a strange feeling to see it, as if her helmet's visor was a window into some long-lost childhood memory. She wondered what would happen if she knocked on the door. Would they even recognise her?

Angel put some speed on, keeping her gaze fixed on the road as she passed her dad's favourite drinking haunt, the New Barrack Tavern. She was afraid what she might do if she saw the bastard. In the months leading up to her running away, she used to lie in bed listening to him beat her mum, fantasising about one day being strong enough to stop him. She'd pictured herself hurting him, and hurting him so badly he would never dare raise his fists against her mum again.

She followed the signs for the Manchester Road, which she knew branched off from the north end of the Fulwood Road.

She passed groups of students heading out to the city's pubs and nightclubs. With their smiling, carefree faces, they seemed to belong to another world – one in which they expected to find happiness and fulfilment, not merely survive. That part of Sheffield seemed like a different city from the one she knew – the streets were broader and leafier, the houses bigger and less stained by the soot of steel-mill smokestacks. When she passed a street sign for the Fulwood Road, she started counting house numbers. After half a mile or so, she pulled over outside a two-storey stone house with bay windows on either side of a porch supported by fluted columns.

She took the hammer, screwdriver and torch out of the seat compartment and approached the house across a small car park. There were two silver plaques at the side of the front door, engraved with the names of Herbert's company and a solicitor's firm he shared the building with. She glanced at an alarm box under the eaves. She had no way of stopping it from going off. Once inside, she would simply have to move fast and hope she found what she was looking for before the police turned up.

There were three keys on the bunch Angel had taken from the Winstanley house. She tried them in the lock until she found one that fitted. As she stepped into the broad, high-ceilinged hallway, an alarm keypad began to bip at one-second intervals. She swept the torch along the walls. Its beam stopped on a door with Herbert's name on it. She tried the handle. It was locked. The second of the remaining keys opened it, revealing an office with filing-cabinets lining the walls and a desk to one side of another door. A name plaque on the desk said 'Christina Low'. *Probably Herbert's secretary*, thought

Angel, shoving the final key into the door's lock. After a thirty-second delay, the alarm went off. She was ready for it, but even so she flinched as a piercingly shrill beep echoed through the building.

The door opened into a wood-panelled room with shelves of books covering two of its walls from floor to ceiling. There was an ornate desk with a chair behind it and two in front of it. Angel flicked a light-switch, figuring there was little point trying to hide her presence. There were two drawers in the desk with locks for which she didn't have keys. She hammered the screwdriver between the upper drawer and desktop, wrenching its handle back and forth. The wood around the lock splintered, and after a minute or so of Angel's violent, straining effort, it gave way. She yanked out the drawer, placed it upside down on the floor and smashed it apart with the hammer. No false bottom. She gave the second drawer the same treatment. Again, nothing. Her blood hammering in her ears almost as loudly as the alarm, she felt around behind where the drawers had been. Her delicate fingers found a tiny hole in the wood. Glancing around frantically, her gaze fixed on a sheaf of papers held together by a paper-clip. She removed the clip, unbent it and inserted it into the hole. Its point pressed against what felt like a spring. She let out a triumphant yip as, with a faint click, a section of the desk carved to look like a fluted column popped open.

Angel eagerly upended the secret drawer. A little black leather book dropped into her palm. Names, addresses and telephone numbers were listed in the book. Shoving it into her handbag, she made for the exit. In the darkness of the adjoining office, a flicker of light at the window caught her eye.

She warily parted the blinds. A car had pulled over behind the motorbike. A man of maybe fifty-five with a moustache and dark, receding hair got out of it and approached the bike. The driver, a younger woman with functionally short blonde hair, remained in her seat, talking on a phone, or maybe a radio. Angel guessed immediately that they were police. Over the years, necessity had forced her to become an expert at spotting coppers. What's more, their suits marked them as CID. Her brain started racing like a hamster on a wheel. CID wouldn't be sent to investigate a break-in. Not unless they suspected it was connected to a more serious crime. As far as she could see, that meant only one thing – Marisa and Herbert's bodies had already been found. Her heart dropped hard into her stomach. She'd hoped to have a day or two at least to formulate her next move before the police got on her trail.

As the man scanned the building, Angel jerked away from the window. She had to get out of there. Fast! She ran towards the rear of the hallway, trying doors as she went. All of them were locked. She put the front door key in the back door, but it wouldn't turn. The door was thick and solid. There was no way she could jimmy it with the screwdriver. Her eyes desperately sought a window. There were none. She considered running upstairs, but quickly rejected the idea. Even if there was a way out up there, it would almost certainly involve jumping from an ankle-breaking height. There was only one way to leave – by the front door. Panic swelled inside her. *Be calm*, she told herself. *You need to do this and do it now, before more of the fuckers get here*. She reached into her handbag and wrapped clammy fingers around the Glock's grip.

Chapter Thirteen

Jim knocked on the Kirbys' front door. Linda opened it. She was still wearing her dressing-gown and slippers, as if she hadn't got dressed all day. She put a hand to her mouth, looking from Jim to Amy with a mix of hope and fear in her eyes. Her sleeve slipped down, exposing a hand-shaped bruise on her wrist. Another bruise showed faintly through a thick layer of foundation cream on her cheekbone. Jim felt a spark of anger at the sight. He despised men like Ron Kirby – men who seemed to enjoy nothing more than hurting the ones they were supposed to love. He would have liked to haul Ron down to the station and fling him in a cell. But he knew it would make no difference. In his experience, women who'd been physically and mentally beaten down for as many years as Linda rarely, if ever, pressed charges.

'What is it?' Linda asked through her fingers. 'What's happened?'

'We'd like to get your opinion on a couple of things that may or may not concern your daughter, Mrs Kirby. Can we come in?'

Linda glanced up and down the street as though searching for someone, before motioning for Jim and Amy to come inside. 'You'll have to make it quick. I'm cooking supper.'

'Where's your husband?'

'At the pub.'

'He doesn't have much liking for the police, does he?' said Amy.

Linda chewed her lower lip, reluctant from fear or loyalty to discuss her husband. She stood with folded arms, casting nervous glances out of the living room window. Amy set the laptop down on the sideboard and flipped it open. 'Take a look at this please, Mrs Kirby, and tell us what you see.' She opened the file containing the CCTV footage.

Linda put on a pair of glasses and studied the screen. She stated the obvious. 'It's a woman in a corridor.'

'Do you recognise her?'

'No.' The answer came without hesitation. Linda's brow creased. 'Hang on. You don't think that's my Grace, do you?'

'We don't know,' said Jim. 'That's why we want to get your opinion.'

'Well that woman can't be my Grace. She's much too old.'

'If she's alive, Grace will be nearly thirty-one now.'

Linda winced as though the thought cut through her like a knife. 'I know, but in here,' she touched her chest, 'she's still my little girl.'

'I understand, but I need you to imagine what she might look like as a woman. Can you do that for me?'

'I'll try.' Linda closed her eyes for a moment, then looked at the screen again. Her voice came falteringly. 'I... I suppose she's got similar lips to Grace, but her nose is different and her eyes. My Grace had such beautiful eyes, so full of life. That woman's eyes look... dead.' She shook her head. 'No, it can't be her, it just can't be.'

Jim and Amy exchanged a glance. He indicated the laptop with his eyes. Catching his meaning, she clicked on the audio file of the anonymous call to the hospital. Linda stiffened as though an icy hand had touched her spine. Her lips worked soundlessly. Tears misted her eyes. 'It's her,' she managed to say at last.

'Are you sure?'

Linda nodded. 'Her voice sounds different, but the same.' She reached for the laptop's screen, stroking trembling fingers over the woman's face. 'Oh my baby. My poor baby girl. What have you done to yourself?' She turned to Jim, her eyes burning with the need for answers. 'Where is she?'

'We don't know. That footage and the phone call you just heard were recorded last night at a hospital in Middlesbrough. Can you think of any reason why Grace might be there?'

'No. I've never been to Middlesbrough in my life. Neither has Ron.' Linda jerked around at the sound of the front door opening. 'Ron!' She dashed into the hallway, her arms pressed to her chest as if cradling an imaginary child. 'She's alive! Our Grace is alive!'

'Jesus fucking Christ, woman,' Ron thundered, a slurred edge to his voice. 'I told you I didn't want to hear any more of that talk.'

'But—'

'No! Grace is dead. Do you hear? She's dead, and that's all there is to it. Now where's my supper?'

'Sod your supper. There are more important—' Linda broke off, clapping her hands to her mouth.

Ron's eyes bulged like golf balls. 'More important? What's more important than looking after your husband?'

'I'm sorry, love.'

'Sorry's not good enough, Linda.' Ron reached to unbuckle his belt. 'I can see I'm going to have to remind you of your duties.'

Hearing the threat in Ron's voice, Jim stepped into the hallway. 'Evening, Mr Kirby.'

Ron's mouth twisted into a scowl. 'Oh, now I get it. I should have known you were behind this.' He stabbed a finger into Linda's forehead. 'And you. Didn't I say not to let that lot into my house again?'

'Don't do that.' Jim's voice was steely with authority.

Barging his wife aside, Ron squared up to him. 'I don't give a fuck who you are. No one tells me what to do in my own house.'

'Please, Ron,' said Linda. 'He's got proof that our Grace is alive.'

'What proof?'

Amy entered the hallway, holding the laptop with a close-up of the woman's face on the screen.

Ron squinted blearily at the image. 'Who the fuck's that? Is that supposed to be Grace? It looks nothing like her.'

'There's more.' Linda gestured for Amy to play the recording.

As he listened to the audio file, Ron let out a snort of derision. 'That's a sodding Geordie.'

Linda shook her head, wringing her hands. 'Listen! Can't you hear it?'

'I can hear perfectly fine, woman. It's you who's got shit in your ears if you think that's Grace.'

'We believe your daughter may be somewhere in the north-east,' said Jim.

179

'Based on what?'

'You just heard a recording of a phone call to a Middlesbrough hospital. The same phone was used to call your house a few hours later.'

'So what? That proves nothing.'

'It proves there's a woman out there about the age your daughter would be now who's making anonymous phone calls to you.'

'It was probably a wrong number. Or maybe it was a practical joke. Maybe someone's trying to fuck with our heads.'

'Why would they do that?'

'You're the copper. You tell me.'

Jim reined in a breath of irritation. 'Granted it might not be Grace, but aren't you even interested to find out?'

'The only thing I'm interested in right now is my supper.' Ron jerked his chin at the front door. 'So go on, piss off out of my house. Oh, and if I find you talking to Linda behind my back again, you and me are going to have serious words. Do we understand each other?'

'Likewise if I come back here and see more bruises on your wife.'

The two men eyeballed each other for a moment. Then Jim turned his attention to Linda. 'Thanks for your help, Mrs Kirby. Hopefully we'll be in touch soon.'

Ron flashed Linda a glowering look, and her gaze flinched from Jim's to the carpet. There was fear in her face, but there was also excitement, euphoria even. Everything about her quivered with the certainty that her daughter was alive.

Jim and Amy returned to the street. Ron slammed the door behind them, with the parting shot, 'Fucking pigs.'

'That bastard's going to beat the living shit out of her, you know,' said Amy.

Jim sighed, a bitter feeling of impotence rising within him. It was a sensation he'd experienced many times in his career. He'd learnt to live with it, but not happily. 'So what do you think?'

'I think Mrs Kirby knows her own daughter's voice.'

Jim nodded in agreement. His mobile phone rang. He glanced at its screen.

'Who is it?' asked Amy.

'Scott Greenwood.' Jim put the phone to his ear. 'What's up, Scott?'

'A report just came in of a suspected double shooting of a man and woman at a house out near Greno Woods. And, get this, apparently their bodies were found in a basement.'

'Jesus.' The word whistled from Jim's mouth. 'What's the address?'

'Treetops Farm, Elliot Lane, a couple of miles east of the Penistone Road.'

'Got it. We're on our way.'

'On our way where?' asked Amy.

As Jim filled her in on the situation, he punched the address into the satnav. He didn't need to look at her to know that they both had the same name ringing in their heads – *Grace!* She accelerated away sharply, siren wailing, dashboard lights flashing red and blue. Traffic pulled into the kerb to let them past as they turned onto the Penistone Road. They sped towards their destination, eyes watching for suspicious activity, ears tuned into the information coming over the two-way radio. The Firearms Unit was also on its way to the scene. The call had come in from the son of the victims, a nineteen-year-old male. Just north of the suburb of Grenoside, the satnav directed them to turn right. A couple of miles further on they pulled over at the entrance to Treetops Farm. A police helicopter circled overhead, but they were the first at the scene on the ground.

'We should wait for Firearms,' said Amy as Jim opened his door.

'If Grace is behind this, I'm not going to give those trigger-happy arseholes a chance to put a bullet in her. You get on that radio, let them know I'm on scene.'

Jim grabbed a torch from the glove-compartment and made his way along the drive at a slow jog. He hadn't gone far when a voice behind him hissed his name. Glancing over his shoulder, he saw Amy hurrying after him. 'You're crazy if you think I'm letting you go in alone to get killed,' she said.

As the house came into view, they saw that a motorcycle and a Range Rover were parked outside it. A boy in motorcycle leathers was sitting hunched on the steps, white-faced with shock. He jumped to his feet at the sight of them. 'Stay where you are!' commanded Jim. 'Get your hands up where we can see them. Who are you?'

The boy raised his hands over his head. Blood glistened on their palms. 'I'm Xavier Winstanley. I live here.'

'Was it you who called us?'

Xavier nodded. 'I found my parents in the basement. They're—' His voice faltered. He drew a shuddering breath and managed to say, 'They're dead. I think they've been shot.'

'Is there anyone else in the house?'

'I don't think so.'

'Turn around.'

'I didn't kill them,' Xavier protested as Amy pulled his hands down behind his back and cuffed them.

'Take us to the basement,' said Jim.

Xavier shook his head frantically. 'Please don't make me go down there again.'

'You want to help us find whoever killed your parents, don't you?'

'Of course.'

'Then let's do this and not waste any more time.'

Jim entered the house first, glancing cautiously all around. Amy followed, holding Xavier's arm in case he stumbled. With his head, the boy indicated the open panel under the staircase. He was shaking too much to speak.

As Jim descended the staircase, his nose wrinkled at the unmistakable stench of post-mortem evacuated bowels. The instant he saw the basement he recognised it from the DVD. Following the line that the camera had taken fifteen years earlier, his eyes swept over the whitewashed brick walls, foam-insulated pipes and quarry-tiled floor before coming to rest on the bodies. The upper part of the man's face was missing. Shards of skull protruded through his facial tissue, forming the rim of a grisly crater. His gaze transferred from the man's hair-matted pot belly and barrel chest to the woman. She didn't need to be naked for him to see that she had the same colouring and build as the woman from the DVD.

'Wait here,' Jim said to Xavier. His words were needless. The boy had turned to press his face against the stairway wall.

Taking care not to disturb anything, Jim and Amy approached the bodies. Dropping to his haunches, Jim touched the man with the back of his hand. 'Still warm.'

He sniffed the air. 'Do you smell it?'

Amy nodded. 'Gunpowder.'

'The woman appears to have been shot first. Looks like she refused to go along with the killer's game.' Jim felt in his pockets for a pair of forensic gloves. He pulled them on and parted the man's lips. He did the same with the woman. 'No overlapping teeth.' His eyes drew a line from Marisa's head to the wine rack. He approached it and peered through the gap where the bullet had hit a bottle. 'There's a hole in the wall back there. What are the bets forensics pull a nine-millimetre round out of it?'

Jim's attention was drawn to Xavier by the sound of him sobbing. 'We'd better get him out of here.'

As they made their way back upstairs, Jim asked, 'How did you come to find your parents?'

Between gut-wrenching sobs, the boy replied, 'Their car's in the drive, so I knew they were home. When they weren't in the house, I thought they'd taken Oscar—'

'Who's Oscar?'

'Our dog. I thought they'd taken him for a walk. But then I noticed that his lead was on its hook. I thought that was strange, so I started looking around the house. That's when I found Dad's desk all smashed up.'

'Show us the desk.'

Xavier led them to the study. He gestured in bewilderment at the wreckage of the desk. 'Why would someone do that?'

Jim and Amy exchanged a glance, both thinking the same thought. *Because they were searching for something.* 'What was in the desk?' asked Amy.

Xavier shrugged. 'Just Dad's work stuff.'

'What kind of work stuff?'

'Letters, contracts, business accounts. Things like that. My dad is… was Herbert Winstanley.' Xavier's tone suggested that he expected them to recognise the name. 'He owns Winstanley Accountants and Business Advisors.'

Jim stooped to look at the computer screen. 'This is showing a map of Fulwood.' He read aloud the address in the Google search box.

'That's the address of Dad's office.'

Jim spun towards Xavier, his eyes suddenly bright with urgency. Catching hold of the boy's arm, he drew him rapidly towards the front door. Guessing his intention, Amy said, 'We can't take him to his father's office with us.'

Jim pointed at one of the stone handrails that bordered the steps. 'Cuff him to that.'

As Amy did so, Xavier looked at her with frightened eyes. 'You're not going to leave me here are you?'

'You're not in any danger. More police will be here any minute.'

Amy and Jim sprinted back to the car. It was only a couple of hundred metres, but Jim was breathing hard by the time they got there. 'I'll drive,' he said. 'Get on the radio and make sure Firearms know about Xavier Winstanley.'

'Shall I request back-up for us?'

Jim shook his head. 'First let's see what we find at the office.'

As Amy spoke into the radio, several police cars screamed past them in the opposite direction. She hung up the receiver. 'I realise this girl might hold the key to breaking this case, but I think you're making the wrong call. If Grace is behind this, she's already killed two, maybe three people. And that's just the victims we know of. What makes you think she'll hesitate to open fire on us if we get in her way?'

'Nothing, except that she isn't out to kill innocent people.' Jim stepped up the car's speed as they hit the Penistone Road, weaving in and out of oncoming traffic. 'To be totally honest with you, Amy, there's a part of me that's not sure it wants to catch Grace. Let's face it, she's doing society a big favour bumping off these sickos.'

A deep frown puckered Amy's forehead. 'Murder is murder, and we have a duty to protect all people equally.'

'Says who?'

'Says the law.'

'Well maybe in this case the law is wrong. Think about it – even if we arrest Grace and she gives us the names of the other men from the DVD, what are the chances of us bringing successful charges against them? Fuck all, that's what. It'll be their word against the word of a murderess. Who do you think a jury is going to believe?'

Amy blew out her cheeks and shook her head. 'I can hardly believe what I'm hearing. This kind of talk isn't like you at all, Jim.'

'Isn't it? Maybe you just don't know me as well as you think you do.'

'I'm starting to think maybe I don't. Have you considered that Grace might be able to give us the names of others who were abused like her and who can back her story up?'

'What, you mean other runaways, prostitutes and assorted cast-offs whose word carries no more weight than hers?'

'Mark Baxley isn't any of those things. There could be others like him out there.'

'Yeah, and if there are, they've no doubt been pumped full of enough Rohypnol to turn their brains into scrambled eggs too.'

'Well what about the desk? Whoever did that was obviously looking for something. Maybe that something is a complete version of the DVD, one that reveals the perpetrators' identities.'

'That was my initial thought too, but then it occurred to me that Grace doesn't care about finding evidence to get those men arrested. She's looking for something that'll lead her to them. A list of names, or something like that.'

'If so, surely it's more important than ever that we catch her and get our hands on that list.'

'At which point we're faced with the same problem I mentioned a moment ago. Without physical evidence or other more credible victims or witnesses, we're screwed.'

'Maybe you're right, maybe not.' There was a sharp note in Amy's voice. 'Either way it's irrelevant. We've got a job to do, and if you want to keep doing it, I suggest you don't repeat any of this to anyone.'

Jim heaved a sigh, wondering why he'd bothered venting his mind. He hadn't really expected Amy to understand where he was coming from. She was still in love with the job, and the job dealt in black and white, innocence and guilt. As she'd said, murder was murder. Regardless of Grace's past, if she was guilty, the law would show no mercy. That was the way it was. The way it had to be. Jim understood that. But the older he got, the less he agreed with it. He'd seen too many victims jailed for taking revenge on those who'd hurt them. And he'd seen too many perpetrators slip through the cracks in the law – people like Bryan Reynolds, Stephen Baxley and the

Winstanleys; people who operated in a world where right and wrong were defined by those who had the power to do so. For them, murder wasn't murder unless you were convicted of it. He found himself wondering, as he had many times in the past few years, whether perhaps the only way to beat their kind was to attack them with their own weapons. He gave a little shiver – it was a thought that never failed to send a chill up his spine.

'Don't worry, Detective Sheridan, as long as I'm doing the job, I'll do it properly.' As if trying to convince himself that his words were true, Jim repeated with slow emphasis, 'Do it properly.'

As they drove on in tense silence, news filtered through the radio that Xavier Winstanley had been taken into custody and the Firearms Unit were securing the house and surrounding area. They heard the burglar alarm's shrill wail before they saw the building that housed Winstanley Accountants and Business Advisors. Jim pulled in behind a motorbike. A light was on in one of the downstairs windows. He caught a shadow of movement behind the blinds. 'There's someone in there.'

Amy reached for the radio. 'That's it, I'm calling for back-up.'

Jim got out of the car and approached the motorbike. The keys were in the ignition. He removed them and turned towards the building, his moustache twitching with uncertainty. Grace was a killer. She had to be stopped. Didn't she? He pushed the thought aside. It wasn't his place to ask such questions. It was his place to do his duty as a policeman. Amy wound down her window. 'Keep the building under surveillance and wait for armed back-up. Those are our orders.'

As she spoke, a figure with a hood pulled tight around their face emerged from the building and advanced rapidly towards them. 'She's got a gun!' Jim shouted, recognising the woman from the CCTV footage.

'You get your hands up!' ordered Angel, her voice trembling. As Jim obeyed, she aimed the Glock at Amy. 'And you get out of the car!'

Amy rose to her feet, hands spread.

'Grace Kirby?' Jim's voice was uncertain. It was the woman from the CCTV, he didn't doubt that, but curiously her eyes were brown, not blue.

'Shut your mouth!'

'You're Grace Kirby, aren't you?'

Angel jerked the gun back towards Jim. 'I said fucking shut it.'

'Put the gun down,' said Amy, her voice calm and forceful. 'We're police officers.'

'I'm warning you. One more word!' Angel pointed at the car. 'Get the keys and the radio receiver.' Once Amy had done so, she continued, 'Put them on the bonnet, along with your mobile phones.'

Again, Jim and Amy complied. With the gun, Angel motioned them to a spot where she could get on the motorbike without taking her eyes off them. She put their things in her handbag, unhooked the helmet from the handlebars and tossed it aside, then felt for the ignition keys. Finding that they were missing, she hissed, 'Which of you has got the keys?'

Jim opened his hand to reveal them. 'I know what Stephen Baxley and the Winstanleys did to you, Grace. I've seen the film they made.'

Angel gave him a narrow-eyed look. 'You're the copper who called me yesterday, aren't you?'

'Yes. I want to help you. Together we can catch the others involved.'

'If you've really seen the film, you know as much about them as me.'

'Their faces were hidden. That's why we need you.'

Shaking her head, Angel echoed Jim's earlier words to Amy. 'Even if I could tell you their names, it wouldn't make any difference. They're beyond your reach. But not mine.'

'Listen to him, Grace,' said Amy. 'You can get these guys, but killing them isn't the way to do—'

'No!' cut in Angel, a dark light kindling in her eyes. 'There's no other way. Now throw me the keys. I don't want to hurt you, but believe me I will if I have to.'

Jim tossed the keys to her.

'Get on your faces.'

Once Jim and Amy were lying down, Angel swung her leg over the bike. For an instant, she was forced to lower her gaze to insert the key into the ignition. Amy started to move into a pouncing position, but Jim caught hold of her wrist. The bike's engine roared into life and Angel accelerated away, speeding towards the city's outskirts.

Amy yanked her wrist out of Jim's grip. 'I could've taken her down.'

'Got yourself killed, more like.'

Amy dismissed his words with a snort. 'And what the hell was all that about you calling her? Have you totally lost your mind?'

'I was just trying to reach out to her. Let her know there was help available.'

'Oh you helped her alright. I can't think of a better way to give someone a heads-up that we're on their arse. No wonder she was wearing fake fucking contact lenses.'

'And what if she'd listened to me? The Winstanleys would still be alive.'

'I bet you'd be jumping for joy if that was the case, wouldn't you?' Amy's tone was laced with sarcasm.

A frown added to the creases carved into Jim's rugged face. 'Are you suggesting I helped her murder the Winstanleys?'

'I wouldn't go that far. But let's face it, Jim, you won't exactly be mourning their deaths.'

'Will you?' Now it was Jim's turn to raise his voice. 'Christ knows how many kids have fallen victim to those perverts. Well, they won't be hurting anyone now. Am I really supposed to mourn that?'

'You're supposed to do your job!'

'I am doing my fucking job, the same as I've been doing it since you were still in nappies.' Jim took a breath and continued more calmly. 'You're right, I was bang out of order phoning Grace. But you seem to be forgetting that at the time I didn't know what had gone down in Middlesbrough. How could I possibly have any idea what she intended to do?'

Amy stared at Jim, her eyebrows knotted. She heaved a sigh. 'OK, look, I'm sorry for saying what I did. But you can hardly blame me after what you said earlier.'

'I don't blame you. But maybe one day, when you've been doing this job for as long as I have, you'll understand why I said what I did.'

'I really hope not.'

'Are you going to tell Garrett?'

'I have to.'

'Why? What good would it do?'

Amy pursed her lips in indecision. 'Our responsibility, our only responsibility, is to arrest Grace Kirby. You've got to get your head straight about that.'

Jim released a leaden sigh. 'I know.'

'Then I'll keep it to myself.' Amy paused, before adding meaningfully, 'For now.'

The wail of fast-approaching sirens drew their attention. Three police cars and a van sped into view. Amy flagged them down. She gave the occupants of the foremost car a description of Grace and pointed them in the direction she'd gone. Two of the cars raced off in pursuit. The van and remaining car blocked off the road in both directions. As a team of six firearms officers geared up to check there was no one else in the building, Amy radioed district headquarters. 'This is Detective Inspector Sheridan. I need a GPS triangulation on a mobile phone.' She gave her phone number and waited for a response.

After a brief pause, she heard, 'GPS indicates suspect vehicle is moving north-east in the area of the Ecclesall Road.'

Amy relayed the information to the cars in pursuit. Then she turned to Jim. 'Well, it shouldn't be long now before we catch up with Grace again.'

'Nice work, Detective.'

'At least say it like you mean it.'

'I do mean it.' With heavy-lidded eyes, Jim watched the firearms officers move in on the building. 'I'm just tired, that's all. Very, very tired.'

Chapter Fourteen

As soon as she was out of sight of the detectives, Angel turned onto a street that cut back towards the city centre. Again, she almost skidded off the motorbike. She forced herself to slow down and take a moment to orient herself. The street descended towards a dark patch in the city, which she guessed was the Botanical Gardens. At that point, she could turn left and skirt along the edge of the park towards the Hallamshire Hospital or right towards the Ecclesall Road. Either route would bring her, after a couple of miles, to the city centre. Over the motorbike's engine and the blood hammering in her ears, she caught a thin whine of sirens away to her left. That made her mind up for her. At the end of the street she turned right.

The pubs, bars and restaurants of the Ecclesall Road were packed with customers, many of them sitting at tables on the pavement. Angel felt too visible. She half expected people to jump to their feet, pointing and shouting, *That's her!*

She turned off the Ecclesall Road and worked her way towards the city centre through a tangle of quiet terraced streets. Houses soon gave way to blocks of flats, shops and office buildings. After negotiating a busy roundabout, she slowed almost to a stop, twisting her head from side to side.

Spotting a boarded-up shop, she mounted the pavement and cut the engine. She wheeled the bike round to the back of the shop and stashed it behind two large metal bins. She pulled off her hooded top and threw it in one of the bins, along with the contact lenses. There was every possibility that her description was already being circulated to the city's hotels, pubs, nightclubs, taxi drivers and the like. She figured the fact that she'd cut and dyed her hair should give her a few hours' breathing space to get her head together and plan her next move.

Angel headed for the hotel, walking fast but trying not to look suspicious. She smiled at the receptionist as she passed through the lobby. The man cast a disinterested glance at her, before returning his attention to the newspaper he was reading. She silently congratulated herself on her choice of lodgings. In a more intimate or upmarket establishment, her appearance alone might have been enough to land her in trouble – her hair was pasted to her forehead with sweat; one leg of her jeans was ripped at the knee; and there were bloody scabs on her elbows.

She caught the lift up to her room and took a long drink of water at the sink. After cleaning and tying a towel around a deep gash on her knee, she removed the carrier-bag containing the tools of her addiction from the toilet cistern. She lay on the bed, staring at the bag, her tongue flicking hungrily for its contents. The heroin itch was almost unbearable, but she knew she couldn't afford to scratch it. She needed a clear head in case she had to make a sudden departure from the hotel. Even more than that, she needed to think. But only one thought kept hammering in her brain – *You did it! You killed the bastards. Now you deserve a little reward, a little treat.*

With a hard shake of her head, Angel shoved the bag under a pillow. Herbert and Marisa were a start, a biopsy before the main operation, that's all. She took out the little black book and started reading the names aloud to herself, fixing them in her memory. 'Thomas Villiers, Sebastian Dawson-Cromer, Rupert Hartwell…' Her voice dissolved into a sigh. There was page after page of names. The sickness, it seemed, went deeper than she'd ever imagined. She was going to need more bullets – lots more.

The first job was to identify the two men still alive from that night in the Winstanleys' basement. But how? Her gaze continued to skim over the names, until she came to one with a Sheffield phone number and address below it. 'Henry Reeve.'

The name meant nothing to Angel. She repeated it softly to herself, summoning up an image of her abusers, wondering how she could find out if it belonged to either of them. She considered phoning the number and seeing if she recognised the voice, but the idea didn't appeal. It would be like holding up a warning sign that said, *I'm on your arse!* An idea occurred to her. She took the detectives' phones out of her handbag. One was an old-fashioned phone with a basic camera. The other was an iPhone. She navigated to Google on the iPhone and did a search for Henry Reeve, Sheffield. 'Dr Henry Reeve, Clinical Psychiatrist' appeared at the top of the hit list. The link led to a chunk of text that read, 'Dr Reeve is a Chartered Clinical Psychiatrist with over twenty-five years' experience working in Child and Family Services. Since setting up in private practice in 2002, Dr Reeve has continued to work with young people. He has particular expertise in treating low self-esteem, depression and bipolar disorders.'

Next to the bio was a head-and-shoulders photo of a late-middle-aged man with short silver-grey hair and a matching beard, chiselled features and the confident eyes of a man used to being listened to. Angel unconsciously curled her fingers into a fist. She knew those eyes. For years she'd seen them in her dreams, leering down at her, swollen with lust and arrogance. Even now, if she closed her eyes, she could recall with chilling vividness the feel of his hand on the back of her neck, forcing her head towards Mark Baxley. She ground her teeth at the thought of him working with young people, wondering how many others had been subjected to similar treatment. *Expertise in treating low self-esteem*. A nauseous rage swept over her at the perverse irony of it. Doctor Reeve's particular brand of therapy had obliterated what little remained of her self-esteem and driven her to the brink of suicide.

At the top of the screen was a 'Contact' link. It took Angel to a webpage with an email address and the instructions, 'To contact Dr Henry Reeve, use the link below. Please include your name, contact number and the nature of your query.' A sardonic smile lifted Angel's mouth at the thought of emailing the doctor something along the lines of, 'Please can we arrange an appointment for me to come over and blow your brains out.'

According to Herbert's book, the good doctor lived on Whirlowdale Road. Angel looked up the address on Google Maps and zoomed in on the house. It was a large detached property, backing onto woods. Reflecting that it should be easy enough to approach the house unobserved, she scrolled the map to her present location.

Very pleased with her bit of investigative work, Angel imagined the satisfaction she would feel at wiping the arrogance off Doctor Reeve's face forever. The need for vengeance throbbed in her veins more powerfully even than the desire to shoot up. As dog-tired as she was, if it hadn't been for the police forcing her to lie low, she would have headed over to his house that very moment.

Angel flinched at the sound of her phone ringing. Warily, as if it might burn her, she took it out of her handbag. A number she didn't know showed on its screen. She frowned at the phone for a moment, before putting it to her ear. A familiar voice came down the line.

****

Torch beams flickered in the building's windows as the team of AFOs moved rapidly from room to room, shouting for anyone hiding to come out. Jim leant against the van, smoking a cigarette and listening to Amy help coordinate the search for Grace over the two-way radio. GPS tracking indicated she was now stationary somewhere in the region of Charter Row, Wellington Street and Furnival Gate – an area of the city centre where there were dozens of pubs, bars, nightclubs, restaurants, a hotel or two and a homeless hostel. It would take a while to check out all the possible hiding places, but even so it was only a matter of time before Grace was found.

A mass of conflicting emotions seethed inside Jim. He knew he should feel pleased at a job well done. But he didn't. He kept thinking about the DVD. Assuming Stephen Baxley was operating the video camera and there was no one else present off-screen, that meant two of the perpetrators were still alive. Two men. Gut police instinct told him that one of those men was Bryan Reynolds. He didn't have a clue as to the other man's identity. But even if he had, it would have made little difference. As things stood, there simply wasn't the evidence to charge anyone. It twisted him up inside to think of Grace going down for life while her abusers remained free to continue their depravity. Especially Reynolds. That scum-sucking piece of filth deserved to be thrown into the deepest darkest hole imaginable. *Other evidence will surface*, he told himself over and again. But each time he did, another voice rose from some remote corner of his mind. *What if it doesn't? What then?*

A firearms officer appeared at the front door and shouted that the building was clear. 'I'll check out Winstanley's office,' Jim said to Amy.

Flicking away his cigarette, he wearily made his way to the office. He knelt at the side of the desk to peer into the empty secret drawer, noting that it was big enough to hold a small book. He glanced around the room. His gaze came to rest on a phone. He stared at it for a moment, a fierce frown on his forehead, a shadow of conflict clouding his eyes. 'Do your job and do it properly,' he muttered under his breath, but there was a hollow ring to his voice.

Jim left the office. He was alone in the building, except for a constable stationed at the front door. He headed upstairs. The door to the office of the solicitor's firm that shared the premises with Winstanley Accountants and Business Advisors had been broken into. He closed it firmly behind himself and approached a desk with a telephone on it. He took out his notepad and found Grace's number. Hesitantly, he reached for the phone. He started to punch in the number, but returned the handset to its base with a shake of his head, murmuring, 'What the fuck are you doing, Jim?'

Again, the sickening images from the DVD flashed through his mind, followed by Reynolds's smug, scarred face. He snatched up the phone and dialled. His knuckles showed white as he gripped the handset. One ring. Two. Three. Part of him prayed that Grace didn't answer. Four rings. Five. *She's not going to pick up*, he thought, releasing a breath that was part relief and part disappointment. He was moving the phone away from his ear when the ringing stopped. For a few seconds there was dead silence, punctuated only by the thud of his heart. Then he heard a voice that was his own, but that sounded strange and distant, as if he was listening to someone else speaking. 'We know you're in the city centre near Furnival Gate. We're tracking the iPhone's GPS. You haven't got long before we find you. You need to move now.'

Another moment of silence passed. Then Grace's voice came down the line, tentative, suspicious. 'Why are you doing this?'

Jim opened his mouth, but no answer came out. He hung up and looked at his hand. For the first time in as long as he could remember, it was shaking. He put it to his eyes, concealing a sadness that went deeper than any bullet could have done.

****

Angel sprang to her feet, swearing at herself for her stupidity. Deano had always been careful to use phones that weren't GPS enabled. She yanked on her old sweatshirt and jeans, dislodging the towel tied around her knee. She didn't understand why

Detective Monahan had warned her, but neither did she doubt that he was telling the truth. There'd been no lie in his voice, just a kind of haunted need. She'd heard that need before in the voices of men betraying their wives. Parting the curtains a finger's breadth, she saw that half a dozen police cars were cruising silently towards the hotel. She grabbed her handbag and the bag of Mexican brown and started towards the door. Almost as an afterthought, she snatched up the iPhone.

She sprinted down a flight of stairs at the rear of the hotel. A fire-exit led to a car park that was accessed from a backstreet with a couple of busy bars and restaurants on it. A group of men emerged from one of the bars. She pulled up her hood. Feigning drunkenness, she staggered into one of the men and flung her arms around him to keep from falling. 'Whoa, easy there, love, I'm a married man,' he laughed.

'Sorry,' slurred Angel, hurrying on her way in the opposite direction to the group. Her heart lurched as the sound of sirens suddenly flared. She ducked into a shop porch, hiding in its shadows until the sirens began to fade. She peered both ways along the high street, then darted across it into an alleyway. Avoiding busy, well-lit streets, she worked her way towards the side of the city she knew best – the north side. Twice she was forced to fling herself out of the sight of passing police cars.

By the time Angel reached the Tinsley Canal, her clothes clung to her with sweat, and not only because of anxiety and exertion. Withdrawal symptoms were starting to kick in. The towpath was deserted, as she'd expected it to be at that time of night. As a teenager she'd spent many aimless evenings wandering along the canal's overgrown banks, smoking, drinking and breaking into derelict factory buildings. She kept on at a steady jog, passing industrial barges moored outside the graffiti-tagged walls of silent factories. When the lights of the city centre were well behind her, she slowed to a walk.

Up to that point she'd been focusing on not getting caught, but now she turned her thoughts to where she was going. She needed a place to hole up until at least the following night. But where? She didn't know anyone in the city who might take her in, except her mum and dad. And she couldn't exactly go to them. In desperation, she considered phoning her policeman ally. But she quickly rejected the idea. His tone had suggested that he'd already gone way beyond what he was comfortable with. Besides, there was no knowing for sure if Detective Monahan was really on her side. There were some influential – and dangerous – people out there for whom things could suddenly get very uncomfortable if she spilled her guts to the police. It was in their interests to keep her out of the law's clutches – at least until after they'd got their slimy mitts on her.

As if seeking inspiration, Angel's gaze skimmed over the canal's algae-flecked surface. It came to her that there was one place where she could hide out, and what's more, the canal and the nearby River Don would lead her almost to its door – the flat where Stephen Baxley had kept her hidden.

****

Jim stared into the darkness behind his hand, until Amy shouted into the building, 'She's on the move again!'

Like someone emerging from a trance, Jim jerked his head up. *On the move? Why the hell is Grace still holding on to the iPhone? Didn't she believe me?* Quickly smoothing the perplexity from his face, he hurried downstairs.

Amy's eyebrows drew together. 'What were you doing up there?'

She doesn't trust me any more, realised Jim. *And she's right not to.* 'Checking to see if anything had been disturbed. Where's she heading?'

'West towards Devonshire Green. Where, if you remember, she was seen talking to someone in a grey mac a week before she went missing. Maybe she's hoping to bump into that same someone.'

I don't think so. 'Maybe,' agreed Jim, the word contradicting the thought.

Amy gestured with her chin at Herbert Winstanley's office. 'Find anything interesting?' Jim told her about the empty secret drawer. She thumbed over her shoulder towards a marked police car. 'Come on, let's get back into the hunt.'

As Jim followed Amy, he glanced back at the office building and was hit by the sudden, almost overwhelming feeling that he'd left something of himself behind in there – something irrecoverable.

Jim sat silent in the back seat as a succession of buildings and streets blurred past, half listening to the updates being relayed over the radio – the suspect was now believed to be hiding somewhere in the area of Devonshire Street. He felt strangely detached from the situation, as if he were watching it happen from a long way off. He found himself thinking about Margaret, wondering what she was doing, and who she was doing it with. He had a sudden longing to be with her, to confide in her about what he'd done. A thought, sharp as a razor, stung him back into the moment. *What you've done is helped a murderer, which makes you an accessory.*

Devonshire Street had been blocked off by three police cars, and firearms officers had taken up positions behind them. A couple of ambulances were waiting silently further back. To the right was Devonshire Green, a triangle of grass bisected by several paths. Its wide-open, well-lit expanse offered nowhere for Grace to hide. To the left a row of bustling bars and restaurants stretched towards the even busier Division Street, where more police vehicles had formed a second road-block. Officers were stopping everyone who came along and showing them printouts of the CCTV still of Grace. Garrett, his chest encased in a bullet-proof vest, was talking to the senior firearms officer. As Amy and Jim approached, he nodded a greeting. Jim could barely bring himself to meet his superior's eyes.

'What's the plan, sir?' asked Amy.

'It's a tricky situation. If we go in hard, more innocent people could get killed.'

Innocent! Jim gave a mental snort at the word. *A drug dealer and a pair of child molesters, by what reckoning are they innocent?* He bit back an urge to spit the question at Garrett.

'So we're going to hold back?'

'For now. This street will be all but deserted in a few hours. Then we can reassess the situation. A negotiator is trying to contact Grace using the number from her mother, but she's not picking up.'

Anyone who emerged from the bars and restaurants was discreetly directed towards officers waiting to question them at whichever end of the street they were closest to. After fifteen or twenty minutes, word came over the radio that the suspect was moving west. A large group comprising both men and women was approaching the road-block. Jim scanned their faces. Grace wasn't among them.

'Where the hell is she?' Amy wondered aloud. 'Surely we should be able to see her.'

'Chief Inspector!' The shout came from one of the officers stopping and questioning people. Garrett, Amy and Jim hurried over to the officer, who continued, 'This man thinks he may have seen the suspect.'

'There's no may have about it,' said the man. He tapped the CCTV still. 'I saw her half an hour ago over near the high street, behind John Lewis. I reckon she must've been pissed, 'cos she almost fell over me.'

The detectives exchanged glances. 'Would you empty your pockets please, sir,' said Amy.

The man pulled a wallet, keys and phone from one of his jacket pockets. His eyebrows drew together as he produced another phone from the opposite pocket. 'This isn't mine.'

Amy took the phone from him and pressed the standby button. A picture of a smiling young boy and girl, flanked by Amy and a thirty-something man appeared on the screen. She showed it to her colleagues, with a wry glimmer of a smile.

'In which direction was the woman heading?' Garrett asked.

'Towards the high street, as far as I could tell. Can I go now?'

'Once you've given a statement.' At a signal from Garrett, a uniformed officer ushered the man into the back of a car.

The DCI told another officer to relay the information they'd learnt to the search teams, then turned to his detectives. 'It would seem we're dealing with a clever girl.'

'Very clever,' agreed Amy, casting Jim a frowning sidelong glance. 'Very clever indeed.'

****

After a couple of miles, Angel came to a place where the canal and the River Don ran parallel to each other, separated by little more than the width of a road. She climbed some steps at the side of a bridge, checked to make sure no one was about, then ran towards the river. She followed the Don's winding bank into the heart of industrial Attercliffe, passing the grimy hulks of steelworks and occasional pockets of lightly wooded scrubland. Every so often she stopped to scan her surroundings for signs of the police search. But apart from the blinking lights of a helicopter circling above the city centre, there were none.

Several more miles of steady walking brought Angel to a dual-carriageway that crossed the river on a steel-framed bridge. She left behind the solitude of the river bank and made her way along the roadside, keeping to the shadows wherever possible, eyes and ears alert for police cars. The factory-flanked road was almost eerily quiet. It struck her, as it had many times during her previous stay in the area, how strange it felt to be in the middle of a heavily populated city and yet so alone.

She managed to make it to the flat without being seen by any passing motorists. The steel door grated inwards a few centimetres at a time as she heaved her scrawny, exhausted frame against it. Once the gap was wide enough, she squeezed through and closed the door. The derelict shop's interior smelt of mildew and old smoke. She sparked her lighter into life, illuminating graffiti-plastered walls and the ashes of a fire containing the half-melted remains of several cider bottles. Someone had clearly been in the building since it was raided. Judging by the bottles, it was probably just kids. She stooped to feel the ashes. Whoever it was, they hadn't been there for a while. The fire was long dead.

Angel approached a door at the rear of the shop that led to a small square of hallway and a flight of stairs. Something twisted in her stomach. The last time she'd climbed those stairs had been the morning after the night in the Winstanleys' basement. She'd been out of it on ketamine, but not enough to stop the memory of what had happened from clawing at her. She would soon learn that there was only one drug that could give her that kind of oblivion.

As though her feet were made of lead, Angel climbed the stairs. The door to the flat dangled off one hinge. The door-frame was split from top to bottom. Something scuttled across the floorboards of a hallway with three doors in its left-hand wall and one at its far end. She didn't flinch or even seem to hear. She advanced towards the first door, her eyes staring hollowly into the past. She saw herself lying on a double bed, with Stephen Baxley thrusting on top of her. She saw herself curled into a tight ball under the duvet, sobbing as if something inside her had been irreparably broken.

Angel opened the door. The bed was gone. There was a mattress on the floor that had been cut to ribbons – no doubt by police searching for drugs. The floorboards had been prised up in several places and a couple of holes had been hammered through the stud wall that separated the bedroom from the bathroom. Angel glanced into the bathroom. The porcelain sink had been smashed. The side of the bath had been levered off. The toilet was intact, but its bowl was brimful of stinking brown water. Next to the bathroom was a tiny kitchen. All the drawers and cupboards were open. The backs of the cupboards had been removed. The linoleum floor and work-surfaces were strewn with broken crockery, pots and pans, and the mould-furred contents of an upturned bin.

The final door, Angel knew, led to a lounge. When she'd lived there the room had been furnished with an old but comfortable brown sofa, a fold-up table with a couple of mismatched chairs, a television and a gas fire. All that remained of the furniture was the sofa, though it had received the same treatment as the mattress. There was a draughty hole in the chimney-breast where the gas fire had been. The green-swirled carpet had been pulled up and flung into a corner. Damp-stained curtains fluttered in a current of air that whistled through a crack in the barred window.

Angel closed the door and wedged the sofa up against it. She turned the cushions over and found that their undersides were intact. She slumped onto the sofa and shut her eyes, letting the silence of the night soothe her ragged nerves. As her sweat began to cool, the dank cold of the room made her shiver. She dragged the carpet over to the sofa and draped it around her shoulders. Then she set about cooking up a hit of Mexican brown. She shot herself up with enough junk to knock her out for the rest of the night. The last thing she saw as she floated off into a chemical haze was Doctor Henry Reeve's face. Only now, instead of being bloated with arrogance, it was crumpled with fear.

Chapter Fifteen

Mark awoke with tears in his eyes. The painkillers that the nurses fed him at regular intervals were wearing off. But that wasn't what had brought tears to his eyes. He'd been dreaming about Charlotte. In his dream, she was standing at the end of his bed, her hair clotted with blood. Her mouth opened and closed, but no words came out, just guttural sounds. Her arms were spread towards him, as if she wanted him to come to her. And there was such an imploring look of sadness in her eyes that he felt it like a physical pain in his chest.

Mark pushed the call button to summon a nurse. 'I want to see my sister.'

'I'm not sure that's possible.'

'Please, I need to talk to her.'

'She's still unconscious.'

'I know. But I can talk to her, even if she can't hear.'

'OK, Mark, I'll see what I can do.'

Mark's features twitched with impatience as he waited. The urge to see Charlotte was so strong he was tempted to get out of bed and wander the corridors in search of her. There was nothing to stop him from doing so – there hadn't been a constable stationed outside his door since forensic evidence had vindicated his story. He resisted the urge, knowing he had little chance of finding her before he was seen and returned to his room.

Eventually the nurse came back. She was accompanied by a policeman, who informed Mark, 'You've been given permission for a brief visit, but I'll have to go in with you.'

Relief gleamed in Mark's eyes. The nurse helped him into a pair of slippers and a dressing-gown. 'Do you need a walking stick?'

Testing his injured leg, Mark found that he could put his weight on it without much pain. 'No thanks.'

The nurse led him to a room at the opposite end of the ward. A stifled sob escaped his lips at the sight of his sister. Her head was heavily bandaged. A tube snaked out from amongst the bandages, draining fluid into a bag hanging on an IV pole. More tubes and wires ran from her arms and chest to a bewildering array of drip bags and monitors. Her chest rose and fell in time to the rhythmic whoosh and hiss of a machine that breathed for her. Looking at her unrecognisably swollen and bruised face, it was hard to believe there was any life left in her that wasn't being artificially maintained.

'I'll be waiting in the corridor,' said the nurse, after she'd drawn a chair to the bedside for Mark. 'Give a shout if you need me.'

Trying his best to ignore the constable standing at his shoulder, Mark took one of Charlotte's delicate, blue-tinged hands between both of his. For a long moment he just sat and stared at her. Then he closed his eyes and wept. Suddenly, almost savagely, he swiped a hand across his eyes.

More tears threatened to come, but Mark stubbornly held

them back. When he trusted himself enough to speak without sobbing, he leant in close to his sister. 'Charlotte, it's me. It's Mark.' He vainly searched her face for any flicker or twitch that might suggest she'd heard him. 'Come on, Charlotte. Move something – a finger, an eyelid, anything. Just give me some sign that you can hear me.' No response. Mark's lower lip began to tremble. He bit down on it hard.

He sat stroking his sister's hand until the nurse stepped back into the room and said, 'Time's up, Mark.'

'Please, just give me five more minutes.'

'I'm sorry, I can't. Doctor's orders. You're still very weak yourself. You can see Charlotte again tomorrow.'

'But what if—' Mark broke off. *What if she doesn't live that long?* That was what he'd been about to say. He shook the words from his head, reluctantly releasing his sister's hand. 'I'll see you tomorrow, sis.' Before standing to leave, he did something he hadn't done in years – he kissed Charlotte's cheek and whispered, 'I love you.'

As soon as Mark was out of the room, the tears pushed their way to the surface again. Between his sobs, he asked, 'What are her chances?'

'I'm sorry, love, but I really couldn't tell you.' The nurse put her hand on Mark's elbow, more to support him emotionally than physically. 'I do know one thing. Your sister's a fighter. And that's the best chance she's got.'

When Mark got back to his room, Doctor Reeve was waiting for him. 'Hello, Mark,' said the psychiatrist. 'It's good to see you back on your feet.'

'I've been to see my sister.'

The nurse helped Mark into his bed, then pressed a button

to raise it into a sitting position. Doctor Reeve waited for her to leave before asking, 'And how did that make you feel?'

'How do you think it made me feel?' There was a defensive edge to Mark's voice. He was tired of being asked questions.

'I imagine it made you feel upset, scared, angry and many other unpleasant emotions besides. I have to say I admire your bravery. If I was you, I'm not sure I'd have the strength to see my sister in that condition.'

Mark released a quivering breath that made his shoulders drop. 'It hurt so much to look at her, but I had to let her know she's not alone. Do you think she heard me?'

'It's impossible to say for sure, but there have been many cases of people who've woken from comas claiming to have been conscious of what was going on around them.'

It gave Mark a little lift to think that Charlotte might have heard him. Their relationship had never been an easy one. Charlotte was prone to behaving with the senseless cruelty of a spoiled child. And he wasn't exactly the easiest person to get close to. But none of that mattered any more. Whatever their differences, they were all each other had left.

Doctor Reeve took out a handheld tape recorder. 'The police have asked me to tape our sessions,' he explained, starting the tape-recording. 'Now, Mark, if you're feeling up to it, I'd like to delve a bit more deeply into what we talked about last night. Have you had any more dreams?'

'I dreamt about Charlotte. She was covered in blood.'

Doctor Reeve nodded as though he wasn't surprised. 'Did she say anything?'

'No. She just looked at me as though she wanted me to come to her.'

'And how about the other dream? Have you had it again?'

'No, but I will do.'

'How can you be sure of that?'

'Because it wasn't a normal dream.'

'But, again, how can you be sure of that?'

'I don't know, I just am.' Mark touched the back of his head. 'It's like I can feel the memories – memories I didn't even know I had – moving around back there. I just need someone to help me reach them.'

'Well that's what I'm here to do, Mark. What I don't want to do in any way is guide you. That's why I was so angry with Detective Monahan. By telling you what he did, he made it all the more difficult to identify whether your memories are real or imagined.'

'They're as real as what happened to me and Grace Kirby.' Mark's voice was sharp with conviction.

'They may well be.' Doctor Reeve spoke with infinite patience, as if he was dealing with a well-meaning but misguided child. 'But for now, Mark, I want to put aside the question of what's real and what's not. What I want to focus on is simply helping you open your mind and seeing what, if anything, comes up.'

'How will you do that?'

'There are several therapies we could explore that might prove effective. But the one that could perhaps produce the most immediate results is hypnosis. By that, I don't mean the kind of thing you've probably seen on the television. What I'm talking about is simply a state of deep relaxation. Right the way through, you'll remain perfectly aware of where you are and what's happening around you.'

'When do we start?'

'Right now, if you feel up to it.' Mark nodded to indicate he did, and Doctor Reeve continued, 'Before we start, Mark, it's very important that you don't try to force your thoughts in any direction. Focus on my voice and nothing else. Do you think you can do that?'

'Yes.'

In a slow, half-whispered monotone, Doctor Reeve began. 'Close your eyes. Take a deep breath, hold it for a few seconds, then exhale, letting all the tension go out of your body as you do so. Now I want you to listen only to the sound of my voice. All the other sounds inside and outside the hospital are fading away. And as you listen to my voice, I want you to concentrate on breathing slowly and deeply, feeling the air go in and out of your lungs. In... out... in... out... And each time you exhale, you feel your body getting heavier and heavier...'

At first, Mark was so stiff with tension and pain that he thought there was no way he'd be able to relax. But gradually and irresistibly the doctor's voice lulled him into a warm, tingling state. A sinking feeling came over him, as though the mattress was sucking him in like quicksand.

'That's good, Mark. Now I want you to imagine you're on the top floor of an office building, where the executives who make all the major decisions have their offices. And now you're walking down some stairs to the next floor, where advertising and marketing people are hard at work, searching for inspiration. You continue on down to a floor crowded with more workers busy at their computers. This is where the real work of the business is done, by people the executives are hardly aware of. And still you continue on down, floor by floor, until you come to the lowest level of the building – the basement.'

Mark had been so deeply immersed in Doctor Reeve's words he was barely conscious of them. They carried him with almost hallucinatory vividness through the scenes they described. But at the word 'basement' a pulse like an electric shock went from his brain to the pit of his stomach. His breathing ratcheted up a notch as the doctor continued, 'This is where the accounts are stored. There are two lines of filing-cabinets, one to either side of a room so long you can't see its far end. On each of the cabinets a year is written, starting with the year we're in now. You're walking between the cabinets. 2012, 2011, 2010...'

As Doctor Reeve counted down the years, Mark's stomach began to squeeze in time to the rhythm of his voice. And each squeeze pushed a churning ball of nausea further up inside him. It was the same feeling he'd had when DI Sheridan had played him the voice from the DVD – the same, only much, much stronger.

'2005, 2004...'

The ball was in Mark's chest, big and tight as a fist.

'1999, 1998...'

Afraid he was going to be sick, Mark tried to speak, but a kind of drugged paralysis weighed down his tongue.

Doctor Reeve's voice quickened, becoming insistent. 'You stop at the cabinet dated 1997 and open the drawer. Inside there's a row of files, each one dated with a month and day. You flick through the files until you come to one dated the first of September. Printed across it in capital letters are the words 'TOP SECRET. DO NOT OPEN. EVER."

Nausea rose painfully up Mark's throat. His head reeled with the effort of holding it back.

'You take out the file. You don't open it. I repeat, you don't open it. You simply place it on top of the filing cabinet.' Doctor Reeve spoke faster still. 'Now you're walking away from the cabinet, you're leaving the basement and climbing back up the stairs. You're climbing past the workers at their computers, past the advertising and marketing people. And as you climb, your body is growing lighter and you're becoming aware again of all the other sounds besides my voice inside and outside the hospital. Now you're at the top floor. I'm going to count slowly back from five, Mark, and when I reach one, you will open your eyes. And when you do, you will feel wide awake and relaxed. Five… four… three… two… one.'

Mark's eyes flicked open. He drew in a deep breath, flexing his fingers as if to check they still worked properly. Doctor Reeve sat silent, letting Mark come fully out of the hypnotic state. Finally, he asked, 'How did that feel to you, Mark?'

'I thought I was going to be sick. Is that normal?'

'There's no normal reaction when you go within yourself and look into your subconscious. Just as there's no normal reaction to abuse. The effects vary from person to person.'

'So the basement was my subconscious?'

Doctor Reeve nodded. 'It's the part of the mind where old memories are stored. It also protects us from our emotions. So when a memory is so traumatic it endangers our survival, the subconscious often buries it in some secret file.'

'Why didn't we open the file?'

'We will do, Mark. This is a gradual process. If we move too fast, it could do more harm than good. Over the next

216

few sessions we'll work on opening the file, and hopefully those buried memories will start to return. But even without opening it, what we've done today may well be enough to bring something new to the surface.'

'Will the memories come back to me in my dreams again?'

'Possibly. Or they may simply pop into your head when you least—'

Doctor Reeve broke off with an exclamation as Mark jerked forward suddenly and vomited down the front of his suit. He grabbed a bedpan for Mark to be sick into, then hurried from the room and returned with a nurse. As the nurse tended to Mark, the psychiatrist cleaned himself with paper towels at the sink.

'I'm sorry, Doctor Reeve,' Mark gasped between retches.

'It's fine, Mark.' Doctor Reeve gave him a tight little smile. 'We've made good progress today. I have to go now, but I'll check in on you tomorrow.'

Once the nurse had mopped up the vomit, changed the sheets and helped Mark into a fresh gown, she left him alone with some anti-nausea pills. He lay there going over the events of the therapy session, full of excited, fearful anticipation. From moment to moment, he half expected some gut-twisting image to hit his consciousness like a lightning bolt illuminating a darkened landscape. But nothing happened. Half an hour, then an hour passed. And still nothing popped into his head.

Doctor Goodwin entered the room. 'I hear you've been unwell, Mark. How are you feeling now?'

'Much better.'

The doctor did a quick check of Mark's vitals and had a look under his bandages. 'Everything seems to be fine. There's no sign of infection. It may be you had a bad reaction to your medication.'

'I think it was something to do with Doctor Reeve hypnotising me.'

Doctor Goodwin tilted an eyebrow at Mark. 'I've never heard of anyone reacting like that to hypnosis before. But then again, I'm no expert on such things. I'd imagine it's extremely dangerous for someone to vomit while under hypnosis.'

'It happened after Doctor Reeve brought me round.'

'So then maybe it had nothing to do with being hypnotised.'

Mark hadn't considered that possibility, but now it struck him with enough force to wrinkle his face.

'I just want to check your shoulder's range of motion.' Doctor Goodwin gently raised Mark's injured arm. 'Tell me if there's any pain.'

If the nausea had nothing to do with being hypnotised, then what did it have to do with? wondered Mark. Simultaneous to the thought, an image rose up like a living dead thing from some dark hole in his mind. He flinched away from it with a whimper.

'Does that hurt?' asked Doctor Goodwin.

Mark didn't hear him. At that instant, he wasn't even in the room. He was back in the basement – not the basement of his subconscious, but the bricks-and-mortar basement where his innocence had been so cruelly invaded. He caught the ghostly white flash of a face – Doctor Reeve's face. Then he found himself staring up into Doctor Godwin's concerned eyes once more. The doctor repeated his question, and when Mark shook his head, he stared at him as if unsure whether to believe him. He took the notes from the end of the bed and wrote on them. 'I'm going to try you on some different medication, and hopefully there'll be no more vomiting.'

Doctor Goodwin told Mark he'd be round to look in on him again in the afternoon and turned to leave. Even before he was out the door, Mark was reaching for Jim Monahan's card. Doctor Reeve had expressly told him not to have further contact with Detective Monahan. Right then that seemed like the best reason possible to put what little remaining trust he had in him.

With a trembling finger, Mark dialled Jim Monahan's mobile number. His call went straight through to an answering service. He tried the detective's home number. No one picked up. He waited a minute or two, then tried both numbers again, with the same results. 'Shit, shit,' he murmured through his teeth.

His eyes darted towards the door at the sound of movement in the corridor. Doctor Reeve had said he wouldn't be back until tomorrow. But the doctor was a lying, twisted bastard. Mark glanced around for something he might use to defend himself. There was only a plastic spoon from breakfast. He snapped its head off to create a jagged point. It wasn't much of a weapon, but it could do some damage if driven into an eye. He concealed it in his sling and turned to the phone. Again the answering service came on the line.

That decided him. He dialled 999 and asked to be put through to the police. 'I need to get a message to Detective Inspector Jim Monahan,' he told the police operator. 'I have some important information and urgently need to speak to him. My name's Mark Baxley.' His mouth twisted on the word *Baxley*. He made a mental note to look into changing his surname to his mother's maiden name. The operator asked for a contact number. Mark gave the number on the phone, adding, 'But make sure Detective Monahan knows I need to actually see him.'

The operator promised to call back and let Mark know when DI Monahan had been located. Eyes fixed on the door, Mark waited. His fingers slid inside the sling and curled around the spoon handle. The minutes passed like hours.

Chapter Sixteen

Jim lowered the passenger window, letting cool air wash over his tired eyes. It had been a long, long night. The search for Grace had continued at a frantic pace into the small hours and beyond into a grey day. The city had been, and was still being, scoured from the air and on the ground. Hundreds of city-centre revellers and motorists had been questioned. Grace's parents had been knocked up out of bed and their house searched. Old school friends of hers had been tracked down. All to no avail. Wherever Grace was hiding, it was off the grid of her former life in the city.

She couldn't remain hidden forever, though. A receptionist at a sleazy hotel on Furnival Gate had seen a resemblance between the CCTV still of Grace and a guest, the only difference being that the guest had short, bright red hair. The word was duly put out that Grace was believed to have cut and dyed her hair. More importantly, she was alone, isolated. Sooner or later, she would have to surface – maybe for food or maybe to feed her craving for another fix of revenge. And when she did, every police unit in the city would be waiting for her. She might elude them for a time, but in the end they'd catch her. The only question was, would she allow herself to be taken alive? Jim doubted she would. When he'd looked into her eyes, he'd seen sadness and pain. But above all he'd seen rage – an insatiable, all-consuming rage that demanded retribution at any cost.

As Amy drove him home in a replacement car from the motor pool, Jim went over and over in his head what he'd done. And the more he thought about it, the less certain he was as to the right or wrong of it. Had warning Grace been a moment of madness or a moment of sanity? Maybe only time would tell. He knew this much – if anyone found out about it, it would cost him a lot more than his job. He would more than likely end up sharing a prison wing with some of the scumbags he'd banged up. He gave a shake of his head, inwardly calling himself an idiot for not having listened to his instinct and walked out on the job. He'd known he wasn't up to it any more. He could have been lying on a beach somewhere, mulling over what he was going to do with the rest of his life. It was too late for that now. The chance to get off the ride was gone. The only choice left was to sit back and see where it took him.

Jim glanced at Amy. Her features were drawn from lack of sleep and set in a stony mask. She'd barely said a word to him since recovering her mobile phone. Her trust in him had been severely shaken. That much was plain. But he was fairly certain she didn't suspect him of anything more than sympathising with Grace's mission. She was too direct a person not to confront him if she suspected such a serious breach of duty.

Amy pulled over outside Jim's house. He hesitated to leave the car. A moment of uneasy silence passed, then he said, 'Look, about last night. What I said.'

'I think it would be best if we both forget what was said.'

'I'm not sure I can. This case has really got under my skin.' Jim's forehead creased. 'Or maybe it's not this case, maybe it's the cumulative effect of every case I've—'

'I'm knackered, Jim,' Amy broke in, her expression becoming even more remote. 'All I want to do right now is go home and sleep.'

Jim gave a little wince. He deserved her cold shoulder, but it stung nonetheless. 'I'll see you later.' He got out of the car and headed for his front door. In years gone by, Margaret would have been waiting to greet him with a mug of tea and an ear that was ready, if necessary, to listen to the story of his night's work. But now the house looked as empty and uninviting as a tomb. Heaving a sigh, he fished his keys out of his pocket.

He turned at the sound of Amy calling his name. She was holding the two-way radio receiver. 'It's dispatch. Mark Baxley wants to see you. Apparently he has some more new information.'

'Tell them I'm on my way.'

'I'd better come along. After all, you're under orders not to speak to him.'

A trickle of relief ran through Jim as he returned to the car. Exhausted as he was, he was in no mood to be alone with his thoughts. 'Something else must have come back to him.'

'Let's hope it's something that can save any more bloodshed.'

Jim bobbed his head, but silently wondered if he agreed. Even if Mark had a name for them, it was unlikely to do more than cast a toxic shadow over that person. The crime was too old. Any forensic evidence was long gone. Added to which, the only possible corroborating witness was a multiple murderer. He knew what Amy would say if he were to point this out to her – even if they couldn't get a conviction on this case, what Mark and Grace knew might lead them to other victims whose cases they could get a conviction on. And she'd be right too. That's what the job was all about, accumulating evidence, building cases. But that took time, and there were no guarantees. Sometimes all you had to go on was hope. *Time* and *hope*. Two things that were in acutely short supply for both him and Grace. Anger burnt his stomach like an ulcer at the thought that she faced the certainty of prison, while there was every chance her abusers would wriggle off the hook of the law.

Amy parked outside the Northern General's main entrance. 'You'd better wait here,' she told Jim. 'If Doctor Reeve catches sight of you, he's going to kick up an almighty stink.'

'I couldn't give a toss about that psychiatrist.'

Amy's voice sharpened. 'You may not give a fuck about orders any more, Jim, but I do. So either you wait here or I'll give the DCI a call and see what he has to say on the subject. Do I make myself clear?'

An acid retort as to exactly what he thought about anything Garrett had to say on any subject rose up Jim's throat. He bit down on it. They were both tired and emotional. Now wasn't the time to push Amy, not if he wanted to salvage what was left of their professional relationship. 'Perfectly.' As she got out of the car, he added, 'But Mark may well not be willing to open up to you. I'm the only one he trusts to believe him. Why else would he have asked to speak to me and not Garrett?'

Ignoring Jim, Amy slammed the door. He watched her head round the corner. Suddenly too tired to think any more, he closed his eyes. Almost at once, he felt himself dropping towards sleep.

****

Mark's fingers tightened on the handle of the broken spoon as the door opened. His grip relaxed when a male constable wearing a peaked cap that shadowed dark eyes stepped quickly into the room.

'Hello, Mark, I'm PC Stone,' the policeman said in a hushed voice. 'Detective Monahan sent me to fetch you. He's waiting to speak to you outside. Can you manage to walk?'

Nodding, Mark swung his legs out of bed. He slid his feet into slippers and pulled on a dressing-gown. PC Stone peered cautiously through the door's observation window. A nurse hurried by. He waited until she was out of sight before motioning for Mark to follow him.

Mark limped after PC Stone, out of the Critical Care ward. As they passed a porter pushing a trolley-bed, the constable dropped his head so that the peak of his cap all but hid his face. They entered a stairwell. Mark leaned heavily on the bannister, wincing with each step he descended.

'We need to hurry it up,' said PC Stone.

'I'm going as fast as I can.'

'Well that's not fast enough.' PC Stone stooped, hooking one arm behind Mark's legs and the other around his back. As Mark was lifted off his feet, he noticed that PC Stone was wearing black leather gloves. PC Stone jogged down the remaining stairs. He set Mark back on his feet and peeped through a door. Taking hold of Mark's upper arm, he drew him into a deserted corridor. Half supporting, half pulling Mark along, the constable headed for a door at the corridor's end.

'Take it easy,' said Mark, stumbling on his injured leg, losing one slipper. But instead of slowing, PC Stone quickened his pace. 'Hey, what about my slipp—'

'Cut the chatter,' broke in PC Stone. 'Someone might hear you.'

'So what? We're not doing anything wrong.'

'You mean, you're not doing anything wrong. I'll lose my job if I'm seen here with you. Is that what you want?'

'Of course not.'

'Then save your voice for Detective Monahan.'

PC Stone cracked open the door. It led onto a quiet road at the side of the hospital. A black car with tinted windows was parked near the door. The constable guided Mark towards it. Keeping hold of Mark's arm, he opened the passenger door. When Mark saw the car's empty interior, he sucked in a sharp breath and tried to shake himself free. But PC's Stone's grip was on him like a handcuff.

'What the fuck is this?' Mark demanded.

In reply, PC Stone – assuming that was really his name – tried to shove Mark into the car. Pain flared in Mark's shoulder. The sensation awoke something inside him – the same something that had caused him to fight back against Stephen Baxley. He clenched his fist and swung wildly. But PC Stone wasn't a businessman whose reactions had been dulled by years of sedentary living. He swayed away from the punch, and with a snake-fast movement, whipped his knuckles across Mark's cheek. Mark rocked on his heels and would have fallen but for the hand on his arm. The bittersweet taste of blood filled his mouth. Tears blurred his vision. Through them he saw a figure emerge from the hospital.

****

Amy took the lift up to the Critical Care ward. Her brow furrowed when she entered Mark's room and saw the empty bed. She approached the nurses' station and asked, 'Where's Mark Baxley?'

'He should be in his room,' replied the nurse on duty.

'Well he's not there.'

'Are you sure?'

'See for yourself.'

The nurse moved from behind her desk and poked her head into Mark's room. She turned, frowning, to Amy. Then, as if something had occurred to her, she hurried towards the far end of the corridor and looked into another room. 'I thought maybe he'd snuck out to see his sister,' she explained. 'But he's not here either.'

'Excuse me,' said a porter. 'Are you looking for the boy from room five?'

'Yes. Have you seen him?' asked Amy.

The porter nodded. 'He was with a policeman.'

The creases on Amy's forehead sharpened. What the hell was going on? Was this Jim's doing? If so, she was going to tear him a new one. 'Where?'

'They went into a stairwell. I thought it a bit odd they weren't using the lifts, what with the boy's leg being bad.'

The porter's words echoed Amy's thoughts. Why would Mark and whoever he was with take the stairs unless they were trying to avoid her? The question reinforced her suspicion that Jim was pulling a fast one. 'How long ago?'

'Two, three minutes tops.'

'Show me.'

The porter led Amy to the stairwell. She thanked him and descended the steps, taking several at a time. Her gaze scoured the corridor, fixing on a slipper left in the middle of the floor. Did it belong to Mark? If so, why had he left it behind? Her irritation turned to unease. What if this had nothing to do with Jim? What if something sinister was at play? Her movements quicker now, but more cautious, she made for the door at the end of the corridor.

As she stepped outside, she saw Mark struggling with a much larger man. The man was wearing a constable's uniform, but she didn't recognise him.

'Move away from him!' Amy yelled at Mark's assailant, mentally filing away his particulars as she flicked open an extendable metal truncheon. He was well built, Caucasian, five foot eleven to six foot, with a squarish face, a flat, boxer's nose, and dark brown eyes peering out from under a thick monobrow. He thrust his hand into his jacket and withdrew something that gave her a sick jolt in her stomach.

'Stop where you are! Toss the truncheon and get on the ground!' The man's voice was hard and flat as a gravestone. It was a voice that meant business. As did the pistol in his hand.

'OK, just don't shoot.' Amy lowered her head submissively, but kept her eyes fixed on the man. It flashed through her mind that whoever he was, he wasn't simply intent on killing Mark, otherwise both Mark and herself would already be dead.

'Shut your fucking mouth and do as I say!'

White-faced with adrenaline, Amy threw aside the truncheon and dropped to her haunches. The man took aim at her head.

****

'Don't!' cried Mark, grabbing for the gun. Again, PC Stone was too fast for him. He drew the gun upwards so that Mark's hand closed on air. Then he slammed its butt down on Mark's bandaged shoulder. Pain exploded through Mark, crumpling his legs. Eyes squeezed into agonised slits, he saw Amy flash past him. Her shoulder brushed his, then connected with PC Stone's chest. Breath whistled through the PC's teeth. He staggered, but didn't go down. Amy seized the gun with both hands. For an instant it seemed she would succeed in wresting it from PC Stone's grasp. But then he let go of Mark and brought his free hand down in a powerful chopping blow to the side of her neck. She sagged to her knees, still holding onto the gun. He twisted its barrel towards her, gradually angling it up beneath her chin.

Mark's eyes expanded into horrified saucers as the gun went off with an ear-shattering blast. The bullet passed through Amy's throat and grazed Mark's right forearm. She was flung backwards against his legs, her body spasming violently, foamy red bubbles oozing from the hole in her neck. Mark gaped down at her, his eardrums whining like a swarm of mosquitoes. Blood dripped from his arm, mingling with the rapidly widening pool of her blood.

'Stupid dumb bitch!' growled PC Stone, catching hold of Mark again, jerking him upright and stabbing the gun into his back.

This time Mark didn't resist as he was thrust towards the rear of the car. His face was devoid of all expression except the sudden blankness of shock. He had an odd, woozy, numb sensation between his ears. The world seemed to be receding and advancing in waves. PC Stone opened the boot, shoved him into it, then slammed it shut. Blackness enveloped him like a coffin.

Chapter Seventeen

Jim's eyes blinked open. A sound had jerked him awake – a sound like an exhaust backfiring. He glanced around. There were no vehicles moving in the car park. A frown wrinkled his brow. The sound had seemed very close. As he turned to check the dashboard clock to see how long he'd been asleep, the roar of a rapidly accelerating engine flared from around the corner of the building. A squeal of tyres biting into the tarmac had him reaching for the door handle. He headed towards where the sound had come from, a sense of foreboding nibbling at his mind, telling him to walk faster. A sudden cry went up. It wasn't a cry of anger, it was a cry of horror. It came again, forming itself into words. 'Help! Somebody help!'

As Jim broke into a run, his cop's brain quickly put together a scenario of what might have gone down. The loud bang, engine and tyre noise could have been a vehicle crashing into something – or someone – before speeding off. In other words, a hit-and-run. He rounded the corner fully expecting to be confronted by someone seriously, maybe even fatally, injured. Not for one second, though, did he expect that someone to be Amy.

Jim came to a stop as though he'd been turned to stone. The instant he saw the coin-sized hole in Amy's neck, he knew it was a bullet wound. The edges of the wound were ragged and blackened, and a fan-shaped area of seared skin radiated upwards from it, indicating that the muzzle of the gun had been pressed against the neck at an angle. Blood oozed rather than spurted from the hole, giving him hope that the bullet had missed the carotid artery. Amy's eyes were closed and she didn't appear to be breathing. But a few faint twitches in her limbs showed that she wasn't yet a corpse.

A woman was staring slack-jawed at Amy, seemingly too shocked to do anything but call out over and over for help. 'Look at me!' Jim shouted at her. She raised her teary gaze to his. 'I need you to go tell the receptionist there's a policewoman down with a gunshot wound to the throat. Understand?'

The woman nodded, then ran towards the hospital's main entrance. Jim dropped to his knees and felt for a pulse in Amy's wrist. He found one, weak and thready as a parched stream. Parting her lips, he saw that her mouth was full of bloody chunks of vomit. He rolled her onto her side and pushed his fingers inside her mouth to clear it away and check she hadn't swallowed her tongue. As he did so, he exposed the horrendous, flared exit-wound at the base of her head. *This is hopeless. She's as good as dead.* The thought dropped on him like a hammer. He thrust it away, telling himself that Charlotte Baxley had survived worse. He returned Amy onto her back and tried to give mouth-to-mouth. Bloody bubbles inflated from the bullet hole. He pressed his palm over it and tried again. This time her chest inflated, but only a fraction. Her windpipe was too full of blood for much air to get through.

Jim lifted his head at the sound of footsteps slapping the pavement. A medical crash team was rapidly approaching. He straightened and stepped away from Amy. One of the doctors quickly attempted to insert a breathing tube into her throat. Another asked Jim, 'What's her name?'

'Amy Sheridan.'

'How long ago was she shot?'

'I'm not exactly sure, maybe three or four minutes.'

'What about you?' The doctor gestured at the blood coating Jim's hands and shirt. 'Are you hurt?'

Jim shook his head. 'It's her blood.'

'I can't get the tube in,' said the doctor who was stooping over Amy. 'We have to get her to surgery right away.'

Jim pressed a hand to his forehead as Amy was manoeuvred onto a stretcher and wheeled towards the main entrance. He followed her as far as the doorway. There was nothing more he could do to help her. All he could do now was his job. He sought out the woman who'd found Amy. 'Did you see what happened?'

Shoulders quaking, she mutely shook her head.

Jim displayed his ID to the busy reception area. 'My name's Detective Inspector Jim Monahan. Did anyone see anything?' He received no replies. 'Make sure everyone remains where they are,' he said to a security guard. Then he sprinted back to the car, his brain whirring like an overwound watch. He couldn't believe the shooting had been random. It had to have something to do with the case. But what possible reason could anyone have for targeting Amy? And who was the shooter? Grace Kirby's face rose into his mind. He thrust it away. Whatever else Grace was, she wasn't a cop-killer.

There was no need to call in the incident. The two-way radio was already abuzz with talk of it. Four words – words

233

every copper dreads hearing – kept coming through the hum of voices. 'Shots fired! Officer down!'

The new mobile phone Jim had been issued buzzed in his pocket. He answered it without looking to see the caller's number, knowing it had to be Garrett. The DCI's voice came urgently down the line. 'We're getting reports that a policewoman has been shot at the Northern General. Where are you?'

'The Northern General.' Jim swallowed a tightness in his throat. 'It's Amy.'

There was a second of stunned silence. Then Garrett said something Jim had never heard him say before. 'Oh fuck. How bad is it?'

'It's bad. She's in surgery. She was hit in the throat.'

'What happened?'

'I didn't see.'

'Then find someone who did. I'm on my way. I'll be with you in ten minutes.'

Jim's voice became even heavier as a thought came to him. 'Someone needs to contact Amy's husband.'

'I'll do it.'

'Are you sure?' Jim tried not to sound as relieved as he felt. 'Maybe it should come from me, seeing as I was with her.'

'That's exactly why you shouldn't do it. Besides, I need you to focus on doing what you do best – your job.'

'Yes, sir.'

Jim returned to the spot where Amy had been shot. A man in a porter's uniform was looking at the blood stain. 'Get away from that!' shouted Jim.

The porter stepped back. 'I just wondered if she'd found him.'

'Who's she?'

'The policewoman. She was looking for that lad from Critical Care. The one who was shot.'

Jim's heart lurched. *Mark! Amy had been out here looking for Mark!* 'Are you saying he's gone missing?'

The porter nodded and told Jim what he'd told Amy. Jim's head throbbed with the realisation that the shooter had been after Mark not Amy. And it seemed they'd got him too. But who was behind his kidnapping? Obviously not Grace. Now another face came into Jim's mind. *Bryan Reynolds*. Jim's hands clenched. It had to be Reynolds. Who the hell else was there with the possible motive and the muscle to pull off something like this?

'What did the cop look like?' asked Jim.

'He was a big bloke. I didn't get a good look at his face. But they'll have him on camera. There's CCTV all over the hospital.'

'Stay here. Make sure no one comes anywhere near this area.'

As Jim rushed back to the main entrance, he phoned Garrett and filled him in on what he'd found out, adding, 'We should send a unit to pick up Bryan Reynolds.'

'We've already been through this, Detective,' said Garrett. 'There's absolutely no proof that Reynolds is in any way connected to this.'

'What? Open your eyes! This has got that fucker's name written all over it.'

'Probable cause!' The words echoed down the line like an insult. 'We need probable cause before we haul someone in for questioning. Or have you forgotten that?'

Jim took a steadying breath. As much as he hated to admit it, Garrett was right. There was no chance Reynolds would voluntarily come in for questioning. And arresting him based on a hunch would do more damage than good. 'No, sir.'

'Then let's find what we need to nail the bastard who's behind this.'

Jim approached the security guard and said, 'Take me to the hospital's CCTV control room.'

He followed the guard along a series of corridors to a door. The guard tried the handle, but the door was locked. He knocked on it. There was no response. 'That's odd,' he said. 'The CCTV's supposed to be manned at all times.'

'Have you got a key?'

'No.'

'Move away from the door.'

Jim withdrew his truncheon and extended it to its full length. Once, twice, three times, he slammed the flat of his foot into the door. The lock gave way with a splintering crack and the door burst inwards. A security guard was lying face down on the floor of the control room, blindfolded and gagged with duct tape, his hands and feet bound with plastic cuffs. Jim peeled away the tape. 'Who did this?'

'I don't know,' said the guard. 'I think there was only one of them. They were wearing a balaclava.'

Jim turned his attention to the bank of CCTV screens. All the displays were ominously blank. He took a pair of latex gloves out of his pocket and handed them to the other guard. 'Put those on and check what the cameras have recorded.'

The guard turned the CCTV system on. 'It's not showing anything. The hard drive seems to have been wiped.'

Jim's expression registered no surprise. It had already become apparent to him that whoever had pulled off this job was a stone-cold professional. He dug his fingers into his forehead. Questions were coming at him faster than he could think. Did Mark's kidnapping have something to do with his recovered memories? And if it did, who could possibly have leaked the information? And why hadn't Mark simply been shot dead? But one question above all others vibrated round and round his head until he felt as though his skull was about to explode: would this even be happening if Grace Kirby had been apprehended?

****

As the car wove its way at breakneck speed through the city's streets, Mark was thrown about inside the boot like a sack of potatoes. He made no attempt to brace himself. The image of the bullet ripping through Detective Sheridan's throat was frozen in his mind's eye, paralysing him with horror. He expected the vehicle to screech to a halt at any second, the boot to fly open and his life to be brought to an equally violent end. His head slammed into something metallic. Rather than dazing him further, the impact snapped him out of his stupor. He groped at the object. It was a jerrycan slosh-full of – from the smell of it – petrol. The car swerved sharply. A nearby vehicle's horn blared.

With his good arm and both feet, Mark hammered at the underside of the boot lid, shouting, 'Help! Help!' But after several minutes of frantic exertion, he gave up, realising he was achieving nothing beyond exhausting what little strength he had. A choking sob rose into his throat. *He's going to kill me, he's going to fucking kill me!* The thought beat against his brain in time to the rhythm of his panicked pulse. *No*, said another part of him. *Whoever he is, he's obviously not just out to kill me. So what's his game? Maybe he wants to find out what I know and who I've spoken to.* That had to be it! The thought held no consolation. If true, it meant he was still facing death, but possibly with torture beforehand.

Once more, helplessness threatened to throw Mark into a catatonic stupor. He fought off the feeling. If he was going to survive this, he had to act now while his hands and feet were free. He felt around the boot. It was bare, except for the jerrycan. He turned his attention to the lock. There was a little rim around it. An idea occurred to him. The boot of his car had a false bottom that concealed a spare tyre and all the tools necessary to fit it. If this boot contained a tyre-jack, maybe he could use it to prise the lock apart. And even if that wasn't possible, at the very least he'd have a weapon to defend himself with other than the broken spoon.

Mark ran his fingers around the edge of the boot's base until he found a gap he could push them into. They curled around the underside of what felt like a sheet of wood topped with a rough material. Wrenching at it, he managed to bend it upwards a few centimetres. A groan whistled through his teeth as he removed his arm from the sling and felt underneath the false bottom. There was a spare tyre but no tools – at least, not within easy reach. He stretched out his arm until it felt as if his wound was about to tear open. His fingers brushed against a metallic handle. With an effort that made sweat pop out all over his body, he wrapped his fingers around it and pulled it free. It was a bolt wrench. He lay still for a few seconds, letting the pain subside. Before he could make another attempt to find a tyre-jack, the car screeched to a halt.

Mark's stomach knotted with indecision. Should he fight? Or should he wait for a better chance to escape? Part of him cried out that it would be crazy to fight a gun with a wrench. But another, louder, part of his brain shouted, *There won't be a better chance. You either fight now or die later!* He rolled onto his front, concealing the wrench under himself. The engine died. There was the sound of a door closing, then the boot popped open. Sunlight flooded in, dazzling him. Through blinking eyes, he saw that PC Stone was no longer holding the gun. As gloved hands hauled him upright, Mark whipped the wrench round. It connected flush with the side of PC Stone's head, sending him staggering. Mark clambered out of the boot, aiming another blow at his captor. This time the wrench was deflected by a forearm. There was a dull crunch of metal against bone, but PC Stone didn't give the slightest indication that he was feeling any pain. He caught hold of the wrench and yanked it from Mark's grasp. He thrust his other hand into his jacket.

Mark turned and ran as fast as his injured leg would allow. He knew it was hopeless. After all, he couldn't outrun a bullet. But he also knew that he would rather die trying to escape than let PC Stone choose the time and method of his death. He was on a narrow road, flanked by trees. He passed a small red car, parked and empty. Maybe two hundred metres up ahead, he could see a broader road with a row of semi-detached houses on its far side. He swerved towards the trees, thinking it would be harder for PC Stone to get a clear shot at him in amongst them. Something hit him hard in the back, knocking him off his feet. Bolts of pain raced through his limbs, stealing their strength. *Have I been shot?* he wondered. His question was answered a second later when PC Stone arrived at his side and stooped to retrieve the wrench.

'Nice try,' growled PC Stone, kneeling on Mark's back. A howl tore from Mark's throat as his wrists were twisted together and bound with plastic cuffs. 'Quiet, or I'll have to kill you.' It wasn't a threat, it was a simple statement of fact.

Mark bit down on his scream. Silent tears streamed from his eyes as he was hauled to his feet and shoved towards the red car. PC Stone opened the boot and took out a scrap of material, which he stuffed into Mark's mouth and secured with duct tape. Then Mark's world went black again as a cloth bag was put over his head. PC Stone pushed him into the boot and flipped his legs in after him. Pain came at him from so many different directions that he couldn't identify them all. His straining ears caught the sound of footsteps moving away from the car. Then another sound like water being sloshed around. There was a faint whoosh. An acrid smoky smell seeped through the cloth bag. For a sickening second, Mark thought the red car had been set alight. Then one of its doors slammed shut and the engine came alive.

At first the car moved fast enough to bounce Mark around. But it soon slowed to a steady pace. Drifting in pain-addled darkness, he struggled to hold on to a sense of time. Unconsciousness pulled at his mind. He refused to give in to it, focusing on slowing his breathing. *Be calm*, he kept telling himself. But no matter how hard he tried, he couldn't keep his body from trembling. He tried to wriggle free of the cuffs, but they were on so tight his hands tingled with numbness. He rolled around, feeling for any sharp edges he might use to saw through the plastic. There were none. More out of desperation than hope, he drove his knees again and again against the underside of the boot. He kept at it until, after what seemed like hours but might have been minutes, the car pulled to a stop.

There was a muffled metallic scraping. The car pulled forwards a few metres. Then the sound came again, suggesting to Mark that a garage door had been opened and closed. The boot clicked open. Hands grabbed him and hauled him out of it. He was manoeuvred forwards until his face came into contact with a wall. A hand pushed him down to a cold concrete floor.

There was a moment of silence that pressed against Mark like a dead weight. Then came the trill of a mobile ringtone. 'I thought we agreed you wouldn't call unless it was an emergency,' said PC Stone. After a brief pause, he continued, 'No, sir, I don't call this an emergency. Everything's under control... She gave me no choice... I don't want to say any more about that right now, sir. I'll give you a full report when I collect payment.'

Sir... full report. The words made the hairs on Mark's neck bristle. They sounded like the sort of thing a policeman would say. Was it possible PC Stone really was who he said he was? *How else could he have known I wanted to speak to Detective Monahan?* Mark asked himself. The question prompted another one: was Detective Monahan involved in the kidnapping? Mark gave a sharp shake of his head. Detective Monahan had gone against Doctor Reeve. Surely that proved he wasn't involved. Unless it had all been an act, a ploy to lure him out of the hospital. No, he couldn't bring himself to believe that. Jim Monahan was the only one who'd been straight with him. Hadn't he? Doubts crowded in on him like an angry mob. For an instant, he burnt with a raw hatred that overrode his fear. Not only had Stephen Baxley crippled his arm, he'd also crippled his capacity to trust.

'I don't think that's a good idea,' PC Stone told whoever was on the other end of the line. As if he'd been reprimanded, he added quickly, in a lower tone, 'I realise that, sir, but you should still be extremely careful what you say to him. I'm putting you on to him now.'

Mark felt the phone being pressed to his ear.

'Hello, Mark.' The voice was as accentless as a BBC newsreader.

Are you certain he won't remember anything? The words from Mark's dream echoed back into his mind. A familiar surge of nausea told him that the person who'd spoken those words and the man on the phone were one and the same.

'You don't remember me, but I remember you.' The man's voice took on a sickeningly sensual thickness. 'How could I ever forget the pleasure you gave me?'

I didn't fucking give you anything, thought Mark. *You took it.*

'That film I had your father – or, more accurately, should I say, your step-father – make is still one of my most treasured possessions.' A sigh filled the line. 'I don't suppose it's any consolation, but I want you to know that I regret it's come to this. Sadly, Stephen's stupidity has forced me into this course of action. I don't blame him so much as I blame myself. I should

242

have known: once a pleb, always a pleb. But there you are, you live and learn. Goodbye, my sweet little boy. We won't speak again.'

The phone was removed from Mark's ear. PC Stone spoke into it again. 'Yes, sir... We sit tight and wait for the whore to come to us... I don't think it'll be long. She'll have to make her next move quickly, if she's going to make it at all... Then we kill all the birds with one stone.'

Mark wondered who *the whore* was. Was it Grace Kirby? Who else could it be? So she was still alive! Although, from the sounds of it, probably not for much longer. It seemed that all the loose ends were being tied up. But what had been meant by *make her next move*? Was Grace out for some kind of revenge? Blackmail maybe? Or maybe something more straightforward and bloody.

'No, don't go home,' continued PC Stone. 'The doctor's the one who's convinced this will work, so let him take the risk... If he's wrong, he'll be dead. Either way, I'll call you when it's over... I'll use the same code as before: three rings, hang up, wait ten seconds, then another three rings.'

Suffocating silence settled over Mark again. He cringed against the wall, wondering how long he had left to live. An hour? Two hours? Since his so-called father's murderous rampage, he'd asked himself more times than he could count whether he'd want to live if Charlotte died. Now the answer stood out in his mind like letters of fire. Yes! He wanted to live, however desolate his life might be.

Chapter Eighteen

What if this is my fault? What if Amy and Mark die because of me? The questions crashed into Jim's brain like stones hurled through glass. He shook his head in an effort to thrust them away. He needed to focus on the job. With every passing second the odds of Mark being rescued alive decreased. There would be plenty of time later to agonise about the possible repercussions of having given Grace the heads-up.

Jim's phone rang. It was Garrett. 'I'm at the main entrance. Where are you?' asked the DCI. Jim told him, and Garrett said, 'Wait there. I'll come to you.'

Moments later Garrett and Scott Greenwood appeared at the door to the CCTV control room. Garrett's eyebrows pinched together at the sight of Jim. 'It's Amy's blood,' said Jim, reading the question in his commanding officer's eyes.

'Have you heard how she's doing?' asked Scott.

'No.'

'So let's go and find out,' said Garrett.

Jim and the DCI went in search of someone who could tell them what they wanted to know, leaving Scott in control of the scene.

'What have you got for me?' asked Garrett.

Jim opened his mouth to reply, but his throat was suddenly too constricted to speak. Again the questions battered at him. *What if, what if...?*

'Detective?'

Focus, you son of a bitch! Clearing his throat with a noise like a strangled groan, Jim relayed all he knew.

'Good work,' said Garrett.

Jim's lips twisted into a grimace. *Good work*. The words stung worse than any insult. Praise was the last thing he'd expected or wanted to hear from Garrett.

'Four bodies in three days. And now this,' continued Garrett, shaking his head. 'I've never known anything like it. This damned city's turning into a warzone.'

The DCI accosted a nurse and asked where the injured police officer had been taken. After making a quick phone call, she informed them that Amy was undergoing surgery. She led them to the Surgical Unit, where they were met by a surgeon. 'I'm afraid it's not good news,' he said. 'The bullet penetrated her trachea and oesophagus, and hit her spinal column.'

'So she's paralysed,' said Jim.

'It's too early to say for sure. We're still trying to establish whether the spinal cord has been damaged. What I can tell you is that we've managed to stop the bleeding and insert a breathing tube.'

'What are her chances?' asked Garrett.

The surgeon's expression suggested they weren't good. 'About the best we can say right now is that the speed with which she received treatment has given her a fighting chance.'

The surgeon went on to say how the next few hours were

going to be critical, but Jim wasn't listening any more. There was a tingling pain in his chest; blood was pounding dizzily in his ears. He dropped onto a chair, head lowered, hands pressed to his face. He looked up at a touch on his shoulder. 'Go and get yourself cleaned up, Detective,' said Garrett. 'Then we need to talk.'

His shoulders slumped under the weight of his thoughts, Jim headed into a nearby toilet. He looked in the mirror and barely recognised the broken-down face that stared back at him with eyes full of haunted questions. He washed the blood off his hands and from around his mouth. But he couldn't wash the blood entirely from his sleeves. Or from his conscience.

Jim rolled up his sleeves and left the toilet. Garrett was talking to Detective Chief Superintendent Knight. The DCS was a tall, broad-shouldered man of about fifty-five, with hooded, serious eyes and a high forehead topped by short, iron-grey hair. He'd been with South Yorkshire Police for over thirty years, during which time he'd risen through the ranks from constable to heading up CID. Jim had got to know him well enough over the years on a professional, if not friendly, basis. He'd proved himself a competent DCI during his time with Major Incidents, gaining a reputation for being ruthless and relentless. But it had quickly become apparent that, like Garrett, he was more of a politician than a policeman. Rumour had it he was marked for one of the top jobs. Possibly even Chief Constable. Jim wouldn't have been surprised if the rumour proved true. Unlike Garrett, the Chief Superintendent possessed a charisma that inspired the officers serving under him.

'Jim, how are you holding up?' asked DCS Knight.

Jim shrugged away the question, as if to say, *What does it matter how I'm doing?*

'I know, I know. When something like this happens it makes everything else seem unimportant.' The DCS put a hand on Jim's shoulder. 'But you've still got to take care of yourself. If you'd like to talk to a welfare counsellor, I'll—'

Jim cut DCS Knight off with a shake of his head.

'There's no shame in it.'

'I know, but there's no need. Really. I'm OK.'

'Well how about taking some time off? You look as though you could do with a bloody good rest.'

'I'd rather drop dead than rest while the bastard who did this is still out there.'

DCS Knight's lips contracted into a grave but friendly smile. 'I expected nothing less from you, Jim.' He turned back to Garrett. 'However many officers you need, I'll see that you get them. We need to send out a clear message that this kind of thing won't be allowed to stand.'

'Thank you, sir,' said Garrett. 'And what about that other matter?'

'I'll leave that up to your judgement.'

Jim wondered what other matter they were referring to. The thought passed from his mind as Garrett gestured towards something behind him. 'I'd better go speak to him,' he said in a heavy voice.

Glancing round, Jim saw a man sitting bent almost double on a chair along the corridor. He recognised him from the photo on Amy's iPhone, although instead of happiness the man's face showed only pain and fear. Jim felt another sharp

247

constriction in his chest. DCS Knight took a dutiful breath. 'I'll do it. What's his name?'

'Justin Sheridan.'

As the DCS headed over to Amy's husband, Garrett fixed enquiring eyes on Jim. 'What do you think Mark was so eager to talk to you about?'

'My guess is he'd remembered more about what happened to him at the Winstanley house.'

'And you think that's why he was kidnapped?'

'I'd say that's a given. Which begs the question, who knows what we've been talking to Mark about?'

'Only Doctor Goodwin and Doctor Reeve.' Garrett pulled at his chin. 'Something doesn't add up here. If this is just about what Mark knows, why isn't he already dead?'

The words struck Jim with the force of an accusation as he found himself wondering whether this was as much about what Grace knew as what Mark knew. Perhaps Mark's kidnapper hoped to use him against her somehow. Jim struggled to keep from wincing away from his DCI's gaze.

Scott Greenwood appeared through a nearby door. 'The helicopter's spotted a burning car in Little Roe Wood, a few hundred metres from the Norwood Road.'

'The kidnapper must have switched cars,' said Jim.

'Get over there and check it out,' Garrett said to Scott.

As Scott headed back out the door, Garrett motioned for Jim to follow him. 'Where are we going?' asked Jim.

'To talk to Doctor Goodwin and anyone else on Critical Care who's had contact with Mark.'

'What about Doctor Reeve?'

'I've already contacted him. He's on his way here.'

When they entered the Critical Care Department, several pairs of worried-looking eyes turned towards them. They belonged to a cluster of nurses who were talking in hushed voices at their workstation. 'I'm so sorry about what's happened,' said one. 'I'm Head Nurse Jess Campbell. What can I do to help?'

'We need to talk to all staff members who've had contact with Mark Baxley since his admission, as well as anyone who was working at the time he went missing,' said Garrett.

'Of course. I'll gather together everyone on duty.' Nurse Campbell turned to one of her colleagues. 'Mary, you'd better start going through the rotas and putting together a list of names.'

'Have you got a room we can use?' asked Garrett.

'You can use the staffroom.'

'I'm also going to have to ask you to seal off Mark Baxley's room until my detectives and a forensics team have looked it over.'

Nurse Campbell's brow wrinkled. 'I hope there's not going to be a lot of people coming and going. The patients on this ward are all seriously ill. They need complete rest.'

'Don't worry. We'll keep a low profile. We won't disturb any patients unless it's absolutely necessary.'

Nurse Campbell led them to the staffroom. Garrett arranged three chairs in such a way that two were directly facing the third. 'I'll lead the questioning, OK?' The DCI said *OK* as if asking for Jim's approval. But he wasn't asking, he was ordering.

There was a knock at the door. Garrett opened it and a shaken-looking Doctor Reeve stepped into the room. There was a paleness at the edges of the psychiatrist's face and a faint sweaty sheen glistened on his forehead. 'I got here as fast I could,' he said, slightly breathless. 'Nurse Campbell just told me about Detective Sheridan. It's terrible. Terrible! What can I do to help?'

'You can start by answering some questions,' Jim put in before the DCI could reply, his voice hard, almost accusing.

Doctor Reeve's eyebrows bunched at Jim. 'I don't care very much for your tone.' His gaze moved to Garrett. 'Am I under some kind of suspicion, John?'

'Of course not, Henry,' Garrett reassured him, shooting Jim a sharp glance.

John. Henry. Jim could barely supress a snort of contempt. Not that it surprised him to learn that the two men were on first-name terms. They were both self-important somebodies. Naturally they would gravitate towards one another. He could just imagine them bonding over a round of golf.

Garrett motioned for Doctor Reeve to sit. Jim lowered himself onto a chair next to Garrett, statement pad in hand. He watched every movement of the psychiatrist's face as the DCI asked, 'Have you discussed the details of Mark's case with anyone other than myself, my detectives and Doctor Goodwin?'

Doctor Reeve swelled with offended dignity. 'Of course not. There's a little thing called patient confidentiality that I take very seriously.'

'I understand you've conducted a therapy session with Mark since we last spoke. How did it go?'

'I taped it as requested. The tape's in my car. I'll fetch it if you like.'

'I'll send a constable along with you for it later. For now just tell us about the session.'

The psychiatrist described how he'd attempted to stimulate Mark's subconscious through hypnosis.

'Did it produce any results?'

'It's far too early to tell. Even if Mark does have repressed memories, it takes time for the subconscious to let go of such things.'

'So Mark didn't mention anything about more memories coming back?'

Doctor Reeve shook his head. 'But if he had done, I would have treated what he told me with extreme caution. Mark's mental state was extremely fragile. I shudder to think what that poor boy must be going through right now.'

Jim gave the psychiatrist a weighing-úp look. His concern appeared to be genuine. But Jim had long ago learnt to trust his instincts over appearances. And his instincts told him there was something slightly off about this guy. It was more than simply being irritated by his condescending manner. He couldn't quite put his finger on what it was, but it gave him an uneasy feeling.

'Can you think of anyone Mark might have confided in?' asked Garrett.

'No. Mark has trust issues. It took me months to get him to open up about his feelings towards his fa… towards Stephen Baxley.'

'He didn't seem to have any problem trusting me,' Jim pointed out.

Doctor Reeve sighed as if dealing with a difficult patient. 'Mark was betrayed by the principal authority figure in his life. You've shown a willingness to go against authority. Hence Mark's readiness to trust you.'

'OK, Henry,' said Garrett. 'I think that's all for now. If we need to find you for any reason—'

'I'll be at home,' said Doctor Reeve, anticipating Garrett's question. 'I couldn't possibly concentrate on work knowing Mark's out there somewhere in mortal danger.'

'Thanks for your cooperation.'

Doctor Reeve waved the thanks away. 'I'm only sorry I couldn't be of more help.'

As soon as the doctor was out of the room, Jim said, 'Is that it? You're just going to let him walk out of here?'

The corner of Garrett's mouth twitched. 'What else do you expect me to do?'

'If it was up to me, I'd haul him down the station and give him a proper going over.'

'But it's not up to you, Detective Monahan. Doctor Reeve said nothing that in any way implicates him. What makes you think he'd do so if we took him in for further questioning?'

'He fancies himself as smarter than us. That arrogance could be his downfall. I think if I pushed his buttons enough, he'd maybe say more than he meant to.'

'And I get the feeling that your obvious personal dislike of Henry Reeve is muddying your thinking on this.'

Jim's voice rose a notch in frustration. 'Mark asks to speak to me urgently. The next thing, he's kidnapped. That's no coincidence.'

'I agree, but what makes you think Henry Reeve had anything to do with it?'

'Reeve is the only one at the hospital who's got history with

Mark. Who else could possibly have reason to want Mark kidnapped? And if the information about Mark didn't come from him or someone else around here, where did it come from? One of our own?'

Garrett's face drew into sharp lines at the suggestion. 'Don't be ridiculous! We don't know that any information was deliberately leaked. Use your head, Detective. Mark called dispatch trying to contact you. Dispatch put the call out over the radio. Anyone listening on a scanner would have heard it and probably come to the same conclusion you did.'

Jim sat in frowning silence for a moment, then conceded begrudgingly, 'Maybe, but—'

Garrett cut him off with an exasperated hiss. 'We can go round in circles all day talking about maybes and perhaps. Let me tell you what I do know: Henry Reeve is one of the country's most respected psychiatrists. The Chief Superintendent knows him personally and has vouched for his integrity. What's more, Doctor Reeve has acted with nothing but the utmost professional propriety. Unlike you, Detective.'

Jim blinked away from Garrett's gaze. *Unlike you, Detective.* There was no arguing with those words. He suddenly found himself doubting his ability to think clearly. Maybe he *was* letting personal feelings get in the way of his professional judgement. After all, wasn't that what had happened with Grace Kirby?

'And I'll tell you something else,' continued Garrett. 'I'm starting to have grave doubts whether you're fit for duty. In the past few days, you've walked off a crime scene, disobeyed orders, and displayed a general lack of judgement. In all honesty, Detective, the only reason you're still on this case is because I need every man in the field right now. Well, that and the fact that the Chief Superintendent remembers when you were one of our best officers.'

Jim recalled Garrett's parting question to Chief Superintendent Knight. *And what about that other matter?* He understood now what that other matter was. They'd been discussing whether he was fit for duty. His eyes dropped as Garrett said, 'Look, I realise there's not much love lost between us. But believe it or not, I have a lot of respect for you. So perhaps against my better judgement, I'm willing to give you another chance. But any more nonsense and I won't hesitate to drop you from the team, and possibly even take other disciplinary action. Do I make myself clear?'

There was an edge of compassion in Garrett's voice that caught Jim off guard. He looked up uncertainly, as if not quite sure of his DCI's motives. 'Crystal.'

'Good. And don't let me hear any more talk about one of our own being involved. I won't have anyone questioning the integrity of the department.'

'Sorry, sir. I was out of order. It won't happen again.'

'Then let's not waste any more time on the subject. There's a young man out there whose life depends on us working fast. Go tell Nurse Campbell we need to talk to Doctor Goodwin.'

As promised, Nurse Campbell was rounding up staff for questioning. She gave Doctor Goodwin a call on the internal telephone system. When he appeared, Garrett subjected him to a set of questions similar to those he had asked Doctor Reeve. In reply, the DCI received a similar set of answers. Jim sat grimly silent throughout, taking notes.

As Doctor Goodwin left the room, Garrett stood to leave

too, saying to Jim, 'I want you to stay here and continue the questioning. I'll send a constable to help organise things.'

'Where are you going?'

'To check on Detective Greenwood's progress. When you've finished here, you're to return to the station and write up your reports. And when you're done with that, go home. You look as though you haven't slept in a week.'

Jim released a heavy breath and rubbed his eyes. As far as he could see, it was a waste of time questioning the rest of Critical Care's staff. He was chomping at the bit to have a real go at Doctor Reeve. Or even better, haul Bryan Reynolds over the coals. Everything in him said they were the ones Garrett should be concentrating the team's resources on. But then again, how could he trust his own judgement when it might be down to him that his partner was now fighting for her life?

Chapter Nineteen

All afternoon Jim took down statements with a growing sense of frustration. After a couple of hours, a constable relayed the news to him that the burning car in Little Roe Wood was a black Subaru. What's more, a dog walker remembered seeing a red car parked in the same location earlier that day – the switch car, no doubt. They had no make or licence number, but it gave the searching officers something to go on. Maybe someone else in the area had seen a red car driving erratically. And maybe that same car had been caught somewhere on CCTV. It was such small details that might make the difference between Mark living or dying.

Jim suppressed the urge to abandon the questioning and rush off to join in the search. By the time he was finished, he felt like flinging his statement pad out of the window. He'd spoken to nearly two dozen nurses, porters, cleaners and laundry workers and had learnt nothing more than he already knew – namely, that no one had got a good look at the kidnapper's face.

He went in search of the Head Nurse and asked her to find out how Amy was doing. 'She's been transferred to the Post-Operative Surgical Unit,' Nurse Campbell informed him.

She pointed out the room where Amy was being kept. 'Her family's in with her at the moment.'

Jim peered through the observation window. Amy was hooked up to the usual array of monitors, tubes and life-support devices. Her neck was heavily bandaged and her hair had been shaved so that a metal halo could be screwed to her skull. The halo was held in place by bars attached to a padded plastic torso brace. Her husband was sitting at her side with his back to Jim. At the other side of the bed was a woman who from her age and looks had to be Amy's mother. The woman's eyes were swollen from crying. A doctor was standing at the end of the bed, making notes.

The woman glanced towards the door. Jim dodged out of sight. The last thing he felt ready to do was look Amy's mother in the eyes. He waited along the corridor for the doctor to come out. 'Excuse me, Doctor, I'm a colleague of Amy's. How's she doing?'

'I'm afraid she's in a critical condition.'

'Has she regained consciousness at any time?'

The doctor shook his head. 'We're keeping her fully sedated. Any neck movement could prove fatal. We believe the bullet nicked her spinal cord.'

'You believe? Does that mean you're not sure?'

'It means we won't be one hundred per cent certain until we've performed further exploratory surgery. We need to wait for the swelling around the wound to subside before—'

The doctor was interrupted by a loud beeping alarm going off on the nurses' station. 'Code blue, room seven,' said Nurse Campbell, rushing out from behind the desk. She followed the doctor into Amy's room. A second later, she ushered

Amy's husband and mother into the corridor.

'What's happening? What's happening?' the mother was frantically asking.

Another nurse hurried towards the room, pushing a crash cart with a defibrillator. A second doctor came running from the opposite direction.

'I think her heart stopped,' Amy's husband said through his hands.

Once all the members of the crash team were inside the room, the door was closed. Amy's mother and husband grasped each other's hands. Jim clutched his chest as though he was the one suffering a cardiac arrest. Every second of waiting was an agony, squeezing more of the breath and hope out of him. Minutes passed like hours. Finally, the door opened and one of the doctors stepped out. From the look on his face, Jim knew Amy was gone.

'I'm so sorry,' said the doctor.

'She's dead?' Amy's husband's voice twanged like a string about to snap.

The doctor nodded. 'The strain was too much for her heart.'

The mother let out a wail, grinding her head against her son-in-law's shoulder. The sound rang in Jim's ears like a death knell. He turned away from the scene, took several steps and swayed against a wall. The floor seemed to be heaving under him. He was vaguely aware that someone took his arm and guided him towards a chair. He shook them off and staggered from the ward. He couldn't seem to catch his breath. He had to get outside into the fresh air. He emerged from the hospital, half sobbing, half gasping. One thought kept screaming at him. *What have you done?*

'You OK, mate?' someone asked.

The voice brought Jim out of his thoughts. He ran to the car Amy had driven them there in. The keys were still in the ignition, where Amy had left them. *Amy. Dead! Oh Christ!* He started the engine and sped from the car park. He pulled over at the first off-licence he saw and bought a bottle of vodka. He gulped half of it down in one, desperately trying to silence his mind. But the torment was unremitting. He thought of the photo on Amy's phone – the happy children and their proud parents. And he thought of the grieving, devastated faces he'd left at POSU. The images tore through his consciousness like shards of shrapnel. Images. Memories. That was all that was left of Amy now.

What the fuck have you done?

Jim drove fast, not thinking about where he was going. Somehow he ended up outside the house where Margaret was living with her new bloke. It was a nice house – detached, decent garden – in a nice area. More than he'd been able to offer her. Not that she'd left him because of money. When she'd first moved in there, he'd spent many evenings watching it, waiting to catch a glimpse of her.

He felt a desperate need to talk to someone, to pour out his troubles, his confusion, his shame. And Margaret was the only person he knew who would understand what he was going through and why. The driveway was empty. The house looked empty too. He knew Margaret's routines. She wouldn't get home from work for half an hour or so yet. He threw back a swallow of vodka, relishing the burn as it hit his stomach. He closed his eyes. Tears trailed down his stubbly cheeks. He took another hit. His mind began to grow hazy. At last the alcohol was working.

Jim didn't realise he'd fallen asleep until the sound of a car door shutting woke him. He'd been dreaming. In his dream Amy was alive and well. But now the awful truth came flooding back, wrenching the breath from his throat. There was a car in the drive. Margaret was unloading shopping bags from its boot. Bobbed brown hair framed her hazel-eyed, strong-featured face. A black trouser suit outlined her solidly built but not overweight figure. She was in good shape for a woman of her age. But then she'd always looked after herself. She'd looked after both of them.

She turned towards Jim as he got out of the car. Her eyebrows lifted. 'Jim, what are you doing here?'

'I... I...' Jim stammered, suddenly afraid that even Margaret wouldn't understand the why of his answer.

Margaret's surprise turned into concern as she took in her ex-husband's haggard face. 'You look terrible. Are you ill?'

'No,' said Jim, but he felt like saying, *Yes, I'm ill. I'm sick of sleeping alone, of eating alone, of all the bitterness and resentment. But most of all I'm sick of the job, of watching good people die and bad people prosper.*

Margaret looked at Jim, caught between concern and uncertainty. 'Do you want to come inside? Alan won't be home for a while.'

Jim shook his head, jaw clenching at the thought of going inside the house where the woman he loved went to sleep and woke up with another man. He wanted to go somewhere where they could talk without fear of interruption, where they could hold each other. But he knew that would never happen. She wasn't his to hold any more. The job had taken her from him. Bryan fucking Reynolds had taken her from him! His fingers twitched into fists. Seeing a glimmer of alarm pass over Margaret's face, he unclenched them and lowered his gaze.

'Don't do that,' she said. 'Look at me and tell me what's wrong.'

The words were as familiar to Jim as his ex-wife's soft but firm voice. She'd said them to him a hundred times before, whenever he used to retreat into himself, overwhelmed by feelings of futility and defeat. He lifted his eyes to hers. He was struck, as he had been the first time they met, by how kind her eyes were. During the years of their marriage a sadness had also crept into them. It wasn't there any more. He knew then that he'd been wrong to doubt whether Margaret would understand. He knew too that he couldn't lay his troubles on her. That burden was no longer hers to carry.

'I'm sorry, Margaret. I shouldn't have come here.' Jim ducked back into his car. As he reversed out of the street, Margaret raised her hand as if unsure whether to wave good-bye or gesture him back to her.

Shudders racked Jim as he drove towards the city centre. He'd never accepted that Margaret was better off without him. He'd always held onto the belief that one day she would wake up and see that she'd made a terrible mistake. But now, after five years, he was the one who'd woken up and seen that she'd made the best decision of her life by leaving him. The realisation winded him. Tears burnt his eyes.

Alcohol swirled in Jim's veins. Faces swirled in his head. Amy. Grace Kirby. Mark Baxley. But one face in particular kept flashing into his thoughts – an angular, scarred, broken-nosed face with a taunting smirk at the corners of its mouth. 'Bryan Reynolds.' The name came with such force that flecks of spittle sprayed the windscreen. He changed gear with a savage movement and punched the horn, forcing his way through the evening traffic.

Jim turned onto a backstreet and pulled over opposite a bar with blacked-out windows and a blue-and-red neon sign depicting a busty woman straddling the words 'The Minx'. A pair of burly bouncers filled the doorway. Knocking back the dregs of vodka, Jim got out of the car and approached them.

The bouncers exchanged an amused glance at the sight of Jim's unshaven face. 'Haven't you ever heard of a razor, mate?' one remarked sarcastically, scanning him with a handheld metal detector.

Jim resisted the urge to smash his fist into the man's face. The detector beeped on his jacket pocket. He took out his car keys. The bouncer scanned him again, and when the detector remained silent, gestured for him to go on in.

'Twenty quid admission,' said a heavily made-up woman in tight leather gear behind a Perspex screen. 'And another twenty for a lap-dance. Touch any of the girls and you're out.'

Jim paid and entered a room gaudily decorated in red and purple. Paintings of scantily clad women adorned the walls. There was a mirrored bar in one corner. Tables and chairs were arranged around a square stage with six dance poles in the centre of the room. Spotlights cut through the gloom, illuminating a woman wearing only a thong and high heels. She pumped her body against one of the poles in time to loud hip-hop music. Several curtained booths where private dances could take place lined the left-hand wall. At this early hour, none of them were occupied. A scattering of punters were watching the performance, sipping overpriced drinks.

Bryan Reynolds was nowhere to be seen. But Jim knew he would be showing his bastard face soon enough. He'd spent sufficient time surveilling Reynolds over the years to learn his routine. Almost every evening between eight and nine o'clock, Reynolds headed out to The Minx. He usually made his way straight to an office at the back of the club, where he'd spend the next few hours locked away, getting down to his real business. Not that any proof that the club was a front for his drug dealing had ever been obtained. The place had been raided several times, but not a single grain of dope had been sniffed out. Reynolds was scrupulous about keeping his clean businesses separate from his dirty ones. Doubtless he would also be scrupulous about sticking to his routine after what had happened at the hospital. And nor was there any doubt that he would have a cast-iron alibi to account for his whereabouts at the time of the shooting.

A woman in a red bikini-top, matching micro-skirt and thigh-high boots teetered towards Jim and asked, 'Do you want a private dance, honey?'

Jim shook his head. He bought a beer and settled himself at a table to wait for Reynolds. He didn't have to wait long. The same dancer was still going through the motions on stage when Reynolds strolled in along with the shaven-headed, brick wall of a man Jim had seen at his house. Reynolds was dressed in a *Miami Vice*-style pastel-blue suit. His thin blonde hair was freshly slicked back. As usual, his wolfish lips were split into a broad grin. 'Send us up a bottle of Cristal,' he shouted to the barman. Clearly he had something to celebrate.

A fresh wave of fury washed over Jim, jerking him to his feet and sending him barrelling towards Reynolds. The smile disappeared from Reynolds's lips as he saw Jim bearing down on him. He stood rooted to the spot, a look in his eyes that said he could barely believe someone was daring to come at him in his own club. Jim grabbed him by the front of his jacket and slammed him against the bar. 'You won't get away with it, you fucker!' he rasped. 'You won't if it kills me. Do you—'

Jim's voice was choked off by a beefy arm wrapping around his neck. As the skinhead wrenched him away from Reynolds, Jim drove his elbow into the bigger man's ribs. The skinhead loosened his hold fractionally, his breath whistling through his teeth. Jim hit him again and he let go, doubling over. Refocusing his rage-swollen eyes on Reynolds, Jim made another grab for him. But the gangster was over his initial surprise. A semi-amused smile played across his face as he dodged out of Jim's reach. Jim drunkenly overbalanced, staggering to one knee. At the same instant, the bouncers charged in. One punched Jim in the face, sending him sprawling.

'Easy, lads,' said Reynolds as the other bouncer aimed a vicious kick at Jim's groin. 'He's a copper.'

The bouncers drew away from Jim as if they'd been told he had the plague. Reynolds jerked his thumb at the doorway. 'Get back on the door.' The skinhead straightened, massaging his ribs. 'You OK, Les?' asked Reynolds.

'I think he's busted one of my ribs.'

Reynolds nudged Jim with his foot. 'Did you hear that? You've hurt him. That's police brutality, that is.'

'Fuck you, you murdering cunt,' Jim gasped through his bloody teeth.

Reynolds touched his heavily muscled chest as if to say, *Murderer? Moi?* He glanced at Les. 'Check him.'

The skinhead patted Jim down and yanked up his shirt, exposing a pale, flabby gut. 'Look at the state of you,' said Reynolds with a sneering laugh. 'You're an embarrassment to your profession.'

Jim fixed him with a look of burning hatred. 'You think you can do whatever you want, don't you? But you're wrong. You've crossed the line this time. No one kills a police officer and gets away with it.'

Reynolds's grin faltered. 'Whoa, killed a copper? I've done some shit in my time, but it's sort of a golden rule of mine not to kill coppers. It tends to be bad for business.'

'Well you've made it the personal mission of every cop on the force to see to it that your business is fucked.'

'Really? So where are they? All I see is one drunken old excuse for a cop.' Reynolds's lips curled upwards again. 'You know what I think, Monahan? I think you're losing the plot, going senile or something.'

'You're going down, Reynolds. I'm going to put you in a hole so deep you'll never see daylight again.'

'That sounds like a threat.'

'It's a promise.'

'Well here's another promise.' Reynolds bent down, pushing his face close to Jim's. His voice dropped to a level audible only to the two of them. 'If you come to my house or club again, you'd better have an army at your back, otherwise I might just be tempted to break my golden rule.' He looked at Les and jerked his chin at Jim. 'Help him up.'

'Put a hand on me and I'll break it,' warned Jim. Grasping a table, he struggled to his feet. He coughed and spat at Reynolds's white suede shoes.

Reynolds attempted without success to dodge the oyster of bloody phlegm. 'You motherfucker! These shoes cost more than you make in a month.' He glared at Jim, his hands twitching as though longing to beat him to a pulp.

Jim returned Reynolds's stare with eyes that seemed to say, *Go on then, do it. Do it if you dare!* A single punch in front of witnesses would be all the excuse he needed to haul him to the station.

Reynolds's tongue flicked at his lips. As if expecting to see a camera, he glanced around suspiciously. 'No chance,' he said, shaking his head. 'You're not getting me like that.'

Now it was Jim's turn to curl his lips into a taunting sneer. 'What's the matter? Lost your bottle?'

Reynolds tried to recover his own smile, but only managed a predatory grimace. 'You really are fucking crazy, Monahan. You're out of control. You want a piece of advice, get a new line of work before you hurt someone and yourself.'

'Thanks for the suggestion,' Jim said in a tone of mock gratitude. 'And here's some advice for you: let Mark go. If you do that, I'll only put you in prison. Hurt him and I'll destroy you.'

A crease appeared between Reynolds's eyes. 'Do you mean Mark Baxley?' His voice was still laced with menace, but now there was something else in it too – concern? 'Has something happened to him?'

Jim gave a sarcastic clap. 'You're good. I'll give you that.'

'Look, whatever it is you think I've done, you're wrong.'

'Just remember what I said. And believe me, I'll do it.' Although Jim's words were slurred at the edges, his eyes were

266

diamond-hard with promise. He turned to stagger outside to his car.

'Wait,' said Reynolds, following him. 'If Mark's in trouble, I might be able to help.'

For the slightest moment, a splinter of doubt pricked at Jim. Was it possible Reynolds wasn't lying? He shook his head. The bastard didn't know how to do anything but lie. 'Yeah, that's it, keep playing your games. See where it gets you.'

Jim drove out of the city centre towards Doctor Reeve's house. Garrett was right, the doctor hadn't done a thing wrong. What's more, his background was as clean as a whistle. More than clean; it was a shining, exemplary model of hard work and decency. But even so, Jim couldn't bring himself to mentally scratch him off his list of suspects. The doctor exuded the unshakeable confidence of someone who couldn't even conceive of failing at anything. In Jim's experience, that kind of arrogance was often a cover for who a person really was. And the best way he knew to find out who a person really was, was to watch them without their knowledge.

He stopped off at a supermarket to pick up a six-pack of Coke and some ProPlus. If he was going to sit on the doctor's house all night, he needed something to stave off sleep. He swilled back a double dose of the tablets. He hadn't driven much further when he noticed his heart was palpitating. The next second, his breath was coming short and shallow. He wound down the window and sucked at the air, but it was as though he was trying to breathe through a wet blanket. He pulled over and closed his eyes, rubbing at his chest with a tingling hand. Images of Amy's bloody body rushed at him. His eyelids snapped back up. His face was clammily cold and the palpitations were becoming painful.

That reluctantly decided Jim. Doctor Reeve would get a pass – for now. He turned sharply in the road, prompting a chorus of horns to blare. As he raced back to the hospital, cramping pains radiated down his arms. And suddenly, for the first time in as long as he could remember, he felt scared. He wanted to phone Margaret and ask her to be there for him at the hospital. But he knew he had no right to do so.

TV vans clogged the pavement to either side of the car park's entrance. Beyond them, reporters were talking into cameras under the glare of handheld floodlamps. Jim parked up and, clutching his chest, swayed his way into A & E. His breath coming in staccato gasps, he said to the receptionist, 'I think I'm having a heart attack.'

Chapter Twenty

All day long Angel had lain on the sofa thinking about Doctor Henry Reeve, chewing over what she was going to do to him. She would take her sweet time killing him, that much she knew. With Herbert and Marisa things had happened too quickly. There'd been no chance to really savour their fear. She'd been too concerned with finding out the names of their fellow perverts. Well now she had enough names to keep her in the business of revenge for as long as she could evade being killed or captured. Sure, she still didn't know the identity of the other surviving man from the basement – the Chief Bastard – but she would cause all the pain in her power to try and make the doctor give him up. And if he held out, well, she would just have to ferret the name out of Herbert's black book.

A feeling deep inside told her that, one way or another, she would get what she wanted. It was such an alien sensation that it took her a while to identify it. Confidence. She was starting to believe in herself, in her ability to do something other than get men off for money. For years she'd kidded herself that her talent for providing pleasure gave her some sort of control over the men who came to her. But the bitter truth was, they were the ones in control. Even with the submissive punters, she did what they wanted, what they desired. Well not any more. Now she was the one calling the shots, and not only that, she wasn't afraid. Oh God, she wasn't afraid!

The heroin high had long since worn off. But even so, at that moment of realisation, Angel had felt as if she was rising out of her body, leaving the husk of her old self behind. She was changing, becoming something new. Something too powerful to be stopped. She'd thought the gun gave her that power. But she saw then that she was wrong. It came from inside her. It spoke to her in a voice as loud as thunder. It told her that shooting her victims was too easy a way for them to die. She needed to kill them in a way that sent a message to the world. The question was, how? *You will know how when the time comes*, the voice had assured her. *And until then, they will live in fear, always looking over their shoulders, never knowing when death will come for them.*

Several times during the day, Angel had heard the wail of sirens – sometimes so faint as to be barely audible, sometimes loud enough to cause her to peer through the barred window. With teeth-grinding slowness, morning had worn into afternoon. Driven by hunger-pangs, she'd rooted through the wreckage of the kitchen and found a couple of labelless tin cans and a box of stale cereal with mouse droppings in it. She'd forced down a few mouthfuls of the cereal before tossing the box aside in disgust. It had taken over an hour to hack the tins open using a rusty nail and a brick to hammer it in. One contained baked beans, the other chopped tomatoes. She couldn't imagine that drug dealers had much use for chopped tomatoes. She'd wondered whether they dated back to her previous stay in the flat. Stephen Baxley had used to buy in tins of them to make pasta sauces. She'd eaten the beans, but left the tomatoes untouched.

It was dark outside now. Angel checked the time on her phone. Nine o'clock. The waiting was finally over.

As Angel rose from the sofa, a tremor shook her. She stared at the envelope of Mexican brown, wondering whether she should give herself a small hit to stave off the withdrawal symptoms. *No*, said the voice, *you don't need the numbness to survive any more. From now on, you need to feel everything.*

Angel concealed the envelope in the chimney-breast along with the rest of her drug-taking gear, then left the flat. There was little traffic and even fewer pedestrians on the streets of Attercliffe. The ranks of factories had long since shut down for the day. She retraced her steps to the River Don, taking care not to be seen, her mind deadly clear and calm, like the eye of a storm.

Sticking to backstreets, Angel threaded her way through the city centre to the boarded-up shop behind which she'd concealed the motorbike. She was taking a big risk, she knew, but it was a good five or six miles to the doctor's house on Whirlowdale Road. She simply had to have some means of getting there quickly and, if necessary, getting away even more quickly. She'd briefly considered stealing another motorbike. But without knowing how to hotwire an ignition, she would have to mug someone for their keys. And that struck her as an even riskier proposition than retrieving the scrambler.

Angel watched the shop and its surroundings for ten or fifteen minutes from the shadows of an alleyway. Seeing no sign of a police presence, she darted round to the back of the building. The motorbike was where she'd left it behind the bins. Her heart hammering, she kickstarted it and accelerated onto the road. Any second she expected sirens to start up in pursuit, but none did.

She headed south-west through a maze of quiet residential streets. After four or so miles, the band of woodland that shielded Whirlow from the rest of the city forced her onto the Ecclesall Road. By that point she was far away from the busy bars and restaurants that lined the road closer to the city centre. She scanned the street signs on her left. Spotting the sign she was looking for, she pulled over at the end of a broad, leafy street and counted along the houses to Doctor Reeve's. It was a big, detached place set well back from the road behind a privet hedge. There were no cars in the driveway, but a downstairs light was on. Someone appeared to be in. Of course, that someone wasn't necessarily the doctor. There was always the possibility that, like Stephen Baxley, the loathsome little toad hid his perversions behind the respectable facade of family life.

Instead of turning onto Whirlowdale Road, Angel accelerated a short distance further along the Ecclesall Road. The houses on the doctor's side of Whirlowdale Road backed onto a belt of trees that screened them from a playing-field. She mounted the verge and rode far enough into the trees to be hidden from the road. Leaving the motorbike propped against a tree, she felt her way forward in the moon-silvered darkness to the fence at the end of Doctor Reeve's back garden.

A long lawn led to a patio furnished with a table and chairs. There was no swing or slide, or anything else to suggest the doctor had young children living at home. To the right of a conservatory, light filtered through curtains drawn across

French doors. There were motion-sensitive security lights at either corner of the house. An alarm box blinked red under the eaves. The alarm surely wouldn't be set if someone was home, but of course there was always the possibility that a light had been left on in an empty house to ward off burglars.

One of the downstairs windows had been left invitingly open. That decided Angel – someone *was* in. She clambered over the fence and ran towards the house. She dropped to her knees and crawled alongside the conservatory, out of sight of the nearest security light's motion detector. Keeping tight to the wall, she stood and peered through the open window. She found herself looking into a large kitchen. Immediately adjacent to the window was a sink and marble work-surface. At the opposite side of the room a door stood ajar, leading to a gloomy hallway.

Angel carefully moved aside a potted plant on the window-sill. Hardly daring to breathe, she climbed through the window. *You're making it all too easy, Doctor*, she thought, lowering herself to the tiled floor. Clearly the doctor hadn't heard about the Winstanleys' deaths, or he might have been more concerned for his safety. She withdrew the Glock from her handbag. The gun no longer felt alien in her hands. It was a part of her, an extension of her arm.

Silent as a stalking panther, Angel moved into the hallway. To her right, a stairway led up into darkness. To her left, a chink of light came from under a door. She put her ear to the door. Not a sound. The house was almost eerily silent. A frown crossed her forehead. Maybe no one was in after all. Perhaps the kitchen window had been left open by accident. She rejected the possibility. Even if someone had neglected to close the window before leaving the house, surely they wouldn't also have forgotten to set the alarm. A prickle of warning raised the hairs on her neck. Something wasn't right here.

Angel's straining ears caught a sound so faint as to be barely audible – the splash of something being poured into a glass. Her forehead relaxed. Nothing was wrong. The doctor, or at least someone, was simply enjoying a quiet drink. Whoever it was, they were about to get a nasty surprise.

You're going to need a knife, said the voice in Angel's head. She crept back to the kitchen and pulled a knife about ten centimetres long from a block of knives. She slid it into the side pocket of her jeans, then returned to the hallway.

With one smooth motion, Angel opened the door and stepped into a softly lit room. Straight ahead of her was a coffee-table flanked by two unoccupied sofas. Beyond the table was a stone fireplace with bookshelves to either side. A framed photo of Doctor Reeve and a pretty middle-aged woman standing at the shoulders of two equally pretty teenage girls hung above the mantelpiece. *So he does have a family*, Angel thought with a little jolt of her nerves. The girls were smiling and bright-eyed, radiating the easy confidence that privilege brings. There was no trace of sadness or unease in their expressions. Of course, that didn't mean they hadn't been subjected to the same kind of abuse their father had inflicted upon her, Mark Baxley and God knows how many others. But still an uncomfortable feeling squeezed her abdomen at the knowledge that she was about to deprive two children of their father. It wasn't guilt, but something else she couldn't quite define – shame, perhaps. Whatever it was, she fiercely dismissed it. Doctor Reeve's perversion was a cancer in the lives of his daughters. Whether or not they knew of its existence didn't change the need for it to be cut out.

To Angel's left was a piano, a couple of armchairs and a sideboard. A man was standing at the sideboard with his back to her. At the sound of the door opening, he turned, with a crystal decanter and brandy glass in his hands.

Doctor Reeve's face was lined with strain, but no hint of surprise showed in his eyes. 'Hello, Grace.'

Angel's heart gave a thump. *He knows my name. My real name! And he looks as if he was expecting me. What the fuck is this – some kind of trap?* She looked anxiously around the room, as if expecting to be pounced on by someone lurking in a corner.

'There's no one in the house but us, Grace.' The psychiatrist's voice was controlled and reassuring.

'My name's not Grace,' retorted Angel, a dark fire flaring in her eyes. 'Grace died a long time ago. You should know that, you helped kill her.'

'So what should I call you?'

'Call me Death, because that's what I am to you.'

A small spasm of something that might have been fear skittered across Doctor Reeve's face. His Adam's apple bobbed as he swallowed in an attempt to shove it aside. He started to raise his glass towards his mouth.

'What the fuck do you think you're doing?' Angel demanded to know, jerking the gun at him.

Doctor Reeve's hand flinched to a stop. 'I was going to have a drink. Do you want one?'

'I don't want a thing from you, except for you to do

275

exactly as I say. You don't move or speak unless I tell you to. Understand?'

'I understand perfectly. But I'm afraid you don't.'

'What the fuck's that supposed to mean?'

'Simply that I'm not going to play your game. I know what you want. You want me to fall to my knees and beg for my life. You need my fear to make yourself feel powerful. Well I'm not going to give it to you.'

Angel bared her brown-stained teeth in a savage grin. 'We'll see about that when I cut off your little prick and feed it to you.'

Doctor Reeve shook his head with a kind of regret. 'You know, I really wish we had a chance to talk properly. How I'd love to get inside your head and see what's going on.'

Angel stabbed a finger at her temple. 'You already know what's in there, Doctor. You made me what I am.'

'I didn't turn you into a monster, you did that all by yourself.'

'Bollocks! I wouldn't be here if it wasn't for you and your sick-fuck friends.'

'No, you'd most probably be off somewhere else, finding some other justification to hurt someone.'

'That's a fucking load of shit.' Angel's voice quickened, taking on a shrill edge. 'I'd be living a normal life. Do you hear me? A normal life with a normal man and kids of my own. You took that from me. You stole my fucking life! You're the monster, not me.'

'Unlike you, I know exactly what I am.' Doctor Reeve's voice was as calm as Angel's was frenzied. 'I accept that my urges were written into my biological makeup at birth. I don't try to pass responsibility for my actions on to anyone else. Do you know how many victims of so-called abuse I've seen professionally over the years? Hundreds. And do you know how many of those victims have gone on to murder their abusers? None. That's not because of anything I've said to them. It's because they're not killers. You're a killer. A sociopath. It's in your DNA. You think you're on a mission to right the wrongs done to you. Maybe you even tell yourself you're sending a message to society. But you're not. All you're trying to do is justify your own pathetic existence.'

Angel felt herself grow dizzy at Doctor Reeve's words. Was she really a sociopath, a monster without any feelings for anybody but herself? 'My dad beat the shit out of me for years. If I'm some kind of born killer, why didn't I ever fight back?'

'Simple. You knew you weren't strong enough. Tell me, if your father hit you now, what would you do to him?'

'I'd kill the bastard!' The words were out before Angel could stop them.

Doctor Reeve nodded as if to say, *I rest my case*.

What little colour Angel had drained from her cheeks. *You're a killer. A sociopath.* For a second she almost believed the diagnosis. Then she gave a sharp shake of her head. *He's a psychiatrist*, she reminded herself. *He knows exactly what to say to fuck with you.* 'I'm not a psycho. After what happened to Mark Baxley, I hated myself so much I wanted to die.'

'Ah yes, Stephen told me how you tried to kill yourself. And yet here you stand,' Doctor Reeve observed in a wry tone.

Angel jerked her sleeve up, revealing the mottled scars of old needle tracks. 'That's the only way I got through, the only thing that stopped the nightmares. So don't tell me I can't feel anything real.'

Doctor Reeve opened his mouth, but before he could speak Angel cut him off. 'No more. I'm fucked if I'm going to let a man who gets his kicks out of raping children psychoanalyse me.'

'OK, no more small-talk. Let's get down to business.'

Doctor Reeve spoke with a confidence that shook Angel's. Once again she found herself wondering, *What's his game? What tricks, other than his clever gob, has he got up that slimy sleeve of his?* She pointed the gun at his groin. 'You're going to tell me the name of the other man from the Winstanleys' basement.'

'That's not going to happen. But I will tell you something. Actually, maybe it would be better if I simply showed you.' The psychiatrist put down the decanter and reached for an object on the sideboard.

Angel saw that it was a mobile phone. 'Touch that and you'll find yourself missing your bollocks.'

Doctor Reeve drew back his hand. 'There's something you really need to see on that phone.'

'What is it?'

'It's a chance. A chance to prove beyond doubt that you're not what I think you are. A chance for redemption.'

Redemption. The word echoed like thunder in Angel's head. Was it possible? She'd never hoped for redemption. The best she'd hoped for was revenge. The vile degradation Mark had suffered that night in the basement was as irreversible as time. She'd done what she had to do to make it out alive. With hindsight, she would rather have let the bastards kill her – at least, that's what she told herself. There'd been many times, though, when she'd wondered whether that was really true. The question had always seemed arbitrary. As far as she could see, other than the blankness of heroin, death was the only way her conscience would ever find peace. But even death wouldn't bring redemption, not unless... *Unless you give your life for someone else! But who? Who might you be willing to die for?* Her mind raced over the possibilities. There were only two. One moulded out of love, the other out of guilt. Her mother and Mark Baxley.

Angel's heart was suddenly pounding. She gestured with the gun for Doctor Reeve to move away from the sideboard. He retreated towards the French doors. As though fearing it might explode in her hand, she picked up the phone. There was a photo on its screen of a young man with dirty-blonde hair pasted to his forehead with sweat. Blue-grey eyes – eyes wide with fear – stared pleadingly out of the screen, almost as if appealing directly to Angel. A spray of cuts covered the man's cheeks. A thick bandage on his right shoulder bulged from beneath a dressing-gown.

'Do you know who that is?' asked Doctor Reeve.

Angel nodded. *Mark Baxley.* There was no doubt it was him. His features were thinner, his hair shorter and darker, but it was essentially the same face that had been branded onto her consciousness fifteen years ago. In an instant, the sense of control that had coursed through her dissolved like the mirage it always had been. The gun began to tremble in her hand.

'That photo was taken by a man who doesn't kill for pleasure like you,' continued Doctor Reeve. 'He's a man who kills coldly for profit.'

'Is he the other man?'

'Who he is, is of no concern to you. All you need know is that if you don't do exactly as I say, Mark dies. Do I make myself clear?'

Angel gave a weak nod.

'I want to hear you fucking say it, you cock-sucking piece-of-shit whore!' There was a malicious glee in the psychiatrist's voice.

Angel almost visibly shrank under the torrent of obscenity. 'Yes, you make yourself clear.'

'Good girl. Now, first things first, I want the book.'

'What book?'

'Don't lie to me. You know full well what book. Where is it?'

Angel's eyes flicked towards her handbag.

The psychiatrist's lips broadened into a superior smile. 'Ah good, you brought it. Not too bright, are you?' He gestured at the sideboard. 'Put it on there, along with the gun and phone, then step away.'

Angel put down the phone. 'If I do what you say, how do I know you won't kill Mark anyway?'

'Mark has no memory of what happened at the Winstanleys' house. He's no threat to anyone. You have my word that we'll let him go if you hand yourself over to us.'

A hiss of incredulity came from Angel. 'You expect me to take your word?'

'You don't have any choice but to.'

Angel stared at Doctor Reeve, her face twitching with tortured indecision.

The psychiatrist huffed out a breath. 'I can see you need more convincing.'

Angel took several steps backwards as Doctor Reeve strode

over to the sideboard and retrieved the mobile phone. He punched in a number and put the phone to his ear. 'It's me,' he said. 'Put him on.' He switched the phone to loud speaker. There was a moment of silence that was suddenly shredded by a scream. The scream subsided into choking sobs – sobs that flashed Angel's mind back to that long ago but never forgotten night in the basement. Stephen Baxley's words rang out in her mind, as they'd done countless times before. *Give him some more medicine, Angel. Do it.* The screaming came again. Angel's head jerked to one side as though she'd been slapped. *Give him some more medicine, Angel. Do it.*

'OK!' she cried in a voice as ragged as broken glass. 'I'll do what you want. Just stop hurting him.'

Angel lowered the Glock. Tears spilling silently from her eyes, she approached the sideboard. As she set the gun down, her thumb flicked on the safety-catch with an almost imperceptible motion. She unhooked her handbag from her shoulder and put it down too, then stepped back.

'That'll do, for now,' Doctor Reeve said into the phone. The line went dead. He looked at Angel with a curl of triumph on his lips. 'Congratulations, Grace, you've proved me wrong.' He emptied the detritus of her life out of her handbag – rape-alarm, condoms, a blister-strip of morning-after pills, assorted bits of makeup, purse, the little black book. He flicked through the book before putting it in his trouser pocket. Very carefully, almost fearfully, he picked up the gun and aimed it at Angel. She tensed automatically, though she guessed Doctor Reeve had no intention of killing her in his house. She would have been surprised if the psychiatrist had any intention at all of doing the deed. He was the kind who preferred to watch others get their hands dirty. A voyeur. He'd proved that in the Winstanleys' basement.

'I can see why you like the power a gun gives you. One pull of the trigger and someone dies.' Doctor Reeve's tongue flicked excitedly at his lips. 'I have this incredible urge to do it right now just to see what it feels like to take a life.'

You haven't got the balls, Angel resisted the urge to retort. She dropped her eyes to the floor, seemingly resigned to her fate. But a plan of sorts was forming in her mind.

'I bet the feeling is amazing, Godlike even,' continued the psychiatrist. 'Of course you know, don't you, that a gun doesn't give you control, it only creates the illusion of control?' He raised his hand as if a ball was balanced in its palm. 'Shall I tell you what real power, real control over people is? It's holding their mind in your hand, knowing you can squash it with one squeeze. And young minds are the easiest to squash. Or mould. They're like soft putty.' An expression of utter loathing came into his eyes. 'But you wouldn't understand that. In the past, I had to deal with your kind – addicts, layabouts, runaways – every day. It's people like you who are sending this country down the toilet. You sit on your arses all day, rotting your brains with daytime TV and your bodies with drugs and junk food. And then you come to me expecting me to sort your miserable, ignorant little lives out. Well I'm fucking sick of it. I'm sick of you people. You make me want to vomit!'

When Doctor Reeve had finished his rant, his face was almost as red as Angel's hair. He glared at her as though daring her to deny the truth of his words. She held her silence, chills of rage coursing through her as she wondered how many young minds he'd closed his sadistic hand on.

Doctor Reeve scooped Angel's belongings back into her handbag and picked it up. He motioned to the door with the gun. 'Move.'

Angel headed into the hallway. The psychiatrist followed close behind, prodding her in the direction of the kitchen with the Glock. At the far end of the kitchen, a door led to a garage with an Audi in it. Doctor Reeve aimed a keyring at the car and pressed a button. The car's lights flashed and its doors unlocked. He opened the boot. It was lined with black plastic. 'Get in.'

The knife in Angel's pocket jabbed into her thigh as she folded her thin frame into the boot. She didn't believe for one second that Doctor Reeve and his final remaining partner in perversion had any intention of releasing Mark. Even so, she had no choice but to comply if Mark was to have any chance of surviving. It all depended on whether she was right about Doctor Reeve not being the sort of man to do his own dirty work. If she was, he would take her to this so-called stone-cold killer. And then she would have a chance, albeit a miniscule one, to free Mark. If she was wrong, he would probably drive out to some isolated spot and attempt to kill her.

'I strongly suggest you lie as still and quiet as possible,' said Doctor Reeve. 'Because if for some reason we don't make it to where we're going, Mark will find his young life brought to a sudden and painful end. Do I make myself clear?'

'Yes.'

A satisfied smile played around Doctor Reeve's lips. 'Good girl, you're learning.'

Chapter Twenty-One

Doctor Reeve closed the boot, sealing Angel in darkness. Her hand moved to the knife. It gave her little reassurance. Knife vs gun promised to be a very short fight. But she wouldn't simply lie down and die. She would go down slashing and stabbing with every ounce of her strength, every fibre of her being. Her blood was thumping in her veins. She concentrated on breathing slowly. She needed to be calm – calm and ready. When the time came, she might only have a split second to act.

Angel heard the garage door opening. The Audi's engine purred into life and the car pulled out. Adrift in darkness, she had no sense of the direction the car was taking. She focused all her energy, all her thoughts, on what she would have to do when it reached its destination, constantly shifting position to keep her circulation going. She visualised herself driving the knife deep into Doctor Reeve's flesh, piercing his vital organs, ripping open his arteries.

After maybe half an hour, the Audi came to a stop and its engine fell silent. With an immense effort of will, Angel forced herself to let go of the knife. Before she struck, she had to be sure Doctor Reeve had taken her to Mark. The boot popped open. Cold air rushed in, stinging her eyes. She caught a glimpse of the star-spangled dome of the night sky. Then Doctor Reeve loomed into view. 'Out,' he said, pointing the gun at her.

Angel uncoiled herself from the boot. The car was parked on an unlit lane bordered by hedgerows and fields. The encircling darkness was dense, but not complete. Over Doctor Reeve's shoulder, maybe a mile away, the lights of a busy road flickered brightly.

The psychiatrist's breath quivered and his eyes gleamed as though he was working himself up to something.

I was wrong, thought Angel. *He intends to kill me himself.* Then she noticed the barn. It was a windowless, one-storey building of wood and corrugated iron set a few metres back from the lane. Light seeped from around the edges of double doors. *No, I was right. Someone's waiting in there, waiting to kill me.*

Doctor Reeve motioned towards the barn. 'Move.'

Angel approached the doors, her heart beating fast, her footsteps dragging, her head a whirl of uncertainty. Should she make her move now or wait until she was inside? There was no way she could be a hundred per cent sure Mark was in the barn unless she waited. But by then she would almost certainly have to tackle two men at once, and her chances of success, already slim, would be reduced to virtually zero.

'This is the end of the line for you, Grace,' said Doctor Reeve.

That decided Angel. If she was going to do anything, it had to be now. She pulled out the knife and turned to face the psychiatrist. His eyes widened momentarily, then a smile of cruel amusement spread across his lips. 'And just what do you think you're going to do with that?'

'I'm going to kill you.'

'Only if you can dodge bullets.' Doctor Reeve pulled the Glock's trigger. Nothing happened.

In the blink of an eye, Angel covered the few paces between them. Doctor Reeve just had time to let out the first note of a scream before she sunk the knife deep into his throat. 'Not too clever, are you?' she spat, wrenching the knife out and lodging it between his ribs.

Doctor Reeve swung the gun at Angel, catching her a glancing blow to the head. The gun span out of his grasp, clattering to the ground several metres away. With the knife still in him, he pushed past Angel and staggered towards the barn, emitting a gurgling, wheezing sound from his throat.

Angel dove for the gun. She snatched it up at the same moment the psychiatrist began hammering his palms against the barn. One of the doors scraped open. Light flooded out, framing a powerfully built man in black military-style fatigues and a bomber jacket. The man had dark brown hair and eyes. She'd never seen him before in her life. In his gloved hands, he held a handgun.

Angel flicked off the safety catch, took aim and fired. The first shot hit Doctor Reeve in the shoulder. He twirled like a crazed dancer before he fell. The second hit the man, punching him onto his back.

Warily, Angel got to her feet and approached the doorway. The psychiatrist was lying on his side, limbs flung out at odd angles. He didn't appear to be breathing. His accomplice lay unmoving too, his eyes closed. A wisp of smoke rose from a bullet hole in his chest. The impact had knocked the gun from his hand onto the bonnet of a black Range Rover. Next to the four-by-four was an inconspicuous little red car. And slumped on the floor beside the car was a figure in a dressing-gown with a cloth bag over their head. *Mark!* The name rang out in her mind, but instead of relief it brought gut-twisting anxiety. He was here, but was he alive? The bandages had been cut away from his shoulder, exposing a bloody mess of torn stitches.

Oh God, let him be alive. Please let him be alive. The plea filled Angel's mind as she stooped to retrieve the knife from Doctor Reeve's body, then darted to Mark's side. She removed the bag, revealing eyes wide and blinking with fear. The fear faded to uncertainty as the eyes took in Angel's relieved expression. She peeled the duct tape away from his mouth. He spat out a rag and gasped, 'Grace?'

Angel wanted to say, *No*, but she made herself nod. 'You're safe. Everything's going—' She broke off. She'd been about to say, *Everything's going to be OK*. But that would have been a lie. Everything was not going to be OK. Not now. Not ever. Her eyes dropped away from Mark's.

He groaned as she started sawing at the plastic handcuffs. When the knife cut through the cuffs, his right arm dropped to his side and hung there like a dead thing. He examined the red welts where the cuffs had bitten into his wrists, slowly flexing the life back into his left hand.

'Can you walk?' asked Angel.

'I think so.'

Angel helped Mark to his feet. With him leaning heavily on her, they made their way to the doors. 'I was right,' Mark exclaimed upon seeing Doctor Reeve. 'He is one of them.'

Them. The way Mark's mouth twisted on the word made

it clear to Angel who he was referring to. She jerked her chin at the other man. 'Who's he?'

'He called himself PC Stone.'

'Well I'd say it's a fair bet that's not his real name. Let's see if he's got any ID.'

Angel rifled through PC Stone's pockets but came up empty-handed. She turned her attention to Doctor Reeve, remembering that he had Herbert's book. She reached into one of his trouser pockets and pulled out a bunch of keys. At that instant, PC Stone's eyes flicked open.

'Watch out!' cried Mark, but his warning came too late.

PC Stone grabbed the Glock and twisted it from Angel's grasp. His other hand drove deep into her stomach. She crumpled, breath whistling through her teeth. PC Stone righted the gun in his hand and swung it towards her.

'No!' shouted Mark, kicking the gun out of PC Stone's grip. It skittered away underneath the Range Rover. He snatched the broken spoon out of his sling and stabbed it at PC Stone's left eye. His aim was good, but there was little strength behind the blow. The sharp plastic tip pierced the eyeball, but didn't push through it into the brain behind. PC Stone screamed, clutching at the spoon and flinging it aside. Tears of blood spilled from his eye. In an attempt to stem them, he pressed his palm against the wound. His other hand groped for the gun.

Mark pulled weakly at Angel. 'Come on.'

Still winded, she pushed herself to her feet. Leaning against each other like wounded soldiers, Mark and Angel staggered away from the barn. 'Can you drive?' she gasped as they neared the Audi.

'Yes, but you'll have to work the gears. I can't move my right arm, so I'll have to steer with my left.'

Angel stopped suddenly, muttering, 'Fuck.'

'What's wrong?'

'The book. I've got to go back for it.'

'What book? What are you talking about?'

Angel started to turn towards the barn, but Mark grabbed her arm. 'You're crazy. You can't go back there.'

'I have to!'

Angel jerked her arm free, sending Mark stumbling to his knees. At that instant, the crack of a gunshot echoed through the night. PC Stone emerged from the barn, swaying like a drunkard, gun in hand. Angel threw herself towards the Audi as a second shot rang out. Sparks flashed off the bonnet. She yanked open the door and dived across the driver's seat. Mark crawled in behind her. 'Where are the keys?' His voice was loud and panicked.

Angel thrust them at him. Staying hunched low, he put the car in gear. Then he reached across himself to start the engine. Another shot. The rear passenger window exploded, spraying glass over them. Mark pressed down hard on the accelerator. The front wheels span and screeched, but the car didn't move.

'The handbrake!' cried Angel. 'Release the fucking hand-brake!'

Mark did so and the car lurched forward, climbing a verge and hitting a hedge. He wrenched the steering-wheel leftwards and the car veered back into the lane. A fourth shot sounded, the bullet thunking into the back of the car. Then they rounded a bend and the barn was hidden from view.

'We did it!' Mark laughed shrilly, a wave of euphoria rushing through him. 'We fucking got away.'

'We're not home free yet,' warned Angel. 'He's got a car, remember?'

Mark's eyes flicked to the rear-view mirror. There was no sign of pursuit. 'He won't come after us. Not with his eye all messed up.' He sounded as though he was trying to convince himself of what he was saying.

They were on a long, straight stretch of road that cut between hedgerows overhung with trees. A mile or two in the distance streetlights marked the outskirts of a built-up area. 'Where are we?' asked Mark.

'No idea.' Angel hugged her arms across her stomach as though she was cold, her forehead gathered into deep furrows. 'I shot him in the chest. Why wasn't he dead?'

'Maybe he was wearing a bullet-proof vest.'

Angel nodded, knowing Mark must be right. She hugged herself tighter, exhaling a strangled groan of despair. She'd lost the Glock. Even worse, she'd lost the little black book. She had no way of tracking down the Chief Bastard. It was over. Everything was over! The Chief Bastard would remain unpunished and free to continue destroying children's lives. Her face twitched with tormented, impotent rage at the thought. It flashed through her mind to tell Mark to pull over and let her out so she could return to the barn. It would be little more than a suicide mission, but it would be better to die that way than to live with the knowledge that she'd failed.

The engine flared and cold air whipped in through the shattered window as Mark put on a burst of speed.

'What is it?' asked Angel.

'I thought I saw headlights in the mirror.'

Angel twisted to look out of the rear window. There was no sign of following headlights. Maybe Mark's fear was making him see things that weren't there. Or maybe their pursuer had cut his vehicle's lights. She realised with a leaden thump of her heart that she couldn't leave Mark, not until she was sure he was safe. *But where's safe?* she wondered. *The hospital? The police station?*

A short distance up ahead the lane split into a Y shape. 'Cut the lights,' said Angel.

Mark did so, plunging them into moonlit darkness. 'Which way?'

Angel pointed to a gap in the hedge. 'Go through there.' Her breath whistled as the Audi juddered along a rutted farm-track. 'Stop and turn off the engine,' she said, when the lane was hidden from view by a grassy hollow.

They sat in silence, ears straining for the sound of approaching engine noise. A minute passed. Two minutes. Nothing except for the slight rasp of Angel's breathing disturbed the silence. Mark blew out his cheeks. 'I think we've lost him. What now?'

'How the fuck should I know?' Angel speared a glance at him, suddenly resentful of his need for her help.

Mark blinked, taken aback.

Guilt tugged at Angel. The last thing Mark deserved was her anger. 'I'm sorry,' she sighed. 'It's just I haven't got a clue what now. I never expected to be sitting here with a hitman on my arse.'

'Is that what he is, a hitman? I thought maybe he really was a po...' Mark's voice wobbled and trailed away. He swayed forward as a wave of faintness washed over him.

Angel caught him, her hand slipping on the blood streaming from his shoulder. 'We need to sort your bandages out.' She pulled the bandages back up, but it was too dark to see what needed to be done to keep them held in place. 'I'm going to switch the light on.'

'What if he sees us?'

'We'll just have to risk it. Better that than you bleeding to death.'

Angel snapped on the interior light. She cut two strips off Mark's gown. He groaned as she used them to tie the bandages tightly over the jagged gash. 'Thanks,' he said hoarsely, when she was done. 'I owe you my life.'

'You don't owe me a fucking thing.' The sharpness was back in Angel's voice. She switched the light off, more because she couldn't bear to see the gratitude in Mark's eyes than because she feared discovery.

A moment passed, then Mark said tentatively, 'Do you mind if I ask you a question about Stephen Baxley?'

Angel made no reply, but the tension in her silence was so palpable that Mark's voice snagged in his throat. His need for answers quickly overwhelmed his nervousness. 'How did you meet him?'

Angel remained silent for so long, he thought she wasn't going to answer. Then in a low, intense voice, almost as if she didn't want Mark to hear but felt compelled to speak, she said, 'Do you know the Devonshire Green skate-park?'

'Yes.'

'I used to hang out there after school. There was this guy. He must have been about thirty-five or forty, and he always wore a grey flasher's mac.'

Mark frowned. He had a vague recollection of his so-called father owning just such a coat.

'Not that he ever flashed anyone, or anything like that,' continued Angel. 'He just used to sit watching the kids on their skateboards.'

Mark exhaled with revulsion. 'Jesus, what a creep.'

'Yeah, he was one creepy fuck. If I saw him now, I'd spot him for what he was in a second. But back then all I saw was a lonely bloke with nothing better to do than sit on a bench. A harmless saddo.'

'How did you get talking to him?'

Angel was silent for another long moment. Then she began quickly, as though watching her memories flash by on a screen. 'I'd had a run-in with my dad. He'd rolled in from the pub after work with a skinful inside him, same as always. I knew as soon as I saw his bastard eyes that things were going to turn to shit fast. He used to get this look in them, like the sight of Mum and me made him want to puke. He hadn't been in the house for more than a minute when he found some excuse to go off on Mum. I got between them, so he belted me too. I've still got a scar on my chin where his wedding-ring cut me. I ran out of the house. I didn't stop running until I got to Devonshire Green. I can't remember if I was crying. I must have looked sorry for myself because your dad—'

'He wasn't my real dad,' broke in Mark, his voice laced with loathing.

'Sorry. Stephen asked if I was OK. I told him to piss off, but he didn't leave. He offered me a hankie for my chin.' Angel's voice became faraway as she burrowed deeper into the soil of her memory. 'He didn't ask how I'd got cut. He

293

just looked at me, waiting for me to speak. And after a while I did. I don't know why. Maybe it was because of his eyes. I remember thinking he had nice eyes. And once I started talking I couldn't stop. Things I'd never meant to say came out. I told him how my dad was always beating the crap out of me. And how I hated him so badly I wanted to kill him. I'd never talked to anyone about that stuff before. My mum made me promise not to. It felt good to get it all out. He said he understood how I felt because his dad used to beat him up. He told me he ran away from home when he was fifteen and never went back.'

'That was a lie. He lived with his parents until his early twenties. He was just trying to gain your trust, I suppose.'

'Well it worked. Over the next few days I got into the habit of stopping by his bench for a chat. He had this way of listening that was different to any other adults I knew. He made me feel…' Angel searched for the right word, 'special.'

'That's funny. He made me feel the exact opposite,' Mark observed in a wry tone.

'He was very good at making people feel what he wanted them to feel. I found that out later on.' Angel heaved a breath. 'So anyway, I told him how I wanted to run away but didn't know where to go. And I told him how sometimes I thought about killing myself because it seemed like there was no other way out. That's when he offered to help me. He said a friend of his had an empty flat I could use. I was too naive to think he might want something in return.' Another silence. Another heavy sigh. 'We arranged to meet up in a few days. When the day came – I think it was a Thursday – I skipped school, returned home after my parents had gone to work and packed a bag. Then I went to Devonshire Green. Stephen was waiting in his car. He was really nervous. He made me lie flat on the back seat. Then he drove to The Minx and left me in the car while he got the keys to the flat.'

'The Minx? What's that?'

'A strip-club on South Lane. His friend owned the place.'

'What was his friend's name?'

'I don't know. But I'd like to find out.'

Mark's forehead wrinkled. The Stephen Baxley he knew mixed with businessmen, financiers and politicians, not strip-club owners. 'Maybe it was someone he knew from back when he lived in Park Hill.'

'Stephen lived in Park Hill?' Angel said, surprised.

'He grew up there.'

'You wouldn't have known it from the way he spoke.'

'Yeah, well, he made a big effort to lose his accent. The only time it ever came out was when he got angry. Do you reckon this friend of his could be one of the men from the basement?'

Angel thought about the Chief Bastard. She thought about his smooth, respectable face, his polished, cut-glass accent. Not exactly the character traits you associated with a strip-club owner from Park Hill. Of course, the Chief Bastard could have dropped his accent too. A doubtful frown shadowed her face. She'd worked in numerous strip-clubs. Their owners had all been hard-bitten, rough-talking men. In their line of business, such pretensions would be seen as a weakness, not an advantage. 'It's possible, I guess.'

'You don't seem convinced.'

'Whoever they are, they've got some seriously shady connections in the north-east.'

'How do you know that?'

'Because it was a friend of Stephen's friend who took me to Newcastle.'

'Why were you taken to Newcastle?'

Angel rubbed her forehead. Mark's questions were starting to make her head reel. 'Keep your gob shut a minute and I'll tell you. The flat was a grotty little place, but I didn't care. For the first time in my life I didn't have to be afraid of my dad. It's hard to describe how that made me feel. It was… it was like I could suddenly breathe.' As if to emphasise the point, she inhaled deeply. Her breath seemed to snag on something, and she coughed for a moment before continuing. 'Stephen and I talked for hours. I don't remember what about. I do remember that he suddenly kissed me. Then we fucked.'

'He forced himself on you.'

'He didn't have to. I wanted to repay him for his kindness. He didn't want money, so I gave him the only other thing I had to offer.' A snarl came into Angel's voice. 'What I should've done was stick a knife in the dirty bastard.' She paused to swallow her anger before resuming. 'After that first night, Stephen came to see me every few days. He'd bring me magazines and clothes, and he cooked for me. We went on like that for weeks, maybe even months. I lost track of time. I never left the flat. The outside world seemed to barely exist any more. Then one day he said he had some friends who wanted to meet me. He took me to a big house out in the country. I'd never been in a place like that before. I remember thinking to myself that whoever lived there must be really important.' A contemptuous hiss sliced through the darkness. 'What a dumb little bitch I was.'

'Whose house was it?'

'It belonged to Herbert and Marisa Winstanley. Do you know them?'

'No.'

'Well they know you. It was in their basement that you were—' Angel broke off. She couldn't bear to think of what had happened to Mark there, let alone say it.

'Herbert and Marisa.' Mark repeated their names slowly, as if trying to prod his memory. 'What did they do to you?'

'One of them, I don't remember which, gave me some wine. It must have been spiked because I blacked out. When I woke up, I was groggy and my arms were being held down by Marisa. Herbert was raping me.'

'Jesus,' Mark breathed, swallowing hard.

'When they were done, Stephen took me back to the flat. I lay on the bed, not thinking, just numb. He was in tears. Can you believe that? After what'd happened to me, he was the one crying.'

Mark could hardly believe that. He couldn't remember ever seeing Stephen shed a single tear.

'He kept saying how much he loved me,' Angel continued. 'How he'd do anything for me. And do you know what the craziest thing of all is? I believed him. Why did I believe him?' She shook her head, her eyes searching the darkness as if she might find an answer there. 'A few weeks went by before Stephen said he had another friend who wanted to meet me. This time I knew what that meant. I was upset, I said I didn't want to do it. But he pleaded and begged. Said he needed me to help him, like he'd helped me. Said if I truly loved him, I'd do this for him. He kept at it until I eventually agreed to do it.

What else could I say? If I'd refused, he might have chucked me out and I'd have been forced to return home. I'd rather have fucked any number of his friends than risk that happening. So I went back to the Winstanleys' house. A different bloke was there. He didn't tell me his name. He just fucked me and fucked off. And that's how it went from then on. Every few weeks Stephen would take me to the Winstanleys' place, and afterwards he would feed me his lines about how sorry he was and how much he loved me.'

'He was prostituting you,' Mark said, with sudden realisation. 'How could you bear it?'

'At first I couldn't. But it wasn't so bad after a while. There was always plenty of booze and drugs around. A bottle of wine and a snort of ketamine, and you don't feel much of anything.'

'Didn't you ever think about escaping?'

Angel expelled a sharp breath. 'Haven't you listened to a fucking word I've said? Where would I have escaped to?'

'You could have gone to the police.'

'They'd have returned me to my parents.'

'Not if you told them why you ran away in the first place.'

'Maybe, maybe not. You can't trust coppers to always do what's right. And even if they had done, I'd have ended up in a home or some other place under someone else's control. At least with Stephen I had some control over my life.'

'No you didn't.'

Mark was right, Angel knew. Stephen had controlled every aspect of her life – what she read, what she ate, who she fucked. The hold he'd had over her had been deeper and more deadly even than her addiction to heroin – he'd made her believe he loved her, and she'd been convinced she loved him too. It

298

wasn't love they'd felt for each other though. It was something else, something ugly and deformed, born of his perversion and her desperation. But by the time she'd realised that, it was already too late. Her head dropped as though it was too heavy to hold up. She didn't have the energy or inclination to try and explain to Mark how she'd felt. Besides, the rest of the story was waiting to be told. It gnawed at her mind like a malignant tumour that was too deep to be removed.

'On the day *it* happened, Stephen turned up at the flat in a right state.' Angel spoke in a trembling monotone. 'He was a nervous wreck. Said he had something he needed me to do for him, something our whole future could ride on. He took me to the Winstanley place. Two men I'd never met before were there. One was Doctor Henry Reeve. I don't know the name of the other one. I call him the Chief Bastard.'

'What did he look like?'

'He's about your height, but much more well built. And he's bald with tufts of brown hair sticking out above his ears. And he's got these nasty, pissy little brown eyes.'

'What about his teeth?'

Angel was silent a moment, searching her memory. 'I don't remember his teeth. I do remember his breath. It stank of cigars and booze and something else, something rotten. Made me want to puke. He was nervous too. All of them were. I overheard him more than once saying to the psychiatrist, 'Are you certain he won't remember anything?''

'That's got to be him,' exclaimed Mark. 'The man I dreamt about. I heard him say the exact same thing.'

'I assumed what they were talking about had nothing to do with me. I just thought I was there to screw them both. So I got to work on making sure I was too out of it to remember much myself. Next thing I knew, I was in the basement. There was a video camera and all sorts of sex toys down there. And there was a young boy. At first I thought he was asleep, but when I looked closer I saw that he was even more out of it than me. I was horrified. I tried to leave, but they wouldn't let me. The Chief Bastard kept hitting me. He told me what he wanted me to do to you. It was sick. Beyond sick.' Angel's breath came in a shuddering groan. She twisted towards Mark with an imploring note in her voice. 'I didn't want to do it. Oh Christ, I didn't! But you've got to understand. Stephen was a manipulative pervert. But the Chief Bastard, he was something else. When I looked into his eyes I just knew he'd kill me if I didn't obey him. And he'd have enjoyed doing it too. So I... I...' Her words gave way to a strangled sob.

There were suddenly tears in Mark's eyes too. His voice scraped out as though his throat was made of sandpaper. 'What did you do?'

'I... I'm sorry. I can't.'

'Please, Grace. I need to know.'

'No you don't. All you need to know is that you're alive and they're dead. All of them, except the Chief Bastard. And if I ever find him, I'm going to make him pay and pay for what he took from us. I won't kill him fast like the others. I'll slice him up bit by bit until he begs for death.'

There was a thrill of anticipation in Angel's voice that Mark recoiled from. She clearly took pleasure from the thought of hurting the Chief Bastard, just as her abuser had taken pleasure from hurting her. That didn't make her the same as him, but it did stir up a deep unease in Mark. He silently waited for the rest of the story.

A long while passed before she continued. 'After that night, I was done with Stephen, with the Winstanleys, with everything. Stephen tried his usual lines on me, but I wasn't listening any more. I hardly slept. And when I did, I had nightmares. I wanted to die. I thought about it constantly. I even tried to OD on some sleeping-pills Stephen brought me. But he found me and walked me round until they wore off. That's when he said I couldn't stay at the flat any longer. I begged him to change his mind, but he wouldn't. He said I had to leave Sheffield for my own good. His friend from The Minx knew someone in Newcastle who could put me up. He warned me never to come back to Sheffield. Said if I did there'd be dire consequences for me and my family.'

A tremor of disgust passed across Mark's face. 'The fucker used you and threw you away like a broken toy.'

'He could've let me OD. Dumped my body somewhere for the coppers to find. Runaways die like that all the time. Nice and easy, no questions asked. It was a big risk letting me leave. I think maybe in his own fucked-up way he really did care for me.' Angel frowned in silence for a moment, as though trying to gauge the truth of her words. With a shake of her head, she continued. 'So one night this Geordie bloke came to the flat. He took me to a house in Newcastle where some other girls were living. Turned out this friend of Stephen's friend owned a string of brothels and strip-clubs. Most of the girls were junkies. Within days, I'd had my first hit of H.' A sigh slipped from her lips. 'And all the hurt, all the guilt, all the memories went away. After I came down, all I could think about was getting another fix, and another, and… And the rest is hardly worth telling. They bounced me from brothel to brothel, kept me back of house until I was old enough to work the clubs. And when they'd got all they wanted from me, when I started to look like the scag-whore I was, they let me go off with a pimp from Middlesbrough.'

'So what made you come back here after all these years?'

'Something happened. Something that made me realise it was time to start fighting back against all the beatings, the abuse, the rapes. Then I saw on the news what Stephen had done and I knew I had to get payback for what they did to us. And to make some kind of amends for what I did to you.'

Mark could sense – could almost smell – the guilt emanating from Angel. Hesitantly, he reached over and touched her arm. She stiffened, but didn't move away. 'You don't need to make amends for that. You only did what you had to do.'

'No.' Angel spat the word out vehemently. 'I had a choice. There's always a choice. I chose to survive when I should've let them kill me.'

'Bollocks you should have. You were fifteen. A fifteen-year-old shouldn't have to make choices like that. No one should.' Mark's voice was suddenly imploring. 'If you truly want to do something for me, let go of this thing. I don't want anyone else to die because of what happened to us.'

'This isn't just about you and me. It's about all the other kids whose lives have been or will be destroyed by the Chief Bastard.'

'Go to the police. Tell them what you know. Let them track him down and deal with him.'

'I told you, you can't always trust the police.'

'So who can you trust?'

'No one. I'd have thought you'd see that after everything you've been through.'

'Sure I see it.' Mark's tone became steely, forceful even. 'But I can't, I won't, allow it to define who I am. Don't you see? If I do that, Stephen Baxley and the Chief Bastard will have won.'

Angel's pained face drew into even deeper creases. Mark's words struck deep and true. For most of her life this thing... this guilty rage had consumed, directed and, until the past few days, weighed on her with a paralysing force. She hated it with every ounce of her being. But what would she do without it? Who would she be? 'I can't let it go. It's too late for that. I have to see this to the end.'

'When does it end? When the Chief Bastard's dead?'

'No. It ends when they're all dead. Every one of them who's ever hurt a child.'

'Then it'll never end, because you'll never be able to kill them all.'

'Maybe not, but I can try.'

Mark removed his hand from Angel, releasing a breath heavy with sadness at the thought of her insane quest and the world that had driven her to it. A powerful feeling suddenly came over him that he had to get away from this place, get back to the city, to the hospital, to Charlotte. It seemed to him that if he didn't do it now, he might be stuck here forever, sharing a dark, lonely limbo with Angel. 'Do you think we've waited long enough?'

'More than long enough.'

Mark twisted the ignition key so that the dashboard lit up. He turned on the satnav. A blip on the GPS tracking

303

screen pinpointed their location. 'We're a few miles south of Rotherham. East of the M1. Where do you want to go?'

Angel turned the question over in her mind. The priority was to make sure Mark was safe. But where was safe? And what about herself? Where was she to go? Trying to come up with answers seemed to make her limbs feel impossibly heavy. 'Just head towards Sheffield. When we get there, I'll tell you where to go.'

Mark started the engine. 'Can you put the car in reverse for me?'

'I don't think so.'

'It's easy. You just shift the gearstick into the slot marked—'

'It's not that. I can't move my arms.'

Mark turned towards Angel with a concerned frown. By the light of the dashboard, she looked like a sickly child. 'Why can't you move your arms?'

Angel's eyes moved, and Mark's followed them to her stomach. He gasped at the sight of blood welling through her vest. 'You've been shot!'

She shook her head slightly. 'It was when that fucker hit me in the barn. He had a knife. Take a look at it, will you? Tell me how bad it is.'

Carefully, Mark lifted Angel's sopping vest. The wound yawned like a cave in her abdomen. Something dark bulged through it. His mouth filled with bitter saliva at the sight. 'It's bad. Very bad.' He shrugged off his dressing-gown, bundled it up and pressed it against the wound. Angel gave out a hoarse groan. Blood almost instantly soaked through the material. 'We've got to get you to hospital.'

'No! If I go there, I'm fucked.'

'You'll be even more fucked if you don't. You'll be dead.'

Angel closed her eyes. She knew Mark was right. She hadn't felt much when the knife went in, except for a winding sensation. But as the adrenaline had worn off, pain had begun pulsing outwards from the wound in white-hot waves. At the same time, numbness had come on in her arms. Now it was creeping through her legs, merciful but terrifying. Her face contorted with savage frustration. That she was dying didn't matter. It only mattered that she would die before she'd had the chance to kill the Chief Bastard. She looked at Mark, her eyes burning with a fevered light. 'Promise me you'll find the Chief Bastard.'

'But I wouldn't know where to start.'

'There is someone you can possibly trust to help you. Jim Monahan. He's a cop.'

'How do you know Detective Mo—'

'It doesn't matter how I know him. Just promise me you'll find the Chief Bastard. And if the law can't get to him, promise me you'll make him pay.'

'OK, OK, but only if you'll let me take you to hospital.'

'Say it. I want to hear you say it.'

'I'll find him and...' Mark hesitated to make the second part of the promise. The Chief Bastard had already taken part of his innocence. There was no way he was about to lose the rest of it over him. No matter what Angel said, he had to trust the law. But he saw that it was necessary to lie if she was to survive. 'And if the law can't get him, I will.'

The wild light in Angel's eyes faded to a weary resignation, an acceptance that she'd done everything she could, given everything she'd got. Suddenly there was only one place she wanted be, only one person she wanted to see. 'There's someone you can take me to. A doctor I know. She'll patch me up.'

'You need more than patching up.'

'Either you take me to her or I'll get out of the car right here.'

Mark looked at Angel uncertainly for a second, then heaved a sigh. 'Where does this doctor live?'

Angel told him the address and he punched it into the satnav. He put the Audi in reverse and they set off again. At every rut and pothole the car exploded over, pain blazed up Angel's spine into her throat, choking off her breath. Her vision was fraying at the edges. Darkness seemed to be seeping into the car like ink, staining its interior blacker and blacker. She focused on the satnav's robotic voice, holding on to every word like a drowning person clutching a lifebuoy. The road and street names were gradually becoming more familiar. She gagged. Something acrid and coppery-tasting filled her mouth. She spat it out.

'Hold on,' said Mark. 'It's not far now.'

'Not far now,' Angel repeated, slurring the words. 'Not far now, not far...'

Then she saw it. Looming through the night like the rampart of some ancient fort. Hillsborough Stadium. Mark turned onto her parents' road and pulled over outside their house. He eyed the two-up, two-down terrace doubtfully. 'A doctor lives here?'

He jumped out of the car and hammered on the door. A light came on in the upstairs window. A moment later, the door opened on a safety chain. A woman peered through the gap between door and frame. As soon as he saw her timid, questioning eyes, Mark guessed he'd been lied to. Her face was lined with age and worry. It was the face of someone used to taking instructions, not handing them out. 'Are you a doctor?'

The woman shook her head, looking at Mark in his blood-stained pyjamas as though she suspected he was a madman.

'Then a doctor doesn't live here?'

'No. What gave you that idea?'

'I was told...' Mark tailed off as it struck him that the woman's eyes had the same feline shape and porcelain-blue colour as Angel's.

An inarticulate groan rasped from the car. The woman squinted over Mark's shoulder. 'Who's that?'

'Someone's hurt. Can I use your phone?'

The woman blinked, uncertain. 'Look, I don't want any trouble. My husband—'

'Please. She's dying!'

'Dying?' The woman's uncertainty gave way to frowning concern. 'Who's dying?'

The groan came again. This time it contained a word, only just audible. 'Mum.'

The woman stiffened as though she'd heard a voice from a coffin. 'Grace?' She breathed the name through trembling lips. 'Is that you?' She fumbled at the security chain, struggling with unsteady hands to unhook it. She stepped into the street in her dressing-gown, barefooted. She didn't seem to notice the cold of the pavement as she approached the car and stooped to look inside it. Her hand shot to her mouth, partly stifling a sound that expressed both shock and horror. Mark's gaze darted back and forth between the women, and it was like looking at two photos of the same person taken twenty-odd years apart.

'Hello, Mum,' said Angel, her voice fading even as she spoke.

'Grace, Grace,' Linda Kirby murmured as if in a trance.

'Help...' Angel's voice caught on her pain. She swallowed, then continued, 'Help me into the house.'

Linda slid an arm under her daughter's armpit. 'I don't think we should move her,' said Mark. But Angel was already standing, out of the car, her face as grey as the soot-stained brickwork of the little terrace. Step by tottering step, Linda guided her into the living room and lowered her onto the sofa.

'Oh my angel, my poor little lost angel,' whispered Linda, cradling her daughter's head, fearfully tender.

Mark grabbed some towels from a radiator in the hallway and handed them to Linda. 'Press them against the wound.'

As Linda did so, Angel grimaced and air wheezed between her lips.

'I'm sorry,' said Linda. 'I'm sorry. I'm so sorry.' It wasn't clear if she was apologising for the pain or for something else.

'Where's your phone?' asked Mark.

Linda pointed at a sideboard. Mark snatched up the phone he saw there and dialled 999.

Angel's eyes drifted around the living room. Nothing much had changed. Same three-piece suite, same carpet, same curtains. It was almost as if she'd only been away a few hours. Her gaze lingered on the shrine of photos of herself cluttering the mantelpiece.

'I never gave up hope,' said Linda. 'I always knew you'd come back to me one day.'

Angel looked into her mum's eyes. Her lips formed three silent words. *I love you.* Then a terrible stillness stole over her.

Linda pressed her face against her daughter's, letting out a low keening sound that quickly built into a wail.

'What is it?' asked Mark, jerking round to face them.

'She's dead.' Linda's voice came muffled and choking.

Mark rushed to Angel's side and searched vainly for a pulse. He thought about trying mouth-to-mouth. Then he looked at her face. All the pain had gone from it. Death had smoothed away the lines of rage and guilt. She looked as peaceful as a sleeping child.

'My baby is dead... She's dead...' Linda gasped between sobs, clutching a hand to herself as if a steel claw was raking through her guts.

Mark stepped away from mother and daughter, suddenly feeling as if he was intruding upon some private rite. He turned towards the door at the sound of heavy footsteps lumbering along the hallway. A burly figure with close-cropped grey hair swayed into view. Mark's heart lurched. Was this man another hired killer? Then he smelt the booze-reek steaming off him and saw the dull glaze over his eyes. If it was a hitman, he wasn't in much of a state to do his job.

'What the hell's going on, Linda?' Ron demanded, his eyes shifting between surprise, anger and wariness as he surveyed the grisly scene. 'Who are these people?'

Linda shot her husband a look of pure, visceral hate. 'This is our Grace.'

Ron squinted back at her as if uncertain he'd heard correctly. 'What the fuck are you on about, woman? Grace is dead.'

'Yes, she's dead!' Linda lifted her daughter's head, so that her eyes gaped sightlessly at Ron. 'Look at her. She's our daughter, and she's dead. Look at her, you bastard!'

Ron's pouchy eyes blinked. He glanced around the room as if to make sure he was in the right house. Then his gaze fell to Angel. His jaw dropping slack, he lurched and put a tattooed hand out to steady himself against the sofa. He slowly reached towards Angel, thick ridges of scars on his knuckles showing bone-white against his tanned skin.

'Don't touch her.' Linda's voice burnt like acid. 'Do you hear me? Don't touch her or I'll kill you!'

Ron's gaze jerked to meet hers. She didn't flinch from it. As his hands curled into fists, she thrust out her chin as if daring him to take his best shot. He loomed over her like an enraged bear, seemingly big enough to take off her head with a single punch. For a breathless moment they glared at each other. Mark found himself looking around for something he might use to defend Linda. He started to reach for a vase, unsure whether he had the strength to lift it, never mind use it to fight the bigger man off. But Ron's hands suddenly dropped like a beaten boxer's. With a noise that was half growl, half whimper, he turned and shuffled from the room. His feet dragged back along the hallway.

At the sound of the front door closing, Linda's bony body seemed to collapse in on itself. Like a penitent, she folded her head against Angel and clung to her as though she would never let go.

Chapter Twenty-Two

Jim woke at the sound of a nurse tending to a patient in a neighbouring bed. He glanced at his watch. It was just after midnight. His mouth was like sandpaper. He reached for a glass of water, wincing as the memory of his drunken encounter with Bryan Reynolds kicked him in the head. *Christ, what were you thinking?* In the cold glare of sobriety, the answer was clear. He hadn't been thinking. He'd been overwhelmed by anger and self-pity. *You're out of control.* His thoughts echoed Reynolds's words. Reynolds had been right about another thing too – he was a pathetic excuse for a copper. Just as he'd been a pathetic excuse for a husband. His threats against Reynolds were as empty as his personal life. He could no more bury Reynolds in a prison or a grave than he could make Margaret come back to him.

Margaret. Jim winced again at the thought of her. She would never have allowed things to get this far. She'd have seen the warning signs and forced him to take a step back from the job. Without her, he was blind to himself. He thought about what the doctor who'd treated him in triage had said. 'You've been lucky this time. Next time it might be a heart attack for real.'

The doctor had performed an electrocardiogram and taken blood measurements to check for enzymes released into the blood from a damaged heart. The tests had shown that Jim wasn't suffering a heart attack. He was relieved, but also confused. If he wasn't having a heart attack, what was wrong with him? 'It could be down to stress, or there might be some other medical condition behind the pain,' the doctor had explained. As a precautionary measure, he'd insisted on admitting Jim to the Coronary Care Unit for observation. Jim had reluctantly agreed to stay.

After swallowing some water, Jim closed his eyes. Once again he saw Amy, saw the blood bubbling from her throat. But even that nightmarish image couldn't keep his exhaustion-addled brain from sleep for long. What seemed like only minutes later, he was woken again, this time by the ringing of his mobile phone. It was Scott Greenwood. There were only two reasons for him to be phoning – either he wanted to talk about Amy's death, or there'd been a development in the case.

A stern-faced nurse appeared at the head of the bed. 'Switch that off,' she said in an admonishing whisper.

'It's police business.'

'I don't care. All mobile phones must be switched off on this ward.'

His heart beating uncomfortably fast, Jim hurried from the ward and called Scott back. One thought kept hammering at his brain. *Please don't let Mark be dead.* 'What's up?'

'A call just came in from Mark Baxley.'

Jim closed his eyes and let out his breath. His relief was quickly tempered by another wave of apprehensiveness – just because Mark was alive didn't necessarily mean he was out of danger. 'Where was he calling from?'

'You're not going to believe this, but he's at the Kirbys' house.'

Jim's eyebrows lifted high. 'What the hell's he doing there?'

'No idea. But Grace Kirby's there too, and she's dead.'

'Dead.' Jim's voice suddenly had a breathless edge. 'Are you sure?'

'Not one hundred per cent. All I know is that's what Mark told the emergency operator. I'm on my way to the Kirbys' house.'

Jim told Scott he'd see him there and returned to his bed. 'What are you doing?' asked the nurse as he pulled his clothes out of the bedside cabinet.

'I've got to go.'

'I really don't think that's advisable, Mr Monahan. Not until we've found out what's behind your chest pain.'

'Thanks for your concern, Sister, but something important has come up.'

'Something more important than your health?'

Jim hesitated for a moment, forehead creased. Then he continued dressing.

His thoughts sped even faster than the car's wheels as he drove. How had Mark ended up at the Kirbys' house with Grace? Had she somehow been involved with his kidnapping after all? He dismissed the question as soon as it came into his head. More likely the kidnapper had used Mark, and Grace's parents, as bait to draw her out, and she'd died trying to protect them.

A constable was standing at the end of the Kirbys' street.

Beyond him the blue flashing lights of police vehicles and an ambulance illuminated the row of terraces. Lights were on in most of the houses. Their inhabitants watched the unfolding scene from their front doors and windows. Recognising Jim, the constable waved him by. As he got out of his car, Scott Greenwood approached him.

'Where's Mark?' Jim asked.

'In the ambulance.'

'Have you spoken to him?'

'No. He's pretty banged up. They're about to take him to hospital.'

'What about Grace?'

Scott indicated the Kirbys' house with his chin. Jim knew what that meant. There was no more doubt. 'How did she die?'

'Well it wasn't from natural causes. How are you holding up?'

Jim made no reply, but his haggard face was answer enough. He headed for the ambulance. Mark was lying on a stretcher. Jim's stomach squeezed at the sight of his bloody pyjamas and bloodless face. One paramedic was applying a dressing to his shoulder. Another was giving him a shot of something.

'How's he doing?' asked Jim, holding up his ID.

'We need to get him to hospital ASAP,' said one of the paramedics.

'Can I speak to him?'

'One of your colleagues already tried to. But what with the blood loss and morphine, Mark's too out of it to—' The paramedic broke off with a surprised look as Mark stirred and lifted his head.

'Jim,' he croaked.

Jim stooped over the stretcher. Mark's eyes were flickering and rolling around. 'It's me, Mark. Who did this?'

'Doc... tor...' The word came slow and slurred.

'Doctor Reeve?'

'Yes.'

Jim's eyes pinched at the corners as he thought, *I knew it! I fucking knew it!* 'Anyone else?'

'Chief... Bastard.'

'Who's the Chief Bastard?'

'Don't know.'

'Where are they?'

'Doc... barn. Grace killed him... Saved my...' Mark's voice dropped away to an inaudible murmur.

'What about the Chief Bastard? Is he dead too?'

Mark gave a barely visible shake of his head.

'I'm done,' said the paramedic who'd been working on the bandage.

'I'm going to have to ask you to leave the ambulance,' his colleague said to Jim.

'I'll see you at the hospital, Mark.' Jim gave Mark's hand a squeeze before turning to leave. He watched the ambulance blare away from the street. *Grace saved my life*, that was surely what Mark had been trying to say. Heaving a sigh, he turned towards the Kirbys' house.

'Did he say anything?' asked Scott.

'Doctor Reeve is involved in this.'

'We know.' Scott pointed at an Audi being worked on by forensics officers. 'That's his car.'

'Did you also know that he's dead?'

'Are you sure?'

'Yes.'

'Where?'

'In a barn somewhere, I think. Where's Garrett?'

Scott nodded at the Kirbys' house. 'Inside, talking to the mother.'

As Jim entered the house, he was greeted by the sound of someone sobbing relentlessly. Linda Kirby was slumped at a table in the tiny kitchen, blood-stained hands pressed to her face, shoulders quaking. A female constable had an arm round her. Garrett was standing to one side, watching Linda with a pained expression. Noticing Jim, a flicker of something that might have been sheepishness passed over his face. He left the kitchen, motioning for Jim to follow him into the living room.

Angel was laid out on the sofa, her sightless gaze fixed on the ceiling. Her vest had been cut open, exposing a wide-lipped wound and her breasts. Even in death, there was no dignity for her. A ball of shame, anger and something else, something close to grief, pushed up inside Jim. Keeping his face carefully expressionless, he forced it back down with a hard swallow.

'We think she was stabbed,' said Garrett. 'Although we won't know for certain until Ruth Magill examines her.'

'Has Linda Kirby said anything?'

'Not much. The woman's almost incoherent with grief. She has told us that Mark and Grace arrived in the Audi parked outside.'

Jim gave his superior a meaningful glance. 'Doctor Henry Reeve's Audi.'

Garrett nodded without looking at Jim. His voice rose, as if the mention of the psychiatrist's name was a personal

316

insult. 'This madness can't go on, Detective. It has to stop. Do you understand?'

Jim looked at Garrett for a moment as if trying to decipher what he was saying. 'Yes, sir.' He thought about telling the DCI what Mark had told him. But then he thought, *No, let the bastard stew on it a while.*

Almost as if they didn't know what else to do, both men continued staring at Grace Kirby's corpse. 'About DI Sheridan...' Garrett began haltingly, but he trailed off, at a loss for words for once.

Scott Greenwood entered the room. 'I was just speaking to one of the guys working on the Audi, sir. There's a route plotted into the satnav from a location east of the city, not far from Thurcroft. Could be where this barn Mark mentioned is.'

'What barn?' asked Garrett, his forehead drawing into a frown.

Scott quickly brought the DCI up to speed. Garrett flashed Jim a sharp look as if to say, *Why don't I already know this?* Then, perhaps realising that he'd been given a bit of what he deserved, he sighed. 'You two get over there straight away. I'm going to follow Mark to the hospital.'

'Mark won't speak to you,' said Jim.

'We'll see about that.' As the detectives turned to leave, Garrett added, 'And for God's sake, be careful. Let's see if we can make it through the rest of the night without any more casualties.'

Jim paused in the hallway and looked at Linda Kirby. In all the years Grace had been missing, she'd refused to accept her daughter was dead, hoping beyond hope that she would return to her one day. Her faith, if that was the right word,

317

had finally been rewarded in the cruellest way imaginable. And now there was nothing left for her but grief. Part of him – the part that had witnessed time and again how living with daily violence sapped at the foundations of a person's being – wanted to reach out and try to console her. But another part of him – the part that said she'd brought this upon herself by failing to protect Grace from Ron – wanted to shake her and shout, *What the fuck did you expect to happen, you stupid, weak woman?*

Jim ducked into his car and reached for his cigarettes. The triage doctor's warning echoed back to him once more. He hesitated, but only briefly. His need for a smoke right then was far greater than any concern he might have about the state of his health.

Scott Greenwood rode in the Firearms Unit van. They sped through the streets, sirens shattering the silence of the city night. Fifteen minutes or so later, they reached their destination. Jim got out and turned full circle, squinting into the darkness. There was no barn. Just hedges, fields and trees. Away to the south a flickering orange glow lit up the sky. 'Something's on fire over there.'

'I'll find out if anyone's called it in.' Scott reached through the van's window for the radio receiver. 'There's a barn on fire,' he called across to Jim. 'They've pulled a body out of it.'

They jumped back into their vehicles and set off again. A few minutes later, their path was blocked by a fireman who waved them to a halt. Beyond him the lane was filled by a line of three fire engines. To the left of the road, flames leapt from the roof of a barn, twitching and hissing in the jets of water from the firemen's hoses. 'Where's the body?' Jim asked.

The fireman led the detectives to a tarp spread over the grass verge. As he pulled it back, the noxious smell of burnt flesh wafted out. Doctor Reeve was lying face down. His hair had been scorched off the back of his head. His shirt was a charred, bloody mess.

'That's how we found him,' said the fireman. 'We were told to leave him like that until the scene of the crime team gets here.'

'Any word on when that'll be?' asked Jim.

'No. Do you need anything else from me?'

'Not for now, thanks.'

'Looks like we're going to be here for a while,' said Scott. 'I'd better let the firearms boys know what the crack is.'

Jim waited for his colleague to turn his back, then pulled on a pair of forensic gloves and rolled the body half over. The flames had barely touched the psychiatrist's face, which was contorted into a frog-eyed mask of agony. The front of his shirt was drenched with blood. Jim unbuckled the psychiatrist's belt and pulled his trousers down several centimetres, exposing a purple birthmark on his left hip. That confirmed it beyond all doubt – Doctor Reeve was one of the men from the DVD. It also confirmed which one of the remaining participants in that vile little piece of perversion was still alive. Jim summoned up a mental image of a broad-shouldered man with a hairless body and a circumcised penis. 'The Chief Bastard,' he murmured, quickly checking the doctor's pockets. They were empty. He returned the body onto its front and headed for his car.

'Where are you going?' asked Scott.

'The hospital.'

'But the DCI wants us to work this scene.'

Ignoring his colleague, Jim ducked into his car. As he drove, he turned the image of the Chief Bastard over in his mind. The man had a similar physique to Bryan Reynolds. But he needed more than that to go on if he was going to identify him as Reynolds with absolute certainty. He needed whatever, if anything, Grace had taken from Herbert Winstanley's office. Or he needed some extra morsel of information from Mark. Barring either of those things, he needed a miracle. And he didn't believe in miracles.

When Jim arrived at the hospital, Garrett heaved a sigh as if wearied by the sight of him.

'Where's Mark?' asked Jim.

'He's still in with the doctors. I'm told we shouldn't have to wait too long to see him.' Garrett's voice took on a conspiratorial tone. 'I've informed the Chief Superintendent about what was found at the barn. We're going to have to be very careful how we handle this development. If word gets out that the Chief Superintendent personally vouched for Henry Reeve, it could create a scandal that affects us all.'

Jim gave the DCI a look of open contempt. People were dead – good people – and Christ knew how many other people's lives had been scarred beyond repair. And all this prick gave a fuck about was his career. He resisted the urge to tell Garrett exactly what he thought of him, knowing he would be wasting his breath. He sat down a couple of chairs away from him and waited in silence.

He didn't have to wait long. Soon enough, a doctor approached. 'How is he?' Jim asked eagerly.

'About as well as can be expected. He's asking for a Detective Monahan.'

'That's me.'

The doctor motioned for Jim to follow him. Garrett started to stand, but the doctor said, 'Mark was very specific that he only wants to see Detective Monahan.'

Garrett's jaw tightened in irritation, but he sat back down without a word.

The doctor led Jim to a room with an armed constable stationed outside it. Mark was propped up in bed, looking pale and drawn but alert and determined. 'How are you feeling?' asked Jim.

Mark shrugged as though that was of no consequence. 'How's Detective Sheridan? They won't tell me.'

Jim's eyes dropped away from Mark's question, but his pained expression made the answer clear.

'She's dead, isn't she?' said Mark.

The hard lump in his throat bobbing, Jim managed a nod.

His voice vibrating with grief, Mark continued, 'Two good people have died today because of me—'

'No, not because of you, Mark,' cut in Jim, lifting his gaze. 'Because of the evil that was done to you. You're not to blame for any of this.'

'I don't blame myself. I just don't want any more people to die.'

Jim opened his mouth, but closed it without speaking. *You and me both*, he'd been about to say. But he found himself wondering whether the words would have been true.

A moment of silence passed, then Mark asked, 'Did you find Doctor Reeve?'

'Yes.'

'What about the other man, the one who kidnapped me?'

Jim shook his head. 'Is he the Chief Bastard?'

'No. He's a hired killer.'

'How do you know that?'

'Because I spoke to the Chief Bastard. He phoned me to gloat.'

'What did he sound like?'

'He sounded like the man from my dream.'

Wrinkles of surprise formed at the corners of Jim's eyes. He'd fully expected Mark to say the Chief Bastard had a thick local accent, like Bryan Reynolds. 'Are you sure it wasn't Doctor Reeve you spoke to?'

'Yes. This guy's voice was...' Mark gave a swallow as he remembered the nauseating sensuality of the Chief Bastard's voice, 'different.'

'Then who is the Chief Bastard?'

'No idea. All I know for sure is what Grace told me about him.' Mark gave Jim her description of the Chief Bastard.

'Bald with tufts of brown hair above his ears, and brown eyes,' echoed Jim, the wrinkles on his face turning into ridges. However unlikely, Bryan Reynolds could have put on a voice to talk to Mark. But it was beyond doubt that with his long blonde hair and blue eyes, Reynolds didn't match up to Grace's description of the Chief Bastard. He'd been wrong all along. Bryan Reynolds wasn't one of the men in the film. But in that case, who was the Chief Bastard? And if Stephen Baxley and Bryan Reynolds weren't bound together by a mutual perversion, what was it that had made Reynolds take the fall and go to prison for his fellow debt collector?

Jim rubbed at his suddenly pounding temples. 'I want you to give me the whole story of what's happened since this morning.'

As Mark recounted the details of his kidnapping, guilt churned through Jim. The knowledge that his name had been used to lure Mark from the hospital gave added weight to the sense that he bore some indirect responsibility for Amy's death. 'Did you tell anyone other than the police operator that you wanted to talk to me?'

'No, which was one of the things that made me wonder whether...' Mark tailed off uneasily.

'Whether what?'

'Well... whether PC Stone really was who he claimed to be. I mean, how else could he have known what he did?'

'Most probably by listening in on a police frequency. What were the other things that made you wonder?'

Mark told Jim about his kidnapper's phone conversation with the Chief Bastard, adding, 'The way he talked reminded me of how police talk to each other.'

Jim's thoughts turned to Chief Superintendent Knight's friendship with Doctor Reeve. Was it possible? Was the DCS—

He cut his thoughts off with a sharp twitch of his head. If he was going to go down that route, he needed to be as certain as a doctor diagnosing a terminal illness. 'Not only police talk like that. This guy could be an ex-soldier.'

Mark continued his story. Emotion threatened to choke off his words as he described Amy's fatal confrontation with PC Stone. Jim closed his eyes, fists clenched in helpless rage. He opened them when Mark recounted his conversation with the Chief Bastard. Jim noted down in bold letters: 'CHIEF BASTARD HAS A COPY OF THE DVD'. He raised an eyebrow at the line, *Once a pleb, always a pleb*. The Chief Bastard clearly harboured an aristocratic disdain of the nouveau riche.

More importantly, he also knew of Stephen Baxley's humble origins. Maybe he was someone in the same line of business, a fellow industrialist or entrepreneur who'd inherited rather than built his fortune.

When Mark mentioned the code his kidnappers used to phone each other, Jim broke in on him again. 'I want to make sure I've got this right. Three rings, hang up, wait ten seconds, then another three rings.'

Mark nodded, then resumed his story. He described how the hitman had tortured him to bait Grace into coming to the barn, and how a while later he'd heard gunshots. 'I thought that was it,' he said hoarsely. 'I thought I was about to die, but then Grace took the bag off my head and… and I can't tell you how that felt, to go from certain death to possible life within the space of a few seconds.' Tears brimmed in his eyes. He wiped them away, his voice quickening as he relived the fight with the hitman.

Jim showed no surprise on hearing that Mark had stabbed the hitman. Time and again over the past few days, Mark had displayed an incredible will to fight for his survival. 'Which eye did you stab him in?'

'The left one.'

'I'll be back in a moment.' Jim hurried from the room. Garrett was waiting with eager, questioning eyes.

Jim handed the DCI a written description of the hitman. 'We need to put an alert out on this guy. He's most probably driving a black Range Rover. I don't have a reg. But I do know that he's urgently in need of medical attention to his left eye.' Before Garrett could say anything, Jim turned to head back to Mark and his story.

When Jim heard how Grace had been desperate to return to the barn for a book, a sharp gleam of interest came into his eyes. Surely it was a safe bet that the book contained a list of the Winstanleys' clients or club members. 'And did she?'

'No. It would have been suicide.'

The light in Jim's eyes faded into disappointment. He listened grimly to the story of how Grace had fallen in with Stephen Baxley. His eyes glimmered again at the mention of The Minx. So Reynolds was involved after all. The question was, how deep did his involvement go? Had he known what Baxley needed the flat for? If so, he'd taken a big risk, letting him keep a fifteen-year-old runaway there. Yet more proof that the two men had shared some kind of bond that gave the industrialist an influence over the gangster that not even his most powerful enemies possessed. There was a soul-destroying inevitability to the abuse Grace had suffered subsequently. Over the years, Jim had come into contact with dozens of runaway children who'd been sexually exploited. Usually the perpetrators of such crimes were bottom-feeders, the dregs of society. Such people tended to be relatively easy to identify. Money and social status, on the other hand, gave offenders a mask of respectability to hide behind. But rich or poor, their motivation always came down to the same two things – money and lust.

It was part of Jim's job to get into the minds of criminals. He understood the ones who were in it purely for the money – the pimps, drug dealers, thieves and thugs. The type he'd always struggled to understand were the ones who were in it for the pleasure – the perverts, freaks, sadists and psychopaths. Stephen Baxley fell into the latter category. And what had happened in the Winstanleys' basement took his crimes to a different level of incomprehensibility. As Jim listened to how the Chief Bastard had hit Grace until she gave in to his warped desires, all he could think about was finding him and making him feel the same pain and fear that she'd gone through.

Her ensuing descent into depression and suicidal impulses was almost as inevitable as the abuse. How was anybody – anybody who wasn't a sexual deviant, that is – supposed to cope with such a memory?

Jim shook his head in disagreement when Mark mentioned Grace's belief that Stephen Baxley had shown he cared by preventing her from dying of an OD. 'Men like him never care for their victims. She was just a plaything to him, a commodity. If he kept her alive, it was either because he had further use for her, or because he was too much of a coward to let her die.'

'Well he must have been a coward, because he didn't have any further use for her. After she attempted suicide, he had the friend who let them use the flat arrange for her to work in a brothel in Newcastle.' Mark's face twisted with hate. 'The bastard used her, then got rid of her like an unwanted pet.'

Reynolds's involvement went deep, thought Jim. The question now was, had Reynolds known what went on at the Winstanley house? Or was he merely doing yet another favour for his friend? Jim was inclined to think the latter more probable. If Reynolds had had dealings with the Winstanleys, surely they'd have come onto the police radar before now.

The path Grace's life had taken after she was trafficked off to Newcastle was a depressingly familiar one. The cycle of prostitution and drug addiction would doubtless have continued for the rest of her life, but for the violent pathology of her formative years. Grace was like an unexploded landmine which had lain buried for fifteen years until Ryan Castle stepped on it. His murder was the catalyst for the spree of killings that brought the story full circle.

Mark briefly related what had happened at the Kirbys' house. Then he fell silent with a long breath, his eyelids drooping, as if telling the story had drained his final dregs of strength.

'Get some rest now,' Jim said gently.

Fear flashed in Mark's eyes as the detective started to turn away. 'I don't want to be alone.'

'You're safe here, I guarantee you.' Even as Jim spoke, he wondered what his guarantee was worth. He pushed the thought aside. Even if – and it was an if so enormous he could barely comprehend its size – Chief Superintendent Knight was guilty of anything more than the desire to avoid a scandal, it would be insane to make an attempt on Mark's life in the hospital. 'Close your eyes and sleep.'

'I don't think I'll ever be able to sleep properly again after today.'

'Yes you will.' Jim's voice was full of tender admiration. 'You've got a strength in you that I've rarely seen in anyone.'

'Do you really mean that?'

'I wouldn't say it if I didn't. I don't think I could've survived what you've been through.'

A wry smile touched Mark's lips. 'It's funny, Stephen Baxley always made me feel like a weak person, a good-for-nothing mummy's boy.'

'Yeah well, you showed him just how wrong he was. If I...' Jim hesitated briefly, before continuing with a trace of awkwardness. 'If I was your father, I'd be proud of who you are.'

'If you were my father, none of this would have happened in the first place.' Mark cast a furtive glance at the door. His voice dropped low. 'There's one more thing I haven't told you yet. Grace knew your name. You were helping her, weren't you?'

Cautious uncertainty glazed Jim's eyes. Mark held not only his career but also his freedom in the palm of his hand. He'd tipped off a murder suspect that the police were coming for her. Official misconduct, obstruction of justice and possibly even accessory to murder were just a few of the charges he could be hit with. And in light of what had happened next, even taking all his years of service into consideration, the courts would have no choice but to come down hard on him.

'Don't worry, Detective Monahan,' continued Mark. 'You can trust me like I trust you. I promise I won't tell anyone.'

The thought of Mark making himself an accessory too was almost enough to make Jim wish he would tell someone. He looked at Mark a moment longer, his eyes troubled. Then he turned and left. Garrett was on him the instant he stepped out the door. 'You've been in there a hell of a long time, Detective. He must have had a lot to say.'

Jim handed his notepad to the DCI. 'It's all there.' *Except for Mark's suspicions about the hitman's background*, he added silently.

Garrett's gaze skimmed over Jim's notes, his expression impenetrable except for fine lines of strain around his eyes. When he was done, he was silent for a long while as if struggling to digest the welter of sordid details he'd devoured. Finally, he said, 'It seems you were right about Bryan Reynolds.'

'I think I was right and wrong. Clearly Reynolds knew about Stephen Baxley and Grace Kirby. But I'm no longer convinced he had anything to do with what went on at the Winstanley house. I think he did what he did because Stephen Baxley had a hold over him.'

'What kind of hold?'

'I don't know.'

'Well it's high time we tried to find out.'

'Do you want me to bring him in?'

'No. In fact, I can't allow you to have any further involvement in this, or any other investigation, for the time being.'

Jim frowned. 'What the hell are you talking about?'

Garrett's voice took on a shallow veneer of concern, through which traces of relief were detectable. 'I've been informed you were admitted to this hospital earlier tonight with chest pains.'

'Yes, but I'm fine now. The doctors say it wasn't a heart attack.'

'That's good to hear, but regulations state that I must remove you from active duty with immediate effect pending a clean bill of health. I'm sorry, Jim. I know how much this case means to you.'

Jim scowled. 'Bollocks you're sorry. You've been looking for a way to kick my arse into touch for months.'

Garrett gave a little wince as though the accusation hurt. 'I don't know what gave you that idea. You're a valued team member and it'll be a big blow to lose you, especially in the middle of such a difficult investigation.'

Jim pushed his face towards the DCI. 'Nothing better happen to that boy in there.' His voice was low and hard. 'If it does, I'm going to hold you personally responsible.'

Garrett pulled his head back, his eyes round with astonishment. 'Are you threatening me?'

'That's not a threat, that's just how it is.'

'Let me tell you how it is, Detective,' Garrett returned authoritatively, quickly recovering his composure. 'I'm going to put what you just said down to all the stress you've been under recently, and you're going to go home before you say something else that harms your career beyond repair.'

'I don't give a toss what you put it down to, or what happens to my career, just so long as no harm comes to Mark under your watch.'

The muscles of Garrett's jaw worked as though he was chewing on the sour taste of Jim's words. As Jim headed for the ward's exit, he called after him, 'You're way out of order, Detective!'

Chapter Twenty-Three

The house was as devoid of life as Grace Kirby's corpse. Jim stared at the living room's flowery wallpaper that Margaret had chosen, thinking, *You're going to die here. Alone.* The thought was like a cold wind blowing through him. He fought down an urge to get back into his car and start driving again. Where would he drive to? As much as he'd come to despise the house, it was all he had left. He shook his head. No, it wasn't all he had left. Not quite. Not yet.

He picked out photos of Mark and Stephen Baxley and Bryan Reynolds from amongst the case-notes spread over the coffee-table, and lined them up with Stephen at the centre. He sucked intensely on a cigarette, his eyes shifting between the three faces. What was the connection? Back and forth went his eyes. Round and round the facts of the case went his mind.

Stephen and Bryan grew up together on Park Hill. They went to the same school. They worked together for a short while. Bryan swallowed a prison sentence for Stephen in '88. Stephen moved in with his future wife Jenny Shaw a month or so later. Jim reached for a photo of Jenny and placed it between Stephen and Bryan. She was a curvaceous, busty redhead a couple of years older than Stephen. Definitely not his type. More the kind of woman Bryan liked to have hanging off his arm. So why had Stephen not only got together with her, but married her when she was pregnant with someone else's kid? Was it about building a facade of normality around himself? Or was there some other reason? Jim went through the dates once more. Bryan Reynolds was jailed in March '88. Four months later Stephen married Jenny. Two months after that Mark was born. What was the fucking connection? Was there even a connection, or was he just grasping at straws, searching vainly for answers where there were only random events?

Jim shook his head. Nothing was random. There was a reason behind everything. Reynolds's parting words at The Minx echoed back to him. *Whatever it is you think I've done, you're wrong… If Mark's in trouble, I might be able to help.* Assuming he'd been telling the truth for once in his life, why would he give a shit about Mark? Jim's gaze darted between Bryan and Mark as he turned the facts over again. *Bryan goes to prison. Stephen marries Jenny. Jenny gives birth to Mark. Mark isn't Stephen's child. So whose child is he?* Mark had his mum's dimples, small mouth and blunt nose, but where did his bluish-grey eyes, high forehead and dirty-blond hair come from? Even as the question ran through his mind, the answer hit him with a jolt. And it was so obvious, he knew he would have seen it days ago if he hadn't been blinkered by his belief that Reynolds was in the film. He placed Mark's photo between Stephen and Bryan. It was Mark. Mark was the connection. Bryan wasn't motivated to help his old school friend out of perverse desires. He was motivated by a sense of indebtedness over Mark.

Jim reached for the phone and dialled Ruth Magill. 'What's up, Jim?' she asked.

'I need a favour.'

Ruth gave an incredulous little huff. 'A favour? I'm sure it hasn't escaped your attention, but I'm kind of busy right now.'

'This is urgent, Ruth. I wouldn't ask otherwise.'

'OK,' sighed the pathologist. 'But only because it's you. What do you need?'

'A paternity test.'

'Bit old to be knocking women up, aren't you?'

'It's for Mark Baxley and Bryan Reynolds.'

'Shouldn't be a problem. Obviously Mark Baxley's DNA is in the database. And, if I remember rightly, we took Reynolds's DNA when he was picked up on a GBH charge a few years back. Do you seriously think there's a chance of a match?'

'I don't know. It's just a hunch. How long will it take?'

'I should be able to get back to you by tomorrow.'

'Call me on my home number. I'll be in all day.'

'Why would you be at home at a time like this?'

'I'm on sick leave.'

'Oh, sorry to hear that. Nothing serious, I hope.' Ruth's voice carried a note of genuine concern.

'No. Do me another favour, Ruth. Keep this conversation between us, would you?'

'Yeah, sure. For now. Obviously, if the result comes in positive I'll have to take this to Garrett.'

Jim thanked Ruth and hung up. Moving like an old man, he made his way upstairs. He took off his blood-stained shirt and threw it out of sight. He sat on the edge of the bed, feeling his chest like he was searching for a wound. Ruth's words came back to him. *Bit old to be knocking women up, aren't you?* Those days were long gone. Soon the days of his working life would be over too. Maybe they already were. And what then? What then?

****

Jim paced about the house like a caged animal, waiting to hear from Ruth. The first thing he'd done upon waking was phone the hospital to find out how Mark was doing, only to be passed on to a constable who'd apologetically informed him that he wasn't at liberty to reveal that information. After that he'd phoned Scott Greenwood, asked the same question, and received pretty much the same answer. Scott was a good man, but he was in the pocket of Garrett. Jim didn't blame him for toeing the line. Unlike himself, Scott had a wife, kids and career to think about.

Outside the official loop, Jim felt blind and frustrated. It was all he could do to stop himself from jumping into his car and driving to the hospital. He knew it would be a waste of time. Doubtless, the constable standing guard would be under orders not to let him see Mark.

At midday the phone finally rang. Jim snatched it up. 'I thought you were never going to call. What's the result?'

'What result?' The voice didn't belong to Ruth.

Jim paused a beat, frowning. Then he inhaled, relieved. 'Hello, Mark. How are you feeling today?'

'Like crap, but that's not why I'm phoning. I wanted to find out how you are. I've been told you're ill.'

'I had a heart scare, but it turned out to be nothing.'

'So why are you on sick leave?'

'It's just procedure. I'll be back on duty soon enough.'

'How soon?'

'That depends how long it takes for me to be given a clean bill of health. Could be days, could be weeks.'

'But what about me?' Mark's voice came anxiously over the line. 'Who else can I talk to? You're the only one I trust.'

'My colleagues are all good people. You're just going to have to find it within yourself to trust them. And we can still talk over the phone whenever you want.'

'What if I need to see you?'

'That might be difficult right now. I'm sorry, Mark.'

Mark heaved a sigh. 'No, I'm the one who should be apologising for bothering you when you're ill.'

'It's no bother.'

'Thank you, Detective Monahan, for everything you've done for me and Charlotte.'

'I'm just doing my job.' A moment of silence passed between them. They both knew Jim had stepped well over the boundaries of his job during the past few days.

Jim was eager to get off the phone in case Ruth called, but he hesitated to hang up. There was something reassuring about the sound of Mark's breathing. He found himself wondering suddenly why it was so important to him that Mark lived. Did he truly care for Mark? Or were his motivations more selfish than selfless? Perhaps he was trying to fill the void left by Margaret, find some kind of meaning for his lonely life.

Mark interrupted his thoughts. 'I'm going to see Charlotte this afternoon.'

'How is she?'

'The doctors say a negative outcome is still most likely.'

There was another silence, heavier than the one before. Jim wanted to say something to comfort Mark. But what? Nothing he said would change the fact that Mark's only remaining family member was hanging on to her life by a thread. 'Listen, why don't you call me later? Let's say eight o'clock. Tell me how it went.'

'I'd like that.'

'I'll talk to you then. Bye, Mark.'

The instant Jim hung up, the phone rang again. This time he checked the caller display before answering. 'Hi, Ruth. So what's the verdict?'

'Guilty as charged. The DNA profile shows that Bryan Reynolds is Mark Baxley's biological father.'

'Have you told Garrett?'

'No.'

'Do you mind if I do the honours?'

'Be my guest. I'll email you the test results.'

'Thanks, Ruth. I owe you one.'

Jim stared at Mark's photo, uncertainty washing across his face. There was no question Mark had a right to know who his father was. The question was, would it be right to tell him? Reynolds had given Mark up for a reason. Maybe he simply didn't want to be a father to him. Or maybe there was something else behind it. Whatever the case, Jim couldn't see how the truth could bring Mark anything other than more pain. If Mark approached Reynolds only to be rejected again, it might have a disastrous effect on his already precarious emotional state. But that was almost preferable to the possibility that Reynolds might have a change of heart and decide he wanted him in his life.

Reynolds was a poisonous scumbag who corrupted everything he came into contact with. A tightness formed in Jim's stomach at the thought of Mark falling under his influence. He shook his head. The truth had to be kept from Mark, at least until he was in a less vulnerable frame of mind.

Which led to another question: how was he to convince Garrett that was the right thing to do? It occurred to Jim that perhaps he wasn't the best person to do the convincing. Perhaps the best person for that job was the one who'd given Mark up in the first place. After all, Reynolds was probably the only person left alive who knew why he'd done what he did. Who better to explain why it was necessary for the truth to be kept from Mark.

Jim headed upstairs and opened Ruth's email. It contained illustrations of the DNA test results, followed by a paragraph explaining that they demonstrated to a legal standard that Bryan Reynolds was Mark Baxley's biological father. While he waited for the results to print out, he scanned through his inbox. One email caught his eye. It was an update alert from Peter Nichols's financial blog. He opened it and followed a link entitled 'The Collapse Of SB Engineering: Or Why Politicians Shouldn't Be Allowed To Invest Public Money In Private Business'.

'I was shocked and saddened to hear of the tragic events surrounding the deaths of Stephen Baxley and his wife Jenny,' began the article. Nichols went on to say that he was praying for their children, before getting down to the meat of the article. 'I and many other observers in the financial community greeted today's announcement that SB Engineering is heading into administration with little surprise. Back in the heady days of 1997, the new company was lauded by Edward Forester, the Labour MP for Sheffield South-East, as the embodiment of the even newer government's entrepreneurial spirit. In November of that year, Forester held the company up as a model of job creation in rundown urban areas through the allocation of investment grants to private firms. Fifteen years on, following the collapse of New Labour and the economy, surely it's time to put a stop once and for all to vote-seeking politicians gambling tax money on young businesses that could – and more often than not do – fail and default on the loans.'

Jim's eyes narrowed into scrutinising slits as he scrolled down the webpage and a photo of Forester came into view. He mentally reeled off Grace's description of the Chief Bastard – well built, bald with tufts of brown hair above his ears, brown eyes. Forester was broad-shouldered and bald with salt-and-pepper wisps around his ears. His close-set brown eyes peered out from deep sockets. There was a coldness in them that contradicted the smile on his lips. So far, so close, but Forester's upper front teeth showed pearly white and even. If Mark's dream was really a memory, they should be yellowed and crooked.

Jim opened a new tab and googled 'Edward Forester 1997', bringing up a selection of images from election night – the night Labour was swept to victory by a landslide vote. He zoomed in on a photo of the then newly re-elected MP. Forester was slimmer, but still solidly built. The narrow fringe of hair above his ears was dark brown. He was smiling broadly at his electorate, revealing a row of overlapping, stained upper teeth. In the years between then and now he'd had his teeth fixed to give him a film-star smile.

Jim's fingers dug into his palms. The Chief Bastard's physical description fitted the Forester of 1997 exactly! Still, there was the matter of his voice. Forester had a broad Sheffield accent. It was his trademark. But was it for real? He did a search for videos of Forester. There was footage of him in the House of Commons dating back to the Thatcher era, and of him giving interviews and election speeches. In all of the clips his accent never wavered. He was either a consummate actor or Jim's suspicion was misplaced.

He took a look at Forester's Wiki biography. Forester was born in Handsworth, Sheffield in 1955, the only child of a housewife and a steel worker. In 1956 Forester's father walked out on his family. Edward seemed to be facing a childhood of poverty, but his mother proved herself a resourceful lady. She set up a business making and selling cakes. It was a huge success, and in 1960 she and Edward moved south to Totteridge, Hertfordshire. By the time Edward was seven his mother could afford to send him to Beldamere House, an exclusive boarding school with fees to match. Forester had gone on from Beldamere House to read law at Cambridge. Shortly after graduating, he joined the Labour Party and moved back to Sheffield. He practised criminal law in his home city for several years, before contesting the Attercliffe constituency in the 1983 general election – a seat he'd held, in its various incarnations, ever since.

Deep in thought, Jim pulled his eyes from the screen. Forester had lived in Handsworth long enough to justify his broad accent. But children are masters of fitting in. Surely his accent wouldn't have stayed with him for long in the rarefied environment of a private school. Or maybe he'd got into the habit of modifying it depending on who he was speaking to. Jim lit a cigarette and sat with it between his fingers, wondering how it would be possible to find out if that was the case. The cigarette had burnt itself out, leaving a trail of ash across the keyboard, by the time it came to him that there might be a way. In order to try it he needed Forester's phone number. The easiest way to get that would be to log on to the PNC Vehicle File database, which contained the details of every owner of a registered vehicle. But that would leave a digital trail connecting him to Forester, and for reasons he barely dared acknowledge to himself, he was reluctant to do that.

In hope rather than expectation, Jim searched online for Forester's home address and telephone number. Unsurprisingly, he was ex-directory. The only available address and telephone number were those of his constituency office. Jim navigated to Forester's website and clicked the 'About Edward' link. His gaze skimmed over paragraphs of idealistic guff about why Forester had gone into politics, until he came to the sentence: 'I've been happily married for nearly twenty years to Philippa Horne, the Labour councillor for the Arbourthorne Ward.' Jim wondered why Forester's wife hadn't taken his name. Was it because she wanted to be judged on her own merits? Whatever the case, it pointed him in the direction of a more fruitful avenue of investigation. Councillors who delivered local services needed to be much more accessible to their electorate. He did a search for 'Philippa Horne, Arbourthorne councillor'. A link to Sheffield City Council's website led him to a list of councillors' contact details. The list provided town hall, home and mobile telephone numbers, but not home addresses.

Jim noted down Philippa Horne's home number and printed off photos of her and her husband. The next thing was to locate Forester. There was no point staking out his house if he was working down in Westminster. He took another look at the MP's website. There was no information about Forester's current whereabouts. He followed a link to his Twitter feed. There were five tweets from that morning. Forester – or more likely, his PA – was clearly eager to show he was down with social networking. A two-hour-old tweet read: 'Just returned from visit to Newhall Stainless Steels. Wonderful to see a true local success story. Now off to launch of CTYT.' Jim Googled 'CTYT launch Sheffield'. A link came up to the Craig Thorpe Youth Trust, a charity set up to help young runaway and homeless people in the city. The website announced that Edward Forester was to open their new Arundel Gate premises.

Jim hurried to his car and drove into the city centre as fast as traffic would permit. According to the website, the launch party started at half past one. It was already nearly two o'clock. The charity's premises were at the top end of Arundel Gate, a busy road that ran parallel to the high street. He saw that he hadn't missed the party. A small crowd had congregated on the pavement and was listening to Edward Forester give his speech. Jim parked on a side-street and made his way to the gathering.

Forester was wearing a white shirt with no tie and the sleeves rolled up, like a real working man. He looked a little tired around the eyes, but his voice was strong and full of energy. '...privilege to be here this afternoon,' he was saying, projecting his earthy Yorkshire tones over the traffic noise with practised ease. 'The Craig Thorpe Youth Trust is a charity very close to my heart.' He indicated several smartly dressed youths – no doubt, examples of the charity's good work. 'I don't pretend to understand what you've all been through. I had a mother who worked every hour of every day to give me the opportunity to be whatever I wanted to be. However, for several years of my childhood, our little family was threatened with homelessness. Those days of uncertainty made an impression that has stayed with me all my life. They showed me how fine the line can be between, in my case, ending up in Parliament or on the street. They also showed me that people can make a success of their lives no matter what their background. But not everyone is lucky enough to have a mother like mine. That's where the Craig Thorpe Youth Trust comes in. It's their ambition not only to get this city's young people off the streets, but to give them the tools to build a future for themselves. And not just any old future, but the future they deserve, one of opportunity and hope.'

As Jim listened, he found himself wanting to believe he was wrong about Forester. The politician's voice was so heartfelt, so natural, it seemed incredible to think it might mask a heart as rotten as a month-old corpse. The teenagers at his sides looked at him with open admiration. Christ only knew what neglect and abuse they'd suffered at the hands of adults in their short lives, yet they'd found it within themselves to trust in others again. For Forester to betray that trust, and in the monstrous way that Jim suspected, would be cruel almost beyond belief.

Someone handed Forester a set of scissors, and the crowd broke into applause as he cut a ribbon strung across the entrance to the charity's premises. A woman announced that there were drinks and a buffet inside, and the crowd began to file into the building. Jim took up a position from where he could see into the building without being easily seen by anyone looking out of the windows. Forester was working the room, smiling, chatting, shaking hands, having his photo taken. After half an hour or so, he left the party accompanied by a thirty-something woman in a business suit. They made their way to a black Jag parked a short distance from Jim's car. The woman got in behind the wheel. Forester lit a fat cigar before ducking into the passenger seat.

For the next few hours, Jim followed the Jag around Sheffield. Forester stopped to chat and have his photo taken with factory workers in Attercliffe. Then it was off to another photo opportunity with some people protesting against a mobile telephone mast in Mosborough. Finally, the Jag made its way to the boxy steel-and-glass building that housed his city-centre constituency office. Forester and the woman entered the building. A few minutes later he reappeared with his wife, Philippa Horne, a slim, attractive brunette of about fifty. The two of them got into the Jag and set off, this time with Forester driving. Jim followed them to Woodhouse, a solid working-class suburb to the south-east of the city centre. The Jag turned onto a long driveway that led to a red-brick, bay-windowed Victorian semi. The house was large, but relatively modest compared to those of the Baxleys and Winstanleys.

Forester and his wife entered the house. Net curtains prevented Jim from seeing inside. He glanced at the clock. It was just past six. He wanted to make sure he was back home in time for Mark's call, but he was reluctant to try what was on his mind with Philippa Horne in the house. Time ticked on:

half past six, seven, quarter past seven. His fingers drummed an impatient rhythm on the dashboard. A few more minutes and he would have to make his move no matter what. His fingers stopped drumming as Philippa appeared from around the back of the house dressed in jeans and a sweater, carrying a garden fork.

He drove to a phone box, dialled Forester's home number, let it ring three times, then hung up. He counted off ten seconds, then redialled. As the phone rang again, he put his handheld tape recorder to its earpiece and hit the record button. One, two, three rings. Someone picked up. A voice came down the line. It was Forester, but not the Forester he'd heard in the city centre. This Forester was well spoken, his voice as sharp and cold as a blade of ice. 'What the hell are you doing phoning me at home?'

There was a brief pause. Then the voice came again. 'What if my wife had answered?'

Another silence. Longer than the last one. Punctuated by the eerie sound of Forester's breathing, suddenly shallow with uncertainty. The line went dead.

His heart thumping in his throat, Jim rewound the tape and played the voice back. There was a slight hiss of static, but the recording wasn't bad. He still needed Mark to confirm it, but there was no longer any doubt in his mind – Edward Forester was the Chief Bastard. He felt no sense of triumph at the discovery, only a leaden sadness for all the lies and hypocrisy of the adult world.

He drove back past the red-brick semi. Philippa Horne was digging over the garden's borders, working out the strains of the day, blissfully unaware that her world was about to be shattered. He heaved a sigh and put his foot down. It wasn't quite eight o'clock when he arrived home, but the phone was ringing. He ran to answer it.

'Where've you been?' Mark asked excitedly. 'I've been trying to contact you all evening.'

'I've—'

Before Jim could finish, Mark went on, 'Charlotte moved. I asked her to move her fingers and she did. The doctors think it was probably just a muscle spasm, but I know it wasn't. She heard me.'

'That's wonderful, Mark.' Jim's flat, heavy voice didn't match his words.

'What is it?' Mark's excitement was replaced by concerned curiosity. 'Has something happened?'

'Are you on your own?'

'Yes.'

'Do you trust me?'

'You know I do.'

'There's something I want you to listen to – a recording I made. And whatever you hear, I want you to promise me you'll keep it to yourself until I say otherwise.'

'I promise I won't say a word to anyone.'

Jim hit play on the tape recorder and Forester's coldly furious voice hissed into the phone. When the recording was finished, he returned the phone to his ear. 'Well?'

'It's him,' Mark exclaimed. 'It's—'

'Keep your voice down,' Jim cut in.

Mark's voice dropped to a tremulous whisper. 'It's the Chief Bastard.'

'Are you certain?'

'One hundred per cent. I'd recognise that voice anywhere. Who is he?'

'I can't tell you.'

Mark's voice rose in surprise again. 'Why not?'

'For your own safety. I can't say any more than that right now. I don't want—' *To make you an accomplice*, Jim thought, finishing the sentence in his mind.

'You don't want what?'

'It doesn't matter. All that matters is keeping you safe.'

'What are you going to do?' Mark asked tentatively, as if unsure he really wanted to know.

As Jim thought about the answer to that question, a cold sweat seeped from the palms of his hands. 'Take care of yourself, Mark.' With a trace of regretful longing, he added, 'And don't ever forget, there's nothing more important than the ones you love.'

Jim hung up and looked at his hand that had gripped the phone, flexing fingers that felt tingly and stiff. He winced as a cramping pain streaked down his arm. He breathed out the pain, telling himself that what he was going to do was the only way to stop Forester. The tape recording was incriminating, but it would no more stand up in a court of law than the words of a dead murderess or the questionable recovered memory of an abuse victim. Not that there was any way the case would ever get to court. Without physical evidence, there was no chance of bringing charges against Forester. And all the physical evidence was long gone, except for the DVDs.

As far as Jim knew, Forester possessed the only other copy of the film. It seemed a pretty good guess that the politician had a version in which his face was visible. In order to properly relive the experience, Forester would want to be able to see his face on screen. If that was the case, he would need to be insane or stupid to have kept hold of his copy after Grace's rescue of Mark. And Forester was neither of those things. He was a cruel, calculating sociopath, a master of manipulating his audience and public image.

There was one other piece of evidence that might connect Forester, and possibly a lot of other people, to what had gone on at the Winstanley house – Herbert's book. But that had most probably been consigned to the burning barn.

That just left the hitman. A pro like him would have plenty of places to lie low until the heat died down. And even if he was caught, there would be no incentive for him to give his client up when he was facing a life sentence no matter what. A snitch's life was less than worthless in prison. Better to go down with a stand-up reputation.

Jim took out his police ID. He stared at his photo. It had been taken shortly before Margaret left him, but it might as well have been from a different lifetime. His gaze moved to the South Yorkshire Police logo: 'JUSTICE WITH COURAGE'. He wanted to believe in it. For a long time he *had* believed in it. But bitter experience had taught him that sometimes courage wasn't enough.

Chapter Twenty-Four

Jim pulled into the kerb a couple of hundred metres away from The Minx. He scanned the vehicles parked outside the club. His gaze came to rest on what looked like a builder's van with ladders on its roof. He knew it wasn't a builder's van, though. It was a surveillance van.

If Garrett had the club under surveillance, there was every chance he was listening in on its phones too. He stared thoughtfully at The Minx's flickering neon sign, then turned his car round. He pulled over at a phone box and wrote its number on the printout of the paternity test results. Then he drove to the Xinchun Chinese Takeaway. The takeaway was owned by Li Xinchun, a known associate of Reynolds. It had been shut down for several years after a drugs raid found bags of cocaine, cannabis and cash under the counter. But since Li's recent release from prison, it had reopened.

Jim sat watching the Chinese girl behind the counter serve customers. When a stocky, middle-aged man in chef's whites emerged from the kitchen, Jim got out of his car and entered the takeaway. 'Li Xinchun.'

Li eyed Jim with a kind of weary suspicion. 'What do you want?'

Jim took out his ID badge. 'Just a word, that's all.' He jerked a thumb at his car. 'In private.'

With a sigh, Li followed Jim. 'I'm operating a straight business now, Officer.'

Jim started the engine and accelerated away from the takeaway.

'Hey,' exclaimed Li. 'What are you doing? I'm working.'

'This won't take long.'

'But I haven't broken my parole. I'm clean. Search me if you don't believe me.'

'I don't give a toss about your parole. Now just sit there and keep your gob shut.'

Li gave Jim a measuring look, as though trying to work out whether he was what he claimed to be. Jim pulled over within sight of The Minx. He held out the printout of the test results to Li. 'I need you to give that to Bryan Reynolds.'

'Who?'

A sardonic smile flickered across Jim's lips. 'I haven't got time for games. Tell him to phone me on that number from a payphone in fifteen minutes.'

Li remained motionless, his expression bewildered.

'If you don't do this, Bryan's going to be in deep trouble,' said Jim. 'You know who I am, so you know I'm not bull-shitting you.'

The confusion left Li's face in a heartbeat. He glanced warily at the printout. 'What is that?'

'That's none of your business. And if you value your neck, I'd keep it that way.'

'Why don't you give it to him?'

'For fuck's sake, are you going to sit there asking questions? Or are you going to save Bryan's arse from prison?'

Li looked at Jim a moment longer, then took the printout and put it in his pocket. As he got out of the car, Jim hissed after him, 'Remember, fifteen minutes, from a payphone.'

Jim watched until Li was inside The Minx, then he returned to the phone box. Fifteen minutes ticked by. The phone rang. He picked it up and waited for the caller to speak. Reynolds's voice came over the line in a cautious but menacing growl. 'Is that you, Monahan?'

'We need to talk.'

'We are talking.'

'Not on the phone. Face to face.'

'Why the fuck should I meet you?'

'Because if you don't I'll tell Mark the truth.'

There was a brief pause, then Reynolds said, 'When and where?'

'As soon as it's dark.' Jim told Reynolds where, adding, 'Make sure you're not followed. We've got you under surveillance.'

'Why are you doing this, Monahan? What's your fucking game?'

'This is no game.'

Jim drove almost reluctantly to the meeting place. By the time he got there the sun was dipping behind the hills of Sheffield. The pain in his chest was back, and there were lights like stars in front of his eyes. He sat very still, breathing softly, sweat popping out all over his body.

Twenty minutes later, headlights shone through Jim's rear windscreen as a car pulled in behind him. The headlights flashed. He left his car and approached the other vehicle. It was a red Subaru. A good getaway vehicle. Reynolds was behind the steering-wheel. His skinhead sidekick, Les, occupied the passenger seat. Les got out, motioning for Jim to take his seat.

'Were you followed?' Jim asked, struggling to keep the pain out of his voice.

Reynolds nodded. He spoke without looking at Jim. 'We lost your pals in Darnall.'

'Are you certain of that?'

'I know how to drop a fucking tail. Now what do you want?'

'I want to know why you asked Stephen Baxley to bring up your child.'

The hard mask of Reynolds's face remained intact, except for a twitch at the corners of his eyes. 'Let me ask you something, Monahan. When you look at me, what do you see?'

'A drug dealer, a pimp.'

'A scumbag through and through,' put in Reynolds. 'That's what I am, and that's why I did what I did. Stephen was a good guy, intelligent, ambitious. He could give my child a real future.'

'So you went to prison in return for him taking on Mark.'

'Prison would have ended his career before it had begun, and any chance my kid had of a normal life along with it.'

'And Jenny was happy to go along with your deal?'

'She was when I made it clear I didn't want anything to do with her or the kid. She'd spent her life rotting on Park Hill. That was the last thing she wanted for Mark. Stephen offered her a way out and she took it. It seemed like the best thing for all of us at the time.' Reynolds's eyes twitched again, more violently. He twisted towards Jim as though appealing for understanding. 'Stephen was always such a steady bloke. How was I supposed to know that one day he'd go off his fucking nut and... and do what he did? If he was in trouble, why didn't he come to me? I'd have helped him.'

'He owed millions.'

'I'm not saying I could've stopped his factory from going under, but I could've done something, given him some cash or a place to live.'

'You mean like you did for him and Grace Kirby.'

'Who?'

Jim detected no hint of a lie in Reynolds's voice, but that meant nothing with a man like him. 'In February 1997 you let Stephen use a flat of yours in Attercliffe to hide a runaway named Grace Kirby.'

Reynolds's eyes widened a fraction in realisation, but he remained silent, wary of saying anything that might incriminate him in any way.

'Don't worry, Bryan,' said Jim. 'Whatever you tell me stays between us. You've got my word on that.'

'You expect me to trust your word?'

'No, but bear in mind that I'll be in just as deep shit as you if my DCI finds out about this meeting.'

As Jim had expected, Reynolds pursed his lips in satisfaction at this response – self-preservation was the only law a man like him understood. 'Yeah, I know who you're talking about, but Stephen called her Angel. How do you know about her?'

'I'll get to that in a bit. First tell me what happened with you and Angel.'

'Nothing happened with me and Angel. I never met the girl. Stephen came to me one day and said he needed to use the flat. I didn't ask why. I just assumed he was keeping a bit on the side. A few months later he came to me again, said he needed my help to get a girl out of the city and give her a false identity. Said she was in trouble with your lot. So I arranged for a mate of mine in Newcastle to look after her.'

'Pimp her out, don't you mean?'

Reynolds's eyebrows bunched. 'How the fuck do you know that?'

'I know a lot of things about what went on back then. What I want to know is how much you know. For instance, did you know Angel was only fifteen at the time?'

'I haven't got a fucking clue how old she was. All I know is Stephen asked me for a favour and I gave it to him.'

'Are you telling me it never crossed your mind that she might be underage?'

'It was none of my fucking business. Listen, Monahan, in a business like mine you get used to not asking those kinds of questions.'

'So you're OK with fifteen-year-olds turning tricks.'

Leaning towards Jim, Reynolds said between clenched teeth, 'Whatever else I am, I'm not into that kind of shit. And if I found out anyone who works for me was, I'd cut their bollocks off.'

Jim regarded Reynolds with weary disdain. In a world where people made it their business not to know each other's business, Reynolds wasn't likely to ever be called upon to make good on his threat. 'Stephen Baxley was into that kind of shit.'

Reynolds licked his lips as though his mouth was suddenly dry. It took him a moment to work himself up to asking the question he didn't want to ask. 'He wasn't into boys as well as girls, was he?'

'I don't know for sure. But he knew people who were, and he allowed them to abuse Mark.'

'That's a fucking lie!'

'Why would I lie? And what do you think the insanity that's been going on in this city for the past few days is all about?'

Reynolds shook his head hard. 'Stephen wouldn't...' he started to say, but the denial died on his lips. He pressed a hand to his face, groaning as though a knife had been thrust into him. 'Why?'

'Again, I'm not exactly sure. Money, pleasure, maybe a bit of both.'

'Who are they, these paedo cunts?'

'There were five of them, including Stephen Baxley.'

'Five,' Reynolds repeated in a mumble of despair, digging his fingers into his face as though trying to prise something away.

'Four are dead.'

Reynolds's hand slid away from his face. His eyes were sheened with moisture. There was an odd twist to his expression. It wasn't simply rage. It was something more. Something verging on rabid hunger. 'I want a name.'

Jim's mouth opened and closed silently. The car suddenly seemed airless, and he couldn't find sufficient breath to speak. He looked out of the window, scanning the road almost as if he hoped Reynolds had been wrong about losing his tail. *I just don't want any more people to die.* Mark's words echoed back to him. But Mark had only been talking about good people. Hadn't he?

'Give me a fucking name,' continued Reynolds, his voice rasping like a knife on a whet-stone. 'That's why you're here, isn't it? You want me to do what you can't. Don't lose your balls now, Monahan. You know it's the right thing to do. It's not about the law, it's about justice.'

'Justice.' Jim mouthed the word as though it was foreign to him. What was justice? He wasn't sure he knew any more. The only thing he was certain of was that doing this was necessary to protect Mark and everyone like him from Forester. He reached into his pocket for the printouts and handed them to Reynolds. The simple movement took an effort that left him shaking.

Reynolds studied the photos, running his tongue over his teeth as though in anticipation of a meal. 'I thought you said there was only one.'

'The man is Edward Forester.'

'Forester, why does that name seem familiar?'

'He's a local politician.'

Reynolds nodded with recognition. 'I've seen the fucker on the news.'

'The woman is his wife, Philippa Horne. She's not involved in this.'

'Politicians.' Reynolds spat the word out in a vicious hiss. 'Criminals in business suits. Well this is one suit-wearing fucker who won't be spouting his bullshit much longer.'

Jim snatched back the printouts. Reynolds glared at him, seething with barely restrained violence. 'Philippa Horne is not involved in this,' Jim said again. 'Repeat what I said.'

'She's not involved.'

'Tell me you won't hurt her.'

'I won't hurt the bitch. Now it's your turn to tell me something.' Reynolds stabbed a finger at Forester's photo. 'Where does he live?'

Jim pointed at a house adjacent to the car.

Reynolds's lips peeled back from his teeth in a savage grin. 'You've got it all worked out, haven't you, Monahan?'

'What are you going to do to Forester?'

'You don't want to know.'

'Whatever it is, it should be fast and painless.'

'Fuck that!' The veins in Reynolds's bull-neck bulged. 'I'm going to kill that child-molesting cunt the way he deserves. By the time I'm done with Forester, he'll be begging to be put out of his misery. And if you're not going to help, you should get the fuck out of here.'

What have you done? As Jim looked into Reynolds's eyes, the familiar thought wrapped itself around his consciousness with the sting of a whip. He wrenched himself free of it. It was too late for such questions. He started to turn towards the door. Reynolds put a hand on his arm. He tensed, half expecting the hand to be followed by a fist, or maybe a knife. After all, even though he would be an accomplice to the murder, he was still a witness, and the fewer of those the better. But all that came his way was a low, almost pleading voice. 'You must really care for Mark.'

'I do.'

'Then make sure he doesn't find out about me. I can never be part of his life.'

'Oh, believe me, you won't be if I can help it. Not being a father to him is the only half-decent thing you've done in your whole worthless life.'

Reynolds's fingers tightened on Jim's arm at the scathing words. 'You think you're so much fucking better than me, don't you, Monahan?'

'That's the last thing I think. Now let go of my arm.'

Reynolds frowned at Jim a moment longer, as though unsure what to make of him. Then he released his grip.

Jim returned to his car, his left leg dragging a little. He looked at Reynolds and Les in the rear-view mirror. Reynolds was saying something and the skinhead was smiling as if he liked what he was hearing. Jim closed his eyes briefly, as if to shut out the world with all its anguish and horror. Then he twisted the ignition key. As he drove, a bluish tinge came into his lips and his head kept nodding as if he was fighting off sleep.

At the end of his street, Jim hit the brakes. There was a police car outside his house. A constable was knocking at his door. His first thought was the constable was there to check up on him. But then Garrett got out of the car. Why the hell would Garrett come to his house? Not simply to find out how he was doing, that was for damn sure. Then the answer came to him. The DCI was there to take him into custody! They must have found Grace Kirby's mobile phone. A scan of its caller list would reveal not only his home number, but also that someone had contacted her from the office above Winstanley Accountants and Business Advisors. It wouldn't be hard to work out who that someone was.

Jim's expression registered no alarm. He reached into his pocket for the tape recorder. Fumbling numbly at the buttons, he rewound the tape until he found what he wanted. Reynolds's voice snarled out of the speaker, *I'm going to kill that child-molesting cunt the way he deserves. By the time I'm done with Forester, he'll be begging to be put out of his misery.*

'Got you,' Jim murmured in a tone of grim satisfaction. Reynolds had been right not to trust his word, but wrong to believe everyone valued self-preservation above all else.

A searing pain suddenly exploded through Jim's chest. The tape recorder fell from his nerveless left hand. Grimacing with the effort, he retrieved it with his right and returned it to his pocket. He pulled out his phone and dialled a number. Margaret's voice came on the line. 'Hello?'

Jim's words wheezed out like air from a broken bellows. 'I'm sorry, Margaret.'

'Jim, is that you? Are you OK?'

'I'm sorry for the way I treated you all those years. I never stopped loving you. I just forgot how to show it.'

'Why are you telling me this now? What's going on?'

'Something's happened. You'll find out what soon enough. I've got to go. Goodbye, Margaret. Take care.'

Jim drove to the house, lowering the window as he pulled up alongside Garrett. The DCI frowned into the car. 'You've got some serious explaining to do, Detective Monahan.'

'It's—' Jim's voice faltered as another wave of pain broke over him. For a moment he thought he was going to faint, but the feeling passed and his voice was steady as he said, 'It's not "Detective". Not any more.'

****

'Mark, Mark.'

The voice pulled Mark out of sleep. He opened his eyes and saw that it belonged to a nurse. 'What is it?'

'It's your sister.' Seeing Mark's forehead tighten into anxious creases, the nurse quickly added, 'She's been showing more signs of movement.'

His eyes flicking wide, Mark struggled into a sitting position. 'I want to see her.'

The nurse helped him into a wheelchair and pushed him through the hospital's silent corridors to Charlotte. Doctor Goodwin was stooping over her, shining a pencil torch into her eyes. 'Has the nurse updated you on your sister's condition?' he asked.

'Yes.'

'I don't want you to get your hopes up, Mark. Like I said earlier, they might just be muscular spasms. On the off-chance that that's not the case, it may be beneficial for her to hear your voice.'

Mark gently took Charlotte's hand. 'Hi, sis.'

He felt a quiver of movement against his fingers, so slight he wondered whether he'd imagined it.

'The doctor tells me you're doing much better today.'

Charlotte's hand twitched again. Mark looked excitedly at Doctor Goodwin. 'Did you see that?'

The doctor nodded and gestured for Mark to continue talking to his sister.

Mark's brow furrowed as he searched for something to say that would make Charlotte want to come back into a world that had so cruelly turned against her. He leant in so close that his mouth touched her ear. His voice dropped to a whisper. 'I know we've never really got on, sis. I know I haven't been much of a brother to you. The thing is, I was jealous of you and...' he faltered briefly, then said, 'Dad. I wanted him to love me like I thought he loved you. I realise now that he wasn't capable of really loving anyone other than himself. He tried to hurt us in the worst way. But he failed. And anyone else who tries to hurt us will fail too, because I'll kill them. Do you hear me, sis? I'll kill them all, every single fucking one of them.'

Charlotte's head moved against Mark's. He pulled back to look at her face. Her eyelids were fluttering like the wings of a trapped moth. Then, suddenly, they parted and she looked at her brother.